SILENT SURVIVOR

BY

DEBORAH SHLIAN

This book is dedicated to all the survivors who understand that only by exposing the truth can secrets lose their power

"The United States shall renounce the use of lethal biological agents and weapons, and all other methods of biological warfare. The United States will confine its biological research to defensive measures such as immunization and safety measures."

President Richard M. Nixon in a November 25, 1969 speech titled "Statement on Chemical and Biological Defense Policies and Programs" from Fort Detrick

Prologue

"Jesus!" Shaking his head in disbelief, the sandy-haired post-doc held up the research file. "You're sure about this?"

His younger colleague, also a PhD, ran a hand through thick, disheveled locks. "No doubt, mate. It's there in almost every chimp I've autopsied."

"Have you told anyone?

"Just you," he said, tugging awkwardly at his rumpled jeans.

"What are you gonna do?"

"I've got to let the muckety-mucks at corporate know."

"Whistle blowing can be risky."

"Yeah. Haven't slept for the past few nights wondering how this will affect my career." He gathered all the notes and stuffed them into his backpack. "But then I realized I have no choice. It's not just the company's national reputation at stake. It's the implications for patients."

"Of course, you're right. Are you leaving tonight?"

"I've booked the eight o'clock to Sydney on Virgin Blue."

"It's almost six. Better get a move on. How 'bout I get my car and drive you to the airport?"

"You sure? Wouldn't want to put you out."

"No worries. Meet me outside in fifteen minutes." His smile was genuine. "After all, what are friends for?"

The winter Australian sun had already slipped into the horizon when the young PhD stepped off the curb without looking. He heard the car before he saw it. A moonless sky made it impossible to see it coming - especially since the driver had deliberately neglected to turn on the headlights. Squeal of tires, an engine's accelerating roar were the last sounds he registered as thirty-six hundred pounds of steel slammed into his body, catapulting him onto and then over the hood of the Holden, landing with a horrible thud on the road. He never heard the car door open or the approaching footsteps falling heavily on asphalt, then quickly fading as the driver, having grabbed the backpack, turned and walked back to his car, satisfied that his problem was solved.

Days later, long after the body was discovered and loaded onto the Port Douglas ME's van and the scene analyzed, the final report labeled the "hit and run" a terrible accident with nothing to suggest the real truth.

CHAPTER 1

Stepping into the darkened VA hospital PTSD clinic, Mackenzie Dodd heard the faint click of the revolver before she saw its barrel pressed against the young sergeant's sweat-beaded temple. The stench of his body odor filled the small space. Standing with his back to the far window, he was eerily illuminated by a tiny, bright swath of early morning light.

"Don't come any farther."

Mackenzie couldn't recall his last name. PJ something. He'd joined these sessions only a week before - another victim of multiple back-to-back tours in Iraq. So many of these poor vets sent off to seemingly endless Middle East wars. Like her, he hardly spoke in group, but she remembered the handsome twenty-something because last time he'd dressed in tight jeans and a T-shirt that accentuated a muscular physique. Today he'd chosen a full Marine combat uniform. That and his grim-lipped expression made him appear a much older man.

"Stay back." He pointed the gun at her, the barrel wobbling slightly.

Mackenzie stopped near the open doorway, not sure what to do.

At ten to nine the circle of chairs was empty. None of the other patients had arrived yet. It would probably be after nine before Dr. Mills showed. The laid-back therapy leader was notoriously late. Mackenzie, on the other hand, was obsessive about being on time, even early - just one manifestation of her need to be in control, no doubt a result of a chaotic childhood and these days, the only sense of control it seemed she had left.

Switching to nursing mode, though a member of the group herself, Mackenzie feigned calm. This young man was obviously on an emotional hair trigger. Anything might set him off.

"You're PJ, right?" She spoke slowly, measuring each word like someone tiptoeing around a land mine. "I'm Mackenzie. My buds call me Mac."

PJ remained silent, his stare a blank, but at least he lowered the revolver, holding it shakily at his side.

Desperate to distract him, Mackenzie noticed his half-bitten nails, then spotted the gold band on his left ring finger. She'd discarded her own not long ago. "Think about your wife. Don't leave her like this."

Hesitating, as if trying to determine the value in conversation, he finally responded in a low rasp, his tone bitter. "She left me after my last deployment. Moved from San Diego to her mom's in Deerfield Beach. Sent me a fucking email." He shook his head. "A fucking email. Said I'd changed too much. Refused my calls. I couldn't…" His voice trailed off. "I begged her to start over. Said I'd sign up for therapy at the VA. Took me six fucking months to get into this group." He focused on the ceiling for a moment, then back at Mackenzie. When he blinked, a tear traveled down his cheek. "Last night she said it was too late."

"It's never too late." Mackenzie uttered the words, not sure she believed them. Her own marriage hadn't survived the war. Swallowing hard, she observed PJ's shoulder insignia, remembering Semper Fi tattooed on his bare bicep when he'd worn a T-shirt to the last session. "Thundering Third?" she asked.

An evanescent smile flickered across PJ's angular face at the mention of the nickname given to the "3/1- 3rd" infantry battalion, 1st marine out of Camp Horno.

Mackenzie had also been deployed from Pendleton. "Were you in Fallujah?"

PJ acknowledged her question with the barest nod.

"Me too," she said. "Nursing corps. Which operation?"

"First time. Phantom Fury."

Mackenzie did a quick calculation. That was four years ago. Mid-2004. The 3/1 had been sent in to clear the infamous Jolan District, to reclaim the city of Fallujah from unrest and capture or kill insurgents responsible for the deaths of a Blackwater Security team. Considered the bloodiest battle of the Iraq war, it took its toll on too many youngsters like PJ.

And now the young Marine was recounting how he'd been re-deployed back to Iraq in 2005 and again in 2007. "Operation Phantom Thunder in Western Iraq."

"Wounded?"

Using the barrel of his gun, he traced a thick ribbon of scar that ran from the corner of his mouth to just below his right eye. "I was taking a leak a few yards from our HumVee when the IED killed my two buddies. A fucking leak. Can you believe that? It should have been me."

Mackenzie exhaled, imagining all the horrors this kid must have seen. She was no psychologist, but she'd suffered her own trauma from that war and was well aware of the internal scars most of these vets carried - especially when they'd dodged a bullet only to watch their comrades die. Survivor's guilt had led to more suicides than the Army was willing to acknowledge. Just another of their dirty little secrets, she thought bitterly, reminded of her own buried wounds.

"Listen, PJ. I understand. I do." Her throat was so dry each syllable seemed to stick. "I know about the nightmares, the pain."

"Then you know I see them everywhere. Dead Hajis, dead Americans. And their cries. It's deafening." He looked at her with sad, dull eyes. "But it all makes perfect sense now. I know what I have to do and it makes so much sense."

MacKenzie held her breath, dread slinking down her spine from the sheer inevitability of his utterance. It was quiet enough to hear the ticking of the wall clock as the second hand swept closer to the moment when the others would appear. "Please, PJ. Listen to me," she begged, slowly moving toward him. "You're upset now, but you can get help here. You don't have to do this."

His voice was low and preternaturally calm. "No…no, I have to die. I have to leave this earth and go up to God. I have to be part of God's army with my men. I have to stop the pain. Too much pain. This is the only way." He put his hands over his ears. "The pain keeps screaming in my head. It never stops. Oh God, stop the pain."

Approaching footsteps just outside the therapy room made Mackenzie swivel to look and in that split second she heard the unmistakable blast of PJ's gun. In the small space the sound reverberated like thunder.

"No!" she screamed, turning back to see PJ's body slump to the floor, a pool of blood forming around his head like a crimson halo. His eyes, mercifully, were closed.

"So you were here all alone with the victim?"

"Sorry?" Mackenzie turned to the West Palm Beach police officer seated beside her, his pen poised over a fresh page in a spiral pad. Handsome in his crisp uniform, he couldn't have been more than twenty-five or maybe thirty, she thought, aware that he was watching her curiously, probably wondering why she appeared so calm.

It was a ruse. For the past hour she'd been cocooned in a state of shock, her mind numb, as VA administration, hospital security and local law enforcement had swooped in and begun dealing with the situation.

She was perched on one of the empty metal chairs that earlier had been arranged in a circle, anticipating the members of the therapy group.

Now all but two of the chairs had been pushed off to the corners to make room for the number of people flowing in and out. The moment any therapy patients appeared in the doorway, they'd been whisked off, away from the scene, leaving only Mackenzie to answer what seemed like endless questions, first from hospital security and now local police.

"Why did you arrive so early?"

"Why didn't you call for help?"

"How well did you know the victim?"

All questions she'd already asked herself.

But no one had asked the unanswerable: Why *hadn't* she done more to stop PJ?

Mackenzie stared blankly at the wall, trying to ignore the blood congealing on the floor by the window and the flash of the medical examiner's camera as two men from the ME's office lifted the marine's body onto a gurney and wheeled it past her. Too painful to think of a young man's life reduced to this: a stain others would struggle to scrub away.

"Miss Dodd?"

The officer's voice brought her back to the moment. "You were all alone with the victim?"

The victim.

"Yes, I came in around ten to nine and found PJ standing over by the window with a gun to his head. I only met him last week in group. I really didn't know him." Though her expression remained blank, her voice quivered as she relayed her short conversation with the distraught marine. "I tried to stop..." Unable to continue, her emotional dam burst. Tears streamed down her cheeks.

Seemingly appearing out of nowhere, Dr. Mills stepped over and gave Mackenzie's shoulder a comforting squeeze. "Officer, I'm the psychiatrist leading this therapy group. I don't really think there's anything Ms. Dodd can add."

Mackenzie turned to look at the doctor, grateful for his intervention.

"You need to go home and rest," he told her.

Mackenzie nodded. She wanted nothing more than to escape the nightmare.

"Oh and take the rear entrance," Mills added, handing her a Kleenex. "I hear there's already a couple of TV vans camped out front. No point in making the sergeant's death a sideshow."

The police officer flipped his pad closed. "Of course, doctor. You're right."

Mackenzie noted the policeman's curious look again before he handed her his card.

"Just in case you think of anything that might be helpful," he said. "I realize this is difficult for you. Go home."

Some time after Mackenzie left the hospital, one of the staff grabbed the receiver on his desk phone and dialed a memorized number in Washington. "I'm afraid we've had another suicide."

The curse on the other end was barely audible. "Any physical symptoms?"

"His medical record mentions a complaint of some muscle twitches. Looks like the PA who saw him chalked it up to insomnia related to depression. Gave him a script of Lexapro and sent him back to the PTSD clinic."

"Guess the good news is your staff's not only underpaid, but too overworked to recognize the early signs."

"What do you want me to do?"

"Make sure there's no autopsy."

"That won't be a problem."

"Can you delete the medical note?"

"Can do."

"And follow-up with family. Call if they start asking questions."

"I understand."

"I hope you do." The voice on the other end was cold. "This is too valuable an operation. We can't afford any further leakage."

"Yes sir," the administrator said, adding "God bless America" before hanging up.

CHAPTER 2

Monday August 18, 2008

An hour later, Mackenzie pulled into the parking lot of Shady Palms Apartments. Still shaken, she had no idea how she'd managed to maneuver her ten year old Civic on busy I-95 from the West Palm VA to the rundown neighborhood in West Delray. Known to most Floridians as an upscale oceanside community, Delray Beach actually had miles of dilapidated dwellings stretching from the Atlantic Ocean to the interstate - a well kept secret by the chamber of commerce who daily lobbied its zoning commission to approve expensive condo projects guaranteed to drive the riffraff even farther inland.

The moment Mackenzie shut off the engine and emerged from her car, she was assaulted by the abrasive sounds of pile drivers and Salsa music. Shading her eyes from the bright August sun, she peered through a cloud of dust toward the empty lot across the street. Less than six months before an apartment building identical to the four story stucco where she now lived had been demolished to make way for a luxury highrise. According to the huge billboard hanging on the steel fence surrounding the lot, the new glass and steel condo complex slated to open in January promised luxury living starting at only five hundred thousand dollars.

Sighing, Mackenzie turned and headed up the creaky stairs to the second floor of her own building which was marked for tear-down by year's end. Its residents' only hope for eviction delay was the sudden drop in Florida real estate prices caused by the economic crisis.

The aroma of poverty seeped beneath each doorway she passed on the catwalk - garbage mixed with day old cooking. At 2G she stopped to swipe at a swarm of no-see-ums and shoo away a tiny newt before turning the lock. The door stuck a little in the frame where the pale pink paint had blistered from the overwhelming summer heat.

Nudging it open, she was greeted by a blast of hot, stale air. Even at a humid ninety-nine degrees, the weather in South Florida couldn't compare to her days in the Iraqi sandbox, dressed in pounds of protective army gear while temperatures soared to one hundred thirty degrees and beyond. That was eight months ago and some bitter memories fade. Wiping beads of sweat from her forehead with her palm, she leaned in the doorway to slide the thermostat up a few notches. Air conditioning was a luxury she could ill afford, but she felt she owed her mother some comfort.

"I'm home," she called from the open door.

Go home, the officer had said.

But Mackenzie had no home. Not of her own. Maybe she never really had.

Stepping into the tiny apartment she'd shared with her mother since her Army discharge, she caught a glimpse of her reflection in the hallway mirror. A short-haired brunette looking much older than thirty, pale blue eyes ringed with smudged mascara, stared back at her.

Splotches of reddish brown, like paint spatter, covered her white cotton blouse. Except that she knew it wasn't paint.

Fuck, fuck, fuck!

Her stomach clenched. Waves of grief, pain, and anger flooded over her.

Damn you, PJ. Hadn't she been through enough?

As if in response to her interior dialogue, Viv Wallach, sometime PBU art student and self-proclaimed social networking expert, appeared in the threshold of her mother's bedroom. Tattooed and pierced, dark hair streaked with neon blue, the waif-like twenty-year old who dressed only in black, scared off most of the elderly residents of the building until they learned that her external Goth belied a heart of gold. "Jeez, what happened to you, kid?"

Normally, the "kid" moniker would summon a smile. Most of Mackenzie's friends called her Mac. That is, when she'd had friends. These days, it seemed that Viv was her only real friend - maybe because they each lived with an older relative - Viv with her eighty year old grandfather, Mackenzie with her fifty-five year old mother. They'd found comfort in some kind of generational bond despite the decade between them.

Not ready to discuss the trauma of her morning, Mackenzie asked, "where's Karyn?" Once a week, while Mackenzie attended a mandatory PTSD therapy group, the Jamaican aide came in to help care for Mackenzie's mother.

"School nurse called. Her daughter had a fever and wanted to come home." Viv pointed to the wall clock in the alcove that served as a kitchen. It was after one. "You're usually back by eleven."

Mackenzie stepped past Viv into her mother's bedroom. "Yeah. Long story."

Viv put a finger to her lips. "She slept through the morning."

Mackenzie nodded, quietly approaching the tiny figure in the rented hospital bed. Swaddled in a white blanket, her mother's chest rose and fell with the hum of the ventilator. For weeks, she'd been tethered to the breathing machine, fed through a tube, unable to move beyond this cramped space, forced to spend her waking hours staring at the beige ceiling, waiting to die. The sight of this latest incapacity made Mackenzie's heart twist. Moving closer, she leaned in and placed a soft kiss on her mother's forehead.

Less than a year ago Diane Carter had been a pleasantly plump beauty. Now she had wasted away to a gaunt shadow of her former self. ALS might sound like an innocent triumvirate of initials, but amyotrophic lateral sclerosis was the antithesis of innocence. Its relentless attack on motor neurons left even the strongest athletes like all-star Yankee slugger Lou Gehrig paralyzed and dependent on others for everything from eating to personal care to breathing. For someone who'd been left a widow at thirty-six and found the strength (albeit with some major missteps) to raise three children while working two jobs, ALS was as ignominious a fate as any Mackenzie could imagine.

At the touch of Mackenzie's lips, her mother blinked open her eyes. Unable to speak, pupil size was the best barometer of her emotions. Dime-sized, crowding out once dramatically blue irises. Mackenzie knew she was glad to see her youngest child.

"Hi. Sorry I was late."

Her mother slowly blinked three times - their agreed upon short-hand for "it's okay", then shut her eyes again and dozed while Mackenzie hung a bag of liquid lunch, expertly suctioned the tracheostomy tube, and emptied the urine bag.

Viv popped her head in the doorway. "I'm off. Gramps needs his meds."

"Thanks for being here," Mackenzie mouthed.

"Kid, that's what friends are for." Viv whispered. She cocked her head. "If you want to talk later, text me and I'll come down. I've got to finish the graphics for a mystery author's website. Then I'll have time to check out your new column on <u>Online.com</u> and we can revisit the idea of better marketing." Staring pointedly at Mackenzie's blood stained blouse, she added, "meantime, why not write about what happened for today's entry?"

Mackenzie was always surprised at Viv's insight. For someone so young she had amazing instincts. It was Viv who'd urged her to start writing about the Iraq and Afghan wars, first for herself and then two months ago to apply for a column with a newly launched online newspaper. Her pay was dependent on how many "clicks" the column got and that was dependent on attracting readers.

Viv and Mackenzie had brainstormed pen names since Mackenzie insisted on anonymity. Finally, they'd both agreed on Silent Survivor. Mackenzie began writing about the experiences of the young men and women no one in America not directly involved in the military seemed to know or care about.

At first just a handful of people found the column, but with Viv's social networking expertise, within one month the numbers were up and approaching several hundred hits a day. Viv was pushing for a website and Facebook tie-in, insisting the column could do even better. But that meant giving up anonymity.

"I'll think about it," Mackenzie had said a week earlier when Viv asked, not sure she was ready to come out of the shadows.

"That's it!"

Though the last time he'd seen her was a good twenty years ago, Officer Sam Cantori had been racking his brains since he'd entered the clinic and spotted Mackenzie. Of course in fifth grade she'd been Kenzie Carter. That's why he hadn't realized who she was at first. But now that he had a minute to think about it, he was sure he was right. It was the anguished look in her pale blue eyes that had given her away - the same expression she'd had when the principal called Mackenzie out of class to tell her that her father had died.

Long after General Paulsen slammed down the receiver, his knuckles were still white. How much more fucked up could his day get? First a notice to appear before the House Armed Services committee and now this. It seemed the harder he'd tried to keep a lid on the operation, the more complicated everything had become.

God damn unintended consequences.

He rubbed the bridge of his veined nose and closed his eyes, wondering just how many more loose ends he'd have to take care of before this thing was finally through.

While her mother slept, Mackenzie set her blood-spattered blouse to soak in cold water, took a quick shower, changed into jeans and a T-shirt and grabbed her laptop. Settling into the chair by the rented hospital bed, she logged onto the Online.com site and read her very first, tentative piece dated July 4, 2008:

> *Today is the day that so many in Florida and around the country will be celebrating. But how many of those eating hotdogs and watching fireworks actually know that on this day in 1776, the Continental Congress ratified the Declaration of Independence, that those thirteen colonies declared their independence from Great Britain to become the United States of America? Since that time so many US veterans and military heroes have and are proudly serving America, fighting for the freedoms that our nation guarantees, preserving our independence.*
>
> *Today on local TV one of our state representatives urged Americans to honor and thank our vets and military not just on July 4th but all year long. Somehow, though, for me, it was just words. And that's why I am starting this blog.*

I am writing for you and me - for those of us who've been deployed in the Middle East, fighting for a country that tells us we are the bravest and the best, but seems to forget us when we come home wounded. Not just in body, but in spirit.

You know who you are. I am one of you and I'm hoping that by sharing some of our stories we can get stronger.

So you tell me yours and I'll tell you mine.

- Silent Survivor

Since those first few paragraphs, Mackenzie had tried to write a little something at least every few days. Memorializing her private thoughts was freeing in a way that surprised her. For so long she'd struggled to keep her emotions in check, aware that bubbling just beneath the surface was a cauldron of rage, shame, and feelings of helplessness.

And so many secrets.

What she couldn't say in group she wrote about here. At least some of it. It was like holding up a mirror without having to expose herself to people who actually knew her. In this ethereal world she never had to reveal her true identity.

What she hadn't counted on was the fact that once she'd sent her secret thoughts out onto the Internet they were actually read by people who had their own secrets to confess.

She scrolled back to the first comment she'd received, recalling the exhilaration of not only making a connection, but creating a place where a reader felt safe enough to express herself:

They don't call me a soldier because officially I'm not. I'm a soldier's wife. I haven't been shipped off to Afghanistan like my husband - three times so far in the last five years - and I haven't been shot at or stepped on an IED. Still, I feel as though I'm a silent survivor like you - suffering the pain of the loss of my spouse, trying to keep up with the bills, with my kids. And I have needs. I'm only twenty-eight and I'm not bad looking. I miss having a man holding me at night. I haven't ever cheated - I go to church regularly, but the other day when my son's teacher smiled at me, well...I couldn't help wondering...

I know it's terrible to think this way, but I can't help it. I have trouble sleeping. Actually I'm afraid to close my eyes because my dreams are so filled with fear - fear that my husband will be killed or worse, injured so badly that he'll never be the same. Even now when he does come home between deployments, he's changed. He hardly talks and he never smiles anymore.

I know that if I tell my husband how I feel, it will have a negative impact on his career. The Army wants us all to carry on as though everything's OK. Stiff upper lip and all.

So thank you for this column. And please keep writing

- Just an Army wife in Albuquerque

That first comment gave Mackenzie the encouragement to continue. With her next few entries, more comments arrived, a torrent of sorrow and pain from wives and mothers and soldiers themselves - men and women who hid their true feelings from commanding officers and family, but who poured out their stories anonymously on the web.

Now Mackenzie clicked on *New Entry* and began to write about PJ.

I watched a young soldier die today. Not on the battlefield, but right here in the good old USA. He held a gun to his head...

CHAPTER 3

Tuesday, August 19, 2008

Knowing she was dreaming didn't make Mackenzie's nightmare any less terrifying. She was lying on her cot in the barracks, dressed only in panties and a T-shirt and she'd kicked off the sheet. It was so damn hot. Her roommate was somewhere OC - off campus. They'd both finished a twelve hour shift, but Brittany liked to party. Even though Mackenzie's marriage was done by that point, she just wanted to sleep.

She was so tired all the time - not just from the heavy work schedule, but from the sound of mortars and RPGs going off every night, keeping her on permanent alert.

So when her commander tiptoed in and stood over her, her eyes opened instantly. "No," she whispered.

The way he stared at her left no doubt that he was there to rape her.

"Please, no," she repeated, grabbing the sheet to draw it around her at the same time that the captain pulled it back. He smelled like sweat and beer and he didn't say anything as he ripped off her panties, lowered his two hundred pounds of pure muscle on her lithe frame, and forced her legs apart with his knee.

Frantic, she tried to twist away, but he'd gripped both arms above her head with one meaty hand and pinned her thigh with his shin. Yelling was impossible. She could barely breathe under his weight on her chest. Thrusting himself into her, again and again, the sound of his satisfied grunts made her stomach churn.

When he finished he gripped her jaw so hard it felt as if the bones would crush from the force. "Not a word to anyone or your ass is grass," he whispered, his rank breath hot on her face. "You hear?" He waited for a nod before loosening his hold and rolling off of her.

Numb, Mackenzie didn't react. She just watched him zip up his pants and saunter out, whistling a tune she didn't recognize.

Heart pounding, covered with sweat, Mackenzie squeezed her eyes shut until she was sure the commander was gone. But that sound. It wasn't whistling after all. It took her a full minute to acknowledge her cell's trill.

Half awake, she wiped her hands on her jeans and fished the phone from her pocket. A glance at the bedside clock told her she'd slept for more than an hour. Her mother still dozed, so Mackenzie laid her laptop on the floor and quickly tiptoed into the hallway to take the call. "Hello?" she whispered.

The strident accent was familiar, the greeting characteristically clipped. "You were late today."

Mackenzie felt her stomach tighten as she imagined her frowning sister chewing on an unpolished nail while balancing the receiver under her chin, a restless toddler on one knee and a belly taut from twins due in a few weeks.

Five years her senior, Judith had naturally been the one to keep her younger brother and sister in line when their mother returned to work after their father's death. Only fifteen at the time, Judith had had to grow up much too soon. Mackenzie realized that now. But it didn't change the fact that their relationship was still fraught with emotional baggage - years of bitter disagreements and misunderstood intentions had widened the gulf between them. "I called a few hours ago.

Karyn said you weren't home yet. You promised to take care of mom."

Mackenzie chose her words carefully, handling them like sensitive explosives. "There was a… a situation at the hospital." No point in detailing PJ's suicide. Though Judith had married a soldier, she couldn't relate to the new wave of silent survivors returning to the states from the Middle East. Husband, Colonel Craig McMaster, was in the Jag Corps. A lawyer stationed in Germany for the past nine years, he'd never seen war up close. And to Judith, who considered her term as surrogate mother to Mackenzie and Paul a ten year deployment rivaling Mackenzie's military experience, the idea of leaving the army with PTSD was inconceivable -though she knew what had happened to Mackenzie in Iraq. Some of it anyway.

"You can't afford to pay the extra hours for Karyn."

The accusation in Judith's voice was unmistakable. *Still irresponsible.* The same tone used since the night their nineteen year old brother had died. Exhausted from a back-to-back shift at a local fast foods joint, Paul had agreed to drive fifteen year old Mackenzie to a party miles from home. On the return trip, he'd fallen asleep, wrapping his car around a tree.

How could you be so irresponsible? Judith had screamed at the hospital, repeating the question in the days and months following Paul's funeral. Even after she'd finally stopped, Mackenzie knew her sister would always blame her for the accident. Their mother never said a word, instead descending quietly into a bottle of gin.

Unable to handle the guilt, Mackenzie had run away multiple times until at age twenty she'd dropped out of junior college and left home for good, experimenting with drugs and sex along the way, barely avoiding jail more than once. A nurse who'd treated her STD at a free clinic five years ago finally convinced her to straighten out. That's when Mackenzie had joined the Army reserves, become a nurse herself. Three years ago, she'd married Art, a doctor she'd met at a two week Army summer camp. For the briefest moment, her life had stretched out before her like an unbroken horizon. Endless possibilities. Even Judith had to admit that Mackenzie seemed back on track. That is until everything fell apart in Iraq.

Defensive, Mackenzie blurted "I'm making money."

"How? The deal was no nursing until…."

"I know the deal," Mackenzie interrupted. Judith never stopped reminding her how Craig had saved her from a dishonorable discharge, even managed to convince the Army to let mom keep dad's benefits. A little bureaucratic snafu, they'd said after…. Mackenzie shuddered, reliving her nightmare.

Just keep the secret.

Secrets actually.

Judith didn't know the half of it.

"How then?" her sister was demanding, forcing Mackenzie from her reverie.

"Some freelance writing," Mackenzie said, deliberately vague. Judith wouldn't understand her blogging about the war. The Army was a family tradition - if you weren't a soldier yourself, you married one. Anything negative was not to be shared with the outside world. "It's less than a hundred dollars a month," she hastened to add, minimizing its import.

The baby's wail distracted Judith from probing. "Okay, listen, Craig, Jr's fussing and I've got to pee. These twins leave no room for my bladder!"

The tight laugh surprised Mackenzie who wasn't used to levity from her sister. "Mom's not doing…."

"Just keep your promise," Judith's tone had regained its hard edge. "It's the least you can do."

The connection ended abruptly. Holding a dead receiver, Mackenzie imagined Judith's pursed lips as she hung up - a habit that gave what might have been a lovely face, a perpetually sour expression. Mackenzie wasn't the only one her sister could never forgive. Judith would always blame their mother for becoming a drunk and stealing Judith's childhood. No surprise that she didn't want to hear about their mother's condition. Once Mackenzie had run away for good, Judith considered her responsibilities over, rarely keeping in touch. She'd married Craig and started her own family. She'd been indifferent to the muscle twitches and shakes, attributing them to alcohol and the Xanax her mother took for "her nerves".

Only after Mackenzie had called home from Iraq and heard the nasal tone and garbled speech was a doctor finally consulted. Judith remained unsympathetic despite the diagnosis, implying that ALS was some kind of penance for past sins.

Just keep your promise. It's the least you can do.

Like a probation officer checking on a parolee, Judith's regular calls were meant to remind Mackenzie that this was *her* penance - keeping watch until their mother died.

Feeling low as she always did after hearing from her sister, Mackenzie returned to the bedroom. She'd closed the blinds to reduce the August heat - an attempt to save on the cost of air conditioning. In this softer light, she had to agree with the home health doctor. Her mother's jaundice was much more pronounced this week.

He'd actually said she was lucky - the alcohol induced liver disease would likely kill her before the ALS. He'd meant to be compassionate, Mackenzie knew, but it seemed macabre. Moving closer, she caressed a saffron colored cheek. If Judith saw her mother's ravished body and obvious suffering, would she remain as seemingly unaffected standing here as she could six thousand miles away? Or would all the misunderstandings, all the harsh words be forgotten, made insignificant by the fact of her dying?

For Mackenzie, the time she'd spent as her mother's caretaker had brought an intimacy she'd never experienced growing up. While Judith considered the past eight months penance, for Mackenzie it was a gift, one she wished her sister could share. Probably too late for Judith. The doctor gave their mother weeks at best, maybe just days to live. With the imminent birth of her twins, Judith couldn't travel - even if she wanted to. The lack of closure would haunt her the rest of her life. Mackenzie understood that. She had her own demons to resolve.

No closure. Mackenzie glanced at her open laptop on the nightstand and re-read her post about PJ. By choosing a bullet to his head he'd denied his wife the closure she would need. Not fair.

Life wasn't fair.

Another of her sister's mantras played in her head as she pushed "Publish Post" on the blog site. Then, with a weary sigh, Mackenzie sat back down in the bedside chair to resume her vigil, wondering if Judith would be there for the funeral.

CHAPTER 4

Tuesday, August 19, 2008

An hour later, the telephone rang again. This time it was the land line.

Damn. Not wanting to wake her mother, Mackenzie rushed to grab the portable from the nightstand before the second ring and tiptoed into the kitchen.

"Ms. Dodd?"

"Yes?"

"Mr. Henrick, here. Dr. Mills' admin assistant. He'd like to see you in his office at fifteen hundred hours tomorrow."

Mackenzie glanced toward the bedroom. "Is it really necessary? I don't have anyone to stay with my mom."

"I just follow orders, but he says it is."

Mackenzie let out a long exhale, wondering if she should impose on Viv again. Judith was right. She couldn't afford to pay the aide for extra hours. Even with the few dollars she was making from her blog, Mackenzie was barely keeping up with the bills. But she'd made a promise and that included following orders. "All right," she said finally. "I'll be there."

"Not a problem," Viv said when Mackenzie called to explain her predicament. "Hey listen, about today's post, I was just watching channel 5 news. I had no idea you were at the hospital when that soldier blew his brains out. No wonder you looked like death warmed over. Are you okay, kid?"

"It's on TV?" Mackenzie felt panic rise in her like bile. "Did they mention me?" The last thing she wanted was publicity - reporters coming around to "get her story". *Just keep your promise.*

"No, they didn't mention a witness. But I put two and two together."

"Guess I shouldn't have written that, huh?"

"Are you serious? This is just the kind of piece that could help your blog go viral - not hundreds of clicks, but tens of thousands, maybe millions. You were right there!"

Mackenzie could almost feel Viv's enthusiasm through the receiver. "Whoa. Slow down. I told you from the beginning I don't want to be some kind of celebrity. Especially at the expense of PJ's tragedy."

"First of all, nobody knows your identity. I took care of routing the blog through an international IP server. If you use a proxy server abroad, IP lookups are useless."

Mackenzie had to smile, impressed by Viv's computer prowess.

"Second, you've seen the comments from the folks who read your stuff. You're providing an incredible service for all the other Silent Survivors and their families. Tell you the truth, until I read them, I had no idea there really *was* a war. Gramps says they need to bring back the draft. Except for the big hoo-hah right after the Iraq invasion, only those directly involved have a clue. For the rest of us?" Pausing for effect. "Going shopping. That's our contribution."

Viv shared a bitter laugh with Mackenzie. Given the limited state of their individual pocketbooks, neither could afford to be very patriotic these days. Like Mackenzie, Viv was the designated caretaker in her family. Viv's parents, childless until they'd had their "late baby" well into their forties, had both died last year. With no inheritance to speak of, Viv had dropped out of full time college in Tallahassee to come live with her grandfather. Others might have wallowed in self-pity. Not Viv. Her inner resolve continually amazed Mackenzie. Always finding potential opportunities. Like promoting the Silent Survivors blog.

"Tell you what," Mackenzie said, hoping to put off the issue. "Let's wait to get some feedback and then we can talk."

"Awesome." Doing a one eighty, Viv turned serious again. "It must have been awful being there, trying to talk him out of... of..."

"Yeah," Mackenzie closed her eyes, reliving those moments.

Why had she arrived so early?
Why hadn't she called for help?
How well did she know the victim?
Why hadn't she done more to stop PJ?
How could you be so irresponsible?

The words playing in her head like dissonant chords. "It *was* awful."

"Are you going to the funeral?"

"What?"

"The news said there's going to be a memorial service on Thursday. Maybe you should go. You could tell PJ's wife that it wasn't her fault."

Mackenzie opened her eyes, wondering if Viv was right. She'd been so focused on her own guilt, she hadn't thought about how PJ's wife might react. The grief she felt at that moment wasn't for herself. What rushed before her was the realization of how much pain PJ had caused his family. No matter how gently the news was delivered it had to be a terrible blow. Gazing into the open bedroom where her mother lay quietly dying, she sighed. "I guess I could give her some closure."

"And you too," Viv replied with the wisdom of someone at least twice her age.

CHAPTER 5

Wednesday, August 20, 2008

In the dim orange glow of predawn, Officer Sam Cantori crept cautiously toward the front porch of the tiny West Palm Beach bungalow, heart pounding, one hand hovering above his holstered weapon. You never knew how a "domestic" would play out. Fifteen minutes earlier he and his partner Ed Wilton had responded to the five-thirty 911. A neighbor of Senior Airman Thomas Welkers reported hearing a woman's screams coming from the house, followed by what he insisted were gunshots.

"Scared the beejeebus out of us," the neighbor told Sam when he'd arrived at his door within minutes of the call. "Name's Thompson. Bob and Betty." He indicated his wife, who like him was wrapped in a well-worn terry robe. Both were gray-haired and appeared to be in their late seventies.

"We've lived here twenty years," Bob said. "It's always been a quiet neighborhood. Even when the Welkers first moved in four years ago. Seemed like a decent couple. Two kids, one on the way. Lynette - that's Tommy's wife - and the children spent lots of time with us after Tommy was deployed to Iraq." Bob brushed a wisp of silver hair that had strayed across his wrinkled brow. "We don't have kids of our own, so it's nice to be with young ones."

"Mr. Thompson," Sam had interrupted. "Tell me exactly what you heard tonight."

"Just before we went to bed around eleven there was lots of yelling. We're used to that. Since Tommy got back the third time it's almost non-stop when he's home."

"Any evidence of abuse?"

"You mean did Tommy ever hit Lynette?" Bob shook his head. "Not as far as I know."

"Yes, but Lynette told me he was changed, you know, since the war," Betty had stepped from behind her husband. "They were having lots of problems. He couldn't find a job, was months late on house payments. Then he stopped sleeping and when he did, he had real bad nightmares," she said. "Lately he started with the shakes. That's why Lynette made him go to the VA for help."

"Ma'am are you sure you heard gunshots?"

"Well, I'm not real sure. I got up around five a.m. to pee," she said matter-of-factly. "I remember because I always check the clock when I come back to bed to make sure I don't disturb Bob. Doctor says he needs his eight hours. I guess I dropped off again when Lynette screamed. Thought at first it was a dream. Then there were loud 'pop pop pop' sounds. That's why I woke Bob. He's a heavy sleeper, you know."

Ed's not-so-muffled snicker indicated his impatience with the interview. He'd already told his young protege that the 911 was likely to be a waste of time. Close to retirement, Sam's partner was only interested in getting through his last two months unscathed. "Grab my pension and head over to Pensacola where I'll spend my days fishing and watching the babes on the beach."

Ignoring him, Sam had asked Thompson. "Okay, so after that what did you hear?"

Bob and Betty glanced at each other as if to confirm their recollection. "Nothing," Bob said. "It's been dead quiet since we called you guys."

Ed exhaled audibly while the younger officer thanked the couple, told them to stay inside and lock their doors.

"Please let us know if those poor children are okay."

"Yes ma'am," Sam had promised, then grabbed his flashlight and headed next door followed by his obviously reluctant partner.

Now he slowly ascended the Welkers' front steps and pushed the door bell.

No answer.

Another two rings with no response. This time he tried banging on the door. "Tommy Welkers, open up! Police!"

Nothing.

After a few more moments of silence, he peeked through the front windows, but the house was dark.

"Hey!" His partner pointed to the morning newspaper laying on the bottom step. "Guess we better take a look around."

Sam nodded and aimed the glow from his flashlight on a cracked stone pathway leading to the backyard.

Ed reached the back door before Sam. "Jesus!" Lying across the transom of the open kitchen entrance was a bloody body.

Sam shined the light inside and started to wretch.

His partner grabbed the flashlight, took a second to view the scene himself before pulling the radio from his belt to call for help. "We've got four victims here. Two kids, two adults. Dispatch the ME and a CSI team ASAP."

It didn't take long for the quiet neighborhood to be transformed into a full blown crime scene. Sam and his partner had draped a roll of yellow tape across the entrance of the Welkers home. Inside the CSI team was busy collecting evidence.

Unable to come closer, Bob and Betty Thompson were joined by other robed neighbors clustered on the sidewalk across the street, watching as two technicians from the ME's office slowly rolled out gurneys loaded with covered bodies. Airman Welkers, his pregnant wife Lynette and their two young children. Shocked, the onlookers just shook their heads.

"Such a tragedy."

"Those poor children."

"How could this happen?"

Sam couldn't help wondering the same thing as he watched the ME van take off from the scene. Once he completed the paperwork at the station, he might just visit that VA psychiatrist he'd met yesterday. It wasn't necessary for the investigation. He had his own reasons to search for answers.

A stickler for punctuality, General Paulsen hated to be kept waiting. He also hated being out of uniform, but those were his instructions. "You're late," he grumbled as portly west Texas Congressman Leyton Fremont slowly settled on the bench beside him.

At midday, the summer crowds around the Lincoln Memorial provided appropriate cover - two Washington professionals in business suits grabbing a lunchtime break.

"Couldn't be helped," the white-haired politician drawled. "Just left one fundraiser. Got two more before the day's over. Damn dog and pony shows."

"Yet somehow you've managed time for a sub-committee hearing."

"Not my doing, General. Don't forget, we're the minority party."

Paulsen acknowledged the disappointing truth. "So what am I up against?"

"Nothing you can't handle." Fremont tossed Paulsen a pointed look. "As long as you don't let that famous temper of yours get the better of you."

Swallowing a retort, Paulsen's jaw tightened.

"It's August recess," Fremont explained. "The current committee chair, Jonah Casey, called us in for this session knowing no one from the national press or the public is likely to show. Guy's up for re-election. Needs to score a few points with his hometown vets for the record. Make it clear he supports the troops."

"Don't we all?" Teeth clenched, Paulsen fought hard to hide his contempt for Fremont, though in the almost two decades he'd known the septuagenerian, nothing seemed to deflate the man's self-centered core. Paulsen despised having to be his toady. If the clandestine project hadn't required continued support from this senior member of the Armed Services Committee, he'd be leading the campaign against him.

"Casey will probably want a status report on the PTSD programs," the politician said, ignoring Paulsen's hostile edge. He removed a linen handkerchief from his pocket and wiped the sweat from his brow. "And he might ask about the suicides."

"What about them?" Paulsen asked, his caution flag raised.

"Two in a week from one Florida VA?"

Paulsen was nonplussed. Welkers' murder/suicide was just hours old. "How'd you...?"

"Eyes and ears, General. How'd you think I manage to stay in this town for thirty years?"

At that moment, three middle-aged women leading a troupe of uniformed Asian teens stopped by the bench to snap photos of the monument. Fremont waited until they'd passed before continuing. "I can't afford to have SEDO become another Charlie's War," he said, lowering his voice. "So you better contain this thing or we're all going down."

Waiting for Dr. Mills to complete his phone call, Mackenzie studied the wall behind his desk where a row of perma-plaqued certificates and framed photos hung. Michael M. Mills, M.D. Medical school at the Uniformed Services University, internship in Bethesda, Maryland and psych residency at the VA in Washington, DC. One snapshot of a uniformed Mills shaking hands with a serious looking George W. Bush and another with a smiling Bill Clinton. No pictures of family.

Focusing on the man seated across from her, Mackenzie calculated his age to be around fifty-five, though with his military crew cut and almost creaseless face, he could easily pass for a decade younger. Definitely a lifer, she thought. And that made her wary.

"How are you today, Ms. Dodd?" Mills asked as he re-placed the receiver.

She shrugged. "Okay." What was the point in telling the truth - that she'd barely slept last night and when she had finally closed her eyes, she'd added the pain of witnessing PJ's suicide to her already long list of nightmares? Mills seemed like a decent enough guy, but in eight months he'd never shown interest in probing her psyche. Other than the weekly mandatory PTSD clinic hour during which she rarely spoke, he'd barely acknowledged her. So why now?

Drawn to the standard issue computer monitor on Mill's credenza, Mackenzie was aware that every patient record resided there. The VA had the first and one of the few integrated electronic medical record systems in the country. She wondered what exactly her record contained.

She knew the Army had expunged any mention of her rape. An honorable discharge in exchange for her silence on the subject. That was the deal her brother-in-law had made when months after the deed, out of desperation, she'd told her ex everything, said she couldn't take it anymore and planned to go AWOL. Art had called Craig who'd promised to help. Four weeks later she had her completed DD214 separation form and a seat on a flight out of Baghdad.

No doubt the required VA clinic was less a concern for the stress of her trauma than a way to be sure she kept her end of the bargain. Now she wondered if Mills was just checking that she didn't renege.

Leaning forward on his elbows, the psychiatrist rested his chin on folded hands as if thinking carefully about what to say or how to say it. "I plan to debrief the group at our next session, but I wanted to meet with you first. To hear exactly what happened and how you're feeling. I'm really sorry you had to witness Sergeant Linton's suicide."

There was a kindness in his eyes, a look that suggested he genuinely meant it and Mackenzie felt herself relax. As best she could recall the details, she described how she'd happened to arrive early and found PJ with a gun to his head.

"You told the police officer that you didn't know Sergeant Linton well." Mills said when she'd finished.

"I didn't even know his last name. He'd only been in the group a week."

Mills nodded. "Of course. So you'd never met with him outside of our clinic?"

"No, I tried to talk to him before he…" Mackenzie bit her quivering lip. "I couldn't…" She felt tears touch her eyes.

Mills handed her a Kleenex from the box on his desk, waiting for her to regain her composure before speaking. "Look, what happened yesterday was horrible. But you can't blame yourself."

Despite the words, Mackenzie felt an ache within her, powerless to control as her emotions took a free fall. "I understand that and yet I do somehow feel responsible," she said between sniffles. "Maybe if I could have called for help or done a better job of getting him to open up."

"Magical thinking," Mills said. "Of course I can't divulge confidential information, but suffice it to say, PJ was a very troubled soul. Right or wrong, the choices we make define who we are. When he walked into the clinic yesterday, he'd already made his choice. There's nothing you or I could have done at that point." He punctuated his assertion with an unwavering gaze.

More than anything, Mackenzie wanted to believe him. Lately she'd been feeling guilt about everything in her life - her brother's death, her misspent youth, her failed marriage, the grief she'd given her sister while they were growing up, the abandonment of her mom when she most needed her. And now this young soldier's suicide. Sure she understood on some rational level that all of this wasn't her fault. Still, she wondered how her life might have gone if she'd made better choices.

"I guess you're right," she admitted, dabbing at her eyes.

"I know I am. So many young people coming back damaged from this war." Mills lowered his voice as if sharing a secret. "I wish we had more money for better programs, but with Congress pushing budget cuts, we do the best we can with what we have."

Mackenzie realized the psychiatrist was opening up to her, that he too must feel a certain amount of guilt. So much was out of his control. She nodded her understanding.

Mills sat back. "I hope you'll appreciate that the Army wants to keep this…" He paused, apparently searching for the right word," incident… out of the press."

Although Mackenzie never mentioned Silent Survivors, she readily agreed. After all, with so relatively few readers, it was unlikely to reach a wider audience. Besides, she'd already posted yesterday's blog. "Of course."

"Good." Mills stood, indicating the meeting's conclusion. "Then I'll see you next week in group."

Mackenzie rose to shake his hand before heading for the door. Just as she opened it, Mills asked, "How's your mother?"

The question elicited a jolt of anxiety in Mackenzie. How did he know? She turned back to face him. "My mother?"

"My administrative assistant mentioned you were taking care of your mother. Is she ill?"

Mackenzie swallowed. So that wasn't in her medical record. "She has ALS."

Mills' brows came together in a deep frown. "What did you say?"

Confusing his expression for misunderstanding, she explained. "Lou Gehrig's Disease."

"Yes, yes. Amyotrophic Lateral Sclerosis. Not good." Mills let out a long breath. "You've never brought this up in the group sessions."

"I guess I didn't think it was relevant."

"Everything that adds to your stress is relevant," he said, his tone uncharacteristically sharp. "I think this is something we really should explore further."

Torn between desire to share her bottled up feelings and fear of betraying her promise, Mackenzie remained silent.

As if appreciating her internal conflict, Mills came to where she stood and gave her shoulder an avuncular squeeze. "Go home and take care of your mom. We have time to talk later. Perhaps I can have Mr. Henrick set up a few private sessions."

Keep your promise.

"I don't..."

"Dr. Mills?" Donald Henrick, the psychiatrist's thirty-something administrative assistant stood in the half-open doorway. "Sorry to disturb you, sir, but there was an urgent call for Ms. Dodd."

Mackenzie knew the instant she recognized sympathy in the bespectacled assistant's face. "Is it my mother?"

"I'm afraid she's passed."

"No, no!"

Mills put his arms around Mackenzie as she leaned against him, sobbing.

Seated in the far waiting area, Sam Cantori observed Mackenzie emerge from Dr. Mills' office. He would have liked to say hello, tell her that he remembered her from grade school, but she just flew by him, head down, dashing into an open elevator. He could see that she'd been crying and wondered why. Something to do with yesterday's suicide?

"Officer Cantori?" From the doorway, Mills' administrative assistant called his name. "Doctor is free now."

"Right." As Sam stood, he did a quick check of the elevators, hoping to catch another glimpse of Mackenzie. The doors had already slammed shut. Funny seeing her again after all these years. Even in her distraught state, she looked damn good. As he headed for the psychiatrist's office, he decided that he might just pay his old schoolmate a visit in the next few days.

Paulsen pulled his microphone closer. "Could you repeat the question, Mr. Casey?" Despite the chill in the Rayburn House Office building hearing room, he was beginning to sweat. He'd changed into his uniform for the session and he could feel an uncomfortable wetness around his starched collar and under his arms.

For the first half hour everything had been low key - each member of the Armed Services Committee thanking him for his service, rhapsodizing about the splendid work of today's military and promising to continue to fund the VA. Nothing controversial. Not until the Chairman, Jonah Casey, took his turn. Thank goodness this was a closed session and that Fremont had been right. With Congress on August hiatus, there were no public observers. The sole photographer had left after snapping a few photos of the members to share with their constituents back home.

"Of course, General." Seated on the raised platform flanked by an American flag, Casey smiled down at the witness. More a smirk, Paulsen thought. Everyone knew the Democrat from San Francisco had been against the wars in Iraq and Afghanistan from the start. Now it seemed he was determined to discredit the Army vice-chief of staff's handling of the healthcare issues of his troops.

"I was asking about drugs." Casey leaned over to one of his legislative aides who handed him a sheaf of paper. "How do you explain this internal memo from the Defense Department's Pharmacoeconomic Center at Fort Sam Houston in San Antonio?"

How in God's name did that bastard get his hands on that? Paulsen stared at Leyton Fremont sitting at the far end of the dais, but the politician seemed determined to avoid eye contact.

Slipping on his Ben Franklin reading glasses, Casey leafed through the report. "It says here that twenty percent of the one point one million active-duty troops surveyed were taking some form of psychotropic drugs including Valium, Xanax and even Seroquel, which I understand is used to treat schizophrenia, bipolar disorders and depression." Casey looked up, dramatically removed his glasses and shook his head. "Tell me, sir, how is it that US Central Command's policy allows ninety to one hundred eighty day supplies of these highly addictive drugs before our soldiers deploy? Sounds to me like CENTCOM's pushing pills rather than dealing with the problem."

Heeding Fremont's warning to keep his cool, Paulsen ignored the burning in his gut and forced his lips into neutral. "Congressman, that memo has not been vetted by our experts yet. There are some serious concerns about how the data was collected and analyzed. I will be happy to send you our report once it is completed. In the meantime, my office has submitted a full update of our Post Traumatic Stress Disorder programs to be placed in the record and I am prepared to give you an executive summary of our progress which has been substantial."

Another of Casey's staffers handed him a manila folder. Slipping his glasses back on, the congressman made a show of studying the pages inside before addressing Paulsen again. "I assume sir that you are aware of the Congressional Quarterly's compilation of the latest statistics from the Armed Forces."

Paulsen cleared his throat. "I am."

"It says here that this year almost as many US military personnel took their own lives than were killed in either the Afghanistan or Iraq wars." Casey began rattling off the numbers: "The Army had two hundred and eleven suicides, the Navy, forty-seven, the Air Force thirty-four and the Marine Corps, forty-two. Three hundred thirty four suicides compared with two hundred ninety-seven killed in Iraq and one hundred forty four in Afghanistan."

Casey stared directly at Paulsen. "General, I think you'd have to agree. Those numbers are staggering and tragically, an indication that we are simply not doing the job of adequately providing mental health care for both our active duty service people and our veterans."

Paulsen would have liked to jump over the witness table and ring Casey's neck. How could this forty-something elitist politician who'd never served in the military begin to understand the challenges of fighting today's wars? A POW in Vietnam, wounded in Kuwait, Paulsen had served his country longer than the young congressman had been alive. He'd spent his life making sure men like Casey could live in a free society. But did any of them appreciate his years of dedication? Though he could barely contain his outrage, Paulsen responded as politely as he could. "Again, sir, I believe some of these numbers are not accurate."

Casey nodded. "Actually I probably agree with you there. I suspect the numbers are even higher since we're not capturing the suicide statistics for Marine Corps reservists or vets of Iraq and Afghanistan who've already left the service. In fact, I understand there may have been two such cases in Florida just this week."

If Fremont hadn't given him a heads-up, Paulsen would never have been able to project outward equanimity. "Both are under investigation."

"Would you agree that the rising number of suicides coincides with the US military forces redeploying frequently to Iraq and Afghanistan?"

Paulsen took a deep breath, focusing on carefully answering this question. "I can tell you that we've determined that at least one third of the active duty soldiers who killed themselves this year had no deployment history."

"But two-thirds did," Casey said. "It's hard to believe the stress of a long war with lack of time at home between multiple deployments isn't a major factor here."

"The Army is taking an aggressive approach to prevention through periodic screening and education."

"Yes, I actually read your report, General. And certainly the PTSD clinics in the VA are a good start. But I'm convinced the process of questioning military personnel to make a PTSD diagnosis isn't thorough enough and that there's too much of a stigma attached to honestly speaking about emotional problems." Casey swiveled his wrist to check his watch. "I see our time is up. I would like to propose further hearings in the next few months to look specifically at the whole issue of suicide. General, we'll want a detailed report from you at that time." Without waiting for Paulsen's response, Casey struck his gavel and concluded the meeting.

"So you never saw Airman Welkers?" Sam asked Dr. Mills as the psychiatrist scrolled through the computer screen displaying Welkers' medical record.

"Actually one of our medical providers had referred him to our PTSD clinic a few months ago."

"And he didn't show?"

Mills shook his head. "We're trying to reduce the stigma around seeking care, but it's not easy to change the military macho culture."

"The neighbors said he was having trouble sleeping."

Mills nodded. "PTSD is often characterized by flashbacks in the form of nightmares, a state of hyper-vigilance or a feeling of emotional numbness to the world."

Sam expelled a deep breath. "Or all of the above."

Shifting forward in his chair, Mills stared at him for a moment as if carefully taking his measure. "Sounds as though your visit here may be less a part of the Welkers investigation and more about something personal."

Surprised by the psychiatrist's insight, Sam welcomed an opportunity to talk about a subject too painful to share with friends and even his recently widowed mother. "My kid brother Jake. Did two tours in Afghanistan. Came back last year completely changed."

"How so?"

"He used to be a gentle soul. Lots of friends. A really happy-go-lucky guy. Always accusing me of being too uptight. But since that last tour, he became a recluse. Hardly left the house. Watched cartoons all day. At night Mom said she could hear him pacing back and forth in his room. When he did sleep, he'd wake up in a cold sweat, screaming. Any little noise made him jump."

"Did he seek help?"

"Like Welkers, he refused. I tried talking to him. But he'd become suspicious of everyone. Especially me since I'm a cop. Thought I was out to get him."

"You're speaking of him in the past tense. Is he...."

"No, he's not dead, though he's as good as," Sam said. "Dad finally threw him out, told him to get a job. Instead, Jake started drinking heavily. He'd go to bars and hang out till closing. Six months ago he got into a fight, pulled a knife and stabbed the guy a half-dozen times. He's serving a life sentence without parole for first degree murder at Florida state prison in Indiantown."

"I'm truly sorry."

Sam nodded. "The verdict killed my dad. Had a heart attack the same day. Jake was his favorite." He looked at Mills. "It's just so hard to understand what happened to him over there."

"Isn't that the million dollar question?" Mills said as much to himself as to Sam.

Because the summer schedule had left his office seriously understaffed and the situation seemed so straight-forward, the Florida medical examiner took less than two hours to complete cursory autopsies on the Welkers family and pronounce the official cause of deaths murder/suicide.

As though an illusion, the moment Paulsen glanced up after gathering his papers and shoving them into his briefcase, the entire hearing room had emptied. Fuming, he entered the men's room, surprised to find Fremont standing at the urinal. Without turning, the portly congressman acknowledged him with a nod toward the wall mirror. "Good job, kiddo."

Paulsen kept silent, not sure they were alone.

"Just you and me," Fremont said, as if reading his mind. He zipped his fly and walked to the sink. "I think we're gonna be okay. At least for now."

"How the hell did Casey get those reports?"

"I told you we're the minority party. Less control. Though the fellow at DOD responsible for the leak has been dealt with."

Figuring the less he knew about how that matter had been handled the better, Paulsen did not inquire. Instead he asked, "Did you hear Casey? He wants a comprehensive analysis of the suicides." Paulsen stared at Fremont's reflection in the mirror. "Much as I regret saying this, I think we're going to have to wind down the operation."

"Nonsense." Fremont finished washing his hands, dried them on a hand towel by the sink, then swiveled to face Paulsen. "In three months we're gonna win back the White House and hopefully Congress too. Casey's little investigation, like the man himself, will be a flash in the pan." His smile was conspiratorial. "Just use that great big bureaucracy of yours to stall."

Paulsen was close to revealing another issue that might not be as easy to deal with when one of the Rayburn Building uniformed guards entered.

"Sorry, Congressman. I thought everyone had left after the hearing."

Fremont's ample belly shook with his laugh. "Son, I'm afraid the General here and yours truly are much too old to pass up a pit stop. We'll be out in just a minute."

The young guard nodded. He gave a little salute, wished them both a good day, and exited the men's room.

"Everything will work out," Fremont said once they were alone again. He walked to the door, opened it, and without turning back added, "Trust me. And don't get your bowels in an uproar."

As Paulsen followed him out, all he could think was that he already had severe indigestion.

CHAPTER 6

Wednesday, August 20, 2008

Mackenzie wasn't sure how she'd made it home. She'd driven the whole way in a daze, on autopilot. Nosing into a tight parking space, she shut off the engine, left the car, and sprinted up the stairs to her apartment. The door was unlocked and slightly ajar. Taking a deep breath, she pushed it all the way open and stepped inside.

Viv stood in the tiny kitchen area talking to the home health doctor. Spotting Mackenzie, she hurried over and encircled her in a tight hug.

They stood that way for a moment before Viv partially disengaged, holding Mackenzie by the shoulders at arms length. "I'm really sorry, kid."

"Can I see her?" Mackenzie asked the doctor.

"Of course." He led her into the bedroom where her mother lay enveloped in a white sheet, eyes shut, appearing for all the world as if she were merely sleeping. Except for the complete silence. No more rhythmic hum of the ventilator. The doctor must have pulled the endotracheal tube and shut off the machine. He'd also removed the IVs, feeding tube, and Foley catheter.

Mackenzie stroked her mother's cheek, surprised to find it still warm. She looked over at Viv lingering in the doorway. "What happened?"

"It was so quick," Viv said, her voice cracking. "I was sitting by the bed watching her sleep. I don't think I even looked away, but one minute she was there and the next..."

"Believe me, she didn't suffer," the doctor assured her. "We all knew the end was just a matter of time."

The end.

So final.

Mackenzie nodded, though she couldn't shake the guilt of having missed her mother's last expiratory breath, a sound she imagined must have been as soft as a welcomed sigh. She'd been suffering for so long. Mackenzie knew she was ready to go. Still, she would have liked to be there, to hold her hand, to say her goodbye. "What happens now?" she asked, willing herself not to cry again. She'd used up all her tears with Dr. Mills.

"As the doctor of record I've already signed the death certificate, so there's no need for an autopsy. The funeral home is on their way. They'll help you make burial arrangements." The doctor gave her arm a comforting pat. "Do you have family you need to call?"

The question evoked a jarring reality. Both parents were gone. She was officially an orphan. "I have a sister."

With rush hour traffic backed up on the Baltimore Beltway, the drive from D.C. to Frederick, Maryland made Paulsen late for his meeting. By the time he pulled up to the modest two story brick home, Doug Anders was just sitting down to dinner with his wife and teenage daughter. Still agitated by Casey's questioning at the afternoon's Congressional hearing, he refused Anders' offer to join them, insisting they talk right away. "It's important," he said after apologizing for interrupting their meal.

"No worries," Anders replied, the expression a carry-over from two years as a postdoc in infectious disease near Sydney.

The handsome forty-seven year old researcher hadn't been back for almost two decades, but still actively cultivated the laid-back Aussie style and speech patterns. Paulsen was never sure if Anders didn't amp up the "G-days" and "no worries" just because he knew it irritated the General who didn't want to be reminded of their original connection.

"So, what would you like to hear tonight?" Anders whispered after he'd led the way to his basement office, locked the door behind them and flipped on the light switch. He pointed to a box of CDs on the floor next to an old boom-box. "Ethel Merman, Wagner, or maybe a little heavy metal? My daughter's just discovered Metallica. They make enough noise to mask any conversation."

Paulsen gave his usual response when he and Anders had their clandestine meetings here. "Makes no difference to me. I was tone deaf even before that Kuwaiti bastard shattered my eardrum with shrapnel."

"Don Giovanni, then. Mozart's a lot easier on the ears." Anders slipped the top CD into the boombox and pushed 'play'. "So what's up? he asked once the tenor had begun his aria.

Paulsen took a moment to collect his thoughts, letting his eye wander around the tiny windowless office. Because Anders did most of his work in the bowels of nearby Ft. Detrick, the decor here was minimalist - just a standard government-issued steelcase desk and chair, a couple of wall shelves filled with rows of lined composition books and a stack of scientific journals on a credenza with a brass nameplate declaring him Douglas Anders, MD, PhD, Director, PsyOps - a recent promotion.

Knowing it was a title Anders had long coveted and was loath to jeopardize, Paulsen hoped he would listen to reason. Pacing back and forth in the small space while Anders perched on the edge of his desk, he quickly summarized what had happened at the hearing, including Casey's plan to step up investigations of the military's handling of PTSD cases. "I think we've got to close SEDO down."

Fine lines along the brow of the still young-looking face merged into a frown. "You can't be serious."

"Things are getting too hot." Paulsen removed his army jacket as if to emphasize the point.

Anders shook his head. "Strategic Enemy Defense Operation's the only reason you've been able to wage your war with such a small all-volunteer army. How can you think of shutting it down when you're so close to winning?"

Paulsen regarded Anders, trying to get a grip on his feelings about the man who'd come to him as a baby-faced, sandy-haired, twenty-eight year old wunderkund - the Harvard trained MD/PhD who'd recognized the potential of a pill that was just another molecule in the infectious disease armamentarium. Joe college good looks, a disarming smile and a passion for the marriage of science and psychology easily won over the equally ambitious Army captain who negotiated a position for young Anders on a newly formed secret research team and made deals with devils like Fremont to keep the funding coming. The careers of both men had soared over the years. But now Paulsen wondered if the whole operation was in jeopardy. "How long do you think we can prevent someone like Casey from figuring out what's really going on?"

"You worry too much," Anders replied. "The drug's been out since the Gulf War. It's a military staple. Hell it's still on the CDC's recommended list of malaria therapies. You said Fremont plugged the leak at DOD." Anders pointed to the research notebooks lining the wall behind him. "These and military grade encrypted digital files are the only copies of the study protocol. No one has access but me. All *you* have to do is keep a lid on inquiries from any local military sites and we're home free. Okay?"

Relieved by Anders' confidence, Paulsen felt the tension in his shoulders dissipate. Maybe he was being too paranoid. After all Anders had managed to keep the project a secret for well over a decade. Besides, he had as much to lose as Paulsen if anyone discovered the truth about SEDO. More even, since Paulsen had no doubt that Anders' plain vanilla lifestyle belied a hefty retirement stash somewhere offshore. Slipping on his jacket, he nodded. "Okay."

"Good." Anders hopped off his desk, unlocked the office door, and wrapped an arm around Paulsen's shoulder. "Now what you really need is a nice cold beer and a good Maryland crab cake followed by a piece of my wife's homemade pecan pie."

It was close to midnight when Anders returned to his basement office, picked up the phone, and dialed a number. "I'm afraid you may be right about the good general," he said.

"You think he's a candidate for forced retirement?" the voice on the other end asked. Emphasis on *forced*.

Taking a long moment to consider the implications of the question, Anders finally responded, "It may come to that, but let's wait for now. No reason to create another potential blip in our operation. Meantime let's keep a close eye on the old man."

"You got it, son."

At that same moment, a Southeast Washington Hospital resident was pronouncing 'time of death' for a thirty-eight year old Department of Defense employee. The man had been unconscious for over a week - ever since he'd been pulled from his Mustang that had plunged into the Anacosta River near the Sousa Bridge.

The hospital lab reported an extremely elevated blood alcohol level and an empty whiskey bottle was found in the salvaged vehicle. Lacking any evidence to the contrary, D.C. police had already closed their investigation, deeming the loss of control of the car an unfortunate accident.

CHAPTER 7

Wednesday, August 20, 2008

"Well, I guess that's that," Judith had said when Mackenzie finally reached her in Germany.

The reaction should have come as no surprise and yet her sister's cold indifference only added to Mackenzie's sense of loss. There was no question about Judith's attending the funeral. "My doctor won't let me travel," she said, though they both knew she wouldn't have been there regardless. "Craig will fly over on Monday to take care of the paperwork. Hold off on the burial until then." So dispassionate, there'd been no words of comfort before Judith had summarily hung up.

Now hours after the funeral home had removed her mother's body and the doctor and Viv had gone, Mackenzie felt utterly alone. In the kitchen she discovered a half full bottle of Grey Goose her mother must have stashed before she'd been confined to bed. Pouring herself a glass, Mackenzie sipped the liquid, savoring its warmth as it traveled down her throat.

Another glass left the bottle empty and her mellow and melancholic as she wandered into the sparsely furnished living room, pulled a dusty photo album from the bookshelf and began thumbing through the curled pages of pasted pictures: her mother's winsome smile as a young bride, standing beside her soldier husband, buzz cut, expression somber; several in which her mother was clearly pregnant, standing alone, but always grinning; then three baby pictures - Judith, Paul, Mackenzie. In each, their father held the tiny bundles with an obvious tentativeness, as if anxiously waiting for the moment to hand them back.

Only in the photos featuring him and Paul as the boy grew - the two playing ball or holding up a freshly caught trout or saluting each other, Paul, the Boy Scout, his father dressed in his Army uniform - did he appear to be enjoying fatherhood.

Mackenzie stopped at a snapshot of both her parents hugging Paul the day his little league team won the championship. Everybody beaming in that one. No question Paul was the favorite. Thank goodness her father hadn't lived to bury his son, Mackenzie thought, experiencing recurrent guilt, knowing that the accident was the beginning of her mother's downward spiral into alcoholism.

In the few photos after Paul's death - Christmas dinners, high school graduations, proms, even Judith's wedding, their mother's smile was tinged with almost palpable sadness. Flipping to the last page, Mackenzie found the photomat strip of Mackenzie and Art posing the day they'd eloped. Art must have sent it, she thought, with a special ache. Mackenzie knew that Art had continued to call her mother long after the divorce. Unwilling to accept Mackenzie's terse explanation for the break-up, her mother had mourned his death last February as if he'd been her own child.

So many secrets....

Snapping the album shut, Mackenzie deposited it back on the shelf between a lovely porcelain doll from Vietnam that had been her then nineteen year old father's engagement gift to his future bride and a tiny marble elephant her mother had brought back from a trip to India a few years ago - her first and only travel outside of the country. To Mackenzie, the two knick-knacks sandwiching the photo album represented fleeting happiness in a sea of sorrow.

Working up her nerve, she slowly approached the door to her mother's bedroom and nudged it open. Silence enveloped her like a heavy cloak as she entered and slumped into the chair beside the deserted hospital bed. Here she'd kept an eight month vigil while her mother fought to live, yet prayed to end her misery. Blinking back tears, Mackenzie wished she'd been there for the final moment, but then death had come with such a quiet abruptness, she'd probably have missed it, misdiagnosing drugged somnolence.

I'm so sorry, Mom.

Closing her eyes, Mackenzie felt utterly drained and empty. For the most part, all these months she'd managed to put the past behind her, dragging herself forward, seeing nothing ahead but the exigencies of the day to day. Her self-imposed penance hadn't allowed her to imagine a future. Now, engulfed in the darkness of this dingy apartment, she wondered what she would do with the rest of her life.

CHAPTER 8

Thursday, August 21, 2008

"Jeez, did you sleep in that chair all night?"

It took more than a second to register the voice. Mackenzie's eyes fluttered open. Morning sunlight streaming through the window blinds illuminated Viv, standing in the bedroom doorway dressed in her usual black, though today's pants and blouse were more Ann Taylor, less Goth.

"Phone off the hook, the place unlocked. Have you forgotten the burglary last month in 3B? I was worried about you."

Mackenzie shrugged, the ache in her shoulders a proxy for the pain in her heart. "Didn't want to talk. Guess I must have dozed off."

Nodding her understanding, Viv pointed to the bedside clock. "It's almost nine. If we don't hurry we'll be late."

"Late?"

"PJ's memorial service."

"I can't." Mackenzie sighed, overwhelmed by a torpor born of grief. "I have to get started cleaning out my mother's things."

"Plenty of time," Viv said, crossing the room. "Didn't you say your brother-in-law wasn't coming 'til next week?"

"I don't belong there. I…"

"Not true." Viv grabbed Mackenzie's laptop from the floor beside her chair, flipped open the cover, pressed the power button, and logged onto the Silent Survivors blog. "Take a look at this," she said, sitting on the bed and turning the screen to face Mackenzie. "Almost a *thousand* clicks yesterday. That's the most yet for one post. There were a bunch of nice comments like 'keep up the good work' and 'you speak for all of us' and 'sorry you have to go through that', but the one that stands out…. Here, let me find it."

Viv scrolled down the page and then she was reading:

"Dear Silent Survivor. Like the poor soldier you write about, my husband took his own life. Three tours in Afghanistan - the third protecting a barren hill while he and his buddies were being picked off one by one like fish in a barrel by Taliban snipers. He survived, yes, but when he got home he was a walking dead man. Always afraid to close his eyes because of constant nightmares. Paranoid, volatile, he couldn't rest. Only in death did he finally find peace. So please don't blame yourself in any way. Just as I couldn't help my husband, there was nothing you could do to stop that solider from ending his pain. My husband died alone. At least you were with that young man at the end.

She signed it 'Wyoming War Widow'."

Mackenzie let out a deep breath. "I don't know what to say."

"Say you'll go to the memorial service and talk to PJ's wife."

It was just after ten a.m. when Mackenzie and Viv slipped into a pew near the back of the VA cemetery chapel in Lake Worth. They could have sat almost anywhere - the turnout in the tiny hall for the funeral of Philip Joseph Linton was pitifully meagre.

Mackenzie was glad to see that the press had stayed away, but she was surprised that few of the two dozen or so attendees were uniformed, none of whom Mackenzie recognized from her PTSD group. Hard perhaps for them to show solidarity for a fallen comrade who had taken his own life. And yet, as she thought of the blog post from the woman in Wyoming, how could you not argue that the war had played at least some part in the internal conflict that resulted in his death?

Just outside the door, one Marine began playing "Taps" on his trumpet while two others, capped, gloved and dressed in starched blues, marched in cadence up the aisle, stopping in front of PJ's flag draped closed casket.

In the front pew, wearing a simple black dress, the widow sat silently, her head bowed, as the two Marines carefully lifted the flag between them, caressing it with their white gloves, making tight folds with almost meditative precision. Only after they had handed her the red, white and blue fabric triangle and the rifles rang their twenty-one shots outside - each of seven Marines firing three times in sync - did she burst into a sudden wail.

The surge of emotion took Mackenzie by surprise as the widow's cries evoked memories of her father's funeral. Not quite ten at the time, she could never forget the sound of her mother's sorrowful shrieks. The grief she felt now wasn't for herself. What rushed before her was the notion of how much pain PJ had caused his family. She wished she could offer this woman some comfort.

"You have to talk to her," Viv whispered as if reading her thoughts.

Because PJ was being cremated, the service ended with the minister's short generic praise of a fallen vet followed by the Lord's Prayer. As the congregation stood and slowly filed out, an older woman dressed in black pressed forward to embrace the widow, folding her to her breast, muffling the sobs. The young blonde's mother, Mackenzie guessed. PJ had said his wife had moved in with her after his last deployment. Once the choking sounds subsided, the older woman began escorting her daughter from the church.

Near the entrance, several women Mackenzie assumed were friends or relatives of the widow encircled her like a protective coterie of mother hens offering quiet condolences, eloquent less in their words than in the emotion conveyed by the sadness in their eyes. Not wanting to intrude, Mackenzie held back, feeling as though she didn't belong here, as though the depth of her own grief for PJ, someone she really didn't know, would be misinterpreted.

Finally the group around the widow slowly drifted away. MacKenzie felt Viv nudge her forward just as a four star general pushed past, blocking her path. "Mrs. Linton?" The officer introduced himself. "General Paulsen," he said, taking the short-haired blonde's hand in his. "On behalf of the United States military, I want to extend our sincerest sympathy for your loss. If there's anything you need…"

"Need?" The widow pulled her hand from his, her swollen, tear stained face contorting into an angry mask. "I need my husband back." She wagged her finger at him. "I *need* the man *your* military killed."

The older woman gripped her daughter's arm. "Christine, please."

"Please what, mother? Please don't tell the general here the truth?" Her voice was a hoarse rasp as she faced Paulsen. "PJ didn't kill himself, General. *You* killed him. That's the truth!"

She glared at him for several moments as if deciding to say more, then sighing, brushed hurriedly past him and out the church door. Viv walked out too, leaving Mackenzie too stunned to move.

"Please forgive my daughter, General," the widow's mother was saying. "She's not herself."

If Paulsen was upset by the verbal ambush, his face did not betray him. Instead, his soft smile conveyed sympathetic understanding. "The military grieves for the loss of every good man like your son-in-law." He removed a business sized card from his pants pocket and handed it to the older woman. "My personal phone number and email. When your daughter feels up to it, I'd like to fly down from Washington to talk more about the war."

Placing his arm on hers, he escorted her out the door toward the parking lot. Too far away, Mackenzie couldn't hear what he said there, but she watched as he waved goodbye, then walked to a black sedan where a young Marine stood near the open door to the back seat. As soon as Paulsen settled in, the officer slammed the door shut and signaled the driver who joined the line of cars exiting the cemetery.

"Are you okay?"

Mackenzie pivoted to face Viv who'd reappeared at the chapel entrance. "I'm alright, I guess. Where'd you go?"

"Caught up with Mrs. Linton. Her first name is Christine, by the way." Viv dug into her purse and removed a small rectangular leatherette case. "I wanted to surprise you, but after that scene with the general, I figured Christine wasn't in a mood to talk to us now, so I to gave her your new Silent Survivors business card. Told her to check out the blog. She needs to know she's not alone."

Viv slipped a card from the case and handed it to Mackenzie with a sheepish grin. "The logo took the most time. Hope you like it."

Mackenzie studied the digitized image in the corner of the card - two soldiers in silhouette - one male with a missing leg, one female with a missing arm, supporting each other. Simple, but to the point. No doubt Viv had spent hours on the design.

"It's really great," she said, looking up. "It's just…"

"Just what?"

"Well, I thought we agreed - nothing public 'til I said so."

"But it's not *really* public." Viv pointed to the block letters under the logo. "See, I only put the URL for Silent Survivors on <u>Online.com</u>. The blog might become a social media star. You can stay anonymous if you want to be. I promise."

Mackenzie had to smile at Viv's earnestness. Her young friend's enthusiasm for the blog project was hard to resist. "You know you are a piece of work."

Viv's smile widened. "I'll take that as a compliment."

"It is," Mackenzie said, pulling Viv into a hug. "But I'm going to hold you to that promise."

The moment his driver exited the cemetery, General Paulsen pulled out his cell and speed dialed a Maryland number. "The situation is contained," was all he said before quickly clicking off. Decades spent in the military and the bureaucratic nightmare of Washington had taught him that a little healthy paranoia never hurt anyone. The phone line was supposed to be secure, but you never really knew who might be listening.

And as to his claim that the situation was contained? Well, it probably was. No point in mentioning the widow's outburst. It wouldn't be the first time the wife of a dead soldier had blamed the Army. Still, just to be on the safe side, he'd have his local contact keep an eye on her.

CHAPTER 9

Thursday August 21, 2008

Knowing Viv was late for her one p.m. graphics art class at PBU, Mackenzie pulled her Civic into the Shady Palms lot alongside Viv's parked motorcycle.

"Sorry to run," Viv said as she slid out of the passenger seat and slammed the door. Grabbing her helmet, she strapped it on and straddled the bike.

Lowering her window, Mackenzie was assaulted by a rush of hot humid August air. She shut off the engine so her voice would carry over the noise of the construction work across the street. "Listen," she said, creating a visor with her hand to shield the sun, "thanks for coming to the funeral with me and, uh, thanks for the blog design."

"No problem." Viv revved the motor, slowly backing out of the parking space. "Now get some rest, kid. It's been a rough few days."

Several hours later Mackenzie was lying on her bed with the blinds shut when a loud knock woke her from a troubled sleep. Still dressed in the navy skirt and light blue blouse she'd worn to the funeral, she sat up, raked her fingers through her hair, then slipped on her flats.

Another knock.

Then another.

"Okay, I'm coming!"

Groggy, she stood, glancing at the Timex on her wrist. Five after six. She'd locked the door, put the portable phone back in its base. Viv wouldn't come without calling. Besides on Thursdays Viv rode the church van with her grandfather and helped call the numbers at his weekly bingo game. Mackenzie couldn't imagine who it could be as she made her way to the front door and opened it a few inches.

"Miss Dodd?"

Mackenzie recognized the young policeman who'd quizzed her after PJ's suicide, although she couldn't recall his name. His card was somewhere in the bottom of her purse.

Frowning, alarm bells went off. What the hell was he doing here? "Is this an official visit?" she asked, noting that he was dressed in a Marlins T-shirt and blue jeans. "I already told you everything I know, Officer…"

"Cantori." He smiled. "No, I, uh… listen, may I come in for a minute?"

Unsure, Mackenzie took a quick inventory. At least six feet tall and muscular, his close cropped auburn hair, five o'clock shadow, and strong jawline all screamed macho - something she'd had a little too much of in the Army. But then that engaging dimpled smile softened the look. There was no trace of guile in his bright hazel eyes. Acting on impulse, she swung the door wider. "Sure."

Leading him into the living room, she indicated a chair opposite the loveseat where she settled herself between several boxes stacked in anticipation of packing her mother's things.

"A little late spring cleaning," she said, in lieu of a more truthful explanation. "So, Officer Cantori. What brings you here?"

He cleared his throat. "It wasn't until I saw you leaving Dr. Mills' office that I realized who you were, Kenzie."

Mackenzie's whole body tensed. Her brother had given her that nickname when she was just a toddler. With Paul's death, she'd shed the name and her childhood. Long time since anyone had called her that. In another life. "How did…?"

"I'm Sam Cantori. We were in fifth grade together. You might not remember Miss Lazerick calling the roll alphabetically each morning, but I sure did. She insisted on calling me Samuel Cantori in those days, but you got to be Kenzie Carter. I was really jealous."

"That was my brother's doing," Mackenzie said, taking a deep breath, desperate to control emotions she'd been struggling to keep in check. "And believe me, there's nothing to envy about my life these days."

"Coming from Dr. Mills' office, you looked so upset. It reminded me of the afternoon the principal interrupted class to tell you about your dad's death. When I heard you just lost your mom, I wanted to tell you how sorry I am. See how you're doing."

"It hasn't been my best week," Mackenzie admitted, feeling her eyes brimming with tears. "First PJ, then my mother. I tried," she said, her lip quivering, "but I couldn't help either one of them." Despite her best intentions, the dam finally erupted.

Sam jumped up and came to her, drawing her up and into his arms.

Surprised by the depth of her sorrow, Mackenzie buried her head in the fold of his shoulder and cried like she couldn't remember crying since that day in fifth grade. It took several minutes before her breathing slowed and her tears were spent. Sniffling, she eased herself away from him, embarrassed. "Sorry." She brushed back a loose hair falling over her brow. "I don't know what came over me."

"Nothing to be sorry about," he said softly, sitting back down. "Everyone deserves a good cry now and then."

Mackenzie produced a thin smile as she perched herself on the arm of the loveseat. "Thanks for understanding." By force of habit she did not elaborate, explaining only that she'd left the Army in January to care for her mother. "She had ALS."

"Jeez, that's a tough one."

Mackenzie nodded. "I knew the end was near, but somehow it seems too soon."

"I lost my dad a few months ago," Sam said. "I can't imagine being without both parents."

Now it was Mackenzie's turn to offer sympathy. "Was he sick?"

"No, sudden heart attack. But it was my brother Jake who killed him."

Silence hung between them as Mackenzie waited, sensing he wanted to say more, his own need to unburden himself almost tangible. Then, as if considering how to begin, he told her how his younger brother had joined the Marines at age nineteen, committed to serving his country, how during his second tour in Afghanistan he'd ended up in the Shinwar District of the Nanharhar Province.

"March, 2007. Jake won't talk about it, but I learned that his guys were caught in a bomb ambush and started shooting. Killed nineteen civilians, wounded a whole lot more. His unit was sent home. Brass said the incident damaged the unit's relations with the local Afghan population." Sam shook his head. "No one ever wanted to know how it damaged my brother."

Sam's voice was tinged with the same bitterness Mackenzie had heard from Christine Linton today at her husband's funeral.

PJ didn't kill himself, General. You killed him.

So many of us damaged by this war, she thought.

"Jake was a funny, generous, easygoing kid with lots of friends before the war. He came back completely changed -

refused to leave the house, wouldn't take calls from friends, slammed the door if they came to visit. Eventually they stopped." Sam shut his eyes, opened them. "It was like a dark cloud had come over him. He stopped sleeping, became so anxious that anything could set him off."

"Classic PTSD," Mackenzie said.

"Yeah, and neither of my parents could deal with it - especially dad. Jake wouldn't get help, wouldn't look for a job. When he started drinking, he got really out of control. One night in a bar some dude insulted the Marines, so Jake stabbed him to death." Sam exhaled a long sigh. "My dad had a fatal heart attack the same day the judge sentenced my brother to life in prison. Jake's at Martin Correctional Institution in Indiantown. I see him whenever I can."

Without thinking Mackenzie leaned forward, reached for his hand and gave it a gentle squeeze. Silently she cried for his loss, knowing that in this melancholy moment there was no need for words.

Sam tilted his head and threw her a curious look.

"What?"

"Except for Dr. Mills, I haven't discussed Jake with any-one. Not my mom, not the guys at work, not my friends. You're a good listener."

The blush came unbidden. "I guess maybe it's my nursing training."

"Maybe, but you're a natural." Sam looked over toward the window. The sun was beginning to set, casting a soft orange glow across the room. "Listen, I don't know about you, but I'm famished. There's a great little diner off Atlantic Avenue that serves the best burgers. How about letting me take you to dinner?" He stood. "As long as you don't mind driving in a police car", he said, then added with a shrug, "One of the perks of our department."

About to refuse the invitation, Mackenzie's stomach grumbled its own response. She hadn't eaten all day.

Sam smiled. "Shall I take that as a 'yes'?"

Doug Anders was on his way home from his Ft. Detrick lab when his cell rang.

"Did you see the news?"

Anders didn't need caller ID. Leyton Fremont's southern drawl was unmistakable. "No, I'm in my car, Congressman."

"Well turn on the radio. It's been all over the networks."

"Just tell me. Is it good news or bad news?"

"Depends how you look at it, son," Fremont laughed. "Today US and Iraq negotiators agreed on a withdrawal of all US troops in Iraq by 2011."

"2011, hmmm. That gives us just three more years."

"Like I said there's good news and bad news. That *could* be construed as the bad news. I know how you want to keep SEDO going indefinitely."

"Okay, so what's the good news?"

"Son, the way we've fucked up things in Iraq, the whole Middle East has become a powder keg waiting to explode. Trust me. Iraq and Afghanistan today, tomorrow Libya, Syria, Somalia, Yemen, even Iran. No way we won't be putting more boots on the ground in the near future."

Anders imagined Fremont's ample belly jiggling as he chuckled. "What's the word on the hill?"

"As long as we can dodge Casey's bullet and I think we can, there's nothing to worry about."

"So the General's definitely on board."

"The situation's contained," Fremont said, then added "For now."

Opened in 1951, Doc's was a throwback to the early days of fast food joints with walk-up windows and counter service. The outdoor diner featured an "All American" menu of burgers, shakes, hot dogs, fries, onion rings and soft serve ice cream.

"This brings back memories," Mackenzie said, following Sam who was carrying their order to one of the few outside tables. She sat down and grabbed her burger and fries from the tray while Sam took his seat opposite her. "Best part of living in Delray as a kid."

"Not the beach?" he asked.

Mackenzie held up a french fry. "Couldn't compete with this or the chocolate sprinkles on a swirl."

"Yeah, Doc's an institution."

Mackenzie narrowed her eyes.

"Something I said?"

"Were you really that geeky kid who sat behind me in fifth grade and knew all the answers?"

"Are you kidding?" Sam rolled his eyes. "You'd call a gawky ten year old with bucked teeth and coke bottle glasses 'geeky'?"

Mackenzie pointed her finger at him. "That *was* you!" she said with a wide grin.

"Guilty as charged." Sam held up his hands in mock defense. "Thank goodness for braces and contacts, huh?"

Yes, thank goodness, Mackenzie thought. No question, grown-up Sam was no geek. The man *was* incredibly good looking. And no wedding band. Recalling the feel of the warm hand she'd held earlier made her heart race. His nearness now frightened her. She didn't want to be hurt again.

"So tell me, did you always want to be a cop?" she asked, desperate to change the direction of the conversation.

Sam took a bite of his burger, chewed thoughtfully. "Not always," he finally said. "I was in junior college studying sociology the day the Twin Towers went down. So many guys I knew were signing up to fight the bad guys over there, I thought about it too. But then I decided I wanted to do something to keep us safe over here, so I quit school and joined the force in 2002. Besides, I knew that Jake was Army bound in a few years and my parents couldn't cope with two sons gone." He was quiet for a second, seemingly lost in the memory. "Funny how things turn out, isn't it?"

Mackenzie could only nod her assent.

"And you?" Sam asked, his hazel eyes locked on hers. "Have you always wanted to be a nurse?"

"That's a kind of a long story," she replied, forcing herself to hold his gaze. Just how much she would tell, she wondered. No way Sam could know that sharing any part of her past was a leap of faith. "Let's just say that unlike you I was a screw-up in school." She leaned back in her chair. "Here's the short version. My life took a few zigs and zags" (mostly zags, she admitted to herself) "until I met an amazing nurse who inspired me to get my act together. The Army paid for my nursing education. I acquired a degree, a one way ticket to Iraq, and a very brief marriage to an Army doc I met at summer camp."

Sam's expression remained neutral even when Mackenzie mentioned her marriage, making it impossible to gauge his reaction. Perhaps she'd misinterpreted his interest in her. Still, she was grateful that he didn't probe for more details.

For the next few minutes they ate in companionable silence.

Mackenzie devoured her burger in several unladylike bites and was about to offer to spring for a couple of Doc's famous hand-dipped ice cream cones when Sam's cell phone trilled.

Sam stood and took the call away from street noise. "Afraid we've got to go," he said when he returned to the table.

"Police business?"

Sam rearranged his face into a somber expression. "No, it's my brother. He's been put on suicide watch."

Christine's mother had insisted she swallow a Xanax after the funeral, but hours later, the drug had done little to mitigate the rush of distinct emotions flooding through her.

Self-pity.

Only twenty-three and already a widow.

Sitting in her bedroom, she pulled PJ's photo from the box of personal effects she'd been handed the day after his suicide. Fresh tears welled as she studied his handsome face. Before the IED had left its mark. Before he'd changed.

Longing.

They'd met the summer after she'd finished high school. A girlfriend who'd moved to California invited her to spend a few weeks in Santa Cruz, claiming the view of Monterrey Bay was only second to the cool looking college guys from UC. The very first day they'd hurried to the beach front boardwalk, challenging each other to ride the giant dipper roller coaster. At the last minute, her friend chickened out, forcing Christine to take an empty seat next to a young Marine.

Though PJ had barely acknowledged her when she'd stepped into the passenger car, the moment he heard her screams as the wooden coaster made its successive deep dips and sped around hairpin curves, he put his arms around her and held her tight. At the end of the ride he introduced himself and asked for her number. Three weeks later, following a whirlwind romance, the two eloped and set up house at Camp Pendleton - less than two months before PJ's unit was called up.

Loss.

Christine stayed in San Diego through his first two tours, taking a waitressing job near the base. But she was young and pretty and needy and with each return, the young man she'd married seem to disappear.

"Talk to me," she'd urged, but like so many of the husbands of the women she'd met at Pendleton, he never discussed the war and he refused to get help, saying nothing was wrong with him, though he startled at any noise, tossed and turned in his sleep and occasionally mumbled "Fallujah" as if it was all that was required to explain his endless nightmares.

By the third tour last year Christine snapped. She'd had enough. The young Marine with the easy smile that could light up a room, the man who'd swept her off her feet, had become a total stranger. The moment he left for southern Iraq, she packed her bags and moved to Florida.

Recriminations.

Sending an email was cowardly and cruel. Worse, she'd refused his calls from across the world. Then six months ago he'd shown up at her mother's condo, promising to get therapy at the VA if only she'd take him back. But she'd turned him away. Two days ago she told him she was filing for divorce, that he'd been away for so long she'd learned she didn't need him. The next day he'd gone and blown his brains out.

Her eyes stung with tears of regret.

She reached into the box and retrieved a dog-eared black notebook. PJ's diary.

Bitterness.

Last night she'd read and reread the scribbled entries. Pages filled with his suffering. How could she have known how truly damaged he was? The horrible scar across his face was the least of it.

Anger.

She clenched her fists, reminded of that general's words today: *I want to extend our sincerest sympathy for your loss. If there's anything you need…*

Christine reached into her pocket and removed the business card she'd been handed at the funeral. The young woman said she was not alone, that there were so many others like PJ, that she might find some comfort in reading their stories, and if she felt up to it, she could share hers too.

Curious, she booted up her Acer laptop, typed in the URL for <u>Online.com</u> and searched for the blog titled *Silent Survivors.*

"You don't need to walk me to the door. I know you're in a hurry to get to the prison," Mackenzie said when Sam pulled his police cruiser into the parking lot of her apartment building. "How long's the drive to Indiantown?"

"Not quite an hour on I-95."

As soon as Sam shifted to 'park', Mackenzie exited the car and hurried around to the driver's side.

Sam lowered his window.

"I'm so sorry about your brother," she said.

Sam merely nodded, the sadness in his eyes reflecting his concern.

"Well, thanks for inviting me to dinner."

"No, thank *you*, Kenz…"

Impulsively, Mackenzie placed two fingers on his lips. "My friends all call me Mac."

"Duly noted," he said before the engine squealed to life and he was on his way.

Mackenzie stood watching Sam drive off just as the St. Anthony Church van arrived. Distracted, she didn't hear Viv come up behind her.

"Everything okay?"

"Hmm?"

Viv snapped her fingers in Mackenzie's face. "Earth to Mac."

"Sorry." Mackenzie turned her attention to Viv. "How was bingo?"

Viv glanced over at the curb where her grandfather was waiting and waved. "Gramps hit all the numbers on the two dollar special. You'd think he won the lottery. The man's on cloud nine." She laughed. "But what about you? I saw you talking to that cop. Do you know him?"

"Turns out he's an old classmate." Mackenzie offered a tired smile.

And maybe a new friend.

Keeping that thought to herself, lest she jinx possibilities, she made her excuses and headed upstairs for the night.

Christine's heart ached as she read the Silent Survivors blog, each post a painful tale of a husband, a wife, a brother, a sister, a father, a mother - all victims of the war.

If there's anything you need...

Yes, General, she thought as she started to write her own story. I need the world to know who really is to blame.

Back in her apartment, Mackenzie replayed the evening in her head. For the last few years she'd become the glass half-empty girl, expecting disappointments, her past very much a wound unhealed. Stuffing everything down like a good soldier. Though lonely and wanting, she'd closed herself off to the possibility of new relationships. Viv was the only person she could truly call a friend these days.

What if...

There was no denying that tonight with Sam feelings she'd suppressed for so long flooded throughout her body. Brief imaginings of another life.

What if ...

Drained, exhausted, she undressed, crawled into bed, and shut her eyes. Even if something did come of it, she thought, drifting off, with so many secrets how could it ever work? Divorce, rape, death, and the miserable mess she'd made of it all. No, her life was just too complicated for a relationship that had nowhere to go.

But what if….

The last name on the on-duty officer's badge was Drake. The beefy jowls and beer belly led Sam to guess the man's age at close to Medicare, the bored expression belonging to someone marking time until retirement. Not unlike his partner.

"Sorry you had to make the trip tonight, son," Drake said, "but your brother's been sedated. Besides, we've got orders that no one can talk to him 'til the prison doc gives the okay sometime tomorrow."

Even though Sam had pushed the accelerator past the speed limit, it was close to ten p.m. when he'd arrived, breathless, at Martin Correctional Institution. The place was a sprawling complex of buildings dating back to 1985 when it was built as an International Exposition Center to house cattle. Now it kept just over fifteen hundred adult males who'd committed everything from burglary to murder under lock and key.

The fact that Sam was a cop was the only reason Drake allowed him past the two internal gates and into the staff room where he treated him to a cup of stale, thick coffee.

Sam poured some powdered cream into the sludge. "What the hell happened?" he asked, trying to control his frustration at the officialism.

"I came on after seven, but word is two correctional officers on day shift found inmate Cantori on the floor of his cell just before dinner around five forty-five. Apparently he'd bashed his head against the wall until he collapsed."

"Jesus, why didn't they send him to the hospital?"

Drake shrugged. "He was revived within minutes by the physician's assistant here at the prison. Patched him up. Only needed a few stitches. Dr. Rodriguez was called and ordered the sedatives and observation overnight. There's a two way mirror and a guard watching 24/7."

Sam threw his half-filled paper cup in the trashcan. Damn it. He'd never felt his brother belonged in prison - even after he'd committed murder. Couldn't everyone see how truly troubled he was, that he needed mental help? Unfortunately, a public defender and an immovable jury meant a life sentence in a locked cell.

Appealing to Drake as a father figure, he said, "Listen, Jake's my little brother. My dad's gone. Mom will be devastated when she hears about this. Since I did come all this way, couldn't I at least take a look through that mirror so I can tell her he's all right?"

Drake's cheeks became bellows as he seemed to consider the consequences of breaking the rules. Finally, he expelled a loud whoosh of air, "okay, but just for a few minutes."

Christine had clicked 'mute' on the TV before she began typing her blog post, so she missed the news anchor report that US troops would remain in Iraq for three more years. No doubt if she had, she'd have wondered just how many more tours the guys like her husband could take before they all went mad.

Sam arrived home after one a.m., exhausted and sick at heart. He tried to catch a few hours of sleep, but couldn't banish the image of his brother lying shackled to a prison hospital bed, his head bandaged, his eyes shut, an IV slowly dripping fluids into a vein.

Ironic, Sam thought. Jake had almost looked peaceful tonight. The last time he'd seen him, his brother had been dressed in his orange prison jumpsuit and was so agitated that he'd kept jumping up and down from the chair until the guard had to cut the visit short.

As the day dawned, he woke feeling unrested, his mind foggy with unremembered dreams. Slipping out of bed, he wandered into the kitchen and brewed himself a cup of strong coffee before heading for the bathroom to shower and change into his uniform. He was buttoning the top button on his shirt when his cell phone buzzed.

It was his partner telling him they'd caught a rape case. "PBU freshman. Dispatch says she was brought to Delray Hospital by a friend. That's all we know so far. Chief wants us to take her statement there."

"Okay." Sam checked the time. Seven thirty. "Pick you up in fifteen."

CHAPTER 10

The slender girl on the gurney sat with shoulders slumped and head bent so that all Sam and Ed could see when the ER nurse escorted them into the exam room was a mop of cascading copper curls.

At the sound of their entrance, she looked up, revealing tear-diluted black mascara staining lightly freckled cheeks and downturned, obviously bitten lips. Even in the oversized hospital gown it was clear she had a mature woman's body - slim-hipped and full-breasted - though the nurse told them Maura Holmes had just turned eighteen.

Ed indicated that Sam should take the lead by finding a perch on the corner window ledge.

"Maura, I'm Officer Cantori." Sam rolled a stool closer to the exam table and sat down. He pointed to Ed, "and this is my partner, Officer Wilton." He smiled at the nurse who stood beside the gurney. "Miss Ingalls here says you've been through a tough time. Do you think you can tell us what happened?"

"He raped me," Maura whispered, clenching trembling fists.

Sam retrieved a spiral notepad and pen from his uniform jacket. "Okay. Who is *he*?"

"Tim... Tim Dalton."

At the sound of throat clearing, Sam glanced in Ed's direction, noting a faint quivering of his partner's lips as though he was on the verge of saying something, then changed his mind.

Sam turned back to Maura. "Tim Dalton." He jotted down the name. "Is he also a freshman?"

"He's a senior. On the football team. I met him in art class. He invited me to a fraternity party."

"Had you two dated before?"

"Uh uh. This was the first time."

"So, you went to the party and…"

She murmured something inaudible.

"Sorry, I didn't get that."

Maura fixed Sam with an anguished expression that begged him not to judge her. "I drank too much gin and rum and coke and I don't know what else. I wound up in the bathroom throwing up and then I guess I passed out 'cause the next thing I remember Tim was helping me into a bedroom, taking off my shoes, telling me I needed to lie down." She took a deep, shuddering breath. "I think I must have fallen asleep, but then I felt a weight on me and I opened my eyes and…." She choked down a sob.

The nurse reached across the exam table and squeezed her hand. "It's okay."

"I was naked and he was on top of me and then inside me before I could do anything."

"Did you ever say 'no'?"

"I tried to push him off, I did, but he was too strong. I…I did try." A tear wobbled on her lower lid, threatening to tumble down mascara smudged cheeks.

She started to wipe her nose with the back of her wrist when Sam leaned over and handed her a tissue. He waited for the sniffles to stop before asking, "Did you contact campus police?"

"Yeah. The next day."

Sam cocked his head. "When exactly was the fraternity party?"

"Last Saturday."

"And you're just contacting the police now?" Sam asked, mentally calculating that a full week had passed.

"Campus police told me to go to the disciplinary committee."

"And did you?"

Maura nodded. "First thing Monday morning. The administration said they'd look into it, but they've done nothing. My friend told me that PBU always sides with the athletes." She squared her shoulders slightly, a half-hearted gesture of defiance. "Like it was my fault."

"I see." Sam shot a sideways glance at Ed who was doing little to suppress a yawn. "Well, we'll need to do our investigation. Starting with a chat with Mr. Dalton."

At eight a.m. Mackenzie was awakened by a call from Dr. Mills' administrative assistant reminding her of the grief counseling session that afternoon for the PTSD group.

"The doctor asked me to schedule a one-on-one for you right after. He thought that would be more convenient than making it another day."

Caught off guard, Mackenzie was slow to respond. She'd forgotten the psychiatrist had suggested a few private sessions.

"Ms. Dodd?"

"Oh, sure," she said, not sure at all that she was up for more confessions.

"Good, we'll see you at thirteen hundred."

Hanging up, Mackenzie considered how to spend the next hour. Judith's husband Craig wasn't due until Monday. He was supposed to help with funeral arrangements and any legal issues. No point waiting before tackling the job of clearing out the apartment. Besides, she'd like one last chance to touch her mother's things, feel her presence, before storing all the memories away in cartons.

A summer rain beat against the windows, perfect counterpoint to Mackenzie's melancholy mood. Fortified with a cup of black coffee, she drifted into her mother's bedroom. After yesterday's funeral, she'd returned to find two men from the rental agency standing by her front door, waiting to remove the hospital bed. Now the empty space seemed a silent disclosure: how easy to erase a life.

Only when she opened the closet, did Mackenzie smile. Her mother was a hoarder - not as bad as some, but seemingly unable to discard the most trivial mementoes. The tiny space was filled with dusty luggage, clothes, and accessories from every era since the seventies. Mackenzie spent the next two hours carefully sorting through each item, placing them in the boxes she'd brought. As she nestled an ashtray on a folded jacket, she conjured up the image of her mother as a recent widow, sitting in the dark, the tumbler of whiskey in her hand filled and refilled so many times that the flicked ashes of her cigarette landed haphazardly around the room. The vision was so intense that Mackenzie could almost smell the smoke. She closed her eyes until it passed, willing away the painful memories.

Certain her sister wouldn't want the bright orange cowl neck sweater, low-cut polyester bell bottoms, bangles or big hoop earrings, she ripped off a strip of packing tape with her teeth, planning to donate them all to a veterans' charity. She'd have to wait for Craig before making a final decision about giving away some of the other items.

In the living room, she took some time to wrap the framed photo of Craig, Jr. Born in Germany, his mother had never brought him to Florida. The distance was Judith's cruel excuse for denying a grandmother the opportunity to embrace her grandson.

Leaving the rest of the photos and knickknacks for later, Mackenzie wandered into the powder room which still held the strong scent of bleach the aide insisted on using to scrub down the sink, toilet, and shower. The cheery yellow and white dandelions covering the walls were the one feature her mother had added a few months before she'd become bedridden. The flowers were her favorites, she'd said. They made her happy. Now they just seemed a sad reminder that she was gone.

Staring into the medicine cabinet mirror, Mackenzie examined her features, trying to discover the young girl Sam would have known almost twenty years ago. The wide cheek bones on her oval face that more than a few women over the years had claimed to envy only served to highlight her recent weight loss. Fine lines at the corners of her eyes had deepened, accentuating the strain and worry of the last few months. Trying to soften her look a little, she reached up behind her, pulled the elastic band off the pony tail she'd worn to bed and shook her brown hair loose. Average weight, average height, Mackenzie had never considered herself beautiful, but she'd always thought 'cute' or even 'passably pretty' were fair descriptions. This woman in the mirror now seemed a stranger. How could the handsome cop be interested?

Stop thinking about Sam.

Acknowledging the silly fantasy, she opened the cabinet where she found a crowded collection of amber-colored and clear pill bottles. Each documented her mother's battle with ALS: antidepressants, vitamins, sedatives, pain meds, anti-anxiety meds, skeletal muscle relaxants, laxatives. One by one, Mackenzie picked them up and examined the labels before dumping unused drugs in a plastic bag for disposal.

Patient's name: Diane Carter

Doctor's name: Dr. Martinez

Riluzole.

Mackenzie shook her head. ALS was a disease affecting thirty thousand people a year and this was the only FDA approved drug for treatment. The doctor had told her it would have no real effect on her mother's quality of life, at best prolonging it for two to three months.

Gabapentin.

Dr. Martinez had to bump up the dose as her mother's night cramps and twitches increased.

Baclofen and Diazepam to relax her muscles.

Amitriptyline to control her moods. The tricyclic not only helped her mother's depression, but reduced the drooling until her mouth got so dry, the doctor had to prescribe Salivert, a saliva substitute.

Bisocodyl for constipation.

Anti-oxidant vitamins: Beta carotene, vitamin C, and vitamin E.

Coenzyme Q10. Though studies had shown no benefit.

White, blue, yellow, red. Elliptical, round, even square. Pills and capsules.

Emptying each bottle into the bag, Mackenzie wondered whether any of these had really made a difference. Certainly not in the ultimate outcome.

About to shut the medicine cabinet door, Mackenzie noticed a small plastic container wedged in the corner. She reached in and pulled it out, squinting at the tiny type on the label. Patient's name: Diane Carter.

Flometoquine 250 milligrams.

35.

Date: December 15, 2006.

For malaria.

Take daily after meals. Start one week prior to travel to endemic area, continue one week after.

No refills.

Doctor: Art Dodd, MD.

Mackenzie frowned, reminded of the marble elephant. Two thousand six was the year her mother had traveled to India. As a nurse, Mackenzie knew that mosquito borne diseases like malaria were endemic in many parts of that country. Just like Afghanistan and Iraq. That's why among the many pills and shots she'd had to take for her Iraq tour she'd been given Malarone. So why this drug? And why would Art prescribe it? Her mother could have gone to a VA clinic here. Art had never mentioned anything to Mackenzie at the time. Even though they'd just divorced, they remained on speaking terms.

She stared at the empty pill bottle. What was Flometoquine? She'd never heard of it. Something to check out. But it would have to be later. Glancing at her watch, she realized it was almost noon. She'd better get going or she'd be late for Dr. Mills' group.

Viv was speechless. She checked the tabular stats over and over until she was convinced the numbers were correct. Wyoming War Widow's blog post had produced a thousand clicks. This new one, posted late last night, already had close to seven thousand views.

Viv read and reread the words, certain of the author's identity despite the attempt at anonymity with the moniker "Furious in Florida". Christine Linton had obviously taken her advice to share her story.

As always Viv moderated the more than forty written comments. She had to remove only one. Even without the scatologic language, 'Loveitorleaveit''s declaration that Christine was unAmerican was enough to justify pushing 'delete'. The vast majority of readers empathized with the widow's loss, applauding her courage for coming forward.

Many offered all sorts of coping advice. A surprising number identified with her fury. Several asked for an address where they could send donations to support the site.

Wow. The blog was obviously hitting a nerve. As soon as Mac returned from the VA that afternoon, Viv planned to show her the updated webpage she'd been working on and make the case for a Facebook tie-in. In the meantime, to monitor the blog's growing reach, she set up a 'Google Alert', sure that it was only a matter of time before Silent Survivors really went viral.

"Anyone?"

You could hear a pin drop, as Dr. Mills searched the faces of the members of the PTSD clinic group. Most just studied their shoes, arms tightly folded, blank stares revealing nothing.

Settled on one of the folding chairs in the circle, Mackenzie counted seven vets - not the usual eight now that PJ was gone.

Dr. Mills debriefing session was pro-forma. He spoke of the need to share their feelings and concerns about what had happened, then waited for some response.

No one volunteered a thought.

Not that they didn't have feelings.

Just the opposite.

If they were anything like Mackenzie, they'd pushed those feelings deep inside and wound them into a tight ball, hoping they'd never surface, terrified what might happen if they did.

Taking your own life.

Sure there were whispers that there were more PJ's out there, but that was just it.

Whispers.

Shame.

Man-up.

Keep it all in.

Keep your secrets.

No talking.

Dr. Mills glanced at his watch. "Looks like our time's up." He rose and moved toward the door. "If you or any of your buddies even consider suicide, please call me any time, day or night. I'll have my administrative assistant provide you all with my private line." He eyed each of them before adding, "I want you all to know that I am here to help."

Even after he'd disappeared down the hall, you could hear a pin drop.

No one looked convinced.

Viv's laptop pinged indicating an incoming email. It was a 'Google Alert' letting her know that Furious in Florida's post had just been reposted on another site.

Donald Henrick handed everyone Dr. Mills' business card as one by one they drifted out the door.

"Ms. Dodd," the administrative assistant said when Mackenzie reached him, "Dr. Mills has a quick conference call, but says he'll see you shortly." He led her into his office, told her to take a seat by his desk while he took off, ramrod straight, for an errand. The fact that he walked with a military bearing made Mackenzie wonder if he'd ever been in the service. Certainly the American flag and the display of past presidents' photos on his credenza declared his patriotism.

She had little time for speculation, however, as Dr. Mills suddenly appeared and beckoned her into his office.

"Apologies for the wait," the psychiatrist said when they were both seated. "Washington bureaucrats." His muted laugh had a conspiratorial edge. "Can't live with them, can't live without them."

"No problem. It's not like I have anyone who needs me today," Mackenzie declared as much to herself as to the doctor.

"I am sorry about your mother's passing." Mills' expression reflected genuine concern.

"Thank you."

"You've had an incredibly difficult week. What with Sergeant Linton's suicide and now your mother." Mills leaned forward. "I know it's hard to open up in group. Especially since you're the only female among them." His gaze was intent. "That's why I wanted to try a few private sessions."

Mackenzie shifted in her seat, reluctant to expose herself to the psychiatrist's probing, however gentle.

"Is your father living?"

"No, he died in 1988. He was lifetime Army, wounded in Vietnam in 1972, then killed on a training mission in '88." Mackenzie took a deep breath. "He was thirty-seven. Mom was thirty-six."

The psychiatrist took a moment to calculate."So you were ten at the time."

Mackenzie pressed her lips together. "Right."

"That must have been tough."

"Tougher for my mom," Mackenzie replied.

"How so?"

Leaving out details, Mackenzie sketched the barest outline of her mother's bouts with depression and alcohol, how her older sister took on the role of surrogate.

"Not an easy childhood to be sure," Mills said.

Mackenzie tensed. She didn't want to talk about that part of her life. "No, it wasn't."

Sensing her resistance, Mills changed the subject. "Tell me, how are you coping right now?"

"To be honest, I haven't really had much time to process it all. I'm kind of running on automatic these last few days."

"Perfectly understandable." Mills cocked his head. "You look tired. Are you sleeping?"

"Not well," Mackenzie admitted, though she didn't dare share the source of her nightmares.

Mills frowned. "You said your mother had ALS?"

"Yes."

"One of those devastating neurological diseases with no known cause and no known cure."

Unconsciously, Mackenzie clenched her fist.

No known cause.

Not if you asked her sister Judith who was fond of saying "what goes around comes around", as if her mother's suffering was her due.

"Ms. Dodd?"

Refocusing, Mackenzie exhaled slowly. "Yes, a terrible disease."

Mills steepled his fingers together. "Taking care of your mother was a big responsibility."

"I'm a nurse. I'm trained to be a caretaker."

"You and I both know it's not the same when it's someone you love."

Even as he spoke the words, Mackenzie could feel the ache rise within her. His soft voice made her bite her lip to keep tears at bay. How she wished she could have done more.

"You were her caretaker for…?"

"Eight months."

"A long time."

"Yes."

Mills studied her for several moments as if searching for the subtext. Finally he said, "So losing her means a certain loss of identity for you."

The painful truth of his words created a knot in the pit of her stomach. Uncanny the way the psychiatrist seemed to tap into her innermost fear. Who was she now if no longer a daughter, a wife, a soldier, a caretaker? The thought of facing an unknown future was terrifying.

"Have you considered what you'll do next?"

"I'm really not sure." Mackenzie explained that the funeral was on hold until her brother-in-law flew in from Germany and that in the meantime she'd been busy cleaning out her mother's apartment. "The building is being razed in January, so I'll definitely have to find another place to live by then."

"Sounds like you have a lot on your plate." Mills checked his watch. "Our time is up, but I'd like to see you back again next week." He smiled warmly as he rose from his desk. "Give you a chance to do some processing."

"Unbelievable." Sam shook his head in frustration as he and his partner left the PBU campus after they'd spent several hours interviewing Tim Dalton and talking to the college administration. "Vic was right. The school's not about to do squat."

"Whole thing's a fucking waste of our time."

Sam frowned. "Why'd you say that? Girl's named the perp, she's brought in the underwear she wore that night, doc says she found evidence of rough sex even after a week."

Ed snorted. "Look, she admits to heavy drinking. Blood alcohol level above point one. Now she can't remember any more than she's sure she screamed 'no'. Girl's this side of legal. Though you have to admit, with that body and a little makeup, she could easily be taken for much older."

"So?"

"So even if her panties shows it's his sperm, the time delay's a major problem. Besides our star athlete says she wanted it as much as he did, that it was consensual."

"How can it be consensual when one of the parties is unconscious."

"You *are* green, Cantori. When you gonna learn we're not sociologists? We're cops."

"I know that, but…"

Ed cut him off with a wave of his hand. "But nothing. Trust me, there won't be any further investigation and there'll never be an arrest."

Annoyed, Sam asked, "You wanna tell me how you can be so sure?"

"Because," Ed said with a wink, "this star athlete is Assistant DA Dalton's nephew. So when you write up your report this afternoon, you'll file it under 'he said, she said'. Now let's grab some lunch, then head back to the precinct. I've got an appointment with HR to finalize my pension."

Viv barely said hello before barging into Mackenzie's apartment and placing her laptop on the kitchen table. "Have a seat. You've got to see this." Hovering over Mackenzie, she leaned in to boot up the computer and clicked on Christine's blog post. "Read it out loud."

"Okay. Let's see…

Dear Silent Survivor:

I saw your post - the one where you said you were present when a soldier committed suicide. I think that soldier was my husband. In case you are blaming yourself for not doing more to prevent his death, I want you to know that my husband didn't die a few days ago. When he took a gun to his head, he was shooting a ghost. The Army sent me a box with his personal effects. Yesterday I found a diary he'd kept during his last mission. July 4, 2007. Operation Phantom Thunder. That's the day my husband really died. Ironic isn't it? July 4th! I didn't understand. He wouldn't talk about it, but he never got over watching his buddies burn to death that day after an IED hit their HumVee. Here are some of his words:

'I can't stop the sound of their screaming in my head. My mind is filled with visions of incredible horror. Every night I try to close my eyes, but the nightmares invade my sleep. Every day is agony. I feel such pain in every nerve ending of my body. I can't stand being touched. I can't control the shakes. It's been getting worse and worse until I can hardly speak. The pain, the depression, the anxiety, the rage. These are my demons. Demons of a war that has made me sick. There is no cure. My wife doesn't want this shell of a man. My friends are gone. The world is better off without me in it. My last mission will be a mercy killing.'

I read and reread my husband's words and I can't stop crying. Three tours in Iraq. It was just too much. The war took a good man and changed him until he couldn't cope. That's where the blame lies. So like the Wyoming Widow wrote, please don't blame yourself in any way. There was nothing you could do to stop him from ending his pain. Thank you for being there with him at the end. God bless.

-signed Furious in Florida

Amazing, isn't it, Mac?"

When Mackenzie turned from the computer screen to look at Viv, her eyes were puddled. "I think I'm gonna cry myself," she sniffled. "Poor PJ."

Viv nodded, slipping into a seat beside Mackenzie and pulling the laptop over so she could type. "Check out these feed stats," she said as a new URL revealed an upward curve resembling frosting on a cake. Viv pointed to the numbers on the screen. "This morning there were almost seven thousand onsite views. Now there are more than fifteen thousand and growing. You're going viral, kid!"

"I have to admit, I'm stunned. I never thought the blog would get this kind of response."

"There's more." Viv couldn't control her excitement. "See what some of the readers had to say." She clicked on the return key to retrieve yesterday's blog post, scrolling down to the comment section, then waited for Mackenzie to silently review what had grown from forty to sixty-two written remarks.

"Christine really hit a nerve."

"Now that you're on a roll, you'll need a proper website and I was thinking of a Facebook Fan Page."

"What happened to your promise to wait till I was ready?"

"I know, I know," Viv said, "but I was hoping that when you saw how many people the blog is touching, how much good it's doing, you'd be ready."

Viv's zeal made Mackenzie relax her jaw muscles which had tightened at the notion of going public. There was no denying the blog's impact on those who had read it. And the reach *was* amazing. Still, she couldn't reconcile her own need to keep out of the limelight.

As if sensing the root of her friend's misgivings, Viv tried to explain how she planned to maintain the website, restricting access to anyone who attempted to determine its administrator. "Online.com can continue to send the money you earn through the Paypal account using your Silent Survivor pseudonym and I'll make sure you'll never be named on the Facebook Fan Page."

"You know I don't understand a word of 'Internet'."

"But you trust me, right?"

"Of course, but…"

"Look, before you say no, why not at least sit down with Christine and hear what she has to say?"

Mackenzie thought about this for a moment. "I guess that's a plan."

Viv threw her arms around Mackenzie's neck.

"But only if she'll talk to us."

Viv pulled back from the embrace, looking triumphant. "I already called her. She said to come by around six tonight."

Mackenzie shook her head, allowing a small smile at the same time. "Of course you have."

Among those trolling the Internet that afternoon was a man who read the post signed by Furious in Florida and recognized the need to alert someone higher up who'd know what to do.

After a quick lunch of barbecued ribs and pulled pork at Lucille's, Sam drove to the field office. While Ed took off for a retirement meeting with Human Resources, he sat down at his desk in the squad room and began flipping through the day's interview notes, ambivalent about heeding his partner's warning to short circuit the investigation. The kind of cop who clocked in and clocked out, Ed gave career advice that could be summed up in a few words: do your time with your nose down. Sam wasn't so sure it was a strategy to emulate. He'd joined the police force to make a difference, not as a sinecure.

Looking for an excuse to procrastinate, he picked up the phone and dialed the state prison. It was the third time he'd tried to check on his brother. At six-thirty that morning, Drake had said Jake was still asleep, he was going off duty, to call back later. At eleven the officer on day shift had told him that Dr. Rodriguez was delayed and would be in sometime in the next few hours, that he didn't know the prisoner's condition, Sam would have to speak to the doctor. This time the guard who answered reported that the GP had just finished his exam, placing Sam on hold while he put in a page.

A few minutes later, a man with a deep voice and a distinctly Hispanic accent identified himself as Dr. Rodriguez. "We're moving your brother to a hospital. I'm just preparing the paperwork."

Sam leaned forward in his chair. "Why? What's happened?"

"He's stable for the moment, but I'm afraid his situation is beyond my expertise," the doctor said. "I think at this point a specialist can better determine what's going on."

"You mean a psychiatrist?"

"Actually I want to start with a neurologist. He needs a full neurological workup including a brain scan to make sure there's no permanent damage."

"What hospital are you sending him to?"

"Indiantown General is the closest."

"He's a vet. Could he be moved to the VA here in West Palm?"

"Not without a special court order."

A sudden thought made Sam look down at his spiral notebook which was flipped to the page with the name of the accused perp: Tim Dalton. "Look, doc, I just may be able to swing that. Could you hold off on the transfer for an hour or so while I contact the DA's office?"

A tsk on the other end suggested the doctor was considering the option. "An hour tops," he finally agreed.

Waiting for the caller to pick up, Sam ratcheted up his courage, hoping his anxiety didn't come across the phone line.

"Assistant DA Dalton here."

The musicality of his accent was slightly southern suggesting somewhere between Dothan, Alabama and Pensacola, Florida. Sam put his money on the latter.

"Sir, I'm Officer Cantori, FDLE, Palm Beach office. I was called in on an alleged rape case this morning…."

Dalton interrupted. "Aren't you a little ahead of yourself, Cantori? Have you filed the paperwork, made an arrest?"

"That's just it, sir. I'm not sure how to file my report."

"Excuse me?"

"Well, it seems that the victim has identified a student at PBU by the name of Tim Dalton and I understand that he's your nephew."

"I see."

"My partner seems to think it's too much of a "he said, she said" situation to make a case - even though the young lady made an ID and we've got a rape kit cooking. He thinks it would be a shame to ruin a young man's reputation on the say-so of a drunk co-ed. I thought maybe you could give me advice."

There was silence for a long moment. "What is it you really want from me?"

Sam knew he was taking a big gamble, but he hoped that Dalton felt as strongly about family as he did. "I have a brother in Martin County Correctional. He's in for murder, but there are extenuating circumstances." Sam quickly summarized Jake's history including his military service, his PTSD, and the latest incident at the prison. "The doctor wants to ship him to a community hospital nearby. I'm hoping you could put in a good word and get him transferred to the West Palm Beach VA."

"And if I do, you'll close the alleged rape case?"

The actual idea of letting a potential rapist off repulsed him, but this was his brother he was trying to help. Sam bit his lip as if the pain could somehow atone for the sin he was committing. "Yes sir, I will."

Dalton's laugh was edgy, devoid of humor. "You know you have a set of balls, Cantori?"

Sam breathed out heavily. His instinct told him he had Dalton's attention. He didn't have to wait long to find out.

"Okay, I'll make a call to the prison. And you - do your thing on your end."

"Thank you."

"Now hang up and don't tell anyone we ever talked."

CHAPTER 11

Friday August 22, 2008

Christine Linton lived with her mother in a split level two bedroom townhouse in a quiet Deerfield Beach neighborhood not far from Quiet Waters Park where in happier times Mackenzie and her sibs had spent more than a few hot summer days biking and cooling off by the lake. Before Mackenzie's father died and her family had to move away.

Pushing back old memories, Mackenzie parked her Civic at the curb and followed Viv up to the entrance of the house.

Christine opened the door after the first knock, clearly expecting them. Though Mackenzie and Viv had dressed in the same dark clothes they'd worn to yesterday's funeral as a show of respect, the widow now sported baggy sweat pants and a Marine logo T-shirt. She'd pulled her blonde hair into a careless ponytail from which a few tendrils escaped, softening a pretty face that showed the strain of the last few days despite the forced smile.

"Thanks for coming," she said, acknowledging Viv with a quick hug, before turning to Mackenzie. "You must be 'Silent Survivor'."

"I uh…"

"It's okay, Mac," Viv intervened. "Christine and I talked about it. She understands that you want to keep your anonymity."

Christine nodded, extending her hand as Mackenzie stepped over the threshold. Viv followed. "I hope you two haven't eaten. Mom made her famous southern fried chicken for her church supper tonight, but left plenty for us." She ushered her guests into the kitchen before they could protest. "After dinner I'd like to show you something."

At quarter past six, Sam stepped off the fifth floor elevator of the West Palm Beach VA. The corridor had slipped into the early evening hospital routine: nurses in white shoes with crepe soles dispensing next dose meds and changing IVs, food service employees rolling carts across linoleum to pick up half-eaten dinner trays, orderlies wheeling in a patient or two just admitted from the Emergency Room.

Sam walked down the long hall toward the horseshoe shaped nurses' station where a bespectacled doctor wearing a white coat over green surgical scrubs was seated on a high stool behind the counter busily writing in a patient chart.

"Excuse me, Dr..." he leaned over to read the man's nametag. "Birken. Jake Cantori was admitted this afternoon. Can you tell me where he is?"

The doctor glanced up, noting Sam's uniform. "Ah, you must be the brother."

"Sam Cantori. Jake's my kid brother."

Birken snapped the chart shut, rose and came around to the front of the counter to shake Sam's hand. "Gary Birken. I'm the neurology fellow assigned to his case." At just over six feet tall, he stood almost eye to eye with Sam, though without Sam's toned muscularity.

As if reading Sam's mind, Birken rubbed his stubbled chin and shrugged. "Twelve hour shifts, no time for the gym." He placed a comforting arm around Sam's shoulder. "How about we grab a cup of coffee downstairs where we can talk?"

"Should I be worried?" Sam asked once they'd paid the cashier for their coffees and found seats in a far corner of the basement cafeteria.

Birken, who Sam guessed to be on the far side of thirty, took a deep breath. "Your brother's awake now. Off the sedatives he seems to have pretty good cognitive function. From what I understand he hit his head hard enough to experience at least a few moments of unconsciousness, so we ordered a CAT scan. The good news is that it showed no evidence of a bleed or permanent brain damage. Probably just a mild concussion, though we're monitoring him for any post-concussive syndrome symptoms."

Sam shifted in his seat. "Is there bad news?"

"It's not so much bad news as no news. The prison doesn't keep very complete medical files. I'm wondering if you can fill me in on Jake's history."

"Sure." Sam quickly summarized his brother's two military deployments including the fact that he'd probably been suffering from PTSD since his return stateside. "He refused to seek help once he was discharged, so we never got an official diagnosis." Sam took a sip of his coffee. "My brother preferred gin to doctors."

"No drugs?"

"If you mean cocaine or heroin, I think I would have known."

"How about antidepressants?"

Sam shook his head. "Of course I don't know what he might have taken while he was in Afghanistan. Guess you can check his military medical records."

"What was he like before he went to war?"

"A gentle soul. Happy. Nothing ever seemed to bother him," Sam said trying to find the right words to describe the brother he once knew. "Easy-going. Maybe even too much. Just squeaked through high school. Not because he wasn't smart enough. He'd just rather hang out with friends than hunker down with the books. Dad blamed mom for babying him, kept saying he needed to grow up. He was thrilled when Jake joined the Army. Thought it would give him direction, make a man of him."

"How was he when he got back?"

"Nightmares, restlessness, agitation, sudden rages. The smallest thing could set him off." Sam inhaled sharply. "That's what landed him in prison. He stabbed a man to death in a bar fight." Sam laughed mirthlessly. "Bartender told me it started after the guy made fun of the way his arm shook when he held his glass."

Birken's forehead furrowed. "Did you ever notice this shaking?"

"Sometimes. I assumed it had to do with all his drinking." Sam tilted his head to the side. "Why, do you think it's something else?"

"I can't say at this point. It could very well be related to alcohol or the PTSD, but I did notice some abnormalities in his neuro exam that warrant further study."

"Like what?" .

Birken removed his wire-rimmed glasses and pushed his thumb over the rose colored indentation left there. "It's much too soon to make a diagnosis, but I'm going to recommend that Jake stay here for at least the next few days. Blood work is being processed. I'm ordering an MRI along with a nerve conduction study and electromyography."

"You don't think he needs to see a psychiatrist?"

"The fact that he may have tried to kill himself means he'll definitely need a psych consult, but as long as he's stable and being watched, we can wait until Monday. By then I should have the results of my tests."

Sam nodded. "Can I see him?"

Birken put his glasses back on and checked his watch. "Sure, but make it a short visit. Room five ten. The tech will be taking Jake down for the MRI after his dinner break."

Viv and Mackenzie spent the better part of the next hour in light conversation with Christine as they enjoyed her mother's fried chicken, green beans, and mashed potatoes. A quintessential Southern meal.

"Delicious," Mackenzie raved.

"Your mom's an awesome cook," Viv agreed.

"Mom brought grandma's recipe from South Carolina where she was born," Christine explained.

"But you're a Florida native?" Viv asked.

"Born and bred, though technically natives are the Seminoles. I'm what you'd call a Florida cracker - poor rural white girl."

"I guess that makes three of us," Mackenzie chimed in.

Christine's laugh was genuine. Noting that everyone had cleaned their plates, she rose, gathered them up and placed them in the sink. She declined their offers to help with the dishes. "I'll wash them later," she said, insisting that mindless tasks were just what she'd need after they'd left.

"Come." She extended an arm and led her guests into the adjacent living room.

Sliding glass doors on the far wall provided a stunning view of a pastel Florida sky that within the hour would make its gentle descent into night. The opposite wall was filled with a few framed family photos including one of Christine and PJ at the wedding altar, three nature watercolors, and an oil portrait of a beaming Christine.

Viv moved from the photos to the paintings, examining the artist's signature on each. "Wow, PJ did all these?"

Christine nodded. "The oil was his wedding present to me." Her voice broke. "Painted it from a photo he took at the amusement park in Santa Cruz where we met." There was a note of wistfulness in her voice.

"It's really beautiful," Mackenzie said.

"PJ always loved to draw and paint, but didn't think he had enough talent to make it a career."

Viv tilted her head as she continued to study PJ's work. "I don't know about that. His technique is excellent. Both the watercolor and the oil." She turned to Christine. "Did he study anywhere?"

"No, he was totally self-taught. PJ lost his parents when he was only six," Christine said without relating any details, though no doubt both Viv and Mackenzie could readily empathize with a childhood loss of parents. It also explained why no one from his family had attended his funeral.

"He bounced around from one foster home to another until he aged out and joined the Marines." Christine sighed. "He never talked much about growing up, but I know that for him, drawing became a way to channel his creativity. When we'd go out to dinner, he'd doodle something cute on a napkin and when he went off to war the first time, he'd send me some of his pencil sketches - a mother and child, a landscape, always positive, nothing sad or angry."

Christine grew silent.

"And when he went back for a second and third tour?" Viv prompted.

Christine walked over to the floral pattered sofa in the corner and sat down. "Take a look." She invited Viv and Mackenzie to sit on either side of her.

"I found this among PJ's stuff the Army shipped back. They called it his 'personal effects'," she said with bitterness. "How appropriate, huh? Like something from a murder scene." She picked up an eight by ten manila envelope lying on the nearby coffee table and handed it to Viv. "These are from his two tours. You're an artist. I'd like your professional opinion."

"Art student," Viv corrected as she lifted the flap on the envelope and pulled out a stack of at least two dozen black and white drawings.

Unlike the sunny subjects on the wall or the positive images described by Christine, the first few were realistic portrayals of PJ's war: sketches of soldiers in skivvies lining up for shots and meds, soldiers in camouflage seated in a tented mess hall, and soldiers in heavy desert gear smiling next to armored HumVees.

All were dated so it was easy to follow the flow of PJ's work as the subjects became much darker: men lying wounded from exploded IEDs, their mouths open in obvious agony; a medic loading a one legged Marine onto a helicopter; a sniper on a rooftop aiming at a Birka clad woman shopping at a crowded market. PJ had drawn her looking directly at the viewer. Every picture was disturbing in its brutal honesty.

"You don't have to be an expert to recognize that these are amazing," Viv said, as she held them up one by one for Mackenzie to appreciate.

Looking at the horrors of war portrayed with such truth made Mackenzie shudder.

"Now check out his later drawings, the ones during his last tour," Christine urged. "And tell me what you think."

Viv shuffled through the pile until she found a few dated ten months ago. Those sketches were totally erratic, the lines angular and jagged, the images harder to identify. It was as if PJ had simply dug his pencil into the paper, expressing the depth of his torment in the only way he knew. "Gosh, I don't know what to say. These seem…"

"Like he was going off the deep end? That's what I thought." Christine turned to Mackenzie. "You're a nurse. Do you think these could be a sign that he had some disease?"

"You mean besides PTSD?"

"The Army never actually made that diagnosis. PJ pushed to get into the clinic because he thought I'd take him back if he went. As far as I know he never even had a physical exam at the VA." Christine picked up a few of the later sketches. "Now that I see these and read his diary, I can't help wondering if he had a medical condition that was missed."

"At this point, it would be very difficult to prove."

"You mean because he was cremated," Christine said flatly. "I get that, but I was hoping you might take a look at his diary. Maybe as a nurse, you'd see some clues, something that would help me better understand what was happening to him."

"I don't know…"

"What *I* know is that PJ should be here with me now," Christine said with sudden anger. "We should be growing old together, Mac. He's gone. It's not fair. I think the Army is to blame. Won't you help me find out what made him sick?"

Viv threw Mackenzie a look that could only be interpreted as 'why not'.

Why not? Because she'd promised to stay below the radar, to keep secrets. But this had nothing to do with her, right? This was about Christine and PJ. If reviewing the diary gave the widow some closure, didn't she owe her that? "I suppose it couldn't hurt," Mackenzie finally said as much to herself as to Christine. "But understand, what you're expecting is a long shot."

Back on the fifth floor, Sam found his brother's hospital room just around the corner from the nurses' station. The thick-necked security guard posted by the door acknowledged the police uniform and told him to go right in.

The circulating air reeked of disinfectant. Jake lay in bed, eyes shut, breathing through his mouth. The bandage on his head was gone, but he still had a plastic IV bag dripping clear liquid into the vein in his right arm. Oxygen hissed into his nose from a thin tube connected to a pressurized wall tank while an overhead monitor continually recorded vital signs. As Sam approached the bedside, he noted the fact that his brother's left wrist was cuffed to the bedrail. No doubt orders from the Assistant DA.

"Jake?"

Jake's eyes flickered open. "You came," he whispered.

"I'm your brother."

"The *good* brother."

Sam let the statement hang there for a moment, feeling a deep sense of sorrow at the simple acceptance in Jake's tone. A life tossed away. "And you're the hard-headed brother," he finally said, pointing to Jakes's matted hair and the nub of at least a half a dozen stitches caked with dried blood along the top of his scalp. "What the hell happened?"

"Wish I knew, Sam. I just kinda lost it."

Sam made no effort to hide his exasperation. "You think?"

"I'm just…just…" Jake stuttered, then without warning burst into convulsive sobs.

Sam didn't know how to react at the sight of his brother's obvious distress. He was about to push the call button for the nurse when the crying abruptly ended with one choking sound.

At that same moment a radiology tech entered the room carrying a clipboard. "Jake Cantori?" He checked Jake's wrist band against his work sheet. "Dr. Birken ordered an MRI." He removed Jake's nasal canula, unhooked the overhead monitor, then turned to Sam. "He'll be in X-ray for at least an hour. Maybe more."

Sam placed a gentle hand over Jake's. "You okay?"

Jake's smile was pained. "Sure."

"Visiting hours end in thirty minutes," Sam said. " I didn't sleep much last night worrying about you. Guess I might as well go home, get some rest. I'll be back tomorrow. Promise."

The tech began wheeling the hospital bed out the door.

"Sam?"

"Yeah?"

"Tell mom I'm sorry I'm such a fuck-up."

As Jake waved goodbye, Sam couldn't miss the involuntary calisthenics as individual muscles began twitching all the way down his right arm.

At her front door, Christine handed Mackenzie PJ's diary. "Thank you so much for your blog. It's a godsend for so many of us who are hurting. Viv tells me almost seven thousand people read my post."

"Nearly fifteen thousand when I checked just before we came tonight," Viv chimed in.

"Well, I was thinking that when you set up the website and Facebook page, Viv, you're welcome to use some of PJ's drawings."

"That would be awesome, wouldn't it, Mac?" Viv prompted.

"Awesome," Mackenzie responded, though that was hardly what she was thinking.

Sometime after his wife had gone upstairs to bed, General Paulsen sat in the comfort of his den, nursing a second whiskey while mulling over the phone message he'd received earlier in the day.

Social media.

He hated the very concept.

His grandchildren reveled in it, were actually addicted to it, never without their mobile devices, lest they lose some existential connection to their world. But what could these naive kids understand about the need for security-tight espionage? To them it was all a game - posting everything and anything no matter how personal - even their genitals. Someone had recently dubbed it 'sexting'. Imagine! It wouldn't be long before a United States congressman got caught sending a snapshot of his dick willy-nilly through the Ethernet.

What was the world coming to? In earlier times he and his chosen few could rely on secrets remaining hidden, but today the damn World Wide Web was just as likely to ensnare the good guys as the prey they were stalking.

He replayed the message, glad that his protege was much more tech savvy than he. At least the issue had been discovered. Now it was up to him to figure out what to do about it.

Viv did all the talking on the drive back to Delray, excited by Christine's wholehearted endorsement of the Silent Survivors blog.

"Pretty generous of her to offer PJ's drawings for the website and Facebook page, huh?"

Mackenzie found herself chewing on the inside of her cheek, weighing her response. What was the point in arguing about taking the next step? Viv was like a runaway train. There really was no way to put the brakes on her enthusiasm.

Besides, why should *she* be so ambivalent? What really was the downside, assuming Viv was able to hide her true identity? Would it be the worst thing in the world if the blog reached even more people? Christine was proof that providing a site for others with similar stories to vent and share was therapeutic. Mackenzie had to admit that for herself, writing had been a wonderful release - even if she still kept most of her own secrets private.

As she pulled into the Shady Palms parking lot, she thought about returning to an empty apartment, of the unfilled hours stretching before her like a vast desert. Maybe Viv's pushing and prodding was a sign. Now that her mother was gone, maybe this was just what she needed to give her life new direction.

"Mac?"

Mackenzie switched off the ignition and turned to Viv. "You're right, it's very generous."

Viv beamed. "How about I show you some of my ideas for the website tomorrow?"

"And here I thought you'd be raring to go tonight."

Viv's face morphed into an uncharacteristically serious expression as she unlocked the passenger side door and stepped out of the car. "No can do, kid. I promised a favor to someone in my art class."

Watching her young friend hurrying up the stairs to her apartment reminded Mackenzie of the favor she'd just promised to Christine. She checked her watch. Only a little after eight. Plenty of time to get a start on PJ's diary.

CHAPTER 12

Saturday, August 23, 2008

The sound of knocking jarred Mackenzie awake. Soaked with sweat, her heart slammed against her ribs. Last night she'd spent several hours lying in bed reading PJ's diary before the incessant rhythm of a hard summer rain had lulled her into a troubled sleep filled with his and her own nightmares.

It took several minutes before she realized that someone was at her door. Forcing her way through the cobwebs of her terrifying dreams, she sat up and glanced at the bedside clock. A little after nine a.m. Surprised that she had slept so long, yet still feeling enervated.

"Coming!" she called out, at the same time slipping into jeans, a bra and T-shirt. Without bothering to put on shoes, she padded barefoot to the entrance and opened the door.

"Guess I should have called." Sam Cantori stood in the bright light of morning holding a cardboard tray with two muffins and two Starbuck coffee cups. Just as the other day, he was out of uniform, dressed in jeans. Today's plain green T-shirt highlighted intense hazel eyes. "Sorry."

The apology came with a dimpled smile that made it impossible for Mackenzie to be angry. Self-conscious about her own appearance, she brushed a hand through her hair, a futile attempt at rearranging it into a semblance of presentability. "Bad night."

"I didn't sleep well either," Sam said, the grin dropping from his face, morphing into weariness.

"Your brother?"

Sam sighed. "Yeah. Thought I could run some things by you. I mean as a nurse and a vet." He peered deeply into her eyes. "That is, if you don't mind, Mac."

Mackenzie felt her cheeks flush at the sound of her nickname on Sam's lips. He obviously appreciated what she'd told him the other night and at the very least considered her a friend. How could she refuse? "Sure." She waved him in, shut the door and led the way to the small kitchen off the foyer.

Sam placed the cardboard tray on the table and took a seat. "Hope you like blueberry. The barista said they were baked fresh this morning."

"I happen to love blueberry, but frankly, anything is appreciated." Mackenzie reached into the cabinet for two plates. "Afraid my cupboard is bare. I haven't had time to do much food shopping. Been busy packing up my mom's things."

"I can imagine that's a difficult job."

Mackenzie nodded, sitting down opposite him. "Lots of memories. Some good, some not so."

As if sensing that she wasn't up for sharing details, Sam didn't press. Instead, he raised his coffee cup. "To better days then," he said.

Mackenzie lifted her cup. "And nights," she added.

As Christine Linton and her mother left their townhouse that morning, a man seated in a white Florida Power and Light utility van parked a block away watched through binoculars. He'd been there since before dawn's first light and he was getting antsy. With the air conditioning off and the August humidity close to ninety percent, his shirt was soaked with sweat. At least the rain had finally stopped.

He stared at the entrance for a long time after they'd driven off, making certain they weren't coming back. Finally convinced, he straightened his borrowed uniform, slipped the FP&L cap farther down his forehead, and grabbed a clipboard. Exiting the van, he hurried around to the side of the unit. Hopefully anyone spotting him would take him for a utility worker doing a routine meter check.

He wasn't a professional burglar and though he had an open carry permit for his handgun, he'd left it in his car at home. He expected this would be an easy job. Luckily the occupants had left one first floor window open a crack - a futile attempt to catch a breeze wafting off the ocean a few miles east. With little effort he lifted the window and pushed in the flimsy screen, then hauled himself inside.

Mackenzie watched Sam's face closely as he described how his brother had apparently knocked himself unconscious in his prison cell, was placed on suicide watch, then transferred to the VA. She was touched by how deeply he seemed to care for Jake, even felt a jab of envy, acutely aware that that level of filial affection was missing in her own life.

"So this doctor thinks my brother may have a neurologic disease," Sam said. "That what's been going on with him may not be due to PTSD."

Mackenzie sat up. How odd that Christine Linton had suggested the same thing about PJ. "Did he say why?"

Sam shrugged. "He did ask me about the twitches and shakes he's been having in his arms. But that could be from his drinking, right?"

Mackenzie nodded, at the same time recalling a couple of PJ's diary entries in which he complained of similar symptoms.

"So they're doing a bunch of tests over the weekend."

"Do you know which ones?"

"Let's see. I know Dr. Birken ordered blood work. Jake had a brain scan when he was first admitted that was okay. I think Birken said he was doing an MRI, but I'm not sure about the other two tests. Some study about his nerves."

"Nerve conduction study?"

Sam took a sip of his coffee. "That sounds right and the other one was about his muscles."

"Electromyography?"

"That's it. What does it mean?"

"I uh, well, the electromyography or EMG for short, tests the electrical activity of the muscles and the nerve conduction study measures how well and how fast the nerves send electrical signals." Mackenzie frowned.

"What are you thinking?"

Mackenzie didn't know what to say. How could she tell him that these were the same tests her mother had had before the doctor diagnosed her ALS? "I'm thinking that you have to wait for the results before you can jump to any conclusions."

"I got the same medical mumbo jumbo 'too soon to make a diagnosis' from Dr. Birken, but from the look on your face, I can tell you're concerned about something," Sam pressed.

Mackenzie shook her head, forcing herself back into professional mode. "Look, the list of possibilities is long and it may all be related to the drinking which is likely caused by PTSD." She placed a comforting hand on Sam's forearm. "You said Birken is a neurology fellow, right? That means he's a relative newbie. Those guys are always looking for zebras."

"Huh?"

Mackenzie smiled. "It's one of the things they teach doctors in training. When you hear hoofbeats, think of horses, not zebras."

Sam's contorted expression reflected his lack of understanding.

"Horses are the most likely diagnosis, zebras are the rare diseases and syndromes that get your name in a medical journal," Mackenzie explained.

Sam exhaled a deep breath. "I guess I am a little anxious. Frankly I'm not sure what I want the diagnosis to be right now. I was hoping that transferring him to the VA would give me a chance to have a psychiatrist check him out. Maybe someone like Dr. Mills who deals with PTSD could help me convince the court to reconsider his sentence and get him the care he needs."

Mackenzie was searching for more words of reassurance when her cell pinged an incoming text message. It could only be from Viv. Damn, she'd forgotten they were to meet this morning. She grabbed her phone and read:

Busy. Can U make it later?

Relieved, Mackenzie quickly typed in: *Sure. No hurry.* She looked up at Sam who was smiling.

"What?"

"I'm impressed. You're pretty fast with that thumb of yours."

Mackenzie laughed. "It's my neighbor upstairs. Viv's a decade younger than we are and an IT wiz. She's the one who insisted I learn to text. Says email will be passé soon. But honestly, I can't get used to all the abbreviations."

"I guess I'm really a Luddite. I still like to talk on the phone," Sam admitted just as his cell began to beep. Between "hello" and "yes sir", he stood, motioning that he had to go.

"Is it Jake?" Mackenzie asked when he'd clicked off.

"Uh, no," he stammered. "Work related."

Respectful of his privacy, Mackenzie merely nodded, walked him to the front door and opened it.

Before she could react, Sam leaned in and kissed her tenderly on the mouth. "I've been wanting to do that since fifth grade." His tone was teasing, but his eyes were serious. "Now that we're friends, I hope we can see more of each other."

Mackenzie couldn't deny the desire his kiss had evoked. "I'd like that," she said. Then on impulse, added, "You know I owe you a dinner. As long as I have to stock the pantry anyway, how about I cook something here tonight?"

"You're sure?"

"Yeah. It's been a drag eating meals over the sink. I'd love the company."

"I know the feeling," Sam agreed. "Okay, count me in."

"How's six o'clock sound?"

"Perfect. See you at six."

Less than a half hour after breaking into Christine Linton's condo, the burglar returned to the parked van. He took a moment to catch his breath before fishing in his pocket for the burner phone he'd been instructed to buy and dialing the private number he'd memorized.

"Yes?"

"The diary wasn't in the box."

"You're absolutely sure?"

"Not there, not in the rest of the apartment."

"You didn't leave a mess?"

"No one will know I was there, sir."

Silence for a moment, then, "All right. I want you to keep eyes on who comes and goes. Maybe we can figure out what the widow's up to - if anything."

"Roger that." He'd have to make some adjustments in his schedule, but this was obviously a priority. "God bless America," he said before ending the call. True he'd never seen active duty, but he'd always loved the military and was more than proud to do his part.

Unlike his blonde, lanky, athletic nephew, Assistant DA Dalton was a short, balding fifty year old. The substantial belly bulge in his suit jacket suggested that if he'd ever been into exercise, that time was long past. "I thought we had a deal Cantori."

The verbal attack started the moment Sam slid into a dark-lit back booth at the Boynton Beach strip mall deli. At ten thirty the low priced breakfast special crowd had already departed and the early bird dinner group was busy with mahjong and golf, so the two men had the place to themselves. The Assistant DA did not want to risk being seen.

Sam waited for the frizzy-haired waitress to pour them each a cup of coffee and move out of earshot before responding. "We did. We do," he insisted. "What's the problem?"

Dalton lifted a Macbook Pro from the seat beside him and placed it on the table. Once he'd booted it up, he typed in a URL, then rotated the laptop around for Sam to see. "This is the problem," he said, pointing a pudgy finger at the screen. "Www dot Tim Dalton is a rapist dot com. Take a look at what this Maura wrote about my nephew."

Sam's heart sank as he read silently:

My name is Maura. I'm me. I'm you.

This website is for everyone who has been the victim of rape on a college campus and suffered in silence. Or worse - like me - whose complaints were just ignored. First by the school administration and then by police.

They say over 6 out of 100 college students are raped every year. But that's just the number brave enough to report it.

Universities and colleges are not prepared to handle sexual assault and rape in a careful, just, or timely manner. Even when the attacker is questioned, he is often not punished. At best, he might get an honor code violation which is the same as if he cheated on a calculus exam.

If the assault occurs during a "date", his story of consensual sex is believed and the rape claim is dismissed. And if, as in my case, the rapist is a star athlete in a sport that brings in loads of money to the school, the authorities are even less likely to take the rape claim seriously.

That's why I decided to go to the police to make an official report.

Unfortunately, I learned first hand that the police are often just as bad as the college when it comes to so-called "date rape". If you had a drink too many, they assume your intoxication somehow justified the assault, that you "consented" - even if you were unconscious!!

I did not want to be raped.

That's why I've decided to go public.

This is not revenge. This website is a public service. People need to know that this can happen to anyone if it happened to me.

In my case, I am telling you that Tim Dalton, a senior at PBU, is a rapist. Do not go on a date with this guy. And anyone else who might have been raped by him is welcome to post a warning here. I bet it's not the first time he's done this.

Sam looked up. "I don't know what to say."

"Tell me how this got out of control."

"Sir, I honestly have no idea. I filed my report before I left the precinct last night. The investigation is closed as far as my captain's concerned."

"Apparently this girl doesn't think so. Convening her own trial on the Internet. It's vigilantism pure and simple."

"So it's illegal?"

"Unfortunately the first amendment makes it all too legal." Dalton shook his head. "I wouldn't be surprised if some other coed decides to take up this girl's challenge and make a claim again Tim."

Sam raised his eyebrows. "You think there *are* others?"

Dalton exhaled a deep breath. "Off the record? No one's ever told my brother's kid 'no'. Tim's a big boy with an ego to match. But that doesn't make him a rapist. Girls today want it both ways - freedom to lead guys like Tim on, then to scream rape when it suits them. What do they care if they ruin a star athlete's chance to make it to the big leagues?" Dalton stared in his coffee cup for a moment, then looked up. "Even if he wasn't my nephew I'd have a hell of a time making a case against him with the facts you presented. Right, Cantori?"

Sam squirmed under the scrutiny. Given the bargain he'd struck with the Assistant DA, he was in no position to argue.

Obviously assuming his question was rhetorical, Dalton didn't wait for a response. Instead he placed a few dollars on the table to cover the coffees neither had drunk, shut down his computer, and stood. "You owe me, son. So do what you have to do to get that website shut down ASAP."

What was she thinking?

It was the kiss.

The soft cadence of his voice, the musky smell of his aftershave, the way he'd looked at her as he moved his lips closer to hers. All had worked to melt her resolve so that she'd found herself letting go of long practiced self-control and enjoying the sensation of the moment. Her heart still beat wildly at the thought of Sam's touch.

But offering to cook for him? Had she forgotten that her culinary repertoire was virtually non-existent? Mac and cheese, boiled hotdogs, scrambled eggs, and one very forgettable attempt at a meatloaf that Art had ultimately rescued from certain death. Perhaps the fact that her ex was a great cook was a clue she shouldn't have missed, but even now she appreciated the benefits of the few homemade gourmet meals they'd enjoyed before he deployed to Iraq. Her mother had been a terrible cook, often letting Judith order fast foods or prepare the minimalist meals - mostly pastas - that made up the staples of the Carter kids' diet growing up.

Panicked, she tried to recall the name of a place she'd heard on the car radio advertising prepared foods. 'Farmer's' something. She hurried into her bedroom and sat down at the desk in front of her laptop. Once it was booted up, she googled 'where to buy prepared foods in Delray Beach, Florida'. Instantly there it was. Boys Farmer's Market on Military Trail. Not too far away and what was most appealing was the fact that the website actually urged consumers to 'bring home delicious meals that no one has to know you didn't make yourself'. Would this be another secret she kept from Sam? She wasn't sure, but at least for now she had a plan for their dinner.

About to get up, she decided to take a few minutes to check out the prescription she'd found in her mother's medicine cabinet. The empty bottle's label had clearly noted the patient's name: Diane Carter, the prescribing doctor: Art Dodd and the date: December 15, 2006. That was just about the time she and Art had divorced; the same month her mother had taken that trip to India with a man she'd met a few months before at a local bar, someone she'd hoped would ask her to settle down, but who turned out to be a two-timer as well as a drunk. Even if he hadn't already been married, Mackenzie had no doubt he'd have abandoned Diane the moment her ALS diagnosis was confirmed. Few long-term male spouses were prepared to care for someone with such a debilitating disease, let alone someone in a fairly new relationship.

Carefully googling the drug's name, Mackenzie pushed 'search'. A moment later a half dozen links appeared. She chose the FDA site and scrolled down the page until she located a summary of Flometoquine:

> 'Developed in cooperation with the US Army, brand name Flomet, approved in 1991 for the treatment of mild to moderate acute malaria caused by susceptible strains of *Plasmodium falciparum* and/or *P. vivax*. Prophylaxis of *P. falciparum* and *P. vivax* malaria infections, including prophylaxis of chloroquine-resistant strains of *P. falciparum*. The mechanism for this quinoline methanol derivative has not been established.'

Interesting.

Mackenzie next typed in a new google search for malaria prophylaxis. At the bottom of the CDC's list was Flometoquine. At the top was Malarone, the drug she and her fellow nurse recruits had been given by the Army.

Okay, so why then had Art prescribed Flometoquine to her mother? Shutting down the computer, Mackenzie decided she'd mention it to Craig when he came on Monday. He and Art had remained friends even after the divorce. Maybe he'd know why her mother had asked her ex for her travel med rather than going to the local VA.

It was close to eleven a.m. when she checked her Timex. Better get a move-on. The reviews of Boys Market had included a warning to avoid the place around mealtimes. Something about the old timers and the narrow aisles.

You owe me.

The message couldn't have been more clear.

Tit for tat.

Tim Dalton for Jake.

Wasn't that the bargain he'd negotiated?

That's why Sam had driven all the way from Boynton Beach to the Boca Raton campus of PBU, hoping to convince Maura to take down her website. But when he'd knocked on her dorm room there'd been no answer. With no one around and disinclined to telegraph the fact that he was a cop, he'd jotted down his name and number on a slip of paper ripped from his spiral notepad, adding that he'd be back around ten the next morning to talk about the investigation. Sliding it under her door, he'd headed back to his car, frustrated by the fact that he'd just wasted two hours.

Now it was almost two thirty and he'd dodged traffic on I-95 to catch a quick visit with his brother at the West Palm Beach VA. Jake was fast asleep when he'd arrived. The nurse said he hadn't slept much the night before and was probably exhausted after the muscle and nerve testing that had just been completed.

As he sat near the hospital bed, he listened to Jake's rhythmic breathing, hoping his was a dreamless slumber. His brother deserved some peace - however short-lived. Sam, on the other hand, was plagued by angst. He shut his eyes, trying to convince himself that what he was doing for Jake was right, that he hadn't crossed a moral line, that there was no chance he was letting a rapist go free. Overcome with conflicting emotions, he wished there was someone with whom he could share his feelings. Not that his cynical partner was the right sounding board. Besides Ed had gone down to Key Largo for the weekend to test out the used camper and new fishing gear he'd bought for his impending retirement.

Sam considered Mackenzie, wondering if he dared open up to her. The relationship was still so new. How would she judge him if he revealed his deal with the Assistant DA? He wasn't sure. He was sure, however, that he really was looking forward to seeing her again.

Sam remained at Jake's bedside for another hour, then tiptoed out of the room, asking the nurse to tell his brother that he'd be back sometime tomorrow. On the drive home he stopped to buy a bottle of wine, then headed to his apartment for a quick shower and change of clothes before his dinner date.

The minute Mackenzie turned into the Boys Market lot and tried to maneuver her Civic past the row of slow moving Mercury Marquis and Crown Vics, she understood the Internet's cautionary post. Several employees were strategically stationed outside attempting to direct traffic, but their efforts to avoid fender benders were futile as a tiny white-haired senior who could barely see over the steering wheel suddenly backed out her Cadillac DTS, slamming into one of the two cars competing for her space.

The good news was that the bumper was only minimally dented and no one seemed hurt. While a small crowd gathered around the drivers, Mackenzie managed to slip into an empty parking slot without having to worry about running over pedestrians.

Near the entrance, she grabbed a bouquet of flowers and a fresh peach pie, then joined a line of mostly elderly shoppers leisurely pushing their carts down tight aisles that left little room for passing. The pace allowed her to admire the amazing assortment of fruits, vegetables, gourmet cheeses and wines, though by the time she arrived at the demarcated island of prepared foods, her ankles ached as more than one aggressive "driver" had unapologetically rammed her with their wheels.

Afraid to risk more bumper cars, she circled the rows of hot dishes several times, trying to make a decision. Everything smelled wonderful.

"Special occasion?" The accent was thick New York.

"Excuse me?" Mackenzie turned to face a Betty White doppelgänger dressed in capri pants and an "I LOVE MAJONG" spangled polo.

The woman smiled. "I noticed the flowers and the pie. Just assumed you're looking for something special."

Was this woman psychic or just plain nosy? Either way, Mackenzie figured there was no harm in honesty. "It's actually sort of a first date."

"I thought so. You're young, pretty...." She cocked her head to check out Mackenzie's left ring finger, "and not married. I'm Loretta, by the way."

"Mackenzie."

"Listen Mackenzie. You could do with the rotisserie chicken which is delicious, but if you're looking to make a real impression on your beau, try the lasagna. It's to die for." She leaned in to share a confidence. "It's how I snared my fourth husband last year. Al still thinks I cooked it myself." She chuckled. "Some secrets are just better left, don't you know?"

Mackenzie nodded. She asked the aproned employee for a large portion of the lasagne, then thanked her new friend. The lady *was* psychic, Mackenzie decided. If anyone knew about keeping secrets, it was she.

Except for his unsuccessful attempt to find Sergeant Linton's diary, the man had been parked inside the FP&L van since before dawn, eyes focused on the widow's condo. She'd returned home with her mother around noon and in the past three hours, no one had come or gone. The good news was that the cops hadn't shown up, so she must not suspect a burglary. He'd been careful not to disturb anything.

A thermos of cold, black coffee had kept him from dozing in the blistering heat, but now his bladder was close to bursting. He was considering a quick pit stop at the gas station a few blocks away when a motorcyclist pulled up to the curb in front of the condo. He reached for his binoculars. It was only when the rider removed the helmet and hopped off the bike that he realized it was a young woman, though not anyone he recognized. Dark hair, dark clothes, probably no more than twenty. He quickly picked up the camera he'd brought and zoomed in to take her photo.

Christine Linton answered the young woman's knock and ushered her inside. Unwilling to leave the scene, the man unzipped his trousers and relieved himself in the empty thermos.

Fifteen minutes later the motorcyclist was back at the front door. The widow gave her a hug before handing her a box that looked suspiciously like the one he'd rifled through earlier. He snapped another photo, then watched as the young woman strapped the box on the back of her motorcycle before taking off down the road.

Figuring his contact in Washington would want to know the connection between the girl and the widow, the man zipped up his fly, started the van's motor and began following.

"Aw oh, what's going on here, kid?"

Standing in her kitchen alcove, lost in thought, Mackenzie jumped at the voice behind her, whirling around to face the intruder. "Jesus, Viv, you scared the shit out of me."

"Lucky it was me and not some crazy." Viv shook an accusatory finger. "You forgot to lock your door again."

Mackenzie shrugged. "Guess I am a little absent-minded today."

Viv nodded at the pretty bouquet of white and yellow daisies in the middle of the table and the place setting for two. "Who's the lucky guy?"

"Just a friend."

Viv's brows shot up. "The policeman friend?"

Mackenzie felt her cheeks grow warm. "Sam's an old acquaintance. He sat behind me in fifth grade."

"Wow, had you seen him since?"

"No, we moved away that year." Mackenzie chewed on her lower lip, thinking about how her family had left Delray after her father's death and the way she'd met Sam again after so many years. "He was one of the policeman called to investigate the day PJ...." She sucked in a deep breath.

Recognizing her friend's obvious distress, Viv reached out and gently squeezed Mackenzie's forearm. "Sorry, I didn't mean to tease. It's just that I know it's been a long time since you've had any kind of social life."

"Yeah, well, I'm not sure this was such a good idea. I invited Sam for dinner before I realized I can't cook," Mackenzie said with a self-deprecating laugh. "Thank goodness for Boys Market."

"Listen, guys today aren't into the 'way to a man's heart thing'. That's so September tenth."

Mackenzie acknowledged the popular Gen Y expression with a small smile. The decade between her and Viv put them in different generations: X and Y, each supposedly with its own set of norms and slang. "How is it you're such an expert on the dating scene? If I'm not mistaken, your social life isn't much more impressive than mine."

"True," Viv admitted good-naturedly, "but I am the diva of social networking which means I'm aware of what's in these days."

"And that is?"

Viv affected a mischievous look. "FWB."

"Friends with benefits?" Mackenzie shook her head. "Guess I'm old school." She studied Viv for a moment, wondering how much to share. Truth was, theirs had become the kind of give and take sibling relationship she'd never had with her sister Judith and lost with her brother Paul's death. Though ten years younger, Viv had usurped the big sister role of life coach - an irony not lost on Mackenzie. Somehow despite her own tragic loss of parents, Viv had managed to overcome and move on with her life. Mackenzie was still trying to exorcise ghosts of her past. Wasn't sure if she ever would.

"Look," she finally said, "I made the mistake of moving too quickly once. I'm not about to do it again." She'd never recited the details of her failed marriage and certainly not the rape. She knew Viv assumed it was just the divorce that had made her wary.

"I get that you're afraid of getting hurt, Mac, but what if Sam's your destiny?"

"My destiny?"

"Could be. You know as bad as the circumstances of your meeting Sam after all these years, I think it's a pretty big coincidence that the cop called to the VA just happens to be a kid you knew in grade school. What if he's your destiny and you let your fear keep you from opening up to someone you could care about?"

Mackenzie was thrown by the unexpected question and Viv's serious expression. Destiny? What if? "Look, it's way too soon to know if I have romantic feelings for Sam, let alone if he has any for me."

Viv threw her a look of disbelief. "He'd be a fool not to."

Mackenzie gave Viv a sisterly hug. "At least I know I have one faithful fan, huh?"

"Actually, right now you've got thousands." Viv took Mackenzie by the hand and led her into the living room. "That's why I'm here."

The man in the FP&L van had followed the motorcycle to Shady Palms. Parked near the construction site across the street, he'd aimed his binoculars at the rider as she hopped off the bike, grabbed the box, and took the stairs to an apartment on the second floor.

Once she'd disappeared inside, he left the van and sauntered over to a bank of mailboxes on the side of the apartment building to check the name of the occupant in 2G. The first name, Diane Carter, he didn't recognize, assuming she might be the motorcyclist. But the second was someone he knew very well.

Now that was interesting.

Torn between alerting his D.C. contact right away and learning more, he opted for the latter. Keeping his FP&L cap low on his forehead, he nonchalantly crossed the street and reentered the van to continue his surveillance.

Inside Mackenzie's apartment, Viv pointed to the box she'd brought in and placed on the living floor beside the sofa. "Christine Linton called this morning. Asked me to stop by and pick up PJ's drawings for your website. I just wanted to share the plan I've made. Since this morning you've had over twenty thousand hits on your blog. With the site I've put together, no telling how many fans you'll have. Not to mention the Facebook 'likes'."

"Viv, I never said…"

"Listen," Viv interrupted, "One of my IT friends put me in touch with a new crowdfunding site that just opened this month. It's called GiveForward.com. I put up a request for support for Silent Survivors yesterday and already raised almost a thousand dollars. Meantime, Online.com is so impressed with your blog that I was able to negotiate a lot more money for each click. And," she added before Mackenzie could get a word in, "I plan to encrypt the website. I'll still be using an overseas proxy server for it and the blog, so you can remain as private as you want, although I hope that it won't be long before you change your mind and come out of the closet, so to speak."

Mackenzie didn't know how to respond. The lure of earning more money was undeniable. Today's mail had brought official word that her mother's VA benefits had been terminated. She desperately needed an income. She'd been thinking about finding a nursing job, but that would take time. This would certainly give her a chance to consider the best options. Despite all her intentions to say "no" to a website and Facebook Fan page, Viv's arguments had eviscerated any doubt. "Okay."

Delight bloomed on Viv's face. "Awesome. I promise you won't be sorry." She leaned over and carefully lifted PJ's drawings from the box. I'm leaving these with you. Choose the one you think would look best on the website. We could even do a slideshow if you'd like. Your decision."

They talked a while longer before Viv excused herself, saying she had more work to do on her art school friend's web page and admonishing Mackenzie to have fun on her date that evening.

"Yes, mom," Mackenzie bantered as she walked Viv to the door.

Even with the window open, the air in the FP&L van was stifling. Only the no-see-ums' constant buzzing around his head kept him alert. Fortunately, less than a half hour after she'd entered, the motorcyclist reappeared in the doorway of apartment 2G. She was empty-handed, obviously having delivered the box. This time he grabbed his camera and snapped another photo of her along with a shot of Mackenzie Dodd as she waved goodbye.

He was about to call it a day when he saw that instead of leaving the building, the girl jogged up the stairs to the fourth floor, fished a key from her pocket and opened the door to apartment 4C. Even from where he sat, he could hear her yell "Gramps, I'm home."

Anxious to deliver a complete report to his D.C. contact, he jumped out of the van and walked back across the street to the bank of mailboxes. The two names above Apartment 4 C made it easy to deduce that Vivian Wallach was the motorcyclist and Charles Wallach, her grandfather. He had no idea what tied Mackenzie and Vivian to Christine Linton, but that wasn't his job. He just took orders.

He glanced at his watch. A little after four p.m. He hoped he wouldn't be interrupting Saturday night plans. Once he returned to the van he'd call Washington and let his contact decide what to do next.

Sam knocked at exactly six. "You look terrific," he said when Mackenzie opened the door and ushered him in.

"Thanks." She knew she looked at least above average tonight. She'd spent the last two hours trying on one outfit after the other until she'd decided on a short cotton skirt that showed off her shapely legs and thin waist and a sapphire blue peasant top that the salesgirl had told her made her pale blue eyes seem the color of the Aegean. A little lipstick and even she was satisfied with the reflection in her bathroom mirror.

Sam, on the other hand, dressed in tight jeans and a white shirt open at the neck looked drop-dead gorgeous. His boyish grin made Mackenzie's pulse quicken.

Get a grip. Stop acting like a silly schoolgirl.

"You seem a little more relaxed than this morning," she said, hoping he couldn't tell that she was anything but. "Does that mean your brother's doing better?"

The smile slipped. "Actually, Jake was asleep when I got to the hospital this afternoon, but at least he had those two neurology tests I told you about." Worry lines appeared around Sam's eyes as he spoke. "I haven't even told my mother what happened yet. She still thinks he's in prison. No point in saying anything until I have some news."

"You should have test results by Monday."

Sam nodded. "I'm trying to think positive."

Well aware of the possibilities, Mackenzie found herself saying a silent prayer that the news would be good.

"Hope you don't mind if I ask your advice when I hear."

"Of course. Anything I can do to help."

Sam's smile returned. He held up a bottle of California merlot. "I'm afraid I know diddly about wine. The salesman claimed this would go with most everything." He took an exaggerated deep breath. "Smells delicious, by the way."

Mackenzie produced a sheepish grin. "As long as we're being honest, I'd better come clean before I mislead you about my culinary skills." She explained how she'd never really learned to cook, didn't want to disappoint him, so she'd bought prepared lasagne from Boys Market. Rather than relate the Betty White lookalike's reason for suggesting that particular dish, she improvised. "I figured you're probably used to gourmet Italian."

"Because Cantori is an Italian name?" Sam burst out laughing. "Dad was second generation Ohio and couldn't cook. Mom's third generation Belle Glade and even worse in the kitchen. Besides, she was always too busy helping out at my dad's small, not-so-thriving, plumbing business. Hunt's tomato sauce over a pot of boiled spaghetti was as gourmet Italian as it ever got at my house."

"That does take the pressure off," Mackenzie admitted.

"Absolutely," Sam replied. "No expectations."

Mackenzie could hear Viv in her head saying 'I told you so'. No expectations about cooking, but what about 'friends with benefits'? Mackenzie could feel a flush rise at the back of her neck. It had been a long time since anyone had made her stomach flip. Not wanting Sam to see the hunger in her eyes, she turned and led him into the tiny kitchen alcove.

Sam took the indicated seat at the table while Mackenzie handed him a corkscrew and two glasses. "If you'd do the honors, I'll get the food."

Moments later, she'd served the lasagne, green salad, a side dish of grilled vegetables and taken a seat opposite Sam.

"Wow, everything looks fantastic," Sam said. He'd already uncorked the wine and poured them each a full glass."What shall we drink to?"

"I don't know." Mackenzie looked at him thoughtfully. "How about to renewed friendships?"

Sam smiled his delight. "Perfect." He held up his glass. "You know I'm so glad our paths crossed again."

"Me too," Mackenzie said, clicking her glass with his, wondering if Viv was right. Could their paths crossing again be destiny? Maybe. Though right now all she wanted was to enjoy the evening.

For the next hour they lingered over the meal, sipping merlot, sharing small talk:

When would the summer heat abate?

Amazing that Michael Phelps had won eight medals in the Beijing Olympics.

Would the Marlins beat the Arizona Diamondbacks this weekend?

Why when they lived so close, had they never found time to swim in the ocean?

"Maybe we can go together before the summer ends," Sam suggested.

"Maybe." Emptying her wine glass for the second time, Mackenzie savored its warmth, overcome by a wonderful mellowness. Not only was Sam easy on the eyes, he was very easy to talk to.

They finished dinner with fresh peach pie that Mackenzie had warmed in the oven.

Sam took a final bite, sat back in his chair and patted his stomach. "Best food I've had in a long time, Mac. You did good."

Pleased, Mackenzie stood. She gathered their empty dishes and placed them in the sink. "Coffee?"

"Decaf? I know I've had my fill of caffeine today."

"Me too. Make yourself comfortable in the living room. I'll be right there."

When, ten minutes later, Mackenzie entered carrying a tray with their coffees, Sam was settled on the loveseat, sorting through the stack of PJ's black and white sketches.

Damn. She'd been so busy getting ready for dinner after Viv left that she'd forgotten to return them to the box.

Sam glanced at her. "Did you do these?"

Mackenzie set the tray on the coffee table and took a seat beside him. "No, actually these were drawn by Sergeant Linton."

"The marine who killed himself?"

"Yes." Of course, Sam would know his name. He'd been there that day too. "The ones on top are from his first tour, the later ones, from his third."

Sam turned back to the drawings, studying them one by one, until he came to the last dark image of exploded body parts. He shook his head. "These are amazing. You can really see the progression of his pain."

"That day in the clinic…" Mackenzie's voice cracked. "He told me the pain kept screaming in his head; that he just wanted it to stop." Mackenzie's eyes teared as she mentally blinked away the image of PJ's crumpled body lying in a congealed lake of blood at her feet.

Sam leaned over and laid a hand over hers. "It must have been terrible for you."

"It was," she admitted. "It is."

"I hate thinking that Jake's been experiencing this kind of hopelessness."

Mackenzie sighed. "PJ's widow feels her husband's story should be shared so that people can understand what drove him to commit suicide."

"Shared? How?"

Mackenzie hesitated for a moment, then decided to confide in him. Maybe she was crazy - after all she really didn't know Sam *that* well - and yet somehow she sensed she could trust him. At least with this part of her secret. "I've been writing a blog. It was my friend Viv's idea really." Mackenzie explained how she'd started Silent Survivors as an online journal - a way to put down some of her own thoughts about the war - but that with Viv's social networking expertise, the blog had reached literally thousands of people who wanted to share personal stories.

"Christine Linton saw what I wrote after PJ's death and responded with this." Mackenzie rose and left the room, quickly returning with her laptop. She booted it up and launched the browser, then set it across his knees, leaning over to type in the web address for <u>Online.com</u> and scroll down to Christine's post on the Silent Survivors blog.

Sam took his time, reading silently. When he looked up, his expression was a mixture of surprise and sadness. "This is so moving." His voice was heavy with emotion.

Mackenzie nodded. "In just a few days over fifteen thousand people have read these words. Viv and Christine want me to expand the blog with an official website and a Facebook page. Christine has even offered PJ's sketches for the site."

"Sounds like a no-brainer." His face reflected admiration. "You'd obviously be filling a real need for lots of vets and their families."

"I hope so." Mackenzie let her gaze slip towards her mother's empty bedroom. "It'll definitely help me fill some of my free time."

As if reading her thoughts, Sam said, "You were a wonderful daughter - taking care of your mom the way you did."

The acknowledgement produced a wry smile. *No, not always. I wasn't always a wonderful daughter.* Mackenzie realized she was balancing a minefield of emotional contradictions: the desire to open up completely versus her promise to keep silent. Impulsively, she placed the laptop on the coffee table, wandered over to the bookshelf and pulled out the photo album.

Flipping to the pictures of her family, she handed Sam the album, then without inflection, began to relate the unvarnished version of her wild teen years, her mothers' drinking, her brother's car accident, and her less than optimal relationship with her sister. Even excluding her darker secrets, the telling left her drained. "Paul's death was my fault," she whispered.

"You were just a kid. And you said it yourself, it was an accident." Sam leaned over and took her hand again. "No one is defined by any one thing they've done - or haven't done," he said, gazing at their interlaced fingers. "The truth about most of us is a lot more complicated." As his voice drifted off, he added, "even me."

If not for the loud throaty nocturnal calls of dozens of feisty male tree frogs directed by the recent rain and long summer day to search for mates, the man parked in the white van might have finally fallen asleep. Up since before dawn, he'd hoped to take off once he'd reported to Washington. But his orders were to keep watch and so he sat with leaden lids, documenting the comings and goings of the residents of apartments 2G and 4C.

Around six p.m. he'd grabbed his camera too late to capture a front-on shot of Mackenzie Dodd's male visitor, but he had been able to check the license plate of the man's Ford pickup. With that information, it shouldn't take too long for his contact to identify the owner.

"Even you?"

Sam could tell from Mackenzie's skeptical tone and amused expression that she thought his comment was meant to make her feel better about herself. But it wasn't so. He was battling his own demons and while he recognized that coming clean might screw things up between them when they were just getting to know each other, he didn't want to build a relationship on dishonesty.

"I guess it's going to be a night of confessions." He drew in a long, deep breath. "Just to be clear, I'm not proud of what I did, but I did it for Jake." Slowly, the words rolled out. "When I saw my brother lying unconscious in the prison clinic the other night I knew I had to get him out of there. The prison doctor said he needed a court order for a transfer to the VA Hospital." Sam took a sip of his now cold coffee before continuing. "I made a deal, Mac. Told the Assistant DA I would close the investigation on his nephew in exchange for that court order."

"What did his nephew do?" Mackenzie asked.

"A fellow student says he raped her."

For a brief instant, there was a flicker of something Sam thought resembled pain in Mackenzie's eyes, but after a few blinks it had evaporated. "And do you believe he did?" she asked.

"It's not what I believe, it's what can be proven. Unfortunately date rape often becomes a 'he said, she said' situation." Sam explained that in this case both parties were of legal age, that each told competing stories, that the girl had admitted to drinking that night, then waited a week before going to the police. "Making her case in court would be an uphill battle at best. The fact that the boy's a football star gives him an unfair advantage - even if he wasn't the Assistant DA's nephew."

For a long time Sam's words hung in the air.

Then Mackenzie spoke. "So I guess that's that. Case closed." It was a controlled, matter-of-fact statement that revealed nothing of her feelings about what he'd just told her.

Sam searched her face, wondering what lay beneath the mask of detachment. As hard as he was on himself, he didn't expect her approval, but he had hoped for some sign of understanding his motive for making the deal.

"Actually not quite," he responded. "Maura - that's the girl's name - Maura has started a web page where she names the boy--Tim Dalton--as her rapist and invites anyone who's had any similar experience with him to contact her via the Internet." He related the threat made by Assistant DA Dalton when they'd met that morning in Boynton Beach. "If I don't get Maura to shut down the website, Jake goes right back to prison." His voice was an unmistakable mixture of desperation and despair.

"Can I see the site?"

"Sure."

Mackenzie lifted her computer off the coffee table and placed it on her lap. "What's the address?"

He grimaced, embarrassed. "Www dot Tim Dalton is a rapist dot com."

A few clicks on the keyboard and the computer screen filled with Maura's accusations in a bold eighteen point font.

For a long time, Mackenzie silently scanned the page. Finally she looked up. "What are you going to do?"

"I'm planning to meet with Maura tomorrow." The fact that he'd be trying to convince her to close down the webpage went unspoken.

"Would you like me to come with you?"

Mackenzie's offer was the last thing Sam expected, but he hid his surprise. "Great. I told Maura I'd be there around ten. Sunday traffic should get us there in less than half an hour. Suppose I pick you up around nine thirty?"

Mackenzie nodded, rising to clear away the coffees neither had finished.

Sam took this as a not so subtle dismissal. Just as well, he thought. Though glad to be unburdened by his confession, it had definitely destroyed the romantic mood of the earlier evening. Hopefully there would be future opportunities to connect.

At the front door, he thanked Mackenzie for a delicious dinner and kissed her chastely on the cheek. Turning to leave, he pivoted. "Right and wrong. It's not always clear, is it?"

"No, I guess not," Mackenzie agreed, a sad smile tugging at her mouth.

General Paulsen's wife had left for a girls' weekend with her sister in Manhattan, so he was alone in his home office when at eight thirty the loud clicks and hums of his fax machine indicated an incoming printout.

"2005 Ford King Ranch F150 Supercrew pickup. License # 892 LAQ. Registered to Samuel Cantori. Drivers License Class E. S360-343-54-044-0. DOB: 01-04-1978. Sex: M.

HGT: 6-01. Address in Delray Beach, Florida."

Paulsen stared at the black and white snapshot of the truck's owner. Not someone he recognized, but no doubt his PI source would have enough background by Monday to help him determine if Sam Cantori was any threat to SEDO. Same with Mackenzie Dodd, Vivian Wallach and Christine Linton. At this point there was no reason to alert Senator Fremont or Doug Anders.

Paulsen carefully folded the fax and placed it in a locked desk drawer before neutralizing the burning in his gut with a couple of antacids. Truth was he hoped the investigator's report would be negative. Nearing his sixty-fifth birthday, he was getting too old for all this subterfuge.

Locking the door behind Sam, Mackenzie leaned against the frame. She took slow deep breaths in an effort to recover from the effect of his touch and the lingering aroma of his aftershave. So much for FWB. The irony was that for much of the evening she'd actually fantasized about the pleasure of sleeping in Sam's arms. Until he told her about the rape.

She was aware that he'd been monitoring her reaction. It had taken all her willpower to prevent emotions from rippling the surface of her face. Sam obviously felt guilt about the deal he'd made with the Assistant DA. But who was she to judge? Hadn't she made her own deal with the devil when she'd agreed not to press charges for rape against her commander in Iraq?

As Sam said, right and wrong wasn't always so clear. When he'd told her about Maura, she couldn't help thinking about herself. Unaware of her secret, how could Sam know that even though it had happened to her more than a year ago, she still felt a residue of violation? For her, the assault remained raw, the pain alive.

Wandering into the living room, she sat down with her laptop. She'd left it in 'sleep' mode, so she could easily revisit the girl's webpage. Scrolling down, she read the words again and again. *My name is Maura. I'm me. I'm you.*

Maura was Mackenzie insofar as she'd been raped too and the civilian authorities were apparently just as willing to turn a blind eye as the military. But she wasn't her, was she? Maura was different. That was why Mackenzie had agreed to go with Sam the next day. Not to convince her to shut down her site.

She wanted to meet this girl who was so young and yet so brave that she refused to suffer in silence, to let her rapist go unnamed and unpunished.

My name is Maura. I'm me. I'm you.

Reading those words again sent her emotions plummeting. Suddenly tears were streaming down her face. She did nothing to wipe them away, thinking that she seemed to be doing an awful lot of crying lately.

An hour later, the man in the borrowed FP&L van was awakened by an insistent chirping on his cell phone. The caller said he could take off; the owner of the truck had been identified. Thank goodness, he thought as he shook away a yawn, grateful that Washington seemed pleased with his surveillance. No need to admit that he'd finally succumbed to exhaustion and missed Sam's exit from apartment 2G.

CHAPTER 13

Sunday, August, 24, 2008

Mackenzie was waiting outside when Sam pulled up in his truck at exactly nine-thirty. She wore dark slacks and a white blouse. He was in uniform. Although he greeted her warmly enough, he was quiet all the way from Delray to the Boca Raton PBU campus. Just as well. She wasn't ready to talk about last night either.

It was only after they'd reached Maura's first floor dorm room and Sam knocked that he broke the silence. Placing his hand on Mackenzie's shoulder, he said in a soft voice, "thank you."

"Don't thank me yet," she responded a moment before the door opened.

Today Maura was dressed in jeans and an emerald green T-shirt that complimented her thick head of unruly copper curls. Sam had said she was eighteen, but with no makeup on her freckled face, this girl appeared much younger.

"Officer Cantori." Maura acknowledged Sam while appraising Mackenzie with a wary eye.

"I hope you don't mind that I brought a friend." Sam turned to Mackenzie. "Ms. Dodd is a nurse. I thought you might feel more comfortable talking to me with her present."

Mackenzie smiled at the girl. "Please call me Mackenzie."

Maura's shrug conveyed a surly teen's 'whatever' as she opened the door a little wider and stepped aside for them to enter.

The tiny windowless dorm room was only slightly bigger than a prison cell and had even less character - sandy-colored walls, matching acoustical tile ceiling, narrow twin bed without a headboard against one wall opposite a low steel case desk and metal shelving on the other. Except for a large campaign poster declaring "Yes We Can" in red, white and blue taped to the back of the door and a few bright covers on her college texts, there was no splash of color to add counterpoint to the drabness of the space. As if the room and its occupant had no distinguishing personality.

Maura shut the door, then plopped down on her bed. Mackenzie took a seat on the only chair in the room while Sam perched on the edge of the desk.

"Your note said you wanted to talk about the investigation. Did you interview Tim?" Maura asked Sam.

"I did."

"And?"

"And Tim said the sex was consensual. Just a hook-up as he put it."

"A hook-up." Maura spat out the words, disbelief flickering in her eyes.

"You said you don't remember everything about that night," Sam said. "Is it possible that you didn't say 'no'?"

Maura was silent, but Mackenzie could tell from her rapid breathing that she was becoming increasingly agitated. "You're kidding, right?" Maura shot Sam a hostile glance. "Sure I was flattered that a senior and a football star at that had invited me out. And yes, I drank too much that night. I admit it. I even flirted a little. But I never ever asked to be raped."

"The problem is the kind of rape you're talking about is difficult to prove."

As if struck physically, Maura squared her shoulders. Her hands closed in a fist. "It's not a *kind* of rape. It's rape, plain and simple."

"Unfortunately, it's not that simple when it comes to making a legal case. For one, you waited a whole week to see the doctor."

Maura lowered her gaze to the floor. "I was scared, ashamed. But my friend made me see that I needed to do something, to make sure he's punished."

"Taking matters into your own hands is not the answer." Sam glanced over at the laptop sitting on her desk. "Making wild allegations on the Internet...."

"Wild allegations? I should have known," Maura was shaking, making an obvious effort not to cry. "You didn't come to help me, did you? You want me to shut down the web page. Right?"

Sam's silence served as confirmation.

"So you lied. You're done with the investigation. You're ready to sweep my case under the rug."

Up to that point Maura had ignored Mackenzie. Now she spoke directly to her. "You're a nurse. Do you know that student health hands out pamphlets to all incoming freshman girls? Why? Because the first six weeks of college are considered a time when us newbies are most likely to be raped. They actually call it the 'red zone'. And what's really unbelievable," she said, her voice laced with bitterness, "is how they tell us to protect ourselves - wear a wedding ring, say you have a boyfriend. What kind of advice is that?" Maura shook her head. "I wasn't afraid before I came to PBU. Now I'm scared all the time of getting raped."

"I'm so sorry," Mackenzie said.

"Sorry? You have no idea how *I* feel," Maura snapped. "So don't sit there and pretend we're in this together. You weren't there. You can't know."

Mackenzie released an audible sigh. She'd tried to see Sam's dilemma through his eyes. His brother or Maura. He loved his brother; there were two sides to every story. The problem was that more than anyone, she could see his choice from Maura's point of view. Listening to her relate what had happened to her, Mackenzie felt a disturbing flash of familiarity.

"Officer Cantori. I wonder if you'd mind stepping out for a few minutes so Maura and I could talk."

As if grateful for the respite, Sam rose and left the room without a word.

Once he'd closed the door behind him, Mackenzie moved her chair closer to Maura and took hold of her hand. "I have been there," she said in a voice barely above a whisper. "I do know. It happened while I was a nurse in Iraq." Taking another deep breath, she slowly shared an account of her own rape.

When she'd finished, Maura asked. "Did the guy go to jail?"

Mackenzie shook her head. "The military never brought charges. All anyone was interested in was what I must have done to invite sex with my superior and how I could ruin his career if I refused to recant my complaint."

"So you never got justice."

"No."

Maura pulled a prescription bottle from her pocket and handed it to Mackenzie. "This is how the school handled my situation."

Mackenzie checked the label: Prozac 20 milligrams. A popular antidepressant, it was a prescription straight-jacket, the same antidote she'd been given in Iraq - as if the pain of rape could be medicated away.

"It doesn't help, does it?" Mackenzie said as much to herself as to Maura.

"No," Maura agreed. "Don't you see then how important my web page is?" she asked. "You have to make people accountable. You have to stand up for yourself." The declaration animated her pretty face. "Already two students have emailed requests to post on the site. I'm just waiting for Viv to show me how."

"Viv?"

"Viv Wallach. She's the friend I was talking about. Once I realized the campus cops and the school administration and then the Florida state police were doing nothing, I was ready to give up, to keep quiet… " Her mouth tightened. "Maybe even quit college, but Viv convinced me to own what happened to me."

So Maura was the art student Viv had mentioned she was helping. Recalling the words on the web page, Mackenzie found the irony stunning.

My name is Maura. I'm me. I'm you.

Mackenzie had never discussed her sexual assault with anyone since she'd mustered out of the military--not even Viv who'd spent months chipping away at the protective layers Mackenzie had constructed around herself. Rape had seemed too intimate a subject to talk about and everyone - the Army, her ex, her sister and brother-in-law - had warned her to keep quiet, to get over it. Just another silent survivor. Yet here was this woman - this girl really - twelve years her junior, bravely demanding justice, refusing to join the silent sisterhood.

Face it, Mackenzie. You're a coward. You let your rapist get away with it .

Shaken by her harsh self-appraisal, Mackenzie had an overwhelming sense that she had a choice to make. She squeezed Maura's hand. "I have an idea."

Fifteen minutes later she left the dorm room, shutting the door quietly behind her.

Sam was pacing the hallway. When he saw Mackenzie he hurried over. "I take it Maura won't close down the site?"

"Not exactly. How about we grab a cup of coffee at Starbucks across the street and I'll fill you in."

If Paulsen thought his communication network was secure, he was mistaken. As someone who'd spent his career working with people in the CIA, DIA, NSC, NSA, SAIC, Army Intel and many more lesser known agencies with intelligence operations, Doug Anders had no problem tapping the general's phone.

The head of Psychological Operations - PsyOps for short - understood human nature better than anyone. Aware that Paulsen was getting cold feet about their covert operation, he was surprised the man had let SEDO go on this long without objecting. The general had believed in the mission from the beginning. He was a military man after all. It was the unintended consequences that gave him second thoughts.

Before Anders had joined the unit, PsyOps' focus had been on finding so-called performance degraders--cognitive weapons that could diminish mental performance--a psycho-pharmaceutical that would pacify the enemy, reducing his ability to fight. That's how the original acronym had been chosen for the operation. Sedo was the Latin word for "calm".

It was the serendipitous discovery that redirected that focus. An anti-malarial drug Anders had been researching as a young postdoc in Australia had an unusual side effect. Flometoquine turned out to be a performance enhancer - increasing alertness and above all aggressiveness - perfect for the US's own troops. The fact that it caused neurologic problems in some of the monkeys tested was a shame, but it wasn't found in all of them. To alert the CEO of the pharmaceutical company funding the study would have put the kibosh on a drug whose performance enhancing effect Anders recognized as just what the US Army needed. Almost two decades later, despite hundreds of thousands of taxpayer dollars spent looking for newer ways to influence the brain, nothing had come close to Flometoquine, making its continued use central to current military strategy.

So far Anders had managed to plug all the leaks through which the true nature of its side-effects could escape - starting with the regretful hit and run death of his Aussie friend and junior colleague. The DOD whistleblower's dive over Sousa Bridge two weeks ago had been Fremont's doing. Corruption and treachery came naturally to the politician who never thought twice about silencing the man who'd sent a classified military suicide report to the House Armed Services Committee. The congressman understood that America couldn't afford to lose in the Middle East. If winning included some collateral damage, so be it. The fact that he'd gotten rich skimming his take from oil and weapons contracts certainly didn't hurt either. His greed actually helped Anders sleep well at night.

It was the general's motivations that worried the MD/PhD. Unlike Fremont, money was never a draw for Paulsen whose dream was to be buried at Arlington National Cemetery with full military honors including a riderless caparisoned horse. The man had staked his reputation on a performance enhancing drug that would allow the country to wage a full out war in Iraq and Afghanistan with the smallest army in history.

But now, as the only other member of the triumvirate who knew about the drug's complications, Paulsen was questioning the operation, pushing to shut it down. He didn't share Fremont's conviction that the Republicans would take back Congress in November, let alone win the White House. His recent appearance in front of the Armed Services sub-committee had unsettled him. He feared incoming Democrats would be out for blood, calling for hearings into the false WMD claims that led up to the Iraq War, searching for scapegoats, demanding accountability. And then who knew what else they might discover?

It was the general's growing paranoia that led Anders to monitor his calls. More than anyone, the head of PsyOps wanted to see Paulsen receive his just kudos. As long as the general did his part and suppressed the reports of veterans' suicides, there was no reason why his honorable funeral had to be sooner rather than later.

At eleven-thirty on a hot Sunday morning in late August, the University Commons Starbucks was surprisingly busy. Maybe it was the air conditioning or the free Wi-Fi. Most of the inside seating was occupied by PBU students huddled over laptops, nursing expensive frappacinos, so Sam carried two iced coffees to an outside shaded table.

As soon as he and Mackenzie sat, he leaned in. "Okay, you've got me in suspense. What's the big secret?"

Mackenzie traced her finger along the rim of her glass, trying to decide how much to tell. "It turns out my friend Viv Wallach put up that page for Maura. They're in the same art class."

"Viv who created your Silent Survivors blog?"

"I told you, Viv's a computer genius."

Sam nodded, but said nothing. Instead, he looked expectantly at Mackenzie.

She understood his anxiety, that his brother's fate might depend on this. "Maura's agreed to shut down the site."

Sam heaved a sigh.

Mackenzie raised a hand to interrupt any premature thank-you's. "On one condition only."

Sam's eyes narrowed with suspicion. "What does she want?"

"She wants you to continue your criminal investigation." Mackenzie drained the rest of her coffee, taking the opportunity to moderate the passion she felt about this, lest Sam wonder if there was something more personal there, something she was hiding from him. "Apparently two students have sent emails claiming they were raped by Tim Dalton."

Sam straightened in his seat. "Jesus, are you serious?"

"According to Maura, they both want to post on her site."

"Does she have their names?"

"Just user IDs for now, but if you agree to keep investigating, she'll ask Viv to contact them for you."

"I don't know, Mac."

Mackenzie regarded him, thinking that they were alike now - she and Sam. Each with their secrets, each with their choices. How could she blame him for his ambivalence when she had her own? Leaning back, she threw him a pointed look. "Last night you said that right and wrong isn't *always* clear and I agree - in principle. Just not in this instance."

Sam was quiet, obviously waiting for Mackenzie to continue.

"You asked me to listen to what Maura had to say. I did. I believe she was raped. If Dalton has raped others, he certainly shouldn't get away with it. These students deserve justice. It would be wrong not to give them that opportunity."

"*If* Maura shuts down the site…"

"As soon as I get home, I'll talk to Viv. She'll do it."

Sam 's face reflected his internal struggle. "My brother…" he said softly, as much to himself as to Mackenzie.

"Tomorrow you should have Jake's test results. Keep the investigation going and I promise to help you get your brother the medical care he needs."

They stared silently at each other before Sam finally exhaled a deep breath. "Okay, but somehow I'll need to investigate without the Assistant DA finding out."

An hour later Mackenzie was back in her apartment and on the phone with Viv. "I should have guessed that Viv Wallach designed Maura Holmes' web page."

"How did...? Viv sputtered, clearly caught off guard.

"Maura told me. I just met with her and Sam Cantori."

"Your policeman date?"

"Small world, huh?"

"I'll say."

"Sam and his partner are the officers assigned to Maura's case."

"No offense, Mac, but your boyfriend wasn't going after Tim Dalton any more than our campus cops or the school administration. That's why I convinced Maura to go public. You'd have to agree, the Internet's a great way to get folks' attention."

"No question," Mackenzie replied. "The problem is your site got the Assistant DA's attention. Now he's putting pressure on Sam to have the site shut down."

"No way. It's free speech. Perfectly legal."

"True, but this situation is a little more complicated." At the risk of betraying a confidence, Mackenzie felt she had to share the details of Jake Cantori's military trauma, his life conviction for murder, and the fact that whatever slim shot he might have at a psychiatric pardon was totally dependent on the Assistant DA's willingness to allow a thorough medical examination at the VA.

"I don't understand."

"If the web page is shut down, Sam's brother can stay in the hospital until he's been diagnosed."

"And the rape investigation? Is that shut down too?"

"No." Mackenzie explained the deal she'd made with Sam. "Maura's given her blessing."

"You trust Sam?"

"I do."

There was a long silence on the other end of the line before Viv spoke. "It's just a temporary shutdown, right?"

"Right. Can you do it?"

"Of course." Spoken with the confidence of an expert. "I'll just put up an HTTP 404."

"What's that?"

"Error message. The website hosting server will generate a '404 Not Found' web page when a user attempts to sign onto her URL."

Though she didn't begin to understood the technicalities, Mackenzie thanked Viv and related Sam's pledge to interview the two PBU students who claimed they'd also been raped by Tim Dalton.

"I'll need to get their okays. Then I'll send you their contact information."

"Thanks, Viv. Oh, by the way, I decided to take your advice and use all of PJ's drawings on a slideshow for the new Silent Survivors site."

"Awesome. Drop the sketches off at my apartment so I can scan them. I'll have the site up and running by tomorrow."

Mackenzie didn't have to see Viv's face to know how pleased she was that she'd convinced her to expand the blog's reach.

"So, now can I ask you how the date went last night?"

Appreciating that Viv could read her better than her own sister, Mackenzie kept her voice nonchalant. "I guess you could say at this point we're friends, no benefits."

"Hmm. Well, just remember, kid, life is really short."

Mackenzie burst out laughing. "Is that some of your Gen Y wisdom?"

"No, it's what my eighty year-old grandfather keeps telling me."

Since her brother-in-law Craig was flying in from Germany the following day, Mackenzie spent the next couple of hours finishing the job of packing the remainder of her mother's things that would go to charity. The few items she thought Judith might want she'd already set aside.

As she reached into the very bottom of a chest of drawers, her heart lurched at the sight of a cardboard box with an Armed Services label. She'd almost forgotten it was there. Mailed six months ago, it was addressed to Diane Carter, but Mackenzie knew it contained her ex-husband's personal possessions. With Mackenzie and Art officially divorced and Art's family all gone, he had listed his mother-in-law as next of kin. Despite the divorce, they'd managed to maintain a close relationship. The details of how he died were never revealed - just that it happened somewhere in the field.

Lifting off the lid, Mackenzie was filled with a deep sadness as she ran her hand over the folded desert dress uniform with its caduceus and Major insignia. No matter what issues they'd had between them, she'd always admired Art's dedication to saving the young soldiers risking their lives every day, year after year, in a war he once confided he had doubts could ever be won.

A melodic ping indicating an incoming text brought Mackenzie out of her reverie. She re-covered the box and shut the dresser drawer, postponing a decision about what to do with Art's things.

Removing her cell phone from her pocket, she saw that the text was from Viv: *Names & #'s in email.*

Hurrying into her bedroom, she grabbed her laptop and carried it into the kitchen. She sat down at the table, booted up the computer and clicked on 'mail'. Sure enough there was a message from Viv with two names: Josie Hunter and Sarah Nathan. Both were sophomores and according to Viv's note, both claimed to have been raped the year before by Tim Dalton in similar circumstances to Maura's. They were willing to talk to the police.

Mackenzie punched in Sam's mobile number.

The land line's incessant ring woke Mackenzie. She'd planned a quick catnap, but when she checked her watch as she lifted the receiver from its cradle, she realized over five hours had passed since she lay down on her bed. Ten after eight. The room was bathed in moonlight. Her stomach growled, reminding her she hadn't eaten anything all day. Just a glass of iced coffee.

"Mackenzie?"

Judith's voice sounding like an accusation made Mackenzie's muscles tighten. She did a quick mental calculation. "It's two in the morning in Germany. Everything okay? Are you…" She knew the twins weren't due for another week and a half, but that didn't mean they might not have come early.

"I'm fine," her sister snapped, making it clear she didn't want to discuss her condition. "Craig's already on the red eye from Berlin. His plane lands in Miami at six a.m. your time tomorrow."

"Should I pick him up?"

"No, the Army's sending a driver. They're putting him up at the Boca Resort. He has meetings scheduled with some high level Army personnel while he's in town. He'll stop off at the hotel and settle in before coming to you. Around nine, he said. Make sure you're home."

"Of course." Where else would she be?

"Have you packed mother's things?"

"Yes and I…"

"Okay then. I've got to get some sleep before Craig, Jr. wakes up." The brusque way she clicked off without so much as a 'how are you' or 'let's talk again soon' merely magnified the tension and distance between them - two strangers who bumped up against each other only when absolutely necessary. Mackenzie wondered if they'd ever mend the torn fabric of their relationship. Judith was the only family she had left.

Hanging up, she stretched and yawned. The morning meeting with Maura had left her emotionally drained. Unfortunately her troubled sleep had done nothing to revive her. Her sister's call only seemed to exacerbate her feeling of powerlessness.

Shedding her blouse and slacks for shorts and a T-shirt, Mackenzie padded barefoot into the kitchen where she gobbled two slices of leftover peach pie while standing at the sink, then settled down at the table and restarted her computer.

As she waited for it to power up, she stared at the monitor for a long time, ruminating about the call with Sam. Grateful that Viv was shutting down the site, he'd been surprised at how quickly she'd managed to contact the two students, but promised to follow through and set up interviews within the next few days.

Her phone call had caught Sam at the VA Hospital visiting his brother. She could hear the strain in his voice when he told her there was still nothing to report about Jake's condition. As a nurse and the caretaker of her mother, Mackenzie well understood the anxiety families felt waiting for news about loved ones. It was a challenge keeping emotions under control.

"Talk to you tomorrow."

"Sure."

Their awkward goodbyes had left Mackenzie wishing for more. What did she expect? She'd forced Sam to make an uncomfortable choice - even though they'd both agreed it was right. Hadn't Dr. Mills said that the choices we make define who we are?

Now it was her turn. She took a deep breath, typed in the URL for <u>Online.com</u> along with her password and began to compose a new post. Like Sam, she realized she had no choice really. Like Maura, she was choosing to make a difference, to touch other lives, to do good. Or so she hoped. A non-decision.

Still the words did not come easily:

> *I've asked you to share your stories on these pages in the hope that we can get stronger together. And if the amazing response from literally thousands of you is any indication, I believe that's happening. You've told me yours and I've told you some of mine. But not all. That's because I've been afraid of my vulnerability and because I'd made promises to keep my secret. Today I want to share that secret, to gain strength from all of you who hopefully will understand that even though I have never seen combat, I'm a silent survivor too. I believe it's my duty to speak out because I know I am not alone. You see, I was raped by my commander....*

Later, after she'd completed the draft, intending to review it before officially posting, Mackenzie stripped and jumped into the shower, turning on the water full force. Rotating slowly, she let the needlelike jets crash down on her head, rivulets of warmth running along both sides of her body, relaxing tight muscles. She was doing the right thing, she told herself over and over as she closed her eyes, emptying her mind of everything but the pure pleasure of the moment.

When she finally reentered her bedroom and slid between the sheets, she drifted into the first dreamless slumber she'd had in months.

CHAPTER 14

At seven forty-five on Monday morning, Sam was sitting by Jake's hospital bed waiting for Dr. Birken to finish his rounds. Yesterday, Mackenzie had clued him in to the fact that this was the surest way to catch the neurology fellow before his day got too busy. "Professional secret," she'd joked.

Now the door to the room opened a crack and Birken nodded at Sam, indicating they should talk outside. In private.

As he shook the doctor's hand, Sam studied his face. What he saw there made him blurt out, "bad news?"

"Afraid so," Birken acknowledged, guiding Sam to the tiny alcove off the nurse's station.

When the doorbell rang at exactly nine a.m. Mackenzie knew it had to be Craig. Although she'd only met her brother-in-law a few times, he'd always struck her as rigid and predictable, disciplined to a fault, someone who'd never show up even one minute late.

No doubt, if Judith was the least introspective, she'd recognize that Craig possessed the extra dose of dependability she craved after her chaotic childhood. The fact that he was seventeen years Judith's senior validated Mackenzie's sense that her sister had been seeking a father figure to replace the one she'd lost.

Mackenzie opened the door prepared for a difficult visit, but found herself wrapped in a tight bear hug the moment Craig stepped into the foyer. "How are you?" he asked before pulling back, holding her at arm's length. "So sorry about your mother. These last few months must have been tough."

The sincerity in his voice was disarming. As if they were old friends. No underlying note of criticism. The last thing Mackenzie expected was any measure of empathy from Judith's husband. Maybe Craig Jr. and soon-to be-born twins were mellowing the man.

Still not inclined to let her guard down, she studied her brother-in-law. Dressed in his precisely pressed Jag uniform, he looked the same as she remembered - tall and slim shouldered, chiseled Patrician features, toned physique and short cropped hair - emulating an Army grunt, though he'd never seen combat. The only change in his outer appearance was the fact that since she'd last seen him well over a year ago, his black hair had become generously salted with gray. He was fifty-four after all.

"I'm all right," she finally replied, shutting the door and leading him into the tiny kitchen.

"Judith was sorry she couldn't make the trip, but the babies are due any minute. You understand."

Do I understand that my mother didn't time her death well?

"Of course," Mackenzie said out loud, though she doubted her sister regretted not being there. She lifted a percolator from the stove. "I just made coffee. Would you like some?"

Craig nodded, accepting the brew in a Florida Gators mug.

Mackenzie poured herself a cup and suggested they talk in the living room.

Once they were settled on the loveseat, Craig explained that he'd already contacted the funeral home and arranged a service for the following afternoon at the VA cemetery in Lake Worth. "As the spouse of a vet, your mother is eligible for burial in a national cemetery. Unfortunately, there was no room for her to be buried with your dad at Arlington."

Even though a part of her was grateful for Craig's intervention, Mackenzie couldn't help feeling a little miffed. "I assumed we'd be making plans together."

"Judith thought…"

"That I'm too irresponsible to figure out where to bury my mother?" Mackenzie blurted. "I guess I'll never overcome her low expectations."

Craig shook his head. "Look, I get that you two aren't close," he said, his voice stern, fatherly, "but you need to remember how hard it was for your sister when your father died. Diane fell apart and Judith had to step into a mother role she was too young for."

Mackenzie cast her eyes down, peering into her coffee cup. "I do remember," she said softly, "but don't you think it was hard for me too? I was only ten."

"I can certainly relate. I lost my father when I was ten too." Craig's closed his eyes for a moment as if recalling his own sorrow.

The gesture touched Mackenzie who realized how little she really knew her brother-in-law. Somehow she'd always pegged him as someone devoid of much emotion. "Sorry, I didn't realize.."

Craig held up a hand. "No need to feel sorry for me. I was luckier than you and Judith. My mother remarried soon after and I had a stable life with my stepfather and brother." He placed his mug on the coffee table and gave Mackenzie a parental pat on her arm. "You know you've been lucky having time with your mother these past months. Judith won't get that closure."

Surprised by Craig's insight, Mackenzie gave a resigned sigh. She knew she was acting like a petulant child. "You're right. Taking care of my mom did bring us closer. I'm actually glad she'll be buried nearby." She produced a conciliatory smile. "Thanks for arranging everything."

"You're welcome." Craig's gaze wandered to the far corner where Mackenzie had stored the cardboard cartons packed with her mother's things.

"I've contacted the Vietnam Veterans of America charity to pick them up later this morning."

Craig nodded. "Sooo, have you given any thought to your future?"

Mackenzie shifted uneasily. Figuring Craig might not approve and banking on Viv's promise of anonymity, she had no intentions of telling him about her blog, but she was equally wary about sharing her career ambitions. Still, might as well test those waters. "Actually I'm thinking about becoming a mental health counselor. With my nursing degree, I could probably add some additional psych courses while I worked."

"And where would that be?"

"Maybe even at the VA. I was going to ask Dr. Mills for his advice."

"Dr. Mills?"

"He runs the PTSD clinic I attend."

"Oh yes."

"And recently he's been giving me individual counseling."

Craig's brow furrowed. "I didn't know the VA had the resources."

Mackenzie shrugged. "He definitely has gone above and beyond with me. I thought maybe you had something to do with that." She regarded Craig, searching his face for some indication that he already knew about the one-on-one sessions. Though she owed Craig for her honorable discharge and the continued benefits for her mother, she resented the way he and her sister had continued to monitor her since she'd returned home. She wouldn't be surprised if that included getting reports directly from the psych department at the VA. Craig was a lawyer. He could probably sidestep any HIPPA nondisclosure issues.

"No, of course not. Why would I?" he asked.

The denial seemed genuine to Mackenzie. In fact, Craig appeared upset by the revelation. "You haven't...?"

She'd anticipated the question. "No, I haven't talked to him about what happened in Iraq." Suddenly teetering on the edge of defiance, she added, "but what if I had?"

"What good would it do?"

Maybe help me, Mackenzie thought, though she kept the response to herself.

"Trust me," Craig said. His eyes met hers, direct and unflinching. "How we left things was for the best. Nothing can be gained by opening up a can of worms." He checked his watch. "I'm late for my meeting. Why don't I pick you up at noon tomorrow for the funeral? I imagine Diane didn't have any friends who will be attending."

"Karyn, the aide who helped out is visiting her folks in Jamaica, but my neighbor Viv Wallach might like to be there. She used to spend time with mom when I was at the PTSD clinics."

"Well," Craig said, getting up from the loveseat, "if she wants to ride with us, there's certainly room for one more."

Mackenzie stood, walked over to the bookshelf and re-trieved a wrapped package. "Some mementoes I set aside for Judith," she said, handing it to him.

"Very thoughtful."

Mackenzie lifted the marble elephant from the bookshelf. "My mother brought this back from her trip to India in 2006."

"That's not something Judith would want. She's not into knickknacks."

Mackenzie laughed. "She did always hate my mother's collections. Thought they were just dust collectors." She put the piece back. "Actually I wanted to ask if you knew why Art had prescribed an anti-malarial drug for that trip." She fished the empty pill bottle from her pocket. "I found this in her bathroom cabinet. The label has his name as the prescribing doctor."

"They kept in touch after…"

"The divorce? It wasn't a secret. I knew Art called her from time to time."

"So I guess he was doing her a favor. Saving her a trip to the VA in town. You know how long the waits can be."

Mackenzie nodded. "Yeah that's what I figured, though it seems odd that he'd prescribe this particular drug."

"What's it called?"

"Flometoquine. All I could find online was that it was developed by the Army, but it's not the anti-malarial the nurses were given in Iraq and it's not on the top of the CDC's list for travelers to India."

Craig was silent for a moment. "You're the medical person."

"I just thought since you and Art were friends, maybe…"

"No, he never mentioned it to me." Craig looked at her strangely. Was it sadness? Regret? Mackenzie couldn't be sure, but his reluctant tone made it crystal clear that Art was a subject he felt uncomfortable discussing. Another subject he'd prefer she let be.

All at once the whole notion of maintaining silence about all her secrets seemed just too great a burden.

That's why the second she'd shut the door behind Craig, Mackenzie brought out her laptop, located the draft of her blog post and impulsively pushed: 'Publish Now'.

"That's it?" The heavyset driver from the Vietnam Veterans of America finished loading the donated items onto his truck.

"That's it," Mackenzie said, saddened by the thought that the remnants of her mother's entire life were packed neatly into just three medium-sized cardboard boxes.

Feeling empty, she slowly trudged back up to her apartment. She could hear the phone's ring as she entered, but took her time answering. She really wasn't in the mood to talk to anyone.

"Mac, glad I caught you."

The voice at the other end was clearly agitated, but Mackenzie recognized the caller. "Sam? What's up?"

"Bad news." Sam's voice cracked. "Jake's got ALS."

Mackenzie felt the sharp edge of regret. She knew those three letters represented an ultimate and painful death sentence. "Where are you now?"

"At the hospital."

Mackenzie checked the time. Almost noon. "I'll be there in thirty minutes."

Seconds after she hung up, her phone pinged, announcing an incoming text.

It was from Viv: "*Saw your post. We need to talk.*"

"*Later.*" Mackenzie texted back, then grabbed her purse and hurried out the door.

Yesterday the man was watching the Shady Palms Apartments in a "borrowed" FP&L van. Today he sat in a Toyota. Sure he'd been told he could dispense with the surveillance, but what kind of spy would he be if he didn't give it his all? Besides, he had nothing better to do during his lunch hour.

He'd just finished the burger he'd picked up at the corner MacDonald's when he spotted Mackenzie bound down the stairs, squeeze into her Civic, and pull out of the parking lot.

He slowly eased his car onto the main road, maintaining a discreet distance.

Less than half an hour later, Mackenzie had arrived at the West Palm Beach VA. As soon as she'd parked, the man did the same, carefully shadowing her as she entered the hospital and pushed the elevator button. Once she'd boarded the car and the doors slammed shut, he moved closer in order to observe the floor number where the elevator stopped.

When Mackenzie arrived on five, she found Sam pacing in front of the nurses' station, worry and fatigue etched on his face.

"Thanks for coming." He wrapped his arms around her. "The neurologist said to page him. I told him you were a nurse and could help me understand the situation better."

She pulled back. "Is he sure of the diagnosis?"

"He says the tests are conclusive, though he's still getting a psych consult today because of Jake's possible suicide attempt."

After asking the clerk to page Dr. Birken, Sam led Mackenzie to Jake's hospital room. The security guard sitting just outside took her name, then waved them both in.

Jake's eyes were closed, but fluttered open as Sam and Mackenzie approached his bed.

"This is the friend I told you about," Sam said. "You were too young to know her when she lived in Delray, but Mackenzie and I were in the same fifth grade class."

As Jake raised his right hand in greeting, the muscles along his forearm began to twitch. "Hey, big bro-brover. You di-dinit s-say she was sso pretty." The words tumbled from his mouth in a rash of barely distinguishable syllables.

Easy for someone to assume he was drunk or on drugs, Mackenzie noted. Unfortunately, she recognized the muscle twitching and slurred speech as ominous signs. Forcing a smile, she bantered, "and Sam didn't tell me how handsome you were."

The fact was, even in his obviously disheveled state, Jake *was* good looking. More wiry than his older brother, he had the same hazel eyes and dimpled grin. Mackenzie could imagine that in his better days he'd been a heartbreaker.

While they waited for the neurologist, the three made small talk, cautiously avoiding any mention of Jake's illness.

"Sam sa-said you were in Iraq?"

"Army nursing corps," Mackenzie replied. "Your brother told me you did two tours in Afghanistan."

"H-hot as hell."

"I'll bet."

"Mo-mosquitoes bi-big as m-mothers." Jake's laugh came in gulping guffaws, then faded suddenly as if turned off by a spigot. Another symptom, Mackenzie knew.

"Good thing the Army made us all take those malaria pills, huh?" She chewed on her lower lip for a minute, thinking. "Say, do you happen to remember the name of the drug?"

"Not sh-sure."

"Does Flometoquine sound familiar?"

Jake shook his head.

"How about Flomet?" she asked, wondering if perhaps the brand name might be more familiar.

"Maybe."

"Are we interrupting?"

Mackenzie spun around, surprised to find Mills and a white-coated younger doctor she guessed to be the neurology fellow standing by the door. She hadn't heard them enter.

"Ms. Dodd," Mills said by way of acknowledgement.

Mackenzie expected the psychiatrist to ask what she was doing there, but when he stepped closer to the bedside, he introduced himself to Jake, then shook hands with Sam. "I just ran into Dr. Birken and thought I'd see your brother now. He's on my consult schedule today."

The neurologist came forward and asked Jake how he was doing before suggesting that Sam and Mackenzie talk with him outside while Mills examined Jake.

General Paulsen studied the intel his PI had faxed to him that morning. So far, nothing in the background information on Samuel Cantori, owner of the Ford pickup, had raised any concerns. Born in South Florida, thirty years old, single, officer in the West Palm Beach Police Department for the past seven years. A model citizen.

Paulsen flipped over the second page to check out family history. Mother, Jenny Cantori, age fifty-seven, living; father, Nicholas Cantori, dead the year before at age fifty-nine. Heart attack. One brother, Jake Cantori, age twenty-five. Sentenced to life in Florida state prison for murder.

Noting the boy's conviction so close to the date Nicolas had died, Paulsen shook his head, imagining the pain the father must have felt at his son's fall from grace. Paulsen and his wife had been lucky. Neither of their two daughters had ever been in trouble.

He was about to fire up the shredder when his fax machine began to spit out several more pages. It was a copy of a computerized medical record he quickly recognized as belonging to the VA. Even before its adoption by Veterans Affairs in 1994, Paulsen had been a strong supporter of the clinical information system known as VISTA. It had gone through a number of iterations since the 1970's and it was still far from perfect, but it was one of the only integrated electronic medical records in the country.

He pulled the sheets off the fax. The top of the document listed the hospital: West Palm and patient name: Jake Cantori.

So the brother was a veteran.

Paulsen checked the date of admission: three days ago and the reason for the hospitalization: suicide attempt, head trauma.

As he skimmed through the admitting doctor's notes, he grew increasingly alarmed: 'Twenty-five year old white male…Army private…two tours in Afghanistan…prisoner at Martin Correctional Institution…found unconscious in his cell…revived by guards…head laceration treated by PA…transferred to VA for neuro and psych eval.'

Paulsen hurriedly turned over the page to locate the neurologist's consult. Skipping past the blood and scan reports, it was yesterday's note by a Dr. Birken that made his stomach clench: 'EMG and nerve conduction studies confirm ALS.'

Jesus, how much worse could things get? He thought he had the situation under control, but now he really had no choice. Once again he had to try and convince Anders to terminate SEDO before someone figured out what they were up to.

Seated around a table in a conference room off the main corridor, Mackenzie and Sam listened to Birken patiently explain the results of the neurological tests in great detail. "When I examined Jake on Friday I found weakness and thinning of his muscles - what we call atrophy - along with muscle twitching known as fasciculations. There was also some spasticity."

Mackenzie nodded, feeling a sense of deja vu. Less than a year ago, she'd had a similar conversation with her mother's neurologist.

"Motor neurons are nerve cells that help control muscle movement," Birken related. "My physical exam suggested that there was both upper and lower motor neuron damage. That's why I ordered the electromyogram and nerve conduction studies."

He pulled a folded computerized printout from the pocket of his white coat. "Jake's EMG," he said to Sam. "I'm afraid this, together with the nerve conduction study, detected damage to both the lower and upper motor neurons. As I told you, this is consistent with classic ALS."

Sam let out a shaky sigh. "But how did he get it? Isn't he too young?"

"It's true that ALS most commonly strikes people between forty and sixty years of age, but younger and older individuals also can develop the disease," Birken said. "Men are affected more often than women. Most cases occur sporadically. Given that you don't have a family history, we can rule out a genetic cause."

"What does that mean?"

"Well, it means that you or other family members aren't at increased risk for developing the disease."

"Are there other causes?" Sam asked.

The neurologist removed his glasses, rubbed his eyes, then pushed the frames back onto his nose. "Researchers have looked at environmental factors like smoking, diet, exposure to pesticides, but so far there isn't enough evidence to show a connection. It's one of my areas of interest. I've actually ordered Jake's medical records from the field to see if there's been any unusual exposure."

Mackenzie frowned. "What about drugs?"

Birken touched his forefinger to his lips, considering her question. "There was a paper published last year. I think out of Sweden. The author suggested that statins--the drug to lower cholesterol--might be responsible for an atypical form of ALS, but the sample was way too small and the consensus is that he's off the mark." Birken regarded Mackenzie. "Why do you ask?"

"My mother recently died of ALS."

"Sorry, I didn't know."

"I've just started wondering if there was something she was exposed to or some drug like the Flometoquine she took for malaria that might have triggered the disease."

Birken held his hands out, palms up in a gesture of doubt. "Obviously there'd need to be a whole lot more people with ALS who'd been exposed to the same medication before you could even make such a speculation."

"So we don't know the cause and there's no cure," Sam interrupted, his frustration palpable.

"I'm afraid not."

Sam closed his eyes. When he opened them, they were filled with tears. "Tell me, doctor, what will happen to Jake? I mean, how will…?"

Mackenzie reached out and gave his hand a soft squeeze, an impotent attempt, she knew, to comfort him. She dreaded his hearing how his brother would die.

Birken obviously shared her reluctance. "How quickly the disease progresses varies from person to person."

Sam took a deep breath, studied the ceiling, then exhaled hard. "Please, I need to know what to expect."

Birken nodded gravely. "Well, Jake is already demonstrating emotional lability with outbursts of laughing and crying. His slurred speech is a result of weakness in the muscles involved with swallowing. That puts him at an increased risk of choking and aspiration pneumonia. As things progress and the muscles of the respiratory system weaken, he'll find it harder to breathe on his own. At some point he'll probably need ventilator support for survival. And as his leg and arm muscles lose strength it will get more difficult to stand or walk, to use his hands and arms." He shook his head. "I'm sorry."

Sam blinked away his tears. "Will he know what's happening?"

"ALS doesn't affect thinking or mental capacities, though most patients experience at least some level of depression. Dr. Mills will probably prescribe something if he thinks he needs medication and I'll sit down with you both after we've told Jake the diagnosis to discuss treatment options."

"Tell him he's going to die?" Sam choked back a sob. "He'll fall apart."

Birken's expression was solemn. "It will be difficult, but once he understands that he's got ALS, it'll be most important for him to have friends and family around him for support."

The neurologist's recitation of the disease's progression had sent Mackenzie reeling back in time, recalling how her mother had suffered. Desperate to conceal her own distress, she clenched her jaw, reminding herself that she was there for her friend. Leaning over, she draped an arm around Sam's shoulder. "I'll be there."

Several hours later, back in her apartment, Mackenzie wondered if her being there had really helped.

Mills had just finished his evaluation when Sam, Mackenzie and Birken had returned to Jake's room. The psychiatrist told Sam he'd like to meet with him privately in his office later that afternoon, then left for the clinic, though not before reminding Mackenzie to make another one-on-one appointment with his administrative assistant.

At that point Birken had pulled a chair up to Jake's bed, sat down and in as sensitive a manner as Mackenzie had ever heard from a healthcare professional, delivered the message that Jake's neurons were relentlessly being destroyed.

As a messenger, the neurologist rated five stars. Mackenzie questioned whether she could convey such devastating news with so much compassion. When she met with Mills again she planned to ask his assessment of her future as a mental health counselor.

Sam's stony expression throughout Birken's explanation had belied the anguish Mackenzie knew he felt.

It was Jake's reaction that she hadn't expected. He never shed a tear. Instead, when Birken was done, Jake turned to Sam and declared that he didn't think he'd tried to commit suicide in the prison, but now that he knew his diagnosis, he wished he had. Ironically, he'd said it without slurring one word - a momentary denial of the inevitable.

Stunned, Sam could no longer hold back his sorrow.

Mackenzie would have liked to cry then too, but she was supposed to be there for Sam and Jake. So she suggested that she and Birken leave Sam to visit with his brother. They needed time together.

Agreeing, the neurologist had said, "Tomorrow we can discuss treatment options."

As they both walked out of the hospital room, Mackenzie made her goodbyes, deliberately not mentioning her mother's funeral. Burying a loved one with ALS was the last thing Sam needed to hear.

Now sitting alone at her kitchen table, Mackenzie read through PJ's diary once again. She'd promised Christine Linton she'd give her a call by the end of the week, let her know if she'd found evidence to back her assertion that the Army had missed a medical condition.

Initially Mackenzie considered the idea far-fetched, but as a kaleidoscope of images and snatches of conversations from the past few days played in her head, she was starting to wonder if just maybe there *was* something there.

She poured herself a cup of strong black coffee in an effort to focus on PJ's words: '*I feel such pain in every nerve ending of my body. I can't stand being touched. I can't control the shakes. It's been getting worse and worse until I can hardly speak…*'

Were the shakes he described fasciculations? Twitches like Jake's, like her mother's?

Mackenzie sipped her coffee, then sat staring at the liquid remaining in the cup. What if Christine was right? Could PJ have had a neurological disease too? Even ALS?

Frowning, she reflected on the similarities between PJ's and Jake's stories. Both had apparently had easy-going, even gentle personalities before going off to war, only to return changed - darker, sadder, angrier, distrustful, violent men who couldn't sleep. PTSD might explain some of their symptoms, but not their muscle twitches, difficulty speaking, or nerve pain.

Mackenzie scanned down to PJ's last diary entry, the one Christine had quoted in her blog post: *'The pain, the depression, the anxiety, the rage. These are my demons. Demons of a war that has made me sick.'*

What if the Army *had* made them sick? It would have to have been something they were both exposed to. PJ had been in Iraq, Jake in Afghanistan.

That morning, when Sam had asked about possible causes of ALS, Birken said that researchers were looking at all kinds of possibilities - diet, smoking, pesticides - though so far nothing had panned out. Mackenzie had thrown out the question about the malaria drug her mother had taken. An offhand comment, but was it so crazy? Probably. Still, it would be interesting to learn if PJ had taken Flometoquine. Maybe Dr. Mills would know. She'd make her one-on-one appointment for Wednesday and ask him then. Jake wasn't sure if he remembered taking a drug called Flomet, the brand name for Flometoquine. She'd ask Dr. Birken to check Jake's medical record.

If Jake and PJ and her mother *had* taken the same drug it wouldn't be enough to conclude cause and effect. She knew that. She'd done enough research when her mother was first diagnosed to learn that compared to medical conditions like cancer or heart disease, ALS affected a relatively few. Each year doctors told about five thousand unlucky individuals they had it. As Birken had said, there'd need to be a whole lot more than a handful of people with ALS who'd been exposed to the same medication before she could justify her speculation.

"I don't believe it!"

Startled, Mackenzie swiveled in her seat to face Viv who was shaking her finger like a parent chastising an errant child. "Forgot to lock your door again."

"Sorry, I've been a little preoccupied."

Viv seemed to be mulling this over, regarding Mackenzie with an expression that broadcast concern for her friend. "I saw your post."

It took Mackenzie a minute to realize Viv meant her online rape confession. Since she'd sent it off into the Ethernet last night, she'd pushed it from her mind. Afraid to think of the consequences.

Viv slid into a chair opposite hers. "What you went through," she said softly. "I'm so sorry, Mac."

Mackenzie exhaled. "Well, now you know."

Viv gently touched her hand. "Telling your story was very brave."

Mackenzie waved away the compliment. "Maura made me see that I couldn't keep it secret any longer. No matter what happens." Making it clear that she didn't want to discuss it further, Mackenzie changed the subject, filling Viv in on today's visit with Sam's brother.

"He has ALS too? That's terrible."

Mackenzie nodded. "You know Christine asked me to read PJ's diary to see if the Army missed a medical problem."

"Yeah, did you find something?"

"I'm not sure. I think he might have had symptoms like Jake's."

Viv's eyes narrowed. "You think he had ALS too?"

Mackenzie shrugged. "I'm not a doctor and there's not enough in his diary to be sure, but it is possible."

"Jeez."

"I plan to ask the VA neurologist what he thinks." Without evidence that Jake, PJ, and her mother had all taken Flometoquine, Mackenzie chose to keep her theory about a possible connection to herself. That could be a non-starter. Instead she shared the fact that her brother-in-law had scheduled her mother's funeral for the following day, asking if she'd like to come.

"Of course. I'll be there for you."

It was close to six-thirty when Anders's phone rang. It was the second call to interrupt his family dinner that evening.

This time Caller ID indicated it was from his brother. "Yeah, M?"

"You'll never guess who's been asking about your drug Flometquine now."

"No worries, bro. I've already got eyes on the girl."

CHAPTER 15

Tuesday, August 26, 2008

"Today we lay Diane Carter to rest in this sacred ground. Wife of Major Dwayne Carter, recipient of the Purple Heart, mother of Judith, Paul, and Mackenzie…"

Under a slate colored sky filled with cumulo-nimbus clouds threatening rain, Mackenzie stood at her mother's graveside listening to the Army chaplain's brief eulogy. Next to her, uncharacteristically quiet, Viv held her hand tightly. Craig, dressed in his Jag uniform, was ramrod straight, his expression appropriately solemn.

With only the three of them attending the funeral, Craig had arranged a simple outside service. Because her husband wasn't buried here, Diane would have her own site amid the row upon row of white marble headstones aligned in strict military formation stretching across seamless carpets of soft Celebration Bermuda grass.

"God's will…the Lord giveth and the Lord taketh….Diane left us too soon."

Too soon. Mackenzie felt the sting of tears on her cheeks at the thought of how unfair it was. The seeming randomness of the illness that had taken her mother at age fifty-five. Still young. And now Jake, decades younger, was doomed to share the same fate.

"Ashes to ashes, dust to dust," the chaplain intoned, throwing a handful of soil atop the plain coffin.

At the final "amen", a uniformed solder stepped forward to present Mackenzie, the next of kin, with a folded American flag. She clutched it to her chest. Another reminder of the transience of life.

The service concluded just when a loud crack of thunder broke the silence. Craig urged them not to linger. As they hurried toward the parking lot, Mackenzie couldn't help looking back one last time. Already the workers were lowering the casket into the open grave.

Even though the summer rain shower had come and gone, Craig didn't get out of the town car when his driver pulled into the Shady Palms lot. He had a four o'clock flight back to Berlin out of Miami and with afternoon traffic on I-95, there was little time to spare.

Viv offered a quick goodbye and hurried up the stairs to check on her grandfather. She was already late for her graphics arts class at PBU.

Mackenzie climbed out of the backseat and walked around to the passenger side as Craig lowered his window. "Thanks again." she said, leaning in. "Have a safe trip and wish Judith good luck."

Craig promised to call as soon as the twins were born, adding, "be good" before the driver turned the car around and drove away.

Mackenzie was still standing on the curb, wondering if his words carried a hidden meaning when she heard Viv scream, "Help!"

Scrambling up the stairs she arrived breathless at apartment 4C. The door was wide open. Just inside she discovered her friend kneeling over the prostrate body of her grandfather.

Panic filled Viv's face as she looked up from her crouch. "I found him like this."

The drooping of the right side of the old man's face, together with the unintelligible speech made the diagnosis clear to Mackenzie. She fished out her cell phone and quickly dialed 911, alerting the woman on the other end that an eighty year old male was having a stroke and needed an ambulance right away.

Less than fifteen minutes later, Viv's grandfather had been transported to nearby Delray Hospital's emergency room. Mackenzie drove Viv there in her car. By the time they arrived and Viv filled out admitting paperwork, an MRI and head CT scan had been done.

"His tests confirm a blood clot in the brain," the on-call neurologist explained to Viv. "Your grandfather's lucky. He's in otherwise good health and you got him to the hospital within the three hour window for treatment."

Viv grabbed Mackenzie's hand. "Thanks to my friend. Mac's a nurse."

The neurologist smiled. "So, I'd like to start him on a clot buster drug called tPA. That's short for tissue plasminogen activator. " He handed Viv a consent form.

"Is it dangerous?" she asked.

"It has risks," the neurologist admitted. "Bleeding in the brain or other parts of the body is the most common risk. In six out of one hundred patients bleeding into the brain may cause further damage. For one out of six of these patients, it may cause death or long term serious disability."

Viv turned to Mackenzie, uncertainty written all over her face. "What should we do Mac?"

Mackenzie regarded the neurologist. "Tell me, doctor. If this were your grandfather, would you recommend tPA?"

"Absolutely," he replied without hesitation. "It's his best shot."

Mackenzie gave Viv's hand a squeeze. "I think we should listen to the doctor."

After Viv signed the consent, the neurologist asked one of the ER nurses to escort her and Mackenzie to a family waiting area, then hurried off to begin the treatment. For the next few hours the two women huddled together, drinking coffee and praying.

Finally, at seven thirty, the neurologist returned, appearing haggard, but happy. "Good news. The facial palsy is almost gone, the right sided arm weakness is improving and the speech is returning to normal. Hopefully your grandfather is out of the woods, Miss Wallach."

Viv jumped up and gave the doctor a hug. "Can I see him?"

"Of course. We'll be taking him up to the neuro ICU soon. He'll probably stay there for a day or two. Then if all goes well, we'll move him to the step down unit." He led them to a curtained cubicle at the far end of the ER where Charles Wallach lay on a hospital gurney, an oxygen cannula in his nose, an IV in his arm and a cardiac monitor attached to his chest.

Considering what he'd been through, Mackenzie thought he looked amazingly well.

Viv came over and gave her grandfather a tentative hug. "You know you scared the heck out of me, Gramps."

"Sorry honey."

"You're doing good, but the doctor says they'll need to keep you here for a few days."

"Bingo?"

Viv laughed. "Afraid you're going to miss church bingo this week."

A tech entering the cubicle interrupted, glancing at the patient's plastic identification bracelet. "Mr. Wallach, they're ready for you in ICU."

Mackenzie rode the elevator up with Viv and her grandfather and waited for the ICU nurses to get him settled before taking off for home. Viv was staying over. A kind nursing supervisor arranged for a comfortable chair to be placed by his bed. "I'll check in with you tomorrow," she promised. "In the meantime, I'll let PBU know you'll be out a few days."

On the way out to the hospital parking lot, Mackenzie marveled at what a miracle tPA was, at the same time reminded that for Jake's neurological condition, there was no comparable treatment or cure.

It was after ten p.m. when Mackenzie arrived at her complex, parked the car, and began trudging up the stairs. Exhausted, wrapped in the pain of the long day, she did not see him until she was almost at her front door. "Sam?"

He was sitting on the top step, his head cradled in his hands. At the sound of her voice, he raised his head and stood. The overhead bulb was blown, but even in the shadowy light from a quarter moon, Mackenzie discerned despair on his face.

"Are you okay?"

"Not really," he said softly.

"Come." She unlocked her door and ushered him inside. "Coffee?"

"No, thanks. I just…" His voice cracked. "I didn't want to go home." Fighting tears, he reached for her and she fell into his embrace.

For a long time they simply hugged, holding each other tightly. Suspended between past and future, Mackenzie felt safe in his arms. When she finally pulled back, she regarded him with a tender smile, carefully tracing the outline of his jaw and chin, wiping away the wetness from his cheeks. He drew her to him again, kissing her gently, then with a fierce passion. She couldn't remember when she last experienced such urgency and found herself responding in kind.

Much later, Mackenzie would wonder how they'd ended up in her bedroom, slowly undressing each other, their bodies pressed together, making love in the darkness, then lying naked, communicating their individual sorrows, the inevitability of their losses.

"I buried my mother today," she said as his hand slid lazily down the slope of her hip.

Sam stopped his exploration. "Why didn't tell you me? I would have been there."

Mackenzie flipped on the light over the bed and raised herself on her elbow to gaze at him. "I know." She touched her two fingers to his lips. "You had enough on your plate."

Sam took her palm and held it to his chest. "We are a pair, aren't we?" He managed something close to a laugh. "I told my mother tonight that Jake is sick, but I couldn't..." He shook his head. "I couldn't tell her what's going to happen to him, Mac." He breathed out a deep sigh. "Birken asked about advanced directives like power of attorney and living will. Jake's only twenty-five for God's sake. Too young. Isn't he much too young to die?"

Mackenzie merely nodded her assent, knowing words could never bring the comfort he sought. She turned off the light and lay her head on his bare chest. Joining the rhythm of his breathing, gradually their shared silence lulled them both to sleep.

Slumped in the chair by her grandfather's hospital bed, Viv couldn't keep her eyes open. And because the ICU supervisor had made her shut off her cell, she missed the 'Google Alert' letting her know that Mackenzie's most recent post had just been reposted on not one, but two new Internet sites.

Their bodies were still entwined when Mackenzie woke in the middle of the night screaming. "No!"

She was sheathed in sweat - and not just because she'd set the thermostat higher to save money she didn't have. It was the nightmare that wouldn't let go. "Don't touch me!"

Roused by her outcries, Sam reached for her. "Shh, it's just a dream," he said, trying to soothe her. "It's Sam. I'm here."

Sam, not her commander.

Struggling toward consciousness, Mackenzie fell against Sam's chest and heaved up sobs.

He held her as she wept, stroking her hair, patiently waiting until she stopped gasping for breath. "Talk to me," he pleaded.

Mackenzie moved away, lying on her back beside him, only their fingers touching. "I can't... you won't understand..."

"I think we're more than friends now, Mac," he said quietly. "No more secrets."

Mackenzie reached up and switched on the overhead light. Blowing out a deep breath, she began relating what had happened to her in Iraq in a monotone.

For his part, Doug Anders was having a sleepless night. He stifled a yawn. Three a.m. on his bedside clock. He may have told his brother "no worries" when he'd phoned, but the comment belied his true feelings. It was Paulsen's call earlier that same day that was keeping him awake now.

The general was convinced that the undoing of SEDO was imminent, that a few amateurs could somehow undermine all their efforts to save the world. It was ridiculous, of course, but

Paulsen's angst, if left unchecked, was a danger to the continued success of the operation.

Anders hadn't shared the call with Fremont. He knew there was no love lost between the congressman and the general. Fremont would be more than happy to put Paulsen out of his misery. Literally. A strong sense of loyalty was the reason Anders had decided to wait a little longer before giving up on the old man. After all, without the general, Anders would never have been able to persuade the Army to buy the rights to Flometoquine almost two decades ago.

So for now he'd just have to take care of the potential loose ends himself. No worries. It underscored his long-held belief that he had to attend to every detail if he wanted to get things done right.

Sam listened to Mackenzie's story without interrupting. Her voice was ragged with emotion. "When the commander was done, he threatened me. Told me no one would believe me if I reported him." Her laugh was laced with sarcasm. "You know - 'he said, she said'."

"Like Maura." Spoken as though he'd read her mind.

"Yes," she answered flatly. "I didn't know what to do. He was my CO, he had all the power. When he came back the next night and the one after that, I wanted to die. Shame, guilt, confusion. I thought about suicide, started saving up sleeping pills. But when it came time to take them, I couldn't.

Out of desperation I finally called Art - my ex. He was stationed in a hospital facility near Baghdad about an hour away from my unit in Fallujah. We were divorced by then, though we talked once in while. I told him what happened and that I'd decided to go AWOL. He begged me to wait until he contacted Craig, my brother-in-law.

"Art and Craig had become friends after our wedding. Craig's a senior officer in the Jag Corps. A lawyer. He has the kind of clout that got me an honorable discharge in exchange for keeping my mouth shut." Mackenzie inhaled. "And I've done just that. Until I met Maura." She turned to face Sam. "That young girl made me see I couldn't keep silent any longer."

Naked, Mackenzie rose and retrieved her laptop from the corner desk. She brought it back to the bed. Sitting cross-legged, she booted it up and found her latest blog post. "The military is every bit as bad as your police force when it comes to blaming the victim of rape. Maura gave me the courage to write this," she said, positioning the computer so that Sam could read the entry.

For a long time after he'd finished Sam was silent, trying to absorb everything he'd just heard and read. He put the computer aside and pulled her to him. "I'm so sorry, Mac," he said. "But I'm glad you told me."

Mackenzie's smile was thin. "My sister Judith convinced me that to be raped is to be forever damaged goods, that men didn't want to hear about it." Lips pressed tightly together, her expression was momentarily shuttered.

Sam waited for her to speak again.

"I certainly didn't want pity," she finally said, "but I was afraid the consequence of a confession might be that you'd think….I don't know…"

"Less of you?"

She nodded.

Sam shook his head. "Never." He produced a sheepish grin. "As a matter of fact, I'm pretty sure I'm falling for you."

Mackenzie switched off the light and lay back down next to him. "I think it may be mutual," she whispered.

This time their lovemaking was slower and even sweeter.

CHAPTER 16

The phone's incessant ringing woke them two hours after sunrise. Mackenzie leaned over Sam and grabbed the portable receiver before he could answer. She had no second thoughts about the rightness of their sleeping together. She just wasn't ready to share the news with outsiders.

Especially with Viv who was on the line. "Gramps is chomping at the bit to go home." She laughed. "He's making the nurses crazy."

Mackenzie walked over to her closet where she slid her bathrobe off a hanger. Balancing the phone against one shoulder, she managed to wriggle into the garment. "That means he's feeling a whole lot better," she said, picturing the feisty eighty year old. "I'm so glad."

While she talked to Viv, she watched Sam sit up, then slowly strut naked past her on his way to the bathroom. At the sound of the shower running, she couldn't help but imagine his muscled body covered with soapy water. A serious distraction.

"Mac?"

It took a moment to realize Viv had been trying to get her attention. "Sorry, I'm here."

"You sound sleepy. Did I wake you?"

"Uh, no…well, yeah I guess I have overslept. What time is it anyway?"

"Almost eight-thirty."

"Jeez, I'd better get going. I have a ten o'clock meeting with Dr. Mills. Then I thought I'd try to find the neurology fellow who's taking care of Sam's brother. I want to ask about the symptoms PJ listed in his diary. After that I'll head over to you. We can have a late lunch in the hospital cafe."

"Great. You think you could bring me a change of clothes?"

"Sure." Mackenzie and Viv kept each other's apartment key, so getting in was no problem. And since Viv wore mostly black, Mackenzie didn't need to ask which specific outfit to bring.

"The ICU supervisor is letting me use the nurse's bathroom to shower," Viv explained. "She says I can stay over tonight too. I think Gramps feels better with me here."

"That supervisor sounds enlightened," Mackenzie said. Although there had been much discussion recently in the medical literature about the calming effect of allowing family unlimited visitation in the ICU, few hospitals, including Delray, actually allowed it, so clearly this nursing supervisor was bucking her bureaucracy.

"Oh and bring my laptop." Viv's voice took on a sheepish tone. "I promised to help with the Powerpoint presentation she's giving at the Florida Nursing Association meeting next month."

"No problem." Mackenzie chuckled. You had to admire Viv's capacity to work the system. "Listen, do you think you could ask your grandfather's neurologist something for me?"

"What is it?"

"Ask if he's ever heard of a drug called Flometoquine?" Mackenzie spelled it out for Viv, waiting until she'd written it down, adding, "the brand name is Flomet."

"Anything specific you want me to ask about it?"

"Just if he's heard of it and if he has, does he know about any neurologic side affects."

"Will do."

Before they hung up Mackenzie mentioned that she'd left a voice mail for Viv's graphic arts professor on her way home last night. "I'll call Maura once I check with Sam to see when he plans to interview Josie and Sarah."

"Tell him I'm so sorry about his brother."

"I'll tell Sam," Mackenzie said, clicking off just as he walked back into the bedroom, this time with a towel wrapped around his waist.

Paulsen knew Anders was shining him on, promising to think about shutting down the Strategic Enemy Defense Operation. SEDO. Anders never let him forget that he'd come up with an acronym that would ultimately propel him to the head of PsyOps. Paulsen always felt the man was too ambitious for his own good.

Still, ever the good soldier, the general was resigned to help keep the operation a secret. That's why he'd spent the last few hours making sure the Department of Defense analysts tasked with collating the current suicide stats dragged their feet. Hopefully Congressman Casey would lose the election in November and his committee's investigation would die a nice quiet death.

That done, Paulsen turned his attention to his other worry. And for that he'd need to arrange another trip down to Florida.

"Tell me what?" Sam asked as he shed his towel and started putting on his clothes.

"Viv was calling from Delray Hospital," Mackenzie reported. "Her grandfather had a stroke, but he's doing okay."

"That's good."

"She wanted me to tell you she's sorry about Jake."

Sam let out a long, slow sigh. "Ironic, isn't it? My brother's diagnosis will probably keep him out of prison now. Dr. Mills thinks the state will be only too happy to let the VA foot the bill for his care." He glanced over at Mackenzie as if anticipating a question. "You don't have to ask. I still plan on interviewing the two PBU students. Today. I'll just duck out around lunchtime."

Mackenzie gave a grateful nod, words unspoken. They both knew that continuing the rape investigation after telling the Assistant DA otherwise would likely put Sam's career at risk.

"A promise is a promise."

An hour later, Mackenzie was taking the I-95 exit to the West Palm VA. Sam had refused breakfast. He was late for work. Though they'd parted without discussing what had happened between them, Mackenzie felt sure they both knew it was something special. As she pulled into the hospital parking lot, she couldn't remember ever feeling so much at peace.

Despite being early for her ten o'clock appointment, the moment she stepped off the elevator to the psych clinic, Donald Henrick escorted her into Mill's office.

The psychiatrist had been staring at what Mackenzie guessed to be a patient record on his computer screen. He quickly clicked back to the VA screensaver when he heard them come in. "Hold my calls," he ordered the administrative assistant who nodded before closing the door.

"Ms. Dodd, good morning." Mills stood and motioned her to one of two chairs facing his desk. "So," he said when they were both seated, "how have you been?"

"I'm okay," Mackenzie replied.

"Your mother's funeral was yesterday." A statement, not a question. She couldn't remember telling him, assumed she must have.

"Yes."

"That can't have been easy for you."

Mackenzie puffed out her cheeks and exhaled. "No."

"Did your sister attend?"

Mackenzie fidgeted. She'd come in a mellow mood and suddenly felt as though a scab was being pulled off a wound that had failed to heal. "No. Judith can't travel. She's almost nine months pregnant with twins and she lives in Germany where my brother-in-law Craig is stationed. He's in the Jag Corps. He came to the funeral."

"Well, it was good that you had some family there."

"I suppose," Mackenzie replied, her lips starting to tremble with unspoken emotion.

Mills had been observing her closely. Now his eyes softened as he seemed to search for an appropriate response. "Am I picking up some unresolved conflicts between you and Judith?"

Mackenzie could feel a familiar ache rise within her, powerless to control it. "You could say that," she whispered. Haltingly she recounted virtually the same story she'd shared with Sam - how as a fifteen year old she'd begged her then nineteen year old brother to drive her to a party only to have him die in a car accident on his way home. "Judith blamed me. Fifteen years later she'd still say I'm irresponsible."

Mills leaned forward. "Is that what you'd say about yourself?"

Mackenzie chewed on her lower lip, struggling to articulate her feelings. "No, not anymore, but it doesn't change how much her opinion hurts."

"Understandable." The psychiatrist's voice was gentle. "Hopefully your sister will come to realize how much she's missing by not having a relationship with her only sib. In the meantime, have you given any thought to what you'll do with your life now that your mom has passed?"

"As a matter of fact, I was hoping to talk to you about that. I need a guaranteed income, so I'll probably look for something in nursing, but I'm also considering going back to school to become a mental health counselor. I'd like to work with vets. What do you think?"

Mills tilted his head. "Actually that sounds like a terrific idea. We're terribly understaffed. I'll have to talk to the powers that be, but if I can arrange it, I might be able to get you a stipend to work in the clinic and study counseling here under a mentorship program."

Mackenzie broke into a wide smile. "As my friend Viv says, that would be awesome."

Mills held up a hand. "Don't thank me yet. Remember the VA is a big bureaucracy. It could be a month or even more before I have an answer."

"That's okay. I can pick up nursing shifts around town while I'm waiting." Mackenzie was careful not to mention Silent Survivors. As long as Viv was keeping her identity anonymous, there was no reason to share the fact that she was making extra money writing her blog.

"Sounds like a plan."

"You know Sam Cantori and I are friends. I did want to thank you for helping keep Jake out of prison."

Mills' expression became a complicated mixture of sadness and resignation. "The least I could do for a vet in need. You of all people understand how difficult the time he has left will be."

"I do," Mackenzie said flatly. "Dr. Mills, can I run something by you?"

"Of course."

"I've been talking to PJ's widow."

Mills raised an eyebrow. "You told me you barely knew Sergeant Linton."

"That's true," Mackenzie said. "My friend introduced us after his funeral. She thought it would help me gain closure if I met with Christine."

Mills merely nodded, his silence encouraging Mackenzie to continue.

Leaving out the widow's outburst at the chapel and her subsequent blog post, Mackenzie related how Christine had given her PJ's diary to read. "She thinks the Army missed a serious medical condition."

"Do you?"

"Well, I'm obviously not a neurologist, but honestly, based on the symptoms he listed - muscle twitches, shakes, nerve pain, difficulty speaking, it's possible he had ALS."

"Do you have the diary with you?"

"It's home. I can bring it in if you'd like to see it."

"No, that's more up Dr. Birken's alley. Though at this point, even if Sergeant Linton hadn't been cremated, there's no way to prove he actually had the disease."

"But you could know if he'd been taking certain drugs while in theatre, right?"

"If you mean prescribed drugs, I assume they'd be listed in the medical record." Mills leaned back in his chair, adding, "though I don't see the relevance."

"This might sound really far-fetched, but talking with Dr. Birken the other day got me thinking. There must be *something* my mother and Jake Cantori and maybe others with ALS have been exposed to."

"Not so far-fetched. There have been lots of studies looking for some common source of exposure. It's just that so far the epidemiologists haven't found one."

"That's what Dr. Birken said," Mackenzie acknowledged. "It's just that..." She hesitated, not sure how to present what even she had to admit was a shot in the dark. As long as Mills was considering a mentorship program, she didn't want to say or do anything that might jeopardize his support.

"I'd been cleaning out my mother's things," she finally began, "when I discovered an empty pill bottle in her medicine cabinet. The drug on the label read Flometoquine, the prescribing doctor was my ex-husband. Art was in the Army Medical Corps, stationed in Baghdad." Mackenzie sighed. "He was killed there last year."

Mills voiced his sympathy with a level of emotion that surprised Mackenzie. She assumed he already knew that part of her history.

"Anyway," she continued, "in 2006 mom took a trip to India and I guess she asked Art which meds she needed to prevent malaria. For some reason he chose that drug. It's on the CDC's list, but it's not the usual one prescribed for travelers."

Mills produced a thin smile. "I'm afraid as a psychiatrist I'm not familiar with all the infectious disease agents."

"Well, I'm just wondering if Art happened to choose Flometoquine because he was already giving it out to the troops in Iraq. According to what I learned from my Google search, the drug was developed by the Army, so there'd probably be plenty of supplies."

Mills frowned. "Let me understand. You think that this drug - what is it? Flometoquine?"

"Yes."

"That Flometoquine somehow caused your mother's ALS?"

Mackenzie shrugged. "I realize one person doesn't even begin to make a case, but I was hoping you could check to see if PJ took it."

She watched the psychiatrist's face intently, prepared to see a negative reaction there.

Instead Mils rotated his desk chair to face the computer and typed in his VA password. "Let's see," he recited. "Patient name: Philip Joseph Linton."

Within seconds a medical record appeared on the screen. Although from where she sat Mackenzie couldn't read what was written there, she assumed it was PJ's record. "Just one paragraph." Mills spoke as much to himself as to Mackenzie. "A short note confirming his acceptance to the PTSD clinic, but nothing about drugs here," he said, turning back to face Mackenzie. "I'm afraid Sergeant Linton never had a medical workup at this facility before joining our group and," he added, his voice somber, "he was only with us a week."

Mackenzie sat up. "So this computer doesn't include records before his deployment? There should be a long list of vaccines and drugs like the ones to prevent malaria that we all got before we shipped out."

"Actually I'm not sure. I'm lucky I can work this computer as well as I do. Old school," he admitted with a self-effacing smile. "When I get into trouble I rely on my administrative assistant."

"Would Mr. Henrick know how to find that information?"

"I certainly can ask," Mills said, checking the clock on his credenza. One minute after eleven. "Right now, I'm afraid our time's up." He stood and walked around to the front of his desk. Perched on the edge, arms crossed, he leveled a serious gaze at Mackenzie. "Before you go, though, I want you to understand that you're treading on dangerous ground. Asserting that the Army made people sick would have serious potential implications for the military. Bad publicity, perhaps even malpractice. We could lose desperately needed funding. Worse, there are plenty of Washington politicians who'd be only too happy to shut down the VA altogether and privatize the health system." He shook his head. "I for one will do anything I can to prevent that from happening."

"You're not suggesting I stop asking questions?"

"If I didn't care about the welfare of our vets, I'd tell you to drop the whole subject. No, Ms. Dodd, I'm just advising you to be careful. At this point any investigation has to be under the radar."

"I understand."

"Good." Mills stood, signaling to Mackenzie to stand as well. The psychiatrist led her to the door. "Let's continue to meet once a week. In the meantime I'll get back to you when I speak with Mr. Henrick. I know he gave out my private line after last week's debriefing session, so use it to call if anything comes up between now and then."

The minute Mills shut the door and returned to his desk, he sat down and spent a few minutes reflecting on the session with Mackenzie. Then he picked up his telephone and placed a call.

Mackenzie left Mills' office feeling a mixture of relief and elation. Relief that the psychiatrist hadn't dismissed her theory out of hand, elation that he'd not only promised to help check it out, but was seriously considering her for a psych mentorship program.

Sam had said she was a good listener. More than ever she was determined to become a counselor and help Iraq and Afghanistan vets like the guys in her therapy group who'd come back so troubled.

She took the stairs down from the PTSD clinic and headed over to the main entry to the hospital where she dashed into an empty elevator car and rode up to the fifth floor. At the nurses' station she asked the clerk, a pretty young Asian woman, to page Dr. Birken.

"Oh, I'm afraid he's gone."

"You mean he's off duty?"

"No, I mean his rotation here is over. He's been reassigned to another VA."

"Any idea which one?"

"Sorry." The clerk picked up an emory board, using the quiet time before lunch to file her nails.

"So who's taking his cases?" Mackenzie knew enough about hospital routines to appreciate the fact that most residents and fellows like Birken changed assignments at the end of each month, not in the middle or even near the end. It was only August twenty-seventh. Technically he should have been here for at least four more days.

"Until September first, second and third year medical residents will be alternating call," the clerk said, confirming for Mackenzie that Birken's leaving was unusual.

She wondered what the neurology fellow might have done to deserve an early departure. In the meantime, she was hoping she could coax the clerk into telling her what was in Jake's medical record from the field. Sam said that Birken planned to order it that week. Mackenzie leaned over the counter to read the clerk's nametag. "Angie, I'm a psych nurse and I've been following Jake Cantori's case. He's in 510."

"Uh huh."

"Well, Dr. Birken said he'd be ordering Jake's record from his time in Iraq. Can you tell me if it's arrived?"

"Oh, Dr. Harms, chief of neuro, canceled that yesterday."

"Really?"

The clerk stopped her filing. "Yes, but I overheard him say he'd gotten his orders from someone in Washington."

Jake was fast asleep when Mackenzie peeked into his hospital room. He looked so peaceful in repose, she didn't have the heart to disturb him.

With Dr. Birken gone, she had extra time before a late lunch with Viv. Stopping again at the nurses' station, she asked the ward clerk for directions to Medical Records.

"First floor," the clerk responded, now busy polishing her nails. "Opposite Radiology."

Mackenzie thanked her and rode the elevator down to 'one'. At eleven-forty, an African American woman with graying hair was the only person manning the Medical Records Department. She had her back turned as Mackenzie entered, her footsteps echoing on the linoleum floor. "Excuse me?"

The woman pivoted and moved closer to the counter. "Yes?"

"I'm an Iraq vet. Mustered out in 2007."

"What branch?"

"Army Nursing Corps."

The woman, whose nametag read Lilian Anderson, smiled. "My boy Jimmy's a Marine. On his second tour in Iraq," she said proudly. "Thank the Lord he's never been wounded, so I guess you wouldn't know him."

"No ma'am."

Lilian nodded as if the lack of familiarity was keeping her son safe. "How can I help you?"

"I was wondering how I might get a copy of my personnel records."

"Well, since 1995 they're stored in electronic format. You just need to fill out a request to NPRC."

"NPRC?"

"National Personnel Records Center. It's a department of Veteran Affairs. Do you have a computer at home?"

"Yes."

"Good." Lilian grabbed a pen from the counter and jotted something on a scrap of paper. "This is the online eVetRecs system where you request your records."

"Can anyone use it?" Mackenzie asked as she was handed the information.

"No," Lilian began to rapidly tick off a memorized list. "Veterans like yourself, of course. Then next of kin of a former member of the military who's deceased, a surviving spouse that hasn't remarried, father, mother, son, daughter, sister or brother."

"I assume VA doctors here can request vets' medical records from the field."

Lilian thought a minute. "Sure, I guess. But I can't remember when anyone at this hospital ever has. Why?"

"Just wondering," Mackenzie said, realizing Birken's order never made it past the fifth floor. Angie upstairs had said the cancellation came through Washington. Why the heck would anyone there care what was in PJ's medical record from Iraq? Something to think about. She folded the paper and put in it her pocket. "Thanks so much Ms. Anderson."

"Thank *you* for your service, young lady."

Knowing that Mackenzie was still in the hospital, the man with the Toyota decided to use his lunch hour for a break-in. The workers across the street from Shady Palms were crowded around a Mexican food truck blaring Salsa music. Too busy, he hoped, to notice him as he climbed the stairs to the second floor. Standing in front of 2G, he pulled on a pair of latex gloves, prepared to jimmy the door. To his surprise, it was unlocked. Foolish girl, he thought.

Entering, a billow of air at least ten degrees hotter than the sweltering outside temperature enveloped him. He wiped sweat from his brow, anxious to get in and out.

Hoping to find PJ's diary lying in plain sight, he was disappointed as he moved quickly from room to room, scanning cupboards, tossing cushions, moving photo albums, pushing aside clothes in closets, emptying dressers. Nothing. Where the heck did she hide it?

The last room he entered was devoid of furniture except for one cheap looking dresser on the far wall. Must have been the mother's bedroom, he guessed. He hurried over and pulled open the top drawer. There it was. Mission accomplished.

Feeling vindicated, he grabbed the diary and retraced his steps toward the front door. In the living room he stopped to survey the mess. Checking his watch, he cursed. He'd burned through twenty minutes. No time to put things back in place. On impulse he pocketed the only items that seemed the least bit valuable - a marble elephant and a porcelain doll. That way, at least the cops might assume it was just a run of the mill burglary.

He opened the front door a crack, checking that no one was around, then slipped out. Head down, he nonchalantly ambled down the stairs to his car, softly humming "God Bless America".

Mackenzie reached Delray Hospital at five to one. She'd called on the drive over so Viv was waiting for her in the lobby cafe.

"I already ordered," Viv said after they'd hugged. "Two tunas on toast and a couple of cokes. The waitress said she'd bring them over."

Mackenzie lay Viv's laptop on one of the empty tables positioned around the tiny room and handed her a shopping bag. "Change of clothes," she said, taking a seat.

Viv sifted through the selection Mackenzie had made: black T-shirt, black jeans, black bra and panties. "Good choice."

Mackenzie chuckled. "Easy choice, my Goth friend."

Viv sat down across from her. "So, I asked Gramps' neurologist about Flometoquine and he hadn't heard of any unusual side effects. But he said it's not a drug he normally prescribes."

"Yeah, it's for malaria prevention. A primary care doc or an infectious disease specialist would certainly be more familiar with its side effects. Thanks for asking, though."

"You haven't told me why you want to know about that particular drug."

"It's just a wild theory at this point," Mackenzie admitted as their lunch was delivered. She waited until the waitress returned to the kitchen before relating what she'd told Dr. Mills earlier.

"Let me see if I understand," Viv said. "Your mother definitely took Flometoquine. Jake wasn't sure. And you don't know if PJ had ALS, let alone if he took the same drug."

"That's why I wanted Dr. Birken to check Jake's medical record and maybe have a look at PJ's diary."

"What did he think?"

"He wasn't there." Mackenzie quickly summarized her conversation with the clerk on the neurology floor.

Viv ate while she listened. When Mackenzie stopped talking she put down her sandwich. "Are you suggesting something sinister in Dr. Birken's leaving his rotation a few days early?"

"Well you have to admit it is a little weird that his chief canceled the order for Jake's medical records from Iraq."

"It's the military, Mac." Viv picked up a potato chip and waved it for emphasis. "Birken's still in training. He probably didn't follow proper protocol."

Mackenzie stopped to consider. Viv was always a good sounding board. Maybe she was right. Maybe it was just some bureaucratic snafu. "I guess that's possible. Birken's off the case, they figure he doesn't need the record."

"Besides, even if both Jake and PJ were given Flometoquine, counting your mom that's only three people.

I'm no scientist, but I do know it wouldn't begin to prove your theory that it's what made them all sick."

"You're absolutely right. I need that information and lots more data before the Army would be willing to open an investigation." Between sips of coke, Mackenzie shared her new career goals including the fact that Dr. Mills was considering her for a mentorship program.

"That's wonderful, Mac. You'd be a fabulous counselor."

Mackenzie produced a grateful smile. She could always count on Viv's support. "Dr. Mills said he's going to see about ordering PJ's record. In the meantime, I thought I'd try to get a copy of Jake's medical record myself."

"Don't requests have to come from doctors?"

"Depends." Mackenzie retrieved the folded paper from her pocket and showed it to Viv. "This is an online site where vets can request their own personnel records. I'll check with Sam later. If Jake gives the okay, can you help?"

Viv tapped the top of her computer. "That I can do." She finished the last bite of her sandwich. "Let's go up and visit Gramps. Then we can find a quiet spot," she said with a twinkle in her eye, "I want to show you your amazing new website."

Sam spent his lunch hour interviewing the two PBU sophomores who'd responded to Maura's web challenge. Josie Hunter was an English major - tall and blonde with a heart shaped face and pale green eyes. Sarah Nathan studied music - petite, brunette with a streak of orange in her wavy hair and a metal ring in her nose. They couldn't have been more different in looks other than the fact that they were both, like Maura, very well endowed. Sam wondered if that was Tim Dalton's fantasy.

Although he spoke with each young woman separately, Sam realized their claims reflected a common theme: star athlete flatters a shy freshman during the first few weeks of class, invites her to a frat party where he plies his date with enough alcohol to completely dull her judgement before luring her into his bed.

"I could hear his buddies on the other side of the door," Josie said, her voice shaky. "I don't know if they knew what was happening to me, but they were there, talking loudly, joking. I don't know if they would have heard my screams anyway, but it didn't matter. He was covering my mouth the whole time he held me down."

A single tear began a slow descent down Josie's cheek. "I didn't report the rape," she whispered, casting her eyes downward. "I was ashamed. I'd been a virgin. I tried to block it from my mind. But it's a year later and I still have trouble sleeping. Terrible nightmares." She hiccoughed a sob.

Echoes of the trauma Mackenzie had shared with Sam the night before.

Sarah's story was similar to Josie's. A photo on her 3G iPhone dated August 25, 2007 showed her with a torn dress, her left shoulder bruised, her lip swollen and bloody, mascara smeared down both cheeks."My roommate took this when I got back to the dorm around three a.m.," she told Sam. "But when I showed it to campus police, they didn't believe my story. The disciplinary committee blamed *me* for drinking too much. Kept asking me if I was sure it wasn't just a bad hookup."

She let out a loud sigh. "After that every time Tim saw me on the quad, he'd wink at me and smirk. I barely made it through last year. I wouldn't have come back this semester if I wasn't on scholarship and couldn't afford to transfer. When one of my friends showed me Maura's statement on the Internet, I couldn't believe that Tim was at it again." Sarah appealed to Sam. "Maura says we can trust you, Officer Cantori. Tim Dalton is a serial rapist. You can't let him get away with his crimes this time. If three of us have come forward, how much you want to bet there are more?"

The same question he'd asked Assistant DA Dalton who'd replied: *Off the record? No one's ever told my brother's kid 'no'. Tim's a big boy with an ego to match. But that doesn't make him a rapist.*

Or does it? Sam wondered, tapping his pencil against his notepad and flipping it closed.

Viv and Mackenzie enjoyed a short visit with Viv's grandfather before a radiology tech rolled a gurney into the ICU cubicle to transport him for another brain scan. While they waited for his return, Viv grabbed her computer and led Mackenzie down the hall to an empty conference room.

Once they were seated Viv opened the laptop, booted it up and connected to the hospital's wireless network. "Check this out," she said, typing in the URL for the new website. Within seconds the screen displayed Viv's Silent Survivors logo just above the original mission statement. She unclicked 'mute' and the inspirational hymn "You Raise Me Up" sung by a church choir could be heard over a dramatic slideshow of PJ's sketches.

"Wow, I love it." Mackenzie regarded Viv with admiration. "You've outdone yourself."

"This site is encrypted to protect confidentiality. I've linked the blog posts to <u>Online.com</u> in a way that will protect your anonymity."

Mackenzie nodded, though she didn't understand the explanation of technical details. She was just so impressed with what her friend had accomplished.

Viv clicked on the link. "Your last entry."

Seeing it officially published, Mackenzie felt her heart skip a beat. With all that had happened in the last twenty-four hours, she hadn't thought about its impact. Now she wondered with some trepidation how it would be received.

As if she'd read her mind, Viv said, "I haven't had a chance to examine the feed stats yet. Let's see…" She typed in her administrative password and located the analytics. "Jeez, Mac. Forty-three thousand and twelve views in two days." She clicked back to the blog management area where forty-two comments were awaiting administrative approval.

Mackenzie shook her head. "These are all from my post?"

Viv nodded. "I usually review them first to weed out the trolls who just want to make trouble."

Although she appreciated the desire to shield her from negative comments, Mackenzie decided it was time to face how others viewed her confession. "Mind if we review these together?"

Viv hesitated for a moment before scrolling down to the first one from 'Wronged Recruit' and began reading out loud:

> *"I joined the Army in 2004. After graduating boot camp I was assigned to a unit in Afghanistan. It was there that I was brutally raped by one of the men and warned that if I told anyone my face would be cut up with a knife. I didn't listen and reported the rape to my CO who said he'd investigate. He refused to reassign me so when word spread, I experienced harassment about proceeding forward with the case. I had to see the rapist every day and suffer his smirking. When I requested counseling, the counselor who happened to be a woman blamed me for the rape. I'll never forget her saying; "If women would just say yes there would be no rape." I tried holding all my emotions in so I could continue my service, but as time went on, I experienced headaches, body pains, flashbacks and panic attacks. They got worse and worse until I knew I had to quit the military if I was ever*

going to heal. They gave me a disability retirement along with a warning to keep my mouth shut about the rape. Until your post, I was going to do just that. Now I want to speak out like you."

The next comment was from an ex-Marine.

"I was raped by a fellow Marine. I reported it and was called a liar. I was ridiculed and forced to sit through Sexual Assault Prevention and Response training which contains a reenactment of a rape. Worse of all, I was in a battalion that did not support me. I was forced to work with this Marine, in the same unit, only ten feet away every day. All the Marines I knew would shun me and turn their backs. Marines would drive by and yell obscenities as I walked down the street. I reported this to the Battalion Commander who told me not to complain and 'Duty before self'. I was discharged from the Marine Corps four months later. Several other female Marines came forward with their stories of rape from the same Marine. After seeing how I was treated, they all retracted their statements. I don't blame them. A Marine on duty has no friends. No room for doubt in the Marine Corps Fidelity.

I'm not sure what you can do with this information, but I figure someone should hear this besides the people that have done NOTHING for me. I HOPE YOU CAN USE THIS STORY FOR SOMETHING GOOD!"

A third was signed 'Speaking Out Cost My Career':

"I was sexually assaulted by my army supervisor (e-7) and his Afghan colleague who both worked for the three star Army Command General. I told his supervisor what happened. I thought there would be an investigation and that I would be allowed to continue doing my job, especially when other women in my same shop came forward and reported

similar actions from the same supervisor around the same time. But it was an election year and the rape was covered up. Instead I experienced three years of retaliation and mistreatment that cost me my career. Being assaulted was bad enough. I did not officially enter hell until I spoke up about it and the military commands did everything in their power to distract me, discredit me, demoralize me, and destroy my once promising career as they railroaded me out of the service for political reasons. I miss being a soldier."

Mackenzie was stunned. On and on she read, women from every military service sharing personal stories. So many of them like her own. It was one written by a mother that finally brought her to tears.

"Thank you for letting me share my story. My daughter played softball; she practiced Taekwondo, played both guitar and drums. She participated in Junior Reserve Officer Training Corps in high school. She went to a local technical college and earned a degree in Graphic Arts.

She always wanted to be a soldier. She scored in the 98th percentile on her Armed Service Vocational Aptitude Battery (ASVAB). She wanted to be a Physician Assistant. She was well on her way to success when she decided to join the United States Army. She went to boot camp and excelled, then to technical school at Fort Sam Houston. She became an Army Medic.

Despite a successful career and deployments, my daughter was raped three times by fellow soldiers while in Sharan, Afghanistan. She died in September 2006. The DOD told us that she committed suicide. She was found with a gunshot wound behind her right ear. I never believed that, but my husband refused to do anything about it. Army Investigators told us she committed suicide for the (SGLI) insurance money.

She'd called me from Afghanistan and said, 'Mom send me Ka-Bar, a combat knife, because I cannot go to the bathroom safely. I have more to fear from my own (fellow soldiers) than any enemy Afghani with a grenade.' She was never scared of Afghani citizens. She was afraid of her fellow soldiers."

Seeing Mackenzie's tears, Viv reached over to give her a hug. "That poor girl. It's terrible, Mac, but look at the good you're doing giving her mother a place to tell her story."

"I'm just overwhelmed. I never expected this kind of response."

Viv pulled back from the embrace. "Mac, you and Maura are my heroes. It takes real courage to speak out."

Nothing can be gained by opening up a can of worms.

Reminded of Craig's words, Mackenzie released a deep sigh. More than forty thousand page views.

Just keep the secret.

Too late.

The bell you can't un-ring.

"Guess it's really out there now, huh?"

If Viv heard ambivalence in Mackenzie's tone, she chose to ignore it. "Your blog is giving all these women a voice." She checked her watch. "Listen, I gotta get back to Gramps. In the meantime, you need to reply to these comments and," she added as she shut down her computer, "write a post that describes your feelings about what you've read. You have a forum here, kid. Like that Marine wrote, use their stories for something good."

Despite the oppressive heat, Sam remained in his police cruiser long after he'd pulled into the FDLE parking lot and shut off the engine. The burger and fries he'd bought at the corner Wendy's lay untouched on the passenger seat. He wasn't hungry after all.

Closing his eyes, he replayed the PBU student interviews. Although the claims made by Josie and Sarah sounded credible, he knew without any real evidence there was little chance any DA would be willing to bring an indictment. The photo Sarah's friend had taken proved only that she'd sustained injuries at some point. Where, when, and by whom would be impossible to prove a year later.

Still, the allegations made by the two young women added to Maura's suggested a pattern. What had Sarah called Tim Dalton? A serial rapist? What if she was right and even more students were willing to come forward?

Sam fished his cell from his pocket and switched it back on. Two voice mails. The first was Mackenzie asking him to return the call. "Not an emergency," she said. "Just want to run something by you." She sounded happy which made him smile. He knew how difficult it had been for her to share what had happened to her in Iraq. The second message wiped the grin from his face. Although the caller didn't identify himself, Sam recognized the soft Southern accent. "Good job, Cantori. As promised, I've officially transferred your brother from prison to the VA system. I can see you're a team player. You'll go far."

Sam tensed as he listened to Assistant DA Dalton's words again and again.

You're a team player.

Obviously a reference to his persuading Maura to shut down the website.

Sam sagged against the headrest, the phone still at his ear.

Considering his options, he couldn't help wondering what Mackenzie would want him to do.

About to push 'delete', something made him change his mind. Instead, he slipped the phone back in his pocket before stepping out of the cruiser and walking across the parking lot toward the field office. At the front door he dropped the Wendy's lunch special into the trash bin.

On her way out of Delray Hospital, Mackenzie stopped by the HR office and submitted an application for a per diem position. The nursing supervisor said that until the snowbirds returned to Florida in the fall, there weren't enough patients to fill all the wards. Right now she could only offer last minute shifts, but promised to contact her if the situation changed. In the meantime, she suggested Mackenzie try the VA. "Their beds are always filled."

"Well hey, partner," Ed Wilton greeted Sam as he settled down at his desk. "Thought we'd planned lunch today at that new Mexican joint in Lake Worth, but you ducked out on me. Couldn't even reach you on the phone. If I didn't know you better, I'd wonder if you stood me up for a quickie."

Used to his partner's low brow humor, Sam managed a half smile. "No such luck." Feeling uncomfortable, he averted his gaze.

Ed must have sensed that Sam was in no mood for teasing because he dropped the sarcasm and turned serious. "Jeez, I'm a schmuck." He bumped the heel of his palm against his forehead. "Of course you were visiting your brother." He walked over to Sam and threw an arm around his shoulder. "If I didn't say so before, I'm really sorry about his…." Struggling to find the appropriate word, he finally chose, "situation. Tough break."

"Yeah, it is." Sam said flatly. He drew back and faced his partner. "I didn't visit Jake. He's busy with PT and voice therapy most of the day. I'll see him tonight."

"Okaaay," Ed drew out the word. "Want to share where you did go? I mean if you do, great, if not..."

"I went back to PBU."

Ed looked confused. "Why?"

"To interview two sophomores who claim they were raped last year by Tim Dalton."

"You're kidding, right? How the heck did that happen? I thought you closed the case."

Sam shrugged. "Long story."

Now Ed's tone was tinged with anger. "How about you give me the punch line. In case you forgot, until I retire in October, I'm still your partner."

"You're right," Sam said quietly. Leaving out any mention of Viv or Mackenzie, he explained that despite an initial deal made with Assistant DA Dalton to get Jake transferred from prison to the VA, Maura had managed to create an Internet page naming his nephew and urging others who'd been raped by him to come forward. "I met with Maura on Sunday and got her to shut down the page, but had to agree to interview two students who answered her challenge." Sam took a breath, adding, "Which I did today at lunch."

"And?"

"And I think Tim Dalton may be a serial rapist. At least there's some reason to keep investigating."

In the long silence that followed, Sam kept his eyes on his partner, trying to gauge his reaction.

Finally Ed said, "I've got to hand it to you, Cantori. I didn't realize you had such big cajones." He shook his head. "Guess you didn't hear the news?"

"What news?"

"It was all over local TV and radio, but now I understand that you were otherwise engaged."

"What news, dammit?"

"Oh just that Assistant DA Dalton has announced he's running for Attorney General on a strong law and order platform. How about that?"

"Shit," was the only response Sam could think of at the moment.

About to insert her apartment key, Mackenzie realized the door was open a crack. Frowning, she tried to think. She'd been in such a hurry this morning, had she forgotten to lock it? Again. She could imagine Viv's scolding. *You need to be more careful, kid.*

The minute she stepped inside, her jaw dropped. Photo albums scattered on the floor, loveseat on its side, cushions tossed. And that was just the living room. Racing through the rest of the apartment it was clear neither kitchen nor bathroom nor bedroom had been overlooked. Cabinets were flung open, clothes thrown around, a bookcase upended. *My God, who did this?* She had nothing of value to steal.

No doubt Viv would say *I told you so*. There had already been a burglary in the building the month before. Pulling out her cell phone, she was ready to dial 911 when she decided to try Sam instead. He hadn't returned her earlier voice mail, but now he answered on the first ring.

"Mac, I'm sorry I didn't get back to you. I…"

"Someone broke into my apartment," she interrupted, her voice shaky.

"I'll be there in twenty minutes."

Mackenzie was pacing in front of her door when Sam arrived. Beads of sweat dotted her temple.

"You okay?"

She shook her head. "I'm so stupid, Sam. I think I forgot to lock up this morning." She produced a guilty smile. "I guess I was a little distracted."

"Must have been *some* distraction," he replied, an unmistakable twinkle in his hazel eyes. "Come here." He brushed aside a few tendrils of hair plastered to her forehead and pulled her into his embrace. "As long as you're not hurt," he said softly. "Thank goodness you weren't home."

Mackenzie shuddered at the thought of what might have been. "Guess it could have been worse," she acknowledged. "But take a look." She ushered him inside.

"Jesus." He glanced around the living room. "Whoever did this made a real mess. Obviously in a hurry. What was taken?"

"I haven't checked." Mackenzie released a sigh as Sam helped her lift the loveseat and replace the cushions. She began putting the photo albums back on the shelf. "Oh no."

"What?"

"Two of my mom's knickknacks are gone. A porcelain doll dad brought back from Vietnam before they were married and a marble elephant from a trip to India a few years ago. I don't think they're worth much except for sentimental value."

"Small time thief, maybe a drug addict looking for anything to pawn for a fix." Sam fished out his cell. "I should probably call Delray police. Technically you're out of my jurisdiction."

"Okay."

"In the meantime, walk through the apartment and take inventory. If anything else is missing, they'll need that for their report."

Several minutes later he found her in the second bedroom. Mackenzie was peering into an open dresser drawer. "It's gone."

She turned to Sam. "PJ's diary's missing. Why would anyone take that?"

"You have PJ's diary?"

Mackenzie related how PJ's widow had asked her to review the diary, concerned that the Army misdiagnosed PTSD.

"Did you find anything?"

"As a matter of fact, PJ described symptoms that sounded an awful like my mother's and," she added with a tone of regret, "Jake's. Muscle twitches, trouble speaking, nerve pain."

"Wait a sec. You think PJ had ALS?"

Mackenzie shrugged. "Maybe or at least some neurological problem. I wanted to ask Dr. Birken if he'd take a look at the diary, but when I went to see him this morning I learned he'd transferred to another VA."

"Why?"

"No idea. But something weird's going on, Sam. It's unusual for residents or fellows to change rotations before the end of the month. And then I asked the desk clerk if Jake's medical records from the field had arrived. Remember Birken said he planned to order them? He wanted to see if Jake was exposed to something that could have triggered his illness."

"There was so much he said at that meeting, Mac, but I think I remember."

"Well, the chief of neurology cancelled the order when Birken was transferred. The clerk heard him say it came down from Washington."

"Why would anyone in Washington care who sees Jake's record?"

"Good question. Viv says I'm looking for conspiracies where there's just bureaucracy, but with the diary missing, I'm not so sure."

"Maybe your thief just got tired of looking for valuables and grabbed the diary and the two knickknacks on his way out. So he'd have something for his troubles."

"Maybe," Mackenzie conceded. "But nothing else was taken. I checked all the other rooms. Not even my laptop and that was sitting on my desk. What if it *was* the diary he was after? If that's why he broke in?"

Sam's expression conveyed skepticism.

"Indulge me. I actually ran this by Dr. Mills this morning and he didn't think I was totally crazy." Mackenzie quickly summarized how she'd discovered the empty bottle of Flometoquine in her mother's medicine cabinet and started to wonder if that's what caused her illness. "I'm trying to find out if any vets with ALS took the same drug. I told Dr. Mills what I'd read in the diary and he's going to order PJ's record. Doctors could always get personnel records, but now so can patients and their families. They just need to fill out an online application. That's why I called you earlier. I want Jake to order his records from the field. Viv says she'll help."

"Sure. I guess it can't hurt to know."

"Great. I'm picking up Viv from Delray Hospital around eleven tomorrow. She's been staying overnight with her grandfather. I'll bring her to the VA. She can fill out the application there."

Loud knocking interrupted their conversation. The short, stocky female Delray Beach police officer at the door introduced herself to Mackenzie, then raised her eyebrows when she saw Sam.

"West Palm division," Sam said pointing to his uniform. "Ms. Dodd and I are old friends. She called me when she came home and realized she'd been robbed. I gave your dispatcher the initial report." He turned to Mackenzie. "I've got to get back to the field office. You gonna be all right?"

She nodded. "I know it's not the end of the world, but it still feels like a violation."

"Because it is, Mac." He leaned in and said sotto voce, "If you want to stay at my place tonight..."

"No, I've got to work on my blog. I promised Viv."

"Okay then." With the officer watching he planted a chaste kiss on Mackenzie's cheek, promising to check in with her later.

At seven thirty p.m. Mackenzie's stomach growled, reminding her she hadn't eaten since lunchtime.

For more than three hours she'd been sitting at the kitchen table responding individually to each of now fifty-four comments from military women who'd been raped while wearing the uniform.

Tired and hungry, she stood and stretched. Wandering into the living room, she gazed out the window at the sun just beginning its descent. No matter how many times she viewed the process in Florida, it always overwhelmed her. She was sure there was nowhere else in the world where the sky was so epic, the sunsets painted in such brilliant hues. The beauty served as a counterpoint to the ugliness of what she'd been reading on her blog.

Ten minutes later, the iridescent shades of pink and orange had faded to black. Mackenzie returned to the kitchen and began foraging in the cupboard for something to eat. She settled on a bowl of granola and milk, kicking herself for not having stopped at Boys Market on the way home from Delray Hospital. She would have loved to try the rotisserie chicken Loretta, the Betty White doppleganger, had recommended. Something new to share with Sam.

Sam.

He'd called just after five, on his way to his mother's. "I've got to tell her the truth about Jake. Can't put it off any longer."

Mackenzie knew only too well how difficult that conversation would be. She wished him luck, told him that the Delray Beach officer was going to file a report, but hadn't given her much hope they'd ever find the thief, let alone the items stolen. "Especially the diary," Mackenzie said. "No witnesses, no fingerprints."

"Tough break."

"Yeah."

He'd hung up abruptly. No endearments. No chance for Mackenzie to ask about his interviews with the PBU students. She understood. Sam had a lot on his mind. Still, as she ate the cereal over the sink, she couldn't stop thinking of what he'd told her that morning: *I'm pretty sure I'm falling for you.* Was he? She hoped he was sincere.

He *had* come right away when she'd called about the break-in. He'd invited her to stay over at his place tonight. Should she have said yes? No matter how much coaching she'd gotten from Viv about what was cool these days, she'd never be willing to settle for friends with benefits. Cautious about opening herself to the possibility of love for so long, she knew she was losing her heart to this man with the dimpled smile.

Placing her empty bowl in the sink, she decided to think about it tomorrow. Right now she had to honor her promise to Viv to write about her feelings.

You have a forum here, kid.

Mackenzie smiled at the memory of Viv's expression when she'd made that statement, a directness in her gaze impossible to ignore.

… use their stories for something good.

It was clear she expected no less. Mackenzie was surprised by how much Viv's trust meant to her. With a tired sigh she sat back down at the table and began to type.

Dear Readers:

My heart is filled with gratitude for every one of you willing to share your personal stories of sexual abuse while serving your country. I know how difficult it can be to come for-

ward. For so long I was afraid and ashamed. I thought I was alone. When I gave my own testimony on this blog, I never dreamed how many of us had similar experiences. So many!

Writing about what we went through at the hands of COs, squad leaders, supervisors, and fellow soldiers is giving voice to a terrible truth. The physical and psychological trauma of sexual assault is terrible enough; the military response is as unforgivable as the act of rape itself. We've broken the silence. Words are powerful. So let's continue to do our duty and speak out. We must demand better treatment. Send your suggestions.

On the drive to his mother's, Sam's mind wandered. Preoccupied with routine police work all afternoon, he'd put off dealing with the PBU investigation. His partner's advice to let it be was unequivocal. "You'll have shit to pay if you proceed." On the other hand, how could he ignore what he'd learned?

He'd need to figure out how to handle the situation soon. Right now he couldn't seem to focus. His thoughts kept returning to Mackenzie and what she'd discovered in PJ's diary.

Muscle twitches, trouble speaking, nerve pain.

The same symptoms Jake had experienced.

The more he considered it, the more something gnawed at him. Something that Air Force vet's neighbor had said when he and Ed answered the domestic call. Exactly one week ago. Senior Airman Thomas Welkers. Sam still couldn't erase the gruesome image of his massacred family. Pregnant wife and two children. Officially declared a murder/suicide. But what had driven Welkers to commit such a horrible act?

He replayed the neighbor's words in his head:

Lynette told me he was changed, you know, since the war...

He stopped sleeping and when he did, he had real bad nightmares…
Lately he started with the shakes…
That's why Lynette made him go to the VA for help.

What if those shakes were a symptom of something beyond PTSD? If Welkers had gone to the VA, Sam wondered what his records would show. Pulling up to the curb in front of his mother's Delray Beach bungalow, he decided he would mention this to Mackenzie. She said she was bringing Viv to the VA Hospital tomorrow. Tomorrow he'd be there too. He shut off the engine and stepped out of the car thinking it was high time he met Vivian Wallach, the young woman who caused him such grief.

CHAPTER 17

Thursday August 28, 2008

Mackenzie spent the early morning tidying up the apartment. When she was done she wandered into the living room and plopped down on the loveseat. She stared at the empty space on the bookshelf, her eyes inexplicably filling with tears. While her mother lived, Mackenzie considered the porcelain Vietnamese doll and the marble elephant dust collectors, but now that they were missing they'd become proxies for her mother's memory.

Wiping her eyes, Mackenzie wondered how she was going to break the news of the stolen diary to Christine. Besides PJ's drawings, it was the only tangible record of how he viewed his military life. She could imagine the widow's sorrow at its loss. Not to mention the fact that without it Mackenzie had nothing to show Dr. Mills. She'd missed her opportunity with Dr. Birken.

The musical trill on her cell interrupted fractured thoughts. Caller ID indicated it was Viv.

"Listen, I'll meet you at the VA. I'm getting a ride with the ICU nursing supervisor. In exchange for my Powerpoint presentation, she's helping me check out a few assisted living facilities. The hospital social worker feels Gramps needs more attention than I can give him. Much as I don't want to admit it, I guess she's right - especially with our building coming down soon. We'll all have to find new places to live."

Mackenzie knew Viv well enough to appreciate that despite her upbeat tone, she would miss living with her grandfather. She imagined the expression on her face now - a mixture of sadness and resolve. Deciding not to press, Mackenzie said, "Okay, how's noon?"

"Perfect. I'll meet you outside Jake's room," Viv replied. "By the way, what you wrote last night was awesome. Do you have your computer handy?"

"Yeah." Mackenzie hurried into the kitchen where she'd left her laptop in 'sleep' mode.

"Your Facebook Fan page is on fire. Take a look. I've added a link on the new website."

Mackenzie typed in the website's URL and stared at the tally beside the Facebook 'likes'. "Is this right? Sixty-five thousand, four hundred and five?"

"And growing, kid. I got a text from <u>Online.com</u>. Based on this unprecedented response, they're sending you a five hundred dollar bonus check in the next few days."

"Wow." Welcome news to Mackenzie whose bank account had dwindled down to a pittance. The money would certainly help cover this month's rent.

"Better yet. Remember I told you about the crowd funding site and my request for support for Silent Survivors?"

"Right."

"I've linked <u>GiveForward.com</u> to your blog. From the original thousand dollars, we've raised a little over three thousand."

"You're kidding," Mackenzie marveled.

"You've started something important. Fifteen more women posted their personnel stories, twenty-three have responded to your request for suggestions so far. Let me read you this one from an Air Force sergeant who thanks you for speaking out:

> *I hope that somebody at the VA can read your blog and do*
> *something about it. I am a twenty-five year old woman*

veteran suffering from Post Traumatic Stress Disorder that resulted from being raped while serving my country.

-Signed: 'Women are veterans too.'

"This is just one example. Your post has not only given these women the courage to talk about their trauma, they're suddenly demanding accountability," Viv said. "When I checked emails this morning I saw that your entry had been re-posted twice yesterday and once today."

"What does that mean?"

"It means that anonymous or not, it's just a matter of time before someone in the Army hears about the blog. I hope you're ready."

Mackenzie was silent for a long time, considering Viv's words. She couldn't help thinking how far she'd come - from the keeper of secrets to someone others were counting on. She understood now that only by exposing the truth could secrets lose their power.

"Mac, are you there?"

"I'm here," Mackenzie said finally, adding "and I'm ready."

Arriving at the VA Hospital forty minutes before noon, Mackenzie ducked into the Human Resource office to check on employment options.

The woman manning the desk lit up when she heard Mackenzie's story. "Army nursing corps? Iraq deployment? I assume you've had experience with amputees?"

Mackenzie nodded.

"Talk about right place at the right time. One of our night nurses on ortho just called in sick. I've been on the phone all morning looking for someone to take the night shift. If you're willing to do eleven to seven, I can expedite the paperwork."

Another nod from Mackenzie.

"Then welcome to the VA team, Ms. Dodd." Before Mackenzie could reconsider, the woman urged her to take a seat and began filling out her employment application. "As someone coming from active duty, I assume your TB test and hep vaccine are up to date."

"They are, but I'm planning to request my personnel records today, so I can get the documentation to you as soon as they arrive."

"Wonderful." She smiled. "The only thing left is a photo ID badge, a uniform, and a personal password for our VA computer system."

Sam knew it wasn't going to be easy. Giving his mother that brutal news last night had been a nightmare. Jake's illness was terminal. No cure. Unable to soothe with comforting lies, he'd felt completely helpless. All he could do was hold her as she cried for the inevitable loss of her youngest son.

Now as Sam entered Jake's hospital room, his only hope was that maybe Mackenzie's theory wasn't so crazy and she'd help him figure out what had made his brother so sick.

Mackenzie had just left the first floor HR office when she spied Viv about to enter an open elevator.

"Wait for me," she called, racing to make it before the doors slammed shut.

Extending her laptop as a barrier, Viv pulled her friend in.

"Thanks." Mackenzie used the car's ascent to the second floor to catch her breath and the ride to the third to share the news of the break-in and the missing diary. "The police think whoever robbed the apartment was a druggie looking for cash or items he thought he could sell. They figure once he sees the

diary isn't worth anything, he'll trash it. I actually checked our Dumpster, but no luck."

"Guess you have to look at the bright side," Viv said. "At least you're okay."

Mackenzie nodded, impressed as always by Viv's positivism. "But how am I going to tell Christine?"

Viv didn't miss a beat. "We'll do it together," she replied as the elevator doors opened on five.

General Paulsen could feel his blood pressure rise as he listened to the report from his Florida contact. If the man had not been a relative--albeit distant--he'd have had him fired on the spot. As it was, he'd tried to rein him in - so far with little success. "What in God's name possessed you to break into that woman's apartment?"

"I thought you'd want to to get rid of the item."

They both knew he was talking about PJ Linton's diary, but Paulsen had demanded discretion - even with the use of the burner phones.

"Do you still have it?" Paulsen asked.

"Yes."

"Okay, look. I'll be down to Florida in a few days. Keep it somewhere safe and I'll deal with it when I get there."

"Yes sir."

Hemming and hawing on the other end of the line made Paulsen delay hanging up. "Anything else?"

"Well, the Internet blog that alerted us about the diary. There's been a new post I think you might find interesting."

Paulsen almost groaned out loud. Nothing about the Internet interested him. Still, the minute he heard the nature of the post and the tremendous response it was generating, he couldn't help but perk up. "That *is* interesting," he said, jotting down the blog address.

By the time the call ended, Paulsen's blood pressure had returned to normal. Smiling, he was already busy plotting how this could be just the distraction SEDO needed.

Sam was waiting outside his brother's hospital room when Mackenzie and Viv arrived. He was wearing his uniform, explaining that he'd ducked out at lunch to visit Jake. He gave Mackenzie a quick hug, then turned to Viv and extended a hand. "Miss Wallach. Glad to finally meet you."

"Please, call me Viv," she said, shaking his hand. With a clandestine wink at Mackenzie, she added, "it's good to finally meet you too."

"Jake just left for physical therapy, but I've got all the information you'll need to get his personnel records." He led them to the conference room down the hall where they took seats around the table.

While Viv opened her laptop and waited to join the hospital network, Mackenzie shared the news that she'd just accepted a night shift position there. "I'll be able to look in on Jake more often," she said to Sam. "Viv, when you're finished filling out Jake's application, can you help me with mine? I need to make sure all my shots are up to date for the job."

"Sure." Viv typed in the URL to access the eVetRecs system. "Okay, I'm ready to fill out Jake's application."

Sam took the spiral notebook from the breast pocket of his uniform and flipped open a page. "It's all here. Jake William Cantori. Birth date, social security number, service number, date he left the service."

Within ten minutes Viv had completed the form and printed out the signature verification page on the conference room printer. "That's it, " she said, handing the paper to Sam. "Can you get Jake to sign and fax it to the Saint Louis office?"

"Sure."

"Then we just wait for a response. It should come to the personal gmail account I just created for Jake."

"Thanks." Sam returned the notebook to his pocket. He looked at Mackenzie. "So this should tell you if my brother took the same drug as your mom, right?"

Mackenzie nodded. "Or any other meds he might have been given while in Afghanistan. Like I told you, I may be way off base, but just maybe it will give us a clue to what made him sick."

Sam sighed. "What you said the other day. About the Army being responsible for his illness. I'm starting to think you may be on to something." He recounted how the week before he and his partner responded to a potential domestic incident only to discover the bodies of an Iraq vet and his family. "It was murder/suicide."

Mackenzie and Viv both gasped.

"The vet's neighbor told me that each time he returned from Iraq, he showed more symptoms that might have been attributed to PTSD - moodiness, trouble sleeping, nightmares, but she also mentioned that after the third tour he had developed uncontrollable shakes. Apparently his wife insisted he make an appointment at this VA. Is it possible to find out whether he was seen and what the doctors diagnosed?"

Mackenzie sat up. "You're thinking he might have had ALS too?"

Sam shrugged. "Wouldn't it be important to know?"

"If you give me his name, I'll see if I can check it out tonight when I get my password for the VA computer system."

Sam jotted down Welkers information while Viv quickly filled out the online application for Mackenzie's personnel records. When she was done she turned to Sam."Mac told me you were planning to interview the two PBU students."

"I did."

"And?"

"And their stories were very credible."

Mackenzie studied his face. "Do I hear a 'but' there?"

"But there isn't enough evidence to make a case. It's their word against Tim's."

"And his uncle is the Assistant DA." The sarcasm in Mackenzie's tone was unmistakable.

"Worse," Sam admitted. "His uncle is running for Florida's Attorney General."

Mackenzie shook her head, indicating disappointment.

"Believe me, if I had anything tangible to nail this kid, I would."

Viv, who had been quietly listening, cut in, "what more evidence do you need?"

"To make the case for sexual battery in Florida you have to prove that the victim did not consent. Physical evidence of trauma and DNA helps. Unfortunately Maura waited a week to see a doctor. Josie was too embarrassed to report her rape. Nancy's iPhone photo of her injuries would be good, but she never saw a doctor. All three admit to drinking heavily. Juries hear that and tend to blame the victim."

"Maura was unconscious," Viv protested. "How could anyone say that's consensual?"

Exactly the argument Sam had given his partner.

Mackenzie pursed her lips. "It's the same with the military, but there's got to be some way to make a case."

"Look, I'm just the messenger," Sam declared. "Conflicting statements are generally viewed in favor of the person being accused. That's just the way it is." He paused, studying his hands, then looked up with an expression that said 'it's never gonna happen': "Of course, if Tim Dalton were to confess, it'd be a slam dunk."

Doug Anders locked the door to his home basement office. This time he didn't ask Paulsen for his music preference. Instead he inserted a heavy metal CD in his boombox and pushed 'play' as much to annoy his guest as to muffle their conversation. Having monitored the general's phone, he had a pretty good idea what he'd been up to and he wasn't happy. Still, he was glad he'd trusted his instincts and counted on Paulsen's loyalty to keep him in the loop. "Okay, what's the emergency?"

"I know I've wanted to shut down SEDO, but maybe you and Fremont are right and I've over-reacted."

Anders nodded. "Go on."

Leaving out the name of his Florida contact and the botched break-in, Paulsen shared his surveillance activities, how he'd learned about PJ Linton's diary from an entry on a blog. "I'm too old to keep up with this newfangled social media nonsense, but my guy's on top of things. He's been monitoring the online discussion to see if the widow found anything that could be a problem for us."

"And did he find a problem?"

"So far, no one's mentioned the drug."

"What about the woman you told me was asking questions at the VA?"

"Mackenzie Dodd? I'm keeping eyes on her, but I did arrange to have the neurology fellow transferred and cancelled his request for Jake Cantori's medical records from the field."

"That's the vet with ALS?"

Paulsen winced. "Yes."

Annoyed by what he perceived to be the man's hypocrisy, Anders lashed out, "Soldiers like Cantori are casualties of war. A war I shouldn't have to remind you, General, that you endorsed from day one. A war we couldn't win without SEDO." He paused for effect, lowering his voice. "It's always unfortunate to lose our own."

"Of course, you're right," Paulsen said. "Guess I'm getting too soft in my old age."

Anxious to return to his lab at Ft. Detrick, Anders pressed, "When you asked for this meeting, you had something particular in mind?"

"I have a proposal." Quickly Paulsen recounted what his contact had told him about the latest discussion topic on the blog. "I think we should do something to promote the issue."

Anders frowned. "Sexual assault in the military? Why would you want to stir up that hornet's nest?"

"Because, it could be the perfect diversion we need. My guy says the post attracted over forty-thousand viewers in a few days. With the upcoming elections it should be easy to alert someone in Washington politics looking for a cause. Especially one that women can rally around. They'd demand hearings that would eclipse that bastard Casey's crusade. Right now I've got the analysts who collect data on military suicides dragging their feet for a few months, but I can only do that so long - especially if our friend Congressman Fremont is wrong and the Republicans don't take over congress next time. This could be a no-brainer."

"I assume your unnamed politician would be a female Democrat."

"So?"

"So, you're not worried she might push to take these sexual assault cases outside the chain of command?"

Paulsen smirked. "She might, but she'd get nowhere fast. There are enough hawks among the Dems who understand that the chain of command is sacrosanct. And we can always count on Senator McCain to make a serious fuss."

That made Anders laugh. He shut off Def Leppard and turned to the general. "Okay then. How about we get Fremont on the phone and see who he thinks might be the best Democratic patsy to make this diversion work."

Mackenzie maneuvered through late afternoon traffic in silence, brooding over the conversation with Sam. She'd left the hospital with a tepid goodbye, annoyed by his apparent willingness to drop the PBU rape investigation. Somehow she'd just assumed Jake's permanent transfer to the VA would resolve ambivalence about doing the right thing. Having made a decision to fight for accountability from the military, she'd experienced a sense of liberation she'd hoped Sam would share. She couldn't help wondering how his intransigence might affect their relationship.

Seated in the passenger seat, eyes shut, Viv was uncharacteristically quiet as well. Noting her rapt expression, Mackenzie decided not to disturb her friend's solitude, assuming she was worried about her grandfather's move to assisted living, distressed by a future without him.

As soon as they arrived at the apartment complex, they went their separate ways, promising to touch base the following day.

Mackenzie decided to use the time left before her night shift to reply to the latest blog post comments, then grab a shower, a snack, and a few hours sleep. At five to eight p.m., she leapt from bed ahead of the bedside alarm, still groggy, but anxiously anticipating her return to nursing.

Forty-five minutes later she was back at the West Palm VA, reporting to the supervisor, a big-bosomed Jamaican whose name tag identified her as Annie Dopkin, RN. Dopkin had a wide grin and a faint Caribbean lilt to her voice. "So glad you could join our team, Ms. Dodd. It looks like the nurse you're replacing has a bad case of gastroenteritis. She may be out for at least a few days. Maybe more. Does that work for you?"

"Absolutely," Mackenzie declared, explaining that she'd been a full-time caretaker until her mother's recent death. "I can be flexible now. I'll take any shift, any time."

Dopkin expressed her sympathy for Mackenzie's loss. "My husband passed last year. I've found the best antidote is work," she said with a sad smile. "I see you already have your photo ID. Let's get you changed into scrubs, then I'll take you up to the ortho floor for a quick orientation."

Since asking Sam what it would take to indict Tim Dalton, Viv had made up her mind to bring him that evidence. That's why she'd been so quiet on the ride back from the hospital, why she'd been sitting in her apartment kitchen for hours, hunched over her laptop, chasing a would-be rapist through cyberspace.

At ten-thirty, fourth floor orthopedics had slipped into the eerie half-life suffused with soft lights and muted voices heralding the start of the eleven to seven shift. Annie Dopkin led Mackenzie down the long corridor, past closed doors that muffled an occasional cough and more than a few moans.

"Most of the amputations treated within our system result from diabetes or peripheral vascular disease," Dopkin explained. "These patients are older vets. They'll sleep through the night. Younger amputees are generally victims of combat related injuries who need a longer continuum of care. As I'm sure you know, initial surgeries are performed at forward hospitals, then they're transported through various echelons of care until they arrive back in the states. Right now we have three vets in their twenties, all with below the knee amputations. Two of the BKs - Bolton and Jones - are bilateral. They were injured in Iraq. Stinson drove trucks in Afghanistan. He's got a trans-humeral amputation as well," she said, pointing matter-of-factly to their names on the rooms they passed.

"All three have had months of reconstructive surgeries and are here for additional rehab and prosthetic fittings. I'd like you to take charge of their care. They'll need their joints moved through full range of motion three times at least during your shift. We don't have physical therapists at night."

"How about meds?" Mackenzie asked.

"They're all on meds for phantom pain and depression."

They reached the nurses station where two seated female nurses were giving report to a male nurse whose name tag read T. Torres. "Teodor, this is Mackenzie Dodd. She's an experienced RN. Did a tour in Iraq."

He stood and shook Mackenzie's hand. "Good to meet you. You can call me T. for short." He pointed to his colleagues. "These ladies do."

"And my friends call me Mac," Mackenzie said, already enjoying the easy camaraderie of the unit.

The taller of the two female nurses waved. "I'm Sherrie with an 'ie' by the way and this is Lili." She indicated her partner, a petite young Asian.

"Ms. Dodd will be filling in for Emily who's out with that stomach flu that's going around," Dopkin said.

"You sure it's not food poisoning from the tamales you brought last night?" Sherrie teased Teodor.

"More likely seafood creole she ate in our cafeteria," he bantered.

Dopkin wrapped an arm around Mackenzie's shoulder. "Sorry we don't have a late night supervisor, but you're in T.'s capable hands. Ten years on the job. He'll orient you to our computer system." She waited for the official shift change, then Sherrie and Lili gathered their purses and accompanied Dopkin down the hall.

Teodor watched until they'd all disappeared into the elevator, before turning to Mackenzie. "Let's hope for a quiet night, Mac."

Viv had begun her cyber search with Tim Dalton's Facebook page, digging around the site, scrolling through comments from his three hundred and twenty three 'friends'. Although there were lots of boasts about hot dates and plenty of double entendres, none of their posts implicated Tim as a rapist. His photos showed him enjoying various extra-curricular activities including a number of shots at popular South Florida beaches, always smiling with a different pretty girl wrapped around his arm and a hoisted can of beer.

Needing to focus, Viv honed in on the images of the PBU football team, most of whom it seemed were in the same fraternity. Once she identified all of them by name, she methodically zoomed in on their individual pages, looking for any red flag. It was tedious work and she was getting tired.

About to give up, she spotted a post from one of the guys: "probably shouldn't be leaving this via a wall to wall; V2 again this weekend?"

The date was August tenth. Was he referring to something planned the same weekend Maura was assaulted?

Tim's response was "Not here dude, discuss on BMOC."

Following a hunch, Viv typed in www.BMOC.com. Her cursor hovered over the URL until the screen revealed a website called 'Big Men on Campus'. Viv had to laugh. Big men on campus. Obviously that was how Tim and his buddies viewed themselves. BMOC's home page featured their PBU frat house along with photos of members in tuxedos and a video of last year's initiates singing the Greek theme song in three part harmony. Viv had to admit, it was not a bad rendition. There was a link to August events listing the party Maura had attended. Viv clicked on the last page titled 'Message Board'. Unfortunately it was for members only and required a login.

Viv thought for a minute. Getting in would require some white hat hacking. She'd been developing these so-called ethical hacking skills from online mentors over the past few years, figuring if her graphic arts career didn't take off, she could always apply for a cyber-security job with some corporation or maybe even the FBI.

Right now she hoped the BMOC site was vulnerable. Typing in 'admin' as the user name, she input a number of different strings for the password. Nothing. She tried a new series with the same negative result. Taking a deep breath, she forged ahead, praying for success with each attempt. As expected, a break-in like this required patience and trial and error, but eventually she found a string that allowed her admin access to the entire website including the private chat room.

Once in, she located the thread that correlated with the August tenth Facebook post. As she scrolled through the long string, Viv could feel her heartbeat accelerate. Because the members assumed this area to be completely private, they hadn't bothered with code names and they didn't couch their comments with subtlety.

Aaron Taube: OK,dude, who U bringing to next week's V2 event? The hot chick I saw U with in the mail room?

Tim Dalton: No, she's a junior. V2's just for frosh, bro. Better chance they're virgins.

Ben O'Malley: Right.

Tim Dalton: Met someone in art class. Definitely a V2 girl. Who's your date?

Ben O'Malley: Found one from econ. Seems like a geek, so we'll see.

Disgusted by what she was reading, Viv jumped ahead to the comments after August twenty-second, the date Maura claimed to have been raped.

Tony Abrogado: Bummer night. Got no ass.

Aaron Taube: Mine was no virgin. What's up with these freshmen? She was all over me before I could spike her drink.

Ben O'Malley: Good news, you scored. Bad news, your date won't make the Varsity Virgin list. How'd U do, Tim?

Viv held her breath as she moved her cursor down to view his reply.

Tim Dalton: Didn't need to spike her drink. She was out after 2 gins & a rum & coke. Virgin!!!

Hal Donaldson: Congrats! Looks like you're leading this year again, dude. Name please for our list.

Tim Dalton: Maura Holmes.

Gotcha! Expelling the air she'd held in, Viv sat back and shook her head. Maura's instincts had been right after all. V2, Varsity Virgins. Tim Dalton was a serial rapist and it looked as though his frat buddies were willing participants in this sick competition.

Copying the entire thread to a flash drive, she logged out of the BMOC site. About to power down her laptop and head for bed, she hesitated, concerned that even with this evidence, the Assistant DA might be unwilling to indict his nephew. Especially now that he was running for Attorney General. Viv had enough street smarts to know that a little leverage never hurt. That's why, in spite of her fatigue, she decided to do more digging - this time into the life of the Assistant DA.

"I think you've got it," Teodor declared as he watched Mackenzie demonstrate her understanding of the VA computer system's menu structure. "I can see you're a fast learner. Why don't you review the medical records of the three vets Dopkin assigned to you while I round on my group?"

He pointed to a cart with eleven medicine cassettes labeled with patients' names. "Each day our pharmacy techs assemble a complete twenty-four hour supply," he explained. "Individual doses are separately pre-packaged and labeled." He removed three of the cassettes for Bolton, Stinson and Jones. "When you check the records for these guys, make sure the meds correspond to their online orders." He smiled at Mackenzie. "Okay, Mac. You're on your own. If you need help, just call."

"Thanks, T."

As Teodor rolled his cart down the hall, Mackenzie typed in the name of Zack Bolton and began to read through his history. The twenty-one year old Air Force mechanic had lost both lower legs in a 2007 ground attack in Baghdad. It was his second deployment. Apparently his recovery had been smooth, but it had taken all this time to get an okay for better fitting prosthetics. Other than the amputations, the doctor's note stated that he was in good health, both mentally and physically. As expected, there was no mention here of meds he'd been given in the field. Mackenzie checked the online orders - Oxycontin for phantom pain, Zolpidem for sleep, Sertraline for depression - against the pills in his medicine cassette.

Satisfied, she typed in the next patient. Army Specialist Garth Stinson, aged twenty-three, truck driver, was finishing his third Afghanistan tour when an RPG hit his vehicle, costing him both lower legs and a good part of his right arm.

The third patient, twenty-year old Marine Private First Class Andy Jones was on his first deployment when his unit was ambushed in downtown Ramadi. His armored HumVee overturned. Pinned down for hours, he'd ultimately lost both lower legs. Like Stinson and Bolton, he was on high doses of the antidepressant.

Mackenzie looked up from the computer, overwhelmed with sadness. The stories of these patients had brought back vivid memories of the dozens of wounded young men she'd seen during her tour in Iraq. Some had never made it back at all, many more had been kept alive by amazing new medical advancements, the legacy of prior wars. Returning with traumatic brain injuries, body burns, multiple missing limbs, PTSD of course, and, thinking of Jake and PJ, maybe worse.

Before starting her rounds, Mackenzie signed and faxed the signature verification form for her own personnel records, then quickly reviewed the physical therapist's assessment of her patients. According to the comments, Jones posed the most challenge, apparently dealing with "significant anger issues." Given that he'd probably take more of her time, Mackenzie decided to start with the other two. She restored the computer screen to the home page, placed the medicine cassettes on one of the carts in the corner and rolled it down the hall.

Congressman Fremont couldn't help chuckling as he replayed Anders' earlier phone call in his mind. The minute the head of PsyOps described Paulsen's proposal, Fremont had recognized its possibilities. Gotta hand it to the general, he thought. It really was a doozy of a plan. Finding a Democrat to take on the military sexual assault issue as a cause celebre would certainly take attention away from SEDO. Selecting a female Representative would just be icing on the cake.

For the past few hours he'd sat in his home office, spinning his Rolodex, reviewing potential candidates. By ten forty-five, he made a decision. He lifted the receiver on his desk phone and dialed the home number of a first-time Florida congresswoman.

Mackenzie spent the next few hours caring for her three patients. Garth Stinson and Zack Bolton were thrilled to have someone take time beyond administering meds and performing passive range of motion exercises just to listen.

"Did anyone tell you you were easy to talk to?" Garth asked as he described his truck driver role in Afghanistan. "My troop ran combat logistical patrols between Forward Operating Base Connolly and Fenty, near the city of Jalalabad, about an hour away. On my fateful trip, we were picking up air conditioners, cups, and building materials. It was just two weeks before I was due for leave and a couple clicks from base when that RPG hit. Lost both legs and half my good arm. The other three guys with me including the platoon leader were killed outright. So I guess I'm one lucky bastard, right?"

Self-proclaimed grease monkey, Zack told her how the AH 64 Apache helicopter he'd just repaired was attacked by Iraqi insurgent mortar fire before it got off the ground. "Want to know the real joke?" he asked while Mackenzie inspected his residual limbs for skin abrasions that might inhibit his scheduled prosthetic fitting. "Those fuckers tracked the exact location using embedded coordinates in photographs our own guys published on the web."

It didn't take Mackenzie long to delve beneath the positive facade of both young men who admitted to flashbacks, sleepless nights, and fractured relationships. No doubt each suffered some level of PTSD and Mackenzie was determined to talk with Dr. Mills about getting them counseling. But she couldn't discern any evidence of ALS or other neurologic issue. Neither could recall what meds they'd taken in the field.

Unlike Garth and Zack, Andy Jones refused to acknowledge Mackenzie when she wheeled her cart into his hospital room. The Tonight Show was blaring on the wall mounted TV. Instead of turning the volume down, he used the remote to click it up a notch.

Recognizing a challenge, Mackenzie walked over to the TV and shut it off.

"Hey, I was watching that," Andy shouted.

Mackenzie stepped closer to the bedside and introduced herself. "Sorry, I'm Nurse Dodd. Filling in for Emily." She slipped on latex gloves. "How are you doing tonight?"

"How do you think?" he spat. "Spent my twentieth birthday outside Ramadi pinned under a three ton HumVee." He pushed the sheet down to expose two below the knee amputations. "I'm doing great."

No matter how hard Mackenzie tried to engage the young Marine, he remained remote, fists clenched in anger. Mackenzie could only imagine his inner pain. If she got the VA mentorship program, she thought Andy Jones would be the perfect candidate to tackle.

"Okey dokey, we're done for now." Completing the final range of motion exercises, she carefully positioned Andy on pillows to minimize contractures and pulled up the sheet. "I'll need to put you through your paces twice more tonight, so I'll be back in a couple hours. Try to get some sleep in the meantime."

Andy's face remained set in a stubborn line. Without a word, he grabbed the remote and clicked the TV back on even louder this time. It was only then that Mackenzie noticed a slight twitching of the muscles in his extended arm. She moved in closer to get a better view, but as quickly as they'd seem to appear, they were gone.

Thirty-three year old Elizabeth Cooper was too young and too new to Washington politics to seriously question the motives for Fremont's late night call. Was she aware of the growing reports of sexual assault in the military? he asked.

The senior member of the opposition was a practiced charmer who easily convinced the junior congresswoman that as a member of the House Armed Services Committee he'd been appalled by the lack of interest in this issue. "Someone needs to be its champion and it should be a woman," he drawled. "I believe you'd be ideal, my dear."

Elizabeth was so flattered by his praise for her recent speech advocating increased VA funding, that she never considered why he wasn't talking to one of the female members of his own party. She *was* a newbie, but she was also ambitious. When Fremont told her about the blog post that was going viral, Elizabeth was intrigued. Upwardly mobile and media savvy, she imagined all the ways she could exploit communication outlets.

Feigning indifference, she affected a cool tone. "Thanks for the heads up, Leyton. Let me take a look at that blog. I'll get back to you in a few days."

"Sounds like a plan," Fremont replied, smiling to himself as he ended the call, certain that the Florida congresswoman was already hooked.

At two a.m., Mackenzie was busy inputting her patient notes into the computer when Teodor entered the nurses' station.

"How'd you do?"

"Two out of three." Mackenzie recounted her difficulties with Andy Jones. "I just couldn't reach him, T."

"Join the club. He's a really hard case." He gave her a sympathetic smile. "All these kids have had a tough break. I don't know how I'd handle losing my limbs."

Mackenzie nodded. She considered telling him about the muscle twitches, but decided she needed to be sure they were really there the next time she examined him. The young Marine had enough troubles without adding a potentially deadly neurological disease.

"Hey, I'm gonna make a cafeteria run while it's quiet on the ortho front. Would you like something?" T. asked.

"No thanks, I'm good."

"Okay, see you in a bit."

As soon as he disappeared down the hall, Mackenzie decided to check the medical records for Senior Airman Thomas Welkers. She typed in the name and began to read. On Wednesday June 23, 2008 Welkers was seen by Al Prieto, PA in the VA's walk-in clinic. Scrolling through the page, Mackenzie did a double-take.

The physician's assistant had recorded 'muscle twitches' and 'trouble sleeping' as the thirty year old's chief complaint. A complete physical did note fasciculation in both arms, but the PA attributed them to insomnia which he felt was related to depression. He'd sent the patient home with Lexapro and a referral to the PTSD clinic. Apparently Welkers never followed-up. Instead, two months later he killed his whole family before shooting himself.

Mackenzie returned to the VA home page and sat back. Sam was right. With these symptoms, it was impossible to rule out the possibility of a neurologic problem. Of course that was with hindsight. Making an early diagnosis of ALS was never easy. No one would blame the PA for missing it if that was in fact what Welkers had.

On impulse, Mackenzie clicked on the VA database for a list of health providers. Locating Al Prieto, she saw that he was a regular on the day shift. She copied his email and cell number, planning to contact him in the next few days. It would be interesting to know if he'd seen any other patients with similar symptoms.

Viv knew she had to be especially cautious as she probed the web for dirt on the Assistant DA. That's why she was using international proxy servers to cover her tracks. Moving from one server in Texas to another in Montana, she hopscotched across the pond to the UK, then on to China, India, Croatia, Mexico, Argentina, and Iceland. Each leap from one server to the next guaranteed that she'd be long gone before anyone could trace her actual location. By three a.m., she'd found nothing she could use, so she logged off to produce a dead end for any cyber spies.

Disappointed, she stared at the blank computer screen. Convinced that no one in the public eye could be that squeaky clean, she decided to call it a night. Whatever she'd missed would be there tomorrow.

Mackenzie finished her shift without making any headway with Private First Class Andy Jones. He tolerated her PT ministration in stubborn silence, while she kept up an awkward monologue.

Teodor reassured her with each return to the nurses' station that she shouldn't expect so much - especially on her first night. "You did great, Mac," he said as they rode the elevator down to the first floor at the end of the eight hours. "See you at eleven?"

Mackenzie produced a tired smile. "I'll be here."

While Teodor entered the men's locker room, Mackenzie took a detour to the walk-in clinic.

"Hi, I'm just getting off an eleven to seven on ortho," she said to the clerk sitting at the front desk. "Do you know if Al Prieto is on today?"

"Al? He's visiting his folks in Miami. He'll be back on Monday. Seven to three."

Mackenzie thanked the clerk, saying she'd catch up with the PA after the weekend, then hurried to the nurses' locker room to change back to street clothes before heading home for a well needed rest.

CHAPTER 18

Friday August 29, 2008

Mackenzie bolted upright in bed at the sound of loud buzzing. Half awake, she grappled for her cordless phone. "Yes?"

"Mac, it's Viv. You told me to call at noon. If you need more time…"

"No, no. I'm up." She'd promised to help Viv move her grandfather from the hospital to a nursing home. "Give me a half hour and I'll meet you at the car."

Rubbing sleep from her eyes, she rose and quickly dressed, stopping in the bathroom to brush her teeth and run a comb through her hair. By twelve-thirty she was waiting in her Civic.

A moment later, Viv appeared with a paper bag and her grandfather's suitcase. "I drove my bike over to the Dunkin's on Atlantic. Thought you could use some caffeine and sugar," she said, placing the suitcase in the trunk before stepping into the passenger seat.

Mackenzie accepted the paper bag and pulled out a powdered donut and a cup of coffee. "Just what the doctor ordered." She took a sip of the hot java. "It'll take a little while to get used to the night shift."

"How was it?"

While she enjoyed her breakfast, Mackenzie described the three young vets in her care including her suspicions about

Andy Jones. "I checked all their inpatient medical records. There was no mention of meds given before deployment."

"If you want more data points for your theory about the drug, why not ask if they'd agree to let you order their personnel records?"

"Excellent idea. I'll do that tonight." Mackenzie finished the donut, placed the half empty coffee in the cup holder and started the engine. "So, how is your grandfather taking the idea of moving?"she asked as she pulled into traffic.

"Once he heard that Delray Manor had daily bingo, he seemed fine with it." Viv sighed. "I'm the one with issues."

Mackenzie glanced at her friend. Outwardly so self-assured, it was unusual for Viv to acknowledge any vulnerability. "You want to talk about it?"

Slowly Viv revealed buried feelings about losing her parents - something she'd never shared before. "I wasn't just their only child. I came late in their lives. They were always on my case. Bugging me about my friends, bugging me about my clothes. They'd tell me I was their special gift. They just wanted to make sure I wasn't doing stupid things. When I got to high school I really started to hate them. I got a tattoo and piercing, dressed like the Goths I saw in magazines. They didn't know how to handle me." Viv paused. "It wasn't until they were killed in the car accident that I realized how lucky I'd been. I'm not sure what I would have done if Gramps hadn't insisted I come live with him. And now I'm about to lose the only family I have left."

Hearing the sorrow in Viv's voice, Mackenzie reached out and placed a gentle hand on Viv's shoulder. As much as anyone, she understood loss. "First of all, you're not losing your grandfather. You can visit him as often as you like." She turned to look at Viv again. "And second, as far as I'm concerned, you're closer to me than my own sister. Okay?"

A smile twitched up the corner of Viv's mouth. "Okay."

By the time Elizabeth Cooper finished reading Silent Survivor's description of her sexual assault and the dozens of posted comments, most of which were equally poignant personal confessions, she realized that Fremont was right. This was an important cause and no one was more qualified than she to be its congressional supporter.

Born in Delray Beach, Cooper had overcome difficult obstacles to accomplish her goals. When her father became disabled after a construction accident and couldn't work, her family ended up living for almost two years in an abandoned warehouse with no electricity or running water. After college she earned a master's degree in social work, a law degree and a PhD in justice studies from Florida State. She became a social worker and then a lawyer to help struggling families like her own. Her involvement in politics grew as she recognized that the solution to their problems - poverty, homelessness, job loss, abuse - required bigger thinking than one family at a time. She became active in political causes before she finally ran for national office two years ago, winning a hard-fought Congressional race in a previously Republican district.

During her first year she'd co-sponsored a bill with another female from Arizona that would have equated Minutemen, a citizens group monitoring illegal immigration at the Mexico border, with domestic terrorists. Though the proposal failed, she never backed down, even as kidnapping and rape threats piled up and the blogosphere buzzed with personal attacks. Lately she was championing increased financial support for veterans wounded in Iraq and Afghanistan. How much more appropriate could it be for someone who once worked as a rape crisis counselor to also focus on the needs of female vets who'd suffered sexual trauma while in uniform?

A no brainer, she thought as she emailed her staff to meet in her office first thing Monday morning.

It was late afternoon before Charles Wallach was settled into his semi-private room at Delray Manor and met his roommate, Joseph "call me Joe" Holland, another eighty year old widower and World War II vet who was thrilled to have the company.

"You'll like it here, Charlie," he said after they'd exchanged life stories like long lost friends. "You know the best part?" he confided with a wink at Viv and Mackenzie,"the low ratio of men to women guarantees you'll get plenty of female attention."

"I'm just here for the bingo," Viv's grandfather replied with an impish grin.

"Perfect." Joe pointed to the hallway where a cavalcade of electric scooters, wheelchairs and walkers were passing by. "They're headed for the four o'clock blackout game."

"What's that?"

"You have to fill every square on your card to win," Joe explained. "Last week they gave away a free dinner at Ruby Tuesday's."

"I love their salad bar. Okay, let's go."

Viv eased her grandfather into a wheel chair.

"I can take it from here," Joe offered, grabbing the chair's handles. "Right, Charlie?"

"Right."

"You sure, Gramps?" Viv asked.

"I'm fine, honey. Stop worrying about me. You go on and get back to your schoolwork."

"All right. I'll see you tomorrow." When Viv leaned in to kiss him goodbye, he murmured something too quietly for Mackenzie to hear.

Standing by the open door, they both watched his wheel-chair join the slow parade down the hall toward the recreation room.

Mackenzie wrapped an arm around her friend's shoulder. "He's going to be fine here," she said as he turned and waved, his smile as broad as a youngster's starting a brand new adventure.

"I know."

"So what did he whisper in your ear?" Mackenzie asked.

Viv sighed. "That it's time I started living *my* life."

On the short drive home, Viv sat in the passenger seat, silently gazing off into the distance as if in a daydream.

Imagining what her friend might be thinking, Mackenzie said, "You'll be fine too."

Viv turned her head in Mackenzie's direction. "Yeah, it's just that I figured I *was* living my life."

"Sure. But you see your grandfather doesn't need you the way he did. It's hard to change priorities when you've been focused on being a caretaker. Believe me, I know." Pulling the Civic into a free space in the Shady Palms parking lot, Mackenzie shut off the engine and looked at Viv. "It's about *your* future now."

Viv leaned over and gave Mackenzie a hug. "Thanks for coming with me today. You make a very good sister."

Mackenzie produced a thin smile, aware that her own sister might not think so.

They both stepped out of the car and walked together to the stairs. Viv started laughing.

"What?"

"I was just thinking about all those ladies at Delray Manor chasing after Gramps," she said between giggles.

"I say good for him."

Viv nodded. "Speaking of social lives, how are things between you and Sam? You seemed a little distant yesterday."

Mackenzie shrugged. "You heard what he said. He's done with his investigation." She let out a sigh. "I guess I expected more. Maura and the others Tim Dalton raped expected more. They deserve justice."

"Sam doesn't want to give up, Mac. He just said he needs more to make a legal case."

"Right. Like a confession from the rapist. That's really going to happen."

Viv tapped her lips with her forefinger as if just now struck by a thought. "What if there was a confession?"

Mackenzie's eyebrows flew up. "Something you want to tell me?"

That night, between patients, Mackenzie sat in the ortho nurses' station musing about Viv's discovery. You had to hand it to that girl, she thought. Impressive the way she'd hacked into the fraternity website chat room. Even more amazing was the fact that Tim Dalton was foolish enough to assume the site was invincible, arrogant enough to make an unqualified confession.

Mackenzie had been ready to call Sam right then, but Viv made a good case for waiting until she could dig a little more into Assistant DA Dalton's life. Though the evidence was clear, Viv reminded her that it had been obtained illegally. "We have to figure a way to help Sam convince the Assistant DA that it's in his best interest to indict his nephew."

"Are you suggesting blackmail?"

Viv explained that she was an ethical hacker. "We prefer to call it leverage."

Except for the sneak peak at her vulnerability during the drive to the nursing home, Viv generally maintained a veneer of assuredness and optimism. This revealed a new side to her personality - street smart and more than a little cynical.

"All's finally quiet on the ortho front," Teodor announced, pushing his medicine cart into the nurses' station and forcing Mackenzie from her reverie. "I might as well go on my cafeteria run before another old geezer pushes the call button." He laughed good-naturedly. "We can't all have the young ones with the healthy bladders."

Mackenzie smiled. "Take your time. I'll cover for you."

"Thanks. Listen, they make a decent turkey chili on Fridays. Can I bring you some?"

Mackenzie checked the wall clock. "Chili at three a.m.?"

Teodor shrugged. "One of the perks of the night shift, Mac."

"Afraid I'll have to pass."

"Suit yourself." Teodor waved and headed down the hall.

As soon as he disappeared into the elevator, Mackenzie pulled out two signed papers she'd hidden under a stack of X-rays. Earlier that evening she'd convinced Stinson and Bolton to let her order their personnel records. She'd told them she needed to verify the meds they'd taken before deploying and they'd agreed without question.

Jones, on the other hand, still refused to speak to her. Now she wondered how to deal with the fact that she'd seen muscle twitching in his arms again tonight. Reminded of Viv's defense of ethical hacking, she made an impulsive decision. Waking her computer from 'sleep' mode, she typed in the URL to access the eVetRecs system, filled in the information for Andy Jones' personnel records, created a gmail account as Viv had instructed, printed out the signature form, and forged his John Hancock. Quickly, before Teodor's return, she faxed all three signed documents to the St. Louis office.

At four a.m., unable to sleep, Viv slipped out of bed, grabbed her laptop and began trolling through the Internet. Frustrated by her initial search which yielded nothing of consequence on the Assistant DA, she'd decided to take Mackenzie's suggestion and focus on Dalton's upcoming campaign for Attorney General.

Opening the personal financial disclosure form first, Viv spent fifteen minutes reviewing the modest salary and short list of assets that included a twenty-five year old bungalow in West Palm Beach and a leased 2008 BMW. Under expenses, there was a recent sixty-thousand dollar home equity loan from Miami Mortgage Company and three thousand dollars a month to RS Consulting.

Next she clicked on the state's campaign finance database for the names of donors. Miami and Palm Beach newspapers had endorsed him the day he announced he was running, applauding his recent successful conviction of a Miami crime boss accused of Medicare fraud and money laundering. Although he'd thrown his hat in the ring less than three months before the election, Dalton had a substantial list of contributors. A few individuals, but most were corporations. Except for Miami Mortgage, Viv didn't recognize any of them.

She jotted them all down just as dawn's light filled her bedroom. Stretching, Viv stood and tiptoed over to the window, admiring the fuchsia and tangerine painted sky. Too tired to continue her search, she resolved to postpone until later.

Before shutting down her computer, she checked the gmail account she'd set up for Jake, surprised to find a message from the National Personnel Records Center, acknowledging receipt of his request, promising to send his records within the next forty-eight hours.

At the same time that Mackenzie headed for bed after her night shift and Viv headed for Delray Manor to visit her grandfather, soldiers were loading the latest batch of Flometoquine onto a cargo jet along with dozens of combat troops, many returning to Iraq for their second, third and even fourth tours.

CHAPTER 19

Sunday August 31, 2008

Viv was breathless when Mackenzie opened the door to her apartment late Sunday afternoon. Pointing to her laptop she blurted, "A giant puzzle, Mac, but I finally figured it out."

Mackenzie yawned as she ushered her inside. "A little slower, please Viv. I just woke up."

"Sorry. Guess I forgot you had another night shift."

"Tonight's the last one for a while. Had a voice mail from the ortho supervisor when I got in this morning. Emily--the nurse who was sick--is back tomorrow." Mackenzie led Viv into the kitchen and poured herself a cup of coffee. "Want something to eat? I bought muffins from Dunkin Donuts on the way home."

"No thanks. Just finished lunch with Gramps. By the way, he already has *two* lady admirers."

The image made Mackenzie smile. "His roommate did say the ratio at Delray Manor favored the guys."

"Just so they keep it friends without benefits," Viv bantered, taking a seat at the table and booting up her computer. "I wouldn't want the excitement to give him another stroke."

Mackenzie placed a muffin on a plate, grabbed her coffee, and sat down beside her. "Tell me all about this puzzle."

Viv opened up the webpage with the names of donors to Dalton's campaign. "I spent the last two days digging through the financials of everyone on this list. A lot of the files were locked behind firewalls that resisted my first attempts to throw a ladder over, but eventually I did it," she declared with pride.

Mackenzie, who had a mouthful of blueberry muffin, held up a hand. "Please, no technical jargon," she begged as she finished chewing.

"Okay, these five names are the key: Miami Mortgage, Delray BMW, RS Consulting, Gina Stork and Stan Townsend."

"I see that each contributed three thousand dollars," Mackenzie said.

"That's the amount allowed by the state for the AG position," Viv explained. "Now look here." She pointed to a thirty-thousand dollar loan made by Dalton himself. "Apparently loans made by candidates to their own campaigns are not subject to limits."

"So what's the problem?" Mackenzie asked.

"This is the problem." Viv opened another document. "I wrote it all down so I wouldn't get confused. Miami Mortgage, which recently made a sixty-thousand dollar home loan to Dalton, is owned by Gina Stork. Delray BMW which just leased Dalton a new beemer is owned by Stan Townsend, Gina's son-in-law. RS Consulting, a subsidiary of Miami Mortgage is run by her daughter-in-law Traci who is married to Ray Stork, CEO of Sunshine State Construction, also a subsidiary of Miami Mortgage."

"I don't see Stork Construction listed as a campaign contributor," Mackenzie said.

Viv nodded. "Exactly. But what if I told you that just this month Assistant District Attorney Dalton dropped his investigation of Sunshine State despite the fact that there was more than enough evidence to bring a case against Stork for taking over four hundred thousand in kickbacks from developers?"

Mackenzie frowned. "So you think Dalton dropped the case in exchange for the donations to his campaign?"

"Yeah. When I uh, nosed around Dalton's bank account, I couldn't find a single lease payment to Delray BMW for his shiny new M5. Same for the supposed monthly three thousand dollars to RS Consulting. And," she added, "there's a website called Zillow where you can check property values. Why would Miami Mortgage give him a sixty-thousand dollar loan when Dalton already has a mortgage for more than he could get from a sale of his house?"

Mackenzie sat back and shook her head. "Wow, you're amazing. How did you even know about this Zill…"

"Zillow. In 2006, my dad lost his job and started selling real estate. That was the year Zillow was launched, the year before…" Viv's voice cracked and her eyes misted.

Mackenzie placed a gentle hand on her friend's arm. She already knew the end of the sentence. In 2007 Viv's parents were killed in a car accident. "You okay?"

"Yeah. It's just that sometimes, something will make me think about my folks and I feel that hurt again. *You* know."

"I do." Mackenzie took a long, deep breath. "Okay, so what's the plan?

"Sam suggests that Dalton might want to reconsider indicting his nephew." Viv contorted her face into a fake smile. "After all, sir, you *are* running on a law and order platform."

"Dalton still gets to run for Attorney General?"

"That's got to be Sam's pitch for now." Viv put a finger to her lip as if a thought has just occurred to her. "But once Tim is convicted, who can say what might get leaked to the press?"

"Yes, who can say?" Mackenzie agreed, thinking that would make a perfect wheel of justice. "When do we alert Sam?"

"I called before I left the nursing home. He's at the VA visiting his brother. I asked him to stay there, that you'd be coming by five, you had something important to tell him."

"You're the hero. Don't you want to come too?"

Viv gave her a conspiratorial wink. "You can take it from here, kid."

Sunday late afternoon traffic was so thin that Mackenzie arrived at the West Palm VA well before five. Now that Dr. Mills had arranged a permanent transfer of Jake's care to the VA system, the security guard was gone. Mackenzie walked right into the hospital room.

Jake was snoring loudly while Sam sat slumped in a chair beside his bed, staring out the window. At the sound of footsteps he turned, blinking a few times as if believing Mackenzie was an apparition, before a smile blossomed. He rose, at the same time pointed to the door, indicating they should talk outside.

"Jake had a bad day. Didn't want to wake him," he said when they'd reached the hallway.

"Of course."

"He told me you've been coming by the past few nights. Means a lot. Thanks."

"I like seeing him." Mackenzie sighed. "It's the least I can do."

"I wasn't sure you'd ever want to see *me* again," Sam said softly. "I know I've let you down with the PBU investigation. But honestly, without more evidence against Tim, there's no chance the DA would indict." He gave her an agonized look. "I'm really sorry."

Mackenzie threw her arms around him. "I'm the one who should apologize." She drew back and grabbed his hand. "Come, I need to show you something."

She led him down the stairs to a fourth floor on-call room. The narrow space was taken up with bunk beds, a desk and two chairs. "No one uses this on Sundays," she said, retrieving her laptop from under the lower bunk and settling into a seat at the desk.

Sam sat down beside her as she took a flash drive from her pocket and plugged it into a USB port on her computer. Within seconds the Sandisk icon appeared. She clicked open the file marked 'TD'. "You need more evidence? Here's your confession." On the screen was a copy of the BMOC chat room conversation between Tim Dalton and his fraternity brothers.

Sam's eyes widened as he read the comments. "Varsity virgins. Jesus. This kid is a real predator."

"So now you've got proof he's guilty of rape."

"Tim and his frat buddies. There's a case here for conspiracy to commit rape. Makes it a much bigger crime." Sam turned to Mackenzie. "How did you find this?"

"Viv gets all the credit. She's what's known as an ethical hacker."

Sam frowned. "Please don't tell me she obtained this by less than legal means. Because if that's the case..."

"Wait." Mackenzie held up a hand. "Viv anticipated your concerns. So before you say another word, let me tell you everything she found. Tim Dalton isn't the only criminal in the family." She clicked on a second file marked 'Asst. DA' and for the next few minutes filled him in on the dirty details of the Assistant DA's campaign finances, explaining how Sam could use the information to force his hand. "Either he indicts his nephew or you report him to state officials and end his hopes of becoming the next Attorney General." Mackenzie imitated Viv's impish smile. "And by the way, if you're worried about letting him get away with his crime, once Tim's found guilty, Viv plans to leak this to the press."

Sam shook his head. "I didn't realize you had such a devious side."

Mackenzie turned serious. "I prefer to think of it as standing up for justice. Viv may be a decade younger, but she's taught me a lot about not being afraid to do the right thing."

Sam slid his chair closer to her and put an arm around her shoulders. "Okay, I'm in. Let's do the right thing."

Mackenzie looked up into his gentle hazel eyes. The invitation was clear as their lips touched. He rose and locked the door, then pulled her to him. As her arms encircled his muscled chest, he pressed her close. It felt so natural, so much like home. So right.

At exactly eight p.m. Florida state representative Elizabeth Cooper dialed Congressman Fremont's private line announcing that she'd agreed to take on the issue of sexual assault in the military. They both knew it was a political dance. She'd waited the appropriate interval since Thursday's call to appear as though she'd struggled with her decision. For his part, Fremont acted sufficiently surprised, but pleased, promising to work hard to garner support from his side of the aisle.

As soon as they hung up, the congresswoman finished her comment on Silent Survivors and pushed 'send' while Fremont alerted Anders that General Paulsen's diversion plan was a go.

Mackenzie woke to the sound of her phone alarm. The windowless on-call room made it impossible to distinguish day from night. Dressed only in her underwear, she leapt out of the lower bunk bed and flipped on the light switch near the door. That's when she saw the note lying on top of her computer.

I set your alarm for eight-thirty so you'd have time to grab dinner before your shift. Off to meet with Dalton.

The other day I said I was pretty sure I was falling for you.
Today I' m sure.
- Sam.

His lingering scent on her skin made Mackenzie tingle at the memory of their passion.

Sam.

Slipping on her clothes, she whispered his name. Past mistrust and disappointment had left her gun-shy. Now she could only marvel at how he'd dispelled that wariness, as if the whole world was newly open to her. No more hiding. No more secrets.

Letting go had given her new strength - to speak up for herself, to demand justice for others, and even to love again.

CHAPTER 20

As soon as Mackenzie finished her shift, she said goodbye to Teodor with promises to keep in touch and hurried down to the outpatient clinic. At seven a.m. a half dozen patients were already in line waiting to check in.

The same clerk who'd manned the desk on Friday recognized Mackenzie, waving her around to the nurses' station. "You're looking for our PA, right?"

"Yes."

"Al's in the coffee room. Better catch him before all hell breaks loose. Monday mornings are our busiest. Spillover from the ER," she explained.

"Thanks." Mackenzie wandered down to a small room off the inner hallway where a middle-aged mustachioed man with a stethoscope wrapped around his neck was filling a paper cup from an old coffee maker. "Al Prieto?"

He turned to Mackenzie and nodded. "Want some? Just made a fresh pot for the crew."

Realizing she was still wearing her scrubs, she shook her head. "Oh I'm not on days," she said introducing herself. "Just finished the night shift on ortho."

"Tough gig," Prieto declared. "All those young guys coming home with lost limbs. I started there before getting assigned to outpatient full time." He took a sip from his cup. "So what can I do for you?"

Mackenzie told him she was looking for information about a Senior Airman Thomas Welkers. "You saw him here in June."

Prieto shrugged. "Don't remember him. I see at least thirty patients a day. Sometimes more. What was his chief complaint?"

"Muscle twitches and trouble sleeping."

"Had he been in Iraq?"

"Three tours."

"Sounds like PTSD. Was that my diagnosis?"

"Yeah. You referred him to the PTSD clinic, but he never went. Two weeks ago he killed his whole family before shooting himself."

Prieto crossed himself. "Oh Dios mio." He narrowed his eyes and took on a defensive attitude. "Are you suggesting I missed something?"

"No. Anything missed would have been missed by most doctors." Without mentioning her theory about Flometoquine, she told him she suspected Welkers' muscle twitches might have been a sign of a neurologic disease. "I've got a good friend whose brother's an Afghanistan vet and has the same fasciculations. He's just been diagnosed with ALS."

"Not a good disease."

"No and not easy to diagnose in the early stages."

A nurse suddenly appeared in the doorway with a stack of charts. "Hey Al. We're getting bombed out here."

Prieto gulped the last of his coffee and threw away the cup. "Coming." He looked at Mackenzie. "Gotta go."

Mackenzie took a a piece of paper from her pocket and handed it to him. "My phone number and email. Would you just let me know if you see any other vets coming in with these same symptoms?"

The nurse at the door was impatiently tapping her foot.

Prieto's cheeks puffed. "Sure," he said, accepting his share of the charts from his colleague. Turning to Mackenzie, he added, "If I have time."

Most of the breakfast crowd had gone by the time Assistant DA Dalton stormed into the Boynton Beach mall deli at ten-thirty, his round face red with rage. Instead of his usual business suit and tie, today he wore a polo and shorts suggesting he'd been pulled off the golf course. "What the fuck are you up to Cantori?" he demanded as he squeezed his pudgy body into the same dark lit back booth where they'd had their clandestine meeting the week before.

He placed his Macbook Pro on the table and shoved it toward Sam. "You call my private line. Give me orders to show up here with my computer. God dammit, this better be worth my time."

Sam, who'd been waiting in the booth, forced himself to maintain an even expression. "Oh I think you'll agree this is definitely worth your time, sir." After booting up the laptop, he reached into his pocket for Viv's flash drive and plugged it into the USB port. Within seconds, he'd opened the BMOC chat room file and spun the screen around for Dalton to see.

The Assistant DA stared at it for a long time before looking up. "Where the hell did you get this?" he asked through gritted teeth.

"What's the difference? It's irrefutable evidence that your nephew is not only a serial rapist, but part of a conspiracy targeting freshman girls who are virgins."

"Evidence that's been obtained illegally? Not a chance it would be admissible in court."

Sam shrugged. "You know these days all kinds of things get leaked on the Internet. Legal or illegal, I suspect the public won't take too kindly to a candidate who looks the other way or even conceals evidence." He affected a phony smile. "On the other hand, imagine how this could play in the media. Our next Attorney General doesn't just claim to be a law and order man. He's so sincere he's willing to personally see that his own nephew goes to jail."

Before Dalton could respond, Sam swung the laptop around and clicked on the file listing donors to his campaign. "Just in case I haven't persuaded you to do the right thing, this should do it." He swiveled the computer back to Dalton. "It took a while to connect the dots, but I'm pretty sure no one's going to believe that sixty thousand dollar loan from Miami Mortgage wasn't a thank you for dropping the case against Sunshine Construction." His eyes fixed on the Assistant DA. "If this gets out."

Dalton studied Sam as if taking his measure. "How do I know this won't get out?"

Sam retrieved his phone from his pocket, found the voicemail he'd kept and pushed 'play'. "*Good job, Cantori. As promised, I've officially transferred your brother from prison to the VA system. I can see you're a team player. You'll go far.*"

"You said it yourself, sir. I'm a team player."

A long silence followed by Dalton's loud exhalation suggested a bitter acceptance of the situation. "You've planned this all out."

"I had a little help, but yes."

The Assistant DA pointed his finger toward Sam and pulled down his thumb like the firing hammer of a revolver, leaving little doubt that if he had a real weapon he'd have used it on Sam right then and there.

Mackenzie reached the hospital lot and was about to step into her car when she noticed Dr. Mills leaning against his parked Volvo, smoking a cigarette. The moment their eyes met he quickly ground the butt into the asphalt with his shoe and assumed an embarrassed expression. "Bad habit," he admitted. "Picked up the last time I toured the Baghdad hospital. Now you know the worst of my vices." He stood up straight. "What are you doing here so early?"

"Working as a temp on ortho. Eleven to seven." She stifled a yawn. "I was just getting used to the shift, but the regular nurse is back tonight. So…"

"Actually I'm glad I ran into you," Mills interrupted. "I have good news. For some reason the bureaucratic wheels turned faster than usual and I just got the okay for that stipend we talked about." He smiled warmly. "Congratulations. You'll be working in the outpatient psych clinic while earning a degree in counseling."

"Wow, that's fantastic. Thank you so much, Dr. Mills. Will you be my mentor?"

He nodded. "Since this is a brand new program, I'll be evaluated on how well you do, so I'll be keeping close tabs on your work. Of course, you'll be assigned your own patients."

Mackenzie told him about the three vets she'd been caring for in ortho. "They could really use psych therapy. Maybe I could take them on."

"Maybe so," he said. "Why don't we talk about it at your regular session on Wednesday? Come a little early to sign the forms for the stipend and you'll officially begin your mentorship. How's that sound?"

"Wonderful."

"See you then." He checked his watch. "Oops. I'm gonna be late for a conference call with Washington." He started to walk briskly away, then turned. "Almost forgot. Mr. Henrick tells me the VA's system for retrieving personnel records has a major glitch. The site is down for repair. Some of the records apparently have been deleted. Hopefully not Sergeant's Linton's, but we won't know until it's back online."

"Do you know when that'll be?"

He shook his head and waved. "Check with Donald when you see him on Wednesday."

Not long after Mackenzie drove away from the hospital, the General received a report that the eVetRecs system was temporarily out of service. He thanked his Florida contact, pleased that the caller had sanitized his message. Nothing about how the job had been accomplished. Especially not the fact that Paulsen had ordered it.

"So here's the deal."

A tense silence filled her office as Elizabeth Cooper explained her intention to sponsor a bill aimed at changing the way the military handled sexual assaults.

None of the three junior staffers said a word, waiting to hear from Warren Hoffman, chief of staff who'd been frowning throughout the presentation. "You're absolutely sure you want to take this on, Liz?" he finally asked. "May I remind you that the first rule in congress is to get elected and the second rule is to get re-elected."

"Meaning?"

"Meaning you just squeaked into this office the first time around. If you sponsor a bill proposing to take on rape in the military, you'll be making this the centerpiece of this year's campaign at a time when the state electorate seems to be moving farther to the right on women's issues."

"Such a cynic for someone barely out of their thirties." Cooper shook her head. "I have more faith in my fellow Floridians, Warren. The country is changing and so are the folks in my district."

"Why not resurrect the bill to get more VA funding? This go-round, the polls are definitely swinging in favor of more support for our vets."

"No reason we can't do both. Let me remind you, women are vets too." Cooper opened the laptop on her desk and typed in the URL for the Silent Survivors blog. "I want you all to read this initial post and the dozens of comments - mostly personal stories from women in every service within the military. I'm certain that when you see what these vets have gone through, you'll understand why the blog is going viral with over a hundred thousand "likes" already on the linked Facebook fan page."

She handed each of the four staffers a xeroxed sheet. "Last night I submitted my own comment which I've printed out here. It apparently hasn't been vetted by whoever administers the site yet, but I'm sure it will be posted shortly."

She pointed to the two women in the group. "Talya and Lili, you're our IT gurus. I want you both to make a list of all the social networking avenues we can exploit once my comment goes live. Brett and Oliver, draft a proposal for targeting any other media outlets."

She turned to her chief of staff. "Warren, I'd like your help in calling for a sub-committee hearing of the House Armed Services in the next few weeks. I'm hoping my post will persuade Silent Survivor to come out of the shadows and join me in a public forum. Her testimony would be amazingly powerful."

Mackenzie was stopped at a traffic light when her cell rang. It was the Delray Beach policewoman who'd responded to her apartment break-in. "Wanted to let you know we've recovered a marble elephant and a porcelain doll from Vietnam that I think may be yours. I'm afraid both were in pieces. I'd like to email a photo for you to identify."

"Oh my." Mackenzie recited her email address. "Where did you find them?"

"One of our detectives has been investigating a string of jewel heists and happened to be staking out a pawn shop on North Federal Highway. Saturday a homeless man wandered in with your stuff."

"You think he robbed my place?"

"No, he's a schizophrenic, no car. Claimed he found them in a nearby Dumpster. The pawn shop owner knows the guy for years. Said if he hadn't felt sorry for him he'd never have taken the figurines. Gave him five dollars to buy a meal.

Most likely the perp who broke into your place was an addict in a hurry and just grabbed whatever looked valuable. Once he realized they weren't worth much, he tossed them. I did question the workmen across the street from your apartment. One thought he saw a white Toyota hanging around a few days before the robbery, but he didn't see the driver and he didn't catch the license number. Bottom line, unless your guy commits more robberies, it's unlikely we'll ever catch him."

That was pretty much what Sam had told her. "I assume no one's tried to pawn a diary?"

"Nope and it wasn't in the Dumpster. Sorry."

The light turned green. "Well thanks for the call, officer."

"One piece of advice, Miss Dodd."

"Yes?"

"Next time, make sure you lock your door."

Mackenzie gave her promise, smiling to herself. Delray Beach cop channeling Vivian Wallach.

At exactly nine a.m. Assistant DA Dalton stood on the steps of the Palm Beach County Courthouse before a crowd of local reporters. Facing them, he was conscious of the cameras and his own concealed fury at having to make this announcement. "Ladies and gentleman. This morning at eight fifteen, four members of PBU's Alpha Beta Tau fraternity have been taken into custody." He read the names off the official arrest sheet. "Ben O'Malley, Hal Donaldson, Aaron Taube and," he cleared his throat, "Timothy Dalton."

He forced himself to ignore the audible gasp from several in the assembled group who must have realized his nephew was included on the list. "Later this morning, the suspects will be arraigned and formally charged with multiple counts of sexual assault and conspiracy to commit rape."

He paused, as much as a calming device as for its dramatic effect. "Of course the names of the victims are being withheld for the time being. The fact that this crime was perpetrated on a college campus in our state, a place where parents send their children, expecting them to be safe, warrants a full investigation. As Assistant DA, I will head up the team myself and if I am elected as Florida's Attorney General I will make it my business to see that cases like this are prosecuted to the fullest extent of the law."

Rising murmurs from the crowd, hands going up, all vying for Dalton's attention. He shook his head and waved them away. "Sorry. No questions right now. My office will release an official statement sometime this afternoon."

Embedded in the cluster of reporters, Sam Cantori had been observing the performance. As Dalton hurried inside the courthouse, a handsome older man Sam recognized as a longtime local TV anchor observed, "Didn't think he had it in him."

"Beg your pardon?"

"Indicting his own nephew? Dalton's the last man I'd expect to do the right thing." He shrugged. "Guess you really never know about people, do you?"

The faintest of smiles flickered across Sam's face. "No, you never do," he agreed.

"This is a big deal, kid. Really really big."

Mackenzie was stunned. She'd arrived at her apartment to find Viv anxiously waiting to share the latest comment on her blog. Now sitting together in the living room with her computer balanced on her lap she read the post out loud:

> *"Dear Silent Survivor: Your story is heartbreaking. As a civilian I cannot possibly hope to understand the individual traumas of all the women soldiers who've been brave enough to share their traumas here or those of the many more who suffer in silence. But as a member of the US Congress, I can help to bring this important issue to the nation's attention. I am planning to call for hearings before the House Armed Services committee. When we set a date, I would like to invite you to come to Washington to testify. Here's my private email. Please don't share online, but write and tell me if you accept my invitation.*
>
> *-Elizabeth Cooper, Representative from 22nd congressional district."*

Mackenzie looked away from the laptop screen and blew out a deep breath.

Viv studied her for a few moments. "Mac?"

"Hmm?" Mackenzie turned back to Viv.

Viv quickly summarized the congresswoman's impressive rise from poor Florida Cracker to social worker, lawyer, PhD in social justice and US Congress, including the fact that she'd once been a rape crisis counselor. "If anyone can get things done, it's Elizabeth Cooper, " Viv declared. "I haven't officially okayed her post yet because I wanted to give you a heads up. Once you respond, I'm guessing all hell will break loose."

"Meaning?"

"You already have over a hundred thousand "likes" on your Facebook Fan page. I wouldn't be surprised if a million or more become fans."

Hearing the stats, Mackenzie's heart beat wildly - not from the fear she'd felt any time she considered revealing her secret in the past. Now it was the excitement of being a catalyst for good. She chewed on her lower lip, realizing her life was about to change course. This really was a big deal.

Viv broke the silence with a plaintive, "Please tell me you're not having second thoughts."

Mackenzie shook her head. "No second thoughts. I told you I was ready to go public and I am. Just give me a day to contact my sister and brother-in-law, let them know what I'm doing. I guess I owe them that. Tomorrow you can officially post the congresswoman's comment with my response."

Viv's features eased into a grin. "Sounds like a plan."

Mackenzie's cell pinged an incoming text. It was from the the Delray Beach policewoman. *Check email 4 photo.*

Mackenzie located the message and shared the picture of the smashed figurines with Viv, explaining how they'd been found. "No diary, though. Whatever the reason it was taken, I don't think we'll get it back."

"Guess it's time we let Christine know," Viv said.

Mackenzie yawned. "Let me grab a few hours sleep and I'll drive us over."

A few minutes past noon, fortified by a three hour catnap, two cups of black coffee and an egg McMuffin, Mackenzie was waiting in her Civic with the motor running when Viv bounded down the stairs and slid into the passenger seat. "Maura just called me. Turn on the radio, Mac. 1290 WJNO."

Mackenzie adjusted the dial to the local news station.

"….in light of the serious charges, Assistant District Attorney Dalton requested no bail be set and that the four PBU seniors including his own nephew be remanded to the county jail until trial. In other news…."

Viv lowered the volume on the radio. "Wow, he really did it, Mac. Sam got Dalton to arrest Tim and the other fraternity brothers who raped those girls. He kept his promise."

"Yes he did," she said. As she pulled into traffic she couldn't help thinking there might still be a price to pay for keeping that promise.

An hour later, Mackenzie sat in Christine Linton's living room apologizing for the theft of PJ's diary. Other than admitting she'd probably left her door unlocked, she was honest about the chances for the diary's recovery. "I feel terrible that you've lost the last record of his military experience. I really am sorry."

Christine appeared to accept the situation with more equanimity than Mackenzie would have expected. "At least I have the sketches," she said, adding "the diary's already done a lot of good."

Mackenzie's brow furrowed with confusion.

"It led me to your blog and the stories of so many others like my PJ. I can't tell you how much comfort I've gotten from the Silent Survivors site."

Mackenzie placed her hand over her heart to indicate how much the widow's words moved her.

"Viv told me you got one of the VA doctors to check what drugs the Army gave PJ." Christine reached over and squeezed

Mackenzie's hand. "I'm hoping the records will show what made him sick, so the world will finally know who's to blame."

Mackenzie's shoulders slumped. "I'm afraid there's a possibility his records are lost."

"What?" The question came from Viv and Christine almost simultaneously.

"This morning I bumped into the medical director of the PTSD clinic. Last week I learned that PJ never had a physical at the West Palm VA, so I asked him to check PJ's records before he mustered. Now Dr. Mills says the computerized system broke down and that some of those records may have been deleted. Apparently the site is offline for repair."

Viv frowned. "That's odd." She rose from her seat and grabbed the laptop she'd brought with her. Settling on the couch between Mackenzie and Christine, she booted up the computer, accessed Christine's wireless network and typed in the URL for the eVetRecs website. "404 error message."

"That's what you used to close down Maura's webpage," Mackenzie observed.

Viv nodded, focusing on the screen. "This site must have just gone down," she muttered to herself, then turned to Mackenzie. "What time did you talk with Dr. Mills?"

"Around seven thirty."

Viv quickly clicked on her mail application, locating the Google account she'd set up for Jake Cantori. "Look, two emails from the National Personnel Records Center." She opened the first one. "This arrived on Friday." She read: 'thanks for your request, records will be sent within forty-eight hours.'"

Mackenzie sat forward in anticipation. "And the second?"

"Dated at seven this morning." Viv lifted her eyes from the screen and looked from Christine to Mackenzie. "It's Jake's records."

Seated in his roomy office on Capital Hill, the west Texas Congressman dialed Doug Anders' private line. "Paulsen was right. Gotta hand it to that old coot," Fremont drawled as a way of greeting. "My staff tells me Cooper's meeting with her team this morning to roll out a major publicity strategy. Already has an acronym. MST: Military Sexual Trauma. I can see it now: bumper stickers, T-shirts, coffee mugs." He chuckled at the image. "She wants to schedule a subcommittee hearing ASAP. With the August recess over and a little help from yours truly, it should get plenty of national press. Put Casey's agenda on the sidelines."

"Great," Anders said. "The General's flying down to Florida this week to meet with the widow," Anders reported. "Though he assures me there hasn't been anything on that blog to implicate the drug."

"What about the girl?"

"No worries, old friend. M's keeping tabs on Mackenzie Dodd."

It was Christine who broke the uncomfortable silence. "Since we can't get PJ's records, can we at least see what drugs Jake took? You said he's got ALS, right?"

Viv nodded, opened the document, then transferred the computer to Mackenzie's lap for review.

After scrolling through for several minutes, Mackenzie looked up. "Jake had all the same vaccines and meds I was given before I left for Iraq except one." She pointed to the screen. "On each of his three deployments he received a script for Flometoquine."

"What's it for?" Christine asked.

"Malaria. Lots of mosquitoes in the Middle East, so the Army wants to prevent the disease."

"Then why didn't you get the same drug?"

Mackenzie shrugged. "I have no idea. As far as I know the nurses in my unit all took Malarone. Both drugs are approved by the CDC, though Flometoquine is farther down on the recommended list."

Viv titled her head. "Have you checked your gmail account today, Mac?"

"Actually I haven't opened mail since Thursday. Too busy working the late shift."

"Take a look now."

"Okay." Mackenzie typed in her gmail address. Just as in the Jake's case, there were two messages from the National Personnel Records Center. The first was the receipt for request, the second her actual personnel records. In no time, she'd opened the document and confirmed that she'd been given Malarone as malaria prophylaxis. Nothing about Flometoquine.

"So Jake got that drug and you didn't," Christine said. "Jake is sick and thank goodness, you're not. Doesn't that tell you something?"

Mackenzie shook her head. "Unfortunately, it's not enough to prove anything," she said, omitting the fact that her mother had taken the drug too. At this point it made no sense to raise Christine's hope without sufficient data. "It will take lots more records of vets with neurological problems who also took Flometoquine to get the Army's attention." Frustrated, she let out a loud exhalation. "We can't really do anything more until the website goes back up."

Viv, who'd been very quiet, perked up. "Dr. Mills wasn't able to complete the request for PJ's records, right?"

"I guess not," Mackenzie said. "Why?"

She turned to Christine. "As PJ's widow, you can request those records yourself." She reached in her backpack and pulled out a folded sheet and pen. "I happen to have an extra copy of the fax form. If you'll sign it, I can send it in when the system is working again."

"Sure," Christine said, leaning over to scribble her name.

"I'll also need PJ's birth date, social security number, service number, and the date he left the service so I can fill out the actual request."

The moment Christine left the room to get that information, Mackenzie leaned over and whispered."If I didn't know you better, I'd think you were up to something."

"Up to something. Just not sure what yet," she whispered back as Christine returned.

Sam was focused on typing notes from a recent DUI when Captain Pete Brompton rapped his meaty knuckles on the desk to get his attention. "My office, Cantori."

Though the chief's tone was soft, Sam understood the urgency of his order. He jumped up and followed the boss into a tiny glassed-in cubby hole that served as his private domain. Slamming the door and closing the Venetian blinds, Brompton slid into the chair behind his desk. Before Sam had a chance to settle into the seat facing him, the chief lashed out."What the hell did you think you were doing?" There was no trace of warmth in his voice. "I imagine you were expecting a pat on the back or maybe even a promotion for your performance."

"Sir?"

"Don't sir me, God dammit. I may have been on the job long enough to get these gray hairs, but I haven't lost my marbles yet. I distinctly recall your telling me last week that that rape case was closed." His face was ruddy with obvious rage.

"Yes, but…"

Brompton waved away Sam's attempt at an explanation. "Apparently you continued investigating on your own. Then this morning I'm blindsided by phones ringing off the damn hook around here. National media demanding a comment, not to mention a very, very angry call from our current AG wondering why I never gave him a heads up about an impending arrest, let alone a press conference from his competition in front of the courthouse steps."

"Sir, I planned on telling you. I never imagined the Assistant DA would make the arrests so soon."

The chief snorted. "Surprisingly enough I haven't heard from Assistant DA Dalton today. Bastard's been a thorn in my side ever since he took that job. Elbowing his way to the top. Now he's running for AG on a law and order platform at the same time he's promised to reduce our police budget by sixty percent."

Brompton sat forward. "Don't get me wrong. I've got two teenage daughters. Far as I'm concerned we should lock up every one of those frat boys and throw away the key. But something stinks in this town," he declared, misquoting Shakespeare. "I know Dalton would never have arrested his own nephew without serious pressure from somewhere. Your partner claims he knows nothing. I don't suppose you want to share your secret?" he asked with a dubious expression.

Sam sat in silence.

"So that's how you want to play it, Cantori?"

"Honestly there's nothing to tell right now," Sam said.

Brompton rubbed a hand over the short hair on his scalp and blew out his frustration. "Okay, but I hope that means you'll let me know when there is."

Sam locked eyes with his boss until he knew they both understood. "Yes, sir. I will."

The six hour difference between Florida and Germany meant it was after ten p.m. in Berlin before Mackenzie returned to her apartment and had time to call her sister.

"Hallo?"

Mackenzie recognized the accent as belonging to a young woman who often babysat for Judith. "Brigitte, hi. This is Mrs. McMaster's sister in America. Is she there?"

"Colonel took her to hospital," Brigitte reported in shaky English.

"When?"

"Just now. Wasser broke."

Judith was in labor. Mackenzie knew her sister couldn't wait to have the twins, so she was glad. She just wished she'd had a chance to prepare her for the fact that a Florida congresswoman was about to make Mackenzie's secret very public - a secret that among other things, had driven a wedge between them. Now she wondered if it could ever be repaired.

"Could you please tell the Colonel to call me as soon as he has news?"

"Ja."

"Danke." Hanging up the phone, Mackenzie experienced a fresh bout of melancholia, as deep as she'd felt the night her mother had died. She wandered into the living room, removed the photo album from the bookshelf and settled down on the loveseat. Flipping past pictures of her parents, her brother Paul, and her sister Judith, she stopped at the last page.

Her eyes puddled as she studied the photomat strip of her and Art on their wedding day. They'd met at a two week Army summer camp, a whirlwind seven days before Art proposed and they'd eloped. Just like that. Tall and handsome and a doctor no less, he'd seemed so perfect that even Judith and Craig had applauded. Maybe she wasn't so irresponsible after all.

Until they'd both shipped off to Iraq and everything changed.

Mackenzie set aside the album and walked into the bathroom where she blotted her tears and washed her face. Staring into the mirror, she saw a young woman transformed. Up until just a few days ago she'd been a coward, someone who'd taken her brother-in-law Craig's words to heart, urging her to keep silent, saying that 'nothing can be gained by opening a can of worms'.

Now her features seemed softer, more relaxed, yet more sure. As she shoved her shoulders back there was a new confidence in her reflection. She'd just confronted one of the most painful secrets of her life. Wasn't it time to acknowledge all of it, so she could really move on?

Mackenzie walked into the spare room, empty now except for a dresser. She pulled open the bottom drawer, removed the stored carton, and carried it into her bedroom. Placing it on the bed, she lifted the top and removed Art's desert dress uniform.

Her heart contracted with pain as she held it close, recalling the night she'd hopped a transport from her unit in Fallujah to the Baghdad hospital where Art had been transferred. Excited to be with a husband she'd hadn't seen in weeks, she planned to surprise him. Some surprise, she thought, picturing the scene as she'd opened the door to his bunk: a beam of light captured him performing oral sex on another soldier.

"Please" was all he said at the time.

Please.

Imploring her not to give away his secret. If the Army discovered that Art was gay, he'd be dishonorably discharged. Don't ask, don't tell. Despite an initial sense of his betrayal and even her own shame, Mackenzie tried to imagine Art's humiliation, the inner turmoil, his fear at the possibility of exposure. She knew how much he loved the military, dedicating himself to saving the lives of so many silent survivors.

Eventually they'd agreed to divorce, citing 'irreconcilable differences' - the lie more expedient than telling the truth.

Mackenzie closed her eyes. *I'm sorry, Art. Sorry that we have both been victims of an intolerant system.*

Upstairs in her apartment, Viv stared at her computer screen, frustrated by the error message blocking entry to the eVetRecs site. On the drive home from Christine's she'd asked Mackenzie to stop at the Delray library where she faxed the signed request for PJ's personnel records. But until the system was back online, there was no way to know when they would be sent.

Unless…

She rested her chin on her elbows, mulling over options.

Did she dare?

Hack into the VA site?

It could be risky.

Viv had no illusions that if she got caught she'd be in major trouble. Though most local and state governments didn't give cyber security the priority it deserved, she expected the Feds to do better.

Determined to be very careful, she sat up and set to work breaking in. Not surprising, she was immediately confronted with a firewall.

Damn.

She took a deep breath before launching a standard protocol, acting like someone who actually belonged in the system, someone with legitimate access who just couldn't remember the password.

Nothing.

Perspiration beaded her forehead as she made another attempt.

Still nothing.

And another.

Come on.

The longer she lurked here, the greater the chance of discovery. Heart pounding, she worked methodically. A few more tentative trials until lo and behold, she had a breakthrough. She was in. She couldn't believe it.

Several more keystrokes and there it was on the screen - the file for Philip Joseph Linton.

The ping on Mackenzie's cell announced an incoming text. She lay Art's uniform on the bed and retrieved the phone from her pocket. It was Viv. The urgency of her message: *Come now!* propelled Mackenzie out the door and up two flights of peeling stairs to 4C.

Standing in the open doorway to her apartment, Viv grinned like a Cheshire cat. "I was surprised how easy it was to hack into the VA's site. Computer security is only as good as the programmer. Lucky for us, whoever firewalled this database was sloppy."

A few minutes later they were both hovered over the computer in Viv's tiny kitchen. "I downloaded PJ's personnel records." Viv pointed to the screen which displayed a list of drugs and vaccines prescribed for his first Iraq deployment.

Mackenzie inhaled sharply. "Flometoquine," She pulled the computer over and scrolled down to PJ's second and then third deployment. In each case, he'd been given the same drug. She sat back and looked at Viv. "You think you could get a few more records?"

Viv reproduced her mischievous smile. "Piece of cake."

Ed Wilton pounced the second Sam emerged from the captain's office. His expression left no doubt he was every bit as peeved as Brompton. "One lousy month, Cantori. Thirty fucking days to a sweet pension," he snarled. "Why the hell couldn't you take my advice and leave well enough alone? Now *I'm* gonna be on Dalton's shit list. Bad enough if I'd been in on his nephew's arrest, but my partner didn't have the decency to keep me in the loop."

"I told the chief you didn't know anything."

"Bet that went over big." Ed's laugh was bitter. "Brompton may hate Dalton's guts, but he's still a team player. He knows the Assistant DA would never have made that arrest unless you had something that could destroy his political career." Ed rolled his eyes. "Whatever ace you've got up your sleeve better trump or you're gonna be the fall guy."

"Look, I…"

"Nope. Don't say a word. The less I know, the better. Captain expects me to keep tabs on you and report back." He shook his head. "Whatever else you might think of me, I'm no snitch."

Sam nodded his appreciation.

"My advice, kid? Watch your back. Trust me, Dalton's not a man you want for an enemy."

"I'll keep that in mind."

As Sam turned to walk away, Ed grabbed his upper arm and held him in place."You do that." He locked eyes for several seconds, then sighed. "Hard to believe any good will come out of this for you."

The sun was fading when Mackenzie returned to her apartment. Viv had gone to visit her grandfather, but she'd given Mackenzie a flash drive with copies of all the requested personnel files. Before sitting down to study them, Mackenzie checked phone messages. There were two. The first was from Maura. Her simple "thank-you" made Mackenzie smile, proud of the part she'd played in bringing about Tim Dalton's arrest. The second was from Al Prieto. The Physician's Assistant didn't say why he was calling, only that Mackenzie should try him in the morning at the clinic; he was going to be busy that evening.

That was it. Nothing from Sam, though Mackenzie wasn't surprised. He'd had a very busy day. And nothing from her sister. She checked her watch, calculating the time in Germany. Two a.m. Too early to call. She'd have to wait a little longer to find out if the twins had been born yet.

Less than an hour later, after a quick change into sweat pants and a rumpled T-shirt and a makeshift dinner of grilled cheese and coffee, Mackenzie settled at the kitchen table and powered up her computer. Before she had any second thoughts, she composed her response to Congresswoman Cooper, emailing the draft to Viv, okaying its online publication in the morning. Hopefully she'd hear from Craig or Judith before it went viral.

Anxious to see what Viv had downloaded, Mackenzie inserted the USB flash drive and waited for the file folder to appear. She already knew PJ had taken Flometoquine. She was hoping to learn if any of the three vets she'd been caring for on the ortho ward had also been given the drug.

Clicking open Zack Bolton's file, she scrolled through his record until she located the vaccines and meds prescribed before he first deployed to Iraq. "Hmm." She frowned, surprised to see that like her, the Air Force docs had prescribed Malarone to prevent malaria. A little more than a year later, before his second tour, he received Malarone again.

It took Mackenzie longer to find the list of meds for Garth Stinson, but when she did, she discovered that he too had been given Malarone before all three of his Afghanistan deployments.

Taking a moment to massage the tightness in her neck muscles, she wondered if she was wasting her time, chasing a ridiculous theory. Maybe she'd be better off focusing on her blog and the opportunity to work with Congresswoman Cooper to make a real difference for fellow vets. If the remaining records didn't pan out, she decided she'd shut down her quest.

Exhaling deeply, she opened the file for Andrew Jones. The Marine Private First Class had been wounded during his first deployment, so his medical information was easy to spot. Mackenzie blinked, unsure her eyes weren't deceiving her. Like PJ, Jones had taken Flometoquine. *Oh my God.* She sat up straighter, leaning forward. She'd seen the twitching of his muscles when she'd made her rounds on the ward. Could it be a sign of ALS? Like PJ?

And maybe like Thomas Welkers? According to Sam, he'd complained of uncontrollable shakes after his third Iraq tour. Al Prieto had examined the Senior Airman in the West Palm VA clinic and described the kind of fasciculations often seen with ALS.

Mackenzie had asked Viv to hack into Welkers' personnel records too, so now she clicked open his file and slowly scrolled through. She shook her head as she read the notes. Before each of his three deployments, he'd been given Flometoquine.

Mackenzie jumped up and ran into her bedroom to retrieve a pen and yellow legal pad from her desk. Returning to the kitchen, she sat down again and began a list:

- Zack Bolton - Air Force - two deployments to Iraq - Malarone - no signs of ALS

- Garth Stinson - Army - three deployments to Afghanistan - Malarone - no signs of ALS

- Andrew Jones - Marine - one deployment to Iraq- Flometoquine - signs of ALS

- PJ Linton - Marine - three deployments to Iraq - Flometoquine - signs of ALS

- Jake Cantori - Army - two tours in Afghanistan - Flometoquine - ALS

- Thomas Welkers - Air Force - three tours to Iraq - Flometoquine - signs of ALS

- Diane Carter - Flometoquine - ALS

She stared at what she'd written, searching for a pattern. It wasn't in the branch of the military. Air Force, Army, Marine didn't seem to matter. Neither did Iraq versus Afghanistan or the number of tours. Still, five of the seven names on the list who either had been diagnosed with ALS or who had signs suggestive of ALS had taken Flometoquine. Was there anything else common to the group? Nothing jumped out at her.

No doubt any epidemiologist worth their salt would point out that even if Jones, Linton and Welkers were actually diagnosed with ALS, their cases could still be isolated. And why assume Flometoquine was the cause? Certainly these soldiers were exposed to lots of potential toxic elements. Mackenzie closed her eyes. But not her mother. She wasn't in Iraq or Afghanistan. But she did take Flometoquine.

Mackenzie wished she could show this list to Dr. Birken to get his view. Unfortunately, according to the woman she'd befriended in HR, the neurologist had just been reassigned to a unit near Ramadi. "With all the brain injuries from this war, there's a real need for more experts in the field. Even residents and fellows like Dr. Birken," she'd explained.

Mackenzie considered talking with Dr. Mills, trying to convince him there was enough here to do more digging. But then she realized she'd have to fess up to how she got the files he'd said weren't available. For now, she'd have to go it alone.

The sound of insistent knocking broke through her reverie. Mackenzie glanced at the wall clock. Eight-thirty. Maybe Viv was stopping by on her way home. She set her computer on sleep mode before hurrying to open the door. "Sam!" Out of uniform, dressed in jeans and a polo, he looked so handsome that Mackenzie self-consciously smoothed her wrinkled T-shirt and raked a hand through her hair. "I wasn't expecting you."

"Sorry I didn't call first, but I was driving past Doc's and remembered." He held out an upside down ice cream cone laying in a large dixie cup. "Swirl with chocolate sprinkles. Right?"

"My favorite." Mackenzie chuckled as she accepted his offering and ushered him inside.

Sam followed her into the kitchen where Mackenzie grabbed two spoons, handing him one. "Help me before it completely melts."

Sharing the dessert over the sink, they giggled like a couple of adolescents, becoming for a moment the ten year old fifth graders they'd once been in Miss Lazerick's class not so long ago.

"That really hit the spot," Mackenzie said, licking her spoon clean. "Thanks."

"The ice cream was just an excuse," Sam admitted. "Truth is, I missed you."

His dimpled smile was soft and gentle, reaching deep into her heart. "I missed you too." As Mackenzie wiped a dollop of vanilla ice cream from his upper lip, Sam grabbed her hand and pulled her to him. Holding her tight, his heart beat against hers with obvious urgency.

Mackenzie experienced the same desire. "Come," she whispered, leading him into her bedroom. Without switching on the light, she grabbed Art's uniform from the bed and quickly draped it over the desk chair. Then she turned to Sam, and helped to remove his polo shirt. The sweet scent of his aftershave filled her as they embraced again. Kissing, groping, laughing, they shed all their clothes and fell onto the mattress.

Later, sated from lovemaking, Mackenzie lay in the curl of Sam's arm, her bare leg casually over his. "I meant what I wrote in that note I left yesterday," Sam said, stroking her hair, caressing her face. "I love you, Mac."

It came to her in that instant, clear, and definite. "And I you," she murmured as his lips met hers again.

273

Before going to bed that night, General Paulsen dialed the number for his relative's latest burn phone and relayed the details of his upcoming flight to Florida.

CHAPTER 21

Tuesday, September 2, 2008

An email junkie, Elizabeth Cooper was up and logged onto her home computer before her morning coffee. Encouraging constituents to keep in touch through social media meant her mailbox was always overflowing. Requests, complaints, suggestions. She valued them all.

Scrolling through the day's messages, one email caught her attention. She clicked it open and began to read:

Dear Congresswoman Cooper:

Thank you for your note. Thank you for understanding my pain and the pain of all those of us who are victims of sexual assault in the military. I realize now I have been silent for too long. We've all been silent for too long. I am willing to go public so that the nation will finally hear our stories, realize this is much more widespread than anyone knew, and demand change. I would be honored to meet with you and testify before the House Armed Services Committee.

-Mackenzie Dodd

Delighted, Cooper picked up her cell and dialed Congressman Fremont's private line. He answered on the first ring.

"Leyton, good news. I've been contacted by the woman who blogged about military sexual assault. She's agreed to testify. My chief of staff is trying to set up a subcommittee hearing ASAP."

"That's wonderful, my dear," Fremont drawled. "But why not let me make a few calls on your behalf? I think I probably have a little more clout than your team."

Cooper had to agree. "Thank you very much."

"Least I can do," he said. "Meantime, who's our star witness?"

"Oh yes, her name is Mackenzie Dodd."

Sam woke before Mackenzie. Propping himself up on his elbows he gazed down at her lovely face. Bathed in the warm sunlight from the bedroom window, he admired her fresh beauty. Without makeup, in repose, her brow was smooth, her body relaxed. No signs of the emotional stress she'd experienced in just these past six weeks - PJ's suicide, her mother's death, the revelation of her own rape. So much had happened to him as well - Welkers' murder/suicide, Jake's ALS diagnosis, Maura's rape, Tim Dalton's arrest. He'd said it before. They were indeed a pair.

Quietly, he rose and tiptoed over to the desk where yesterday he'd hurriedly thrown his polo shirt and jeans. As he was dressing, Mackenzie blinked open her eyes. "Good morning," she whispered in a sleepy voice. "What time is it?"

Sam zipped up his jeans. "Almost seven thirty." He lifted the desert dress uniform draped over the desk chair and held it in front of him. "Can I assume you weren't entertaining some other fellow before I arrived last night?" he teased.

Mackenzie sighed. "It belonged to my ex." There was sorrow in the quietly spoken words.

Sensing she wanted to say more, he asked, "what was your marriage like?"

Mackenzie smiled weakly and looked away, as if considering what to confide. Finally she spoke, her voice clear. "My last secret." She sat up and reached over the side of the bed for her T-shirt. Pulling it down over bare breasts, she found her panties tangled in the sheets, slipped them on, then stood. "Art Dodd was gay."

Anticipating his next question, she added, "Of course, I had no idea when I married him. I told you about my wild years, how I finally saw the light, hunkered down and became a nurse in the Army Reserves. Art and I met at a two week summer boot camp at Ft. Jackson, South Carolina. He was tall and handsome and so kind. I was estranged from my sister. I'd lost my brother. Art seemed to understand me in a way no one else really had until then." Mackenzie moved closer to Sam. "Until I met you."

Sam lay the uniform jacket back on the chair, then reached out and gently touched her cheek.

"We married before we really knew each other." Mackenzie produced a cynical laugh. "You know the irony? Everyone loved Art too. My mother, my sister, Craig. They thought I'd finally become a responsible adult. Until one night in Baghdad." Mackenzie took a deep breath before describing how she walked in on Art and learned his secret. "I felt so betrayed, so angry that I filed for divorce the next day."

"Did you tell anyone the reason?"

Mackenzie shook her head. "I knew it would be the end of his Army career. 'Don't ask, don't tell' is no joke. Art loved the military. As mad as I was at his deception, I couldn't do that to him."

She was silent for a long time, obviously lost in painful memories, then spoke again. "Art helped me when I was raped by my CO. At the time, he was the only person with whom I felt I could share my shame."

Sam pulled her to him, wrapping his arms around her. "Until now," he said. "And I told you there's no reason to feel shame."

Mackenzie looked up at him, nodding.

"How did Art die?"

"I honestly don't know. Enemy fire somewhere outside of Baghdad. I never learned details. I asked Craig when he was here last week, but he didn't want to talk about it. He and Art remained friends long after the divorce. Art kept up with my mother too, though he was killed before her diagnosis."

Sam frowned. "Didn't Art prescribe the malaria drug you found in your mom's medicine cabinet?"

"Flometoquine." Mackenzie stepped back from the embrace. "Yes and I still don't know why, but I just found out that Jake took Flometoquine too."

"You're kidding." Sam drew in a sharp breath. "That helps your theory right? That the drug made them both sick."

"Maybe. Maybe not."

Sam arched an eyebrow.

"I need something from the kitchen." Mackenzie hurried out, returning seconds later with her laptop, Viv's flash drive and her yellow legal pad. She grabbed Art's jacket from the chair and lay it on the bed, then sat down at the desk and powered up her computer. Inserting the flash drive, she clicked open the first document. "This is Jake's personnel record."

Sam leaned over to study the screen. "I thought the VA system was down."

"It is." Without looking up, Mackenzie said matter-of-factly, "Last night Viv hacked into it."

Sam shook his head. "Jesus, one of these days that kid's gonna get herself into a shitload of trouble."

"I told you, Viv's a white hat. She only hacks for good."

"Tell that to the judge."

Mackenzie ignored him, instead handing him the legal pad. "The first six names represent vets whose personnel files Viv was able to download. I added my mom because we already knew she took Flometoquine." She squinted as her forefinger moved down the list. "I've been trying to find some pattern here, but so far I'm stumped."

Sam studied the names. "Okay, let's see. These four vets - Andrew Jones, PJ, Jake, and Welkers all took the drug and they all either have ALS or show signs. Right?"

"Possible signs," Mackenzie corrected. "In PJ's case, I made the assumption based on his diary. With Andy Jones I saw the twitching of his muscles when I was on the ortho ward, but he needs a neurologist to make an actual diagnosis."

"Okay," Sam acknowledged, "but let's assume you're right about both of them. And let's also say, the drug can cause ALS. Why did Zack Bolton and Garth Stinson get Malarone instead of Flometoquine? What's different about them?"

The ringing of Sam's cell interrupted any further speculation. It was his partner. "What's up?"

"Chief wants to see us."

"What about?"

"We'll find out when we get there, partner. Pick you up in fifteen."

Sam rubbed his stubbled chin, figuring he'd need a few extra minutes to drive home, change into his uniform and shave. He winked at Mackenzie. "Make it thirty."

In 1952, the Army purchased Nallin Farm in Frederick, Maryland. Three years later, the two hundred fifty acre historical parcel of land was incorporated into Fort Detrick with the post's expansion. Open to Military Service Members and the Fort Detrick community, the farm's recreational area was complete with three pavilions, horseshoe pits, a stocked trout pond, playground, softball field, and driving range.

As the head of PsyOps with offices on the grounds, Doug Anders spent every other morning jogging several times around the three and a half acre pond. Savoring the alone time, it was an opportunity to enjoy the area's natural beauty while contemplating the future of SEDO.

He had just completed a second loop, passing by the fieldstone banked barn and springhouse thought to have been built around 1800, when his cell buzzed. Annoyed by the interruption, but reluctant to miss an important call, he stopped running and fished his phone from the pocket of his Nike running shorts.

"This better be good, Leyton."

"Far be it from me to disturb your morning jog for anything trivial," Fremont said. "I just spoke with Elizabeth Cooper. It seems that the good congresswoman has identified the woman claiming her CO raped her."

"And…" Anders prompted, anxious to get back to his run.

Fremont cleared his throat. "Her name is Mackenzie Dodd. She was going by the moniker Silent Survivor."

"Jesus H. Christ. Paulsen really missed that one."

"How's that?"

Anders explained that since the General had voiced qualms about continuing SEDO, he'd been monitoring his phone calls.

"Smart, but why didn't you tell me?"

"I knew your solution would be 'early retirement'," Anders replied, using the politician's not so subtle euphemism for getting rid of Paulsen permanently. "And I thought the situation was contained," he said with an exasperated sigh. "A few weeks ago Paulsen's contact in Florida discovered a post on the Silent Survivors blog from the wife of that vet who blew his brains out."

"Sergeant Linton?"

"Right. She'd read her husband's diary. Some things he'd written there made her wonder whether the Army made him sick. Now that you tell me Mackenzie Dodd created Silent Survivors, I understand why she started asking about our drug."

"Why make that leap from some vague blog post?"

"Her ex husband was Dr. Art Dodd."

"You're kidding. The doc who almost blew the whistle?"

"Afraid so. M. just learned that Dodd unwittingly prescribed it for a trip Mackenzie's mother took to India. A few years later, the mom came down with ALS. She just died. M's been keeping tabs on her. From what he told me, the idea of a link was just a stab in the dark and between Paulsen and me, we've closed down any avenues that might lead her to learning more. The General's flying down to Florida tomorrow to make sure the widow's no longer asking questions."

"Good." Fremont clucked his tongue. "Thanks for the update. But don't keep anything else from me. Okay?"

"I won't."

"We should keep M. in the loop."

"Of course," Anders agreed. "Meantime, you do your bit making sure Ms. Dodd's kept busy helping Congresswoman Cooper."

"Already on it," Fremont said, adding, "Let's just hope no one going forward needs to take 'early retirement'." The message unmistakable, the tone inviting no argument.

Clicking off, Anders did an about face and walked slowly back to his car, the politician's call having nullified the joy of his morning jog.

Viv was carrying her laptop when Mackenzie opened the door to her knock. "Morning," she said stepping inside. "Couldn't wait any longer. Got something important to show you."

Slamming the door shut, Mackenzie glanced down at her skimpy attire - no bra, just T-shirt and panties. She produced a crooked grin. "Guess I'd better dress."

That brought a bemused smile from Viv. "Sam's a good guy."

"How did you...?"

"Saw his car when I got home last night. It was there when I looked out the window at seven a.m.." Her expression turned serious. "He's more than an FWB, Mac. I think he's a keeper."

Mackenzie nodded. "I think you may be right." She wrapped an arm around her friend.

"Come. I'll make us coffee and we can talk." She led the way to the kitchen and held a kettle under the tap. "Hope instant's okay," she said, turning on a burner to boil the water. "Be right back."

By the time she returned wearing a fresh polo and jeans, Viv had found the Nescafe and set two mugs of steaming coffee on the table. Mackenzie took a seat beside her as Viv booted up her computer and typed in the web address for Online.com .

Clicking open Silent Survivors, Viv located the blog management area. "Amazing how many more people have been moved by your confession," she said, pointing to fifty-two new comments awaiting administrative approval.

"Unbelievable."

"That's what got me thinking," Viv said. "I know you gave me permission to publish your comment to Congresswoman Cooper on the blog, but maybe it's better to wait to reveal your name publicly until you speak to her."

Mackenzie considered the option. "That makes sense. Especially since I still haven't told my sister and brother-in-law what I'm doing."

Viv let out an exhalation, obviously pleased that Mackenzie agreed. "Early this morning I sent your answer to Cooper's private email. She's already written back." Launching Apple mail, Viv clicked on the message while Mackenzie leaned in to read it out loud:

> *"Dear Mackenzie:*
>
> *It takes great courage to come out of the shadows and reveal your true name. But there is no doubt in my mind that by doing so, you will be helping so many women who just need a leader like yourself to show them the way."*

Mackenzie was struck by the very words that described what Viv had done for her and Maura. She glanced over at her friend who seemed to be anxiously monitoring her response. Nodding, she turned back to read more:

> *"I now have the support of Congressman Fremont who has heard about your blog and agrees that military sexual assault is too important an issue to ignore. He has promised to help expedite a subcommittee meeting. So I'd like to fly down to Florida in the next few days and meet with you. Send me a private email and let me know when you can be available.*
>
> *- Elizabeth Cooper, Representative from 22nd congressional district."*

Mackenzie looked at Viv. "Who is Congressman Fremont?"

"I Googled him. Leyton Fremont is a senior Republican representative from west Texas. He's sat on the House Armed Services Committee for almost two decades. Obviously very powerful when it comes to military appropriations. Lots of pictures of him on the Internet with generals and other Army muckety mucks."

Mackenzie tilted her head and pursed her lips in thought. "Makes you wonder why he'd be willing to shame the military."

"He's up for re-election in November. Probably figures supporting a congressional hearing will get him the female vote."

"Makes sense."

"So when do you want to meet the congresswoman?" Viv asked.

"I guess the sooner the better. I'm meeting Dr. Mills tomorrow morning. He wants me to come early to sign forms for the stipend so I can officially begin my mentorship."

"Then why don't we suggest you meet her Thursday sometime after five p.m.?"

"Sounds like a plan."

Pulling the computer closer, Viv's fingers moved quickly over the keyboard. "Done," she announced after a few minutes. "I'll post your note to the congresswoman and her response on the blog after you two meet on Thursday. With your permission, of course." She gave Mackenzie a long look. "When those posts are published, your identity will be out there, Mac. It's only a matter of time before an army of print and TV journalists shows up."

This brought Mackenzie up short. She considered Viv's words. Since her friend had talked her into creating the Silent Survivors blog, she'd begun a journey without knowing where it would end. Publicly sharing what had happened to her in Fallujah and revealing her name was a final, irreversible step. No longer able to hide behind anonymity. No more secrets.

The sound of Viv clearing her throat broke through Mackenzie's introspection. She blinked Viv back into focus. "Sorry, I was just thinking that without your pushing, I never would have had this opportunity to make a difference." She summoned a smile. "Thank you."

"That's what friends are for, kid," Viv said, smiling back. "By the way, with all that's been going on today I forgot to ask. Did you check out those personnel records?"

"Yes." Mackenzie left the room again, returning with her yellow legal pad. "I'm trying to find a pattern so I made a list of the six vets whose files you downloaded, plus my mom's. The five I've circled all took Flometoquine."

"Do they all have ALS?"

"Jake and my mom for sure. PJ and Welkers had symptoms that could go along with ALS. I'm going to ask Dr. Mills if he'll order a neurology consult for Jones who's being rehabbed in orthopedics. The last few nights I did his PT, I could see that he definitely had muscle twitching. Unfortunately, both PJ and Welkers were cremated, so there's no way to know if they actually had the disease."

Viv studied the list. "And what about Zack Bolton and Garth Stinson?"

"They never got Flometoquine. On each of their tours they were given Malarone."

"And they don't have symptoms of ALS?"

"Not that I could see when I cared for them on the ward and there was nothing noted in their charts. I suppose though, for completeness, they should also be checked out by neurology."

Viv stared at the two names Mackenzie hadn't circled on the yellow pad. Her forehead furrowed. "So why didn't they get the drug?" she asked. "What's different about them?"

"That's what Sam wanted to know after I showed him the list this morning. We hadn't figured it out when he had to leave for work. I ruled out age as a factor since my mom was older."

"And it doesn't seem to matter if they were Air Force, Army or Marines."

"Right," Mackenzie agreed. "Iraq or Afghanistan, one tour versus three doesn't do it either."

Viv shook her head. "Nothing obvious."

Once again, the phone ringing interrupted speculation about the drug. This time it was Maura calling on Viv's cell. Excited. "Breaking news. Turn on your TV. Channel 5."

Doug Anders sat in his home basement office savoring tenor Lucciano Pavoratti's soleful Vesti La Giubba aria. Amazing, he thought. Pagliacci's declaration that 'no matter what, the show must go on', mirrored his own feeling that no matter what, SEDO had to continue.

Earlier he'd finished reviewing his latest research notes. For the past few months he'd worked to tweak the initial molecule, hoping to reduce its unintended side effects. It would take much more time to determine its success, but in the meantime, with the potential of expanded war in the Middle East there was no doubt in his mind that Flometoquine was vital to America's ultimate victory.

That was why after Leyton Fremont's call that morning, he'd updated all the critical players, making sure they each understood their roles going forward. That also meant sending an extra pair of eyes to Florida.

Ed held his radar gun out the window as a Mercedes drove by the police cruiser parked near a West Palm Beach school zone. "Thirty-one, let's go." He activated the flasher and siren and took off after the perpetrator.

"This is ridiculous," Sam said as he watched the Mercedes pull over. "Thirty-one miles in a twenty-mile zone? It's nine-thirty for Pete's sake. The kids are already in class."

Ed shut off the siren and exited the cruiser without a word. Only after he'd written the five hundred dollar ticket, watched the very unhappy motorist drive away, and re-entered the patrol car did he turn to Sam. "This is your doing, bud. By putting you on traffic enforcement the chief is sending a message."

"Yeah, what's that?"

"Reverse career trajectory." Ed chuckled. "Of course, for yours truly with only weeks until retirement, this couldn't be a better gig. Unless some angry driver runs me over, I should be able to collect my pension in one piece."

Sam shook his head.

"I told you not to continue the rape investigation. The minute that Maura girl named Tim Dalton as her assailant - football star and nephew of our very ambitious Assistant DA, I might add - you were heading for a bruising."

"Did you know Tim and more than a few of his team buddies are fifth year seniors?" Sam asked.

"A lot of kids these days take an extra year to graduate. So what?"

"That means they've had five years to play their Varsity Virgins game. Those boys aren't just rapists. They're out and out predators. There's a chat room file that's as good as a confession."

"But it's *not* a confession, is it? And since it's only been seen by the Assistant DA so far, I'm guessing it was obtained illegally." Ed gave Sam a hard stare. "I said it before. I don't know what you have on Dalton, but don't underestimate him."

When Sam didn't respond, Ed continued. "Did you know that late yesterday Dalton recused himself and appointed Victor Novak, one of the youngest and weakest prosecutors in his office to take the case?"

"No, I didn't hear."

"Well, get this, the boys' families hired Elliot Van Buren's firm to defend them."

"Jesus." Van Buren had an even better record than OJ's team for beating cut and dried criminal cases.

"He already got the boys bail," Ed said. "I wouldn't be surprised if Van Buren figures out some way to blame the rapes on the girls." He was quiet for a long time as if considering whether to say more and then let out a long breath. "Believe it or not, I was once as dedicated to 'serve and protect' as you."

Sam tried not to roll his eyes. Instead, he asked, "So what happened?"

"Dalton. He was just a young prosecutor then, but he was already a ball buster. In those days the gangs owned the streets in the West Palm Beach slums. One of the mothers came to me with information about a dealer who was pushing 'H' to young kids like her son. A week later she was murdered. I arrested the guy and I won't lie, I didn't go completely by the book to get his confession. The gang had a high-powered defense lawyer on retainer. He claimed the confession had been coerced and was therefore inadmissible. The judge agreed. Dalton lost the case. Afterwards he took me aside and told me that as long as he had breath, he'd make sure I never moved up to detective." Ed shook his head. "And I never have."

"I didn't know."

Ed shrugged. "Yeah well, I thought this might be a good time to share a life lesson." He restarted the engine and headed back to their hiding place. "We've got to ticket at least twelve more hapless drivers to hit our target goal. If we finish early you get to grab a few hours sleep before you need to leave for the night shift."

Mackenzie grabbed the television remote and switched on the twelve inch portable TV sitting on top of her kitchen counter.

On the screen, an attractive local TV anchor was seated at her desk in front of a photo of the US Capital. "...yesterday it was the report of a number of rapes on one of our local college campuses that sent shock waves throughout the state. This morning Elizabeth Cooper, our representative in Washington from Florida's twenty-second congressional district, put out a press release alleging that a similar problem exists in our military. Congresswoman Cooper is calling for a special investigative subcommittee. Although she hasn't told us when it will take place, she insists it will be in the near future and that one of our local vets will be her star witness. News Channel 5 will keep you updated as we learn more. In the meantime...."

The Capital building behind the anchor morphed to a shot of a state weather map. "Good news for you beach lovers. No rain in sight for the next week in paradise...."

Mackenzie depressed the power button on the remote. She took a deep breath. "Guess that day you talked about may be coming sooner than later." She forced a smile.

Viv reached over and squeezed Mackenzie's hand. "Stop worrying, kid. You're gonna do great." She shut down her computer and stood. "I've got to run. My project for art class is due tomorrow morning and I've hours more work."

Sitting alone at her kitchen table, Mackenzie stared at her cell, wishing she'd heard from her sister. Almost one p.m. in Florida meant it was seven p.m. in Berlin. She'd talked to Brigitte, Judith's nanny at ten p.m. last night. Nineteen hours seemed a long time to be in labor--though certainly not unheard of.

As if thinking about it made it so, the land line began ringing. Mackenzie jumped up and hurried over to the base unit that sat on the kitchen counter. Recognizing an international calling code on the ID, she quickly lifted the the receiver.

"Mackenzie, this is Craig. I'm calling from the hospital. Good news." Although the connection was less than optimal, her brother-in-law sounded genuinely happy and much more relaxed than usual.

"How's Judith?"

"Exhausted, but doing well. The twins were just born. A boy and a girl. They were a little jaundiced, so they've put them in the NICU. The doctors don't seem to be concerned."

"No, it's normal for some newborns." Mackenzie blinked back tears. "Can you send pictures?"

"I can do better than that. I've just been called to an emergency military resource meeting in Boca on Thursday, staying at the Marriott. I'm on the red eye tonight to Washington. Then I'll catch a flight to Ft. Lauderdale. Once I know my schedule we can figure out a time and place to meet and I'll show you photos of the babies then."

Craig's uncharacteristic ebullience alleviated Mackenzie's anxiety about what she'd been afraid to tell him. Without taking a breath she quickly filled him in on how the blog she'd created a few months before inviting troubled vets to share personal stories had gone viral and with the encouragement of readers and the recent rape of a young woman at a local college, she'd decided to publicly reveal the torment she'd been feeling since her own rape in Iraq.

"I didn't expect it, but after I published my story, literally hundreds of female vets wrote about similar experiences. Now a Florida congresswoman, Elizabeth Cooper, wants me to testify about military sexual trauma in front of the House Armed Services Committee."

There was silence on the other end, so Mackenzie pushed on. "A senior Republican from west Texas, Leyton Fremont, is supporting the hearing. I know you and Judith wanted me to keep this all a secret, but I just couldn't do it anymore."

"I understand."

Mackenzie was certain the static on the line had somehow masked his response. "What did you say?"

"Congressman Fremont is a member of the military resource group. If he thinks it's time we dealt with this issue, well then, you have my support too."

"Wow, Craig. I can't tell you how relieved I am. You think Judith will understand or will she still think I'm being irresponsible?"

"Now Mackenzie. We've talked about your relationship with your sister. Give her a few days to recover from the delivery and I'll have her call you. I'm sure she'll tell you herself that you're doing the right thing." Before saying goodbye, Craig gave Mackenzie the cell number he'd be using in the states. "You can leave voice mail there if I don't pick up."

For several moments after the call ended, Mackenzie simply stared at the receiver, delighted, but completely nonplussed by Craig's reaction. For so long he and her sister had insisted she keep silent about her rape. Just a week ago he'd sat in her apartment and discouraged her from talking about it with Dr. Mills. *Nothing can be gained by opening up a can of worms.*

This one eighty had her floored. She replaced the receiver and sat down at the table, mulling over their conversation. No matter how she played it, she could find no reason to believe her brother-in-law was insincere. Maybe she was just over-thinking. Perhaps the birth of the babies - especially if one was a girl - was simply the catalyst Craig needed to finally understand her need to go public.

The buzz of her cell grabbed her attention. When caller ID showed Al Prieto's name, she realized she'd forgotten to return his call.

"I wasn't sure you'd gotten my message," he said when she answered."Thought I'd try you during my break."

"If I was older I'd say I had a Florida moment, but the truth is I did forget," Mackenzie confessed. "What's up?"

"You asked me to let you know if I saw any cases with symptoms like Airman Welkers."

Mackenzie sat up straight. "Have you?"

"No, but I was talking with one of the other nurses. She told me that a Dr...." He laughed. "Now *I'm* having a senior moment. Good thing I wrote it down. Just a sec, it's in my notebook here. Okay, yes, Dr. Birken."

"He was the neurology fellow on the ward last month," Mackenzie said.

"Well, this nurse said that around a week ago Dr. Birken came down to the walk-in clinic asking about vets with neuro symptoms."

"Interesting," Mackenzie said as much to herself as to the physician's assistant. The timing of Birken's request coincided with the meeting she and Sam had had with the neurologist. Maybe he hadn't discounted her hypothesis about the drug after all. Unfortunately with Birken's transfer to Ramadi, a particularly active war zone, the doctor was basically incommunicado. "Thanks so much for calling, Al. I'd really appreciate if you'd keep your eyes open for those cases. I'm starting a mentorship with Dr. Mills in the PTSD clinic and I'd like to focus my study on vets with neuro symptoms."

"Will do."

Hanging up, Mackenzie was disappointed. She felt at a bone-deep level that there was a real connection between Flometoquine and ALS, but without a larger sample there was really no way to prove anything. Hopefully once the eVetRecs system was officially back online, she could convince Dr. Mills to let her do a proper search.

In the meantime, she needed to focus on Silent Survivors. She'd promised Viv she'd respond to the fifty-two new posted comments. After gulping down a very late breakfast of granola and milk, she woke her laptop from 'sleep' mode, located the blog's site and began to type.

More than two hours later, Mackenzie had completed the task. Her back ached from hunching over the computer without a break. Standing up, she stretched outward to relax the tension in her neck and shoulders. Although it was only three-thirty in the afternoon, she was overwhelmed by emotional and physical fatigue.

Deciding a short nap was just what the doctor ordered, she walked into her bedroom. Before lying down she lifted her ex-husband's desert dress uniform from the chair. Held at a distance from her, she imagined the times she'd seen Art wearing it in Iraq, so proud to be a member of the Army Medical Corps, serving the brave young men and women who were risking their lives for their country. She closed her eyes, remembering the wide smile that had attracted her when they'd first met.

Damn you, Art.

No matter how angry she'd been when she'd learned of his homosexuality, she couldn't totally expunge the love she'd once had for him. Sighing at the thought of his dying so young, she decided it was finally time to leave that part of her life behind. No point in keeping the uniform, she'd donate it back to the military.

Taking special care, she began to fold the jacket with the same meditative precision she'd seen the Marines use when they'd folded the flag draping PJ's coffin. She was almost done when she felt something in one of the pockets. Patting it down, she reached around to the inside pocket and pulled out a smooth elliptical object. It wasn't until she turned it over in her hand that she identified it as a USB flash drive.

Why would Art need a flash drive? Not only did he have access to the Army's computer system in the field, but he was required to transcribe all patients' medical histories on the official electronic medical record. Doubtful he'd make copies illegally. Art was always a stickler for military protocol.

Knowing how Viv used her flash drives to keep copies of important documents and lately hacked secrets, Mackenzie couldn't help but wonder what Art's contained. Perhaps it was a diary where, like PJ, he could put down his private thoughts. Mackenzie's heart lurched at the thought of discovering more of his personal secrets. She couldn't handle that right now. Whatever was on the flash drive would have to wait to be revealed.

Placing it and the folded uniform on top of the dresser, she lay down on the bed without getting undressed. Within moments she'd drifted into a deep, though troubled sleep.

The trill of her cell jolted Mackenzie awake. Night had fallen. Flipping on the overhead light, she reached for her phone on the bedstand, at the same time checking the time. Seven forty-five. She'd napped for almost four hours. "Sam?"

"Sorry I didn't call sooner, but the captain has me doing a double shift."

Mackenzie sat up in bed and rubbed the sleep from her eyes. "Double shift. Is that normal?"

"Not really. According to my partner, not only am I on Assistant DA Dalton's shit list - which I accept - but my boss isn't too happy with me."

"Why not? You got four serial rapists arrested."

"Apparently the chief hates Dalton, but bottom line, he's not a risk taker, keeps his head down. Ed's known the guy for decades. Says he'd have no qualms sacrificing me if anything goes wrong with the case."

"Why should anything go wrong?"

Sam filled her in on everything he'd recently learned from his partner.

"You're kidding, right? They got bail? Dalton promised no bail."

"No, actually he said he'd request no bail. The boys' high-powered defense attorney walked all over the new prosecutor's argument. When Dalton recused himself, he set things up so that he can act tough to the press, but claim it's not his fault if there's no conviction."

"I can't believe it. No conviction?"

Sam tried to explain the finer points of the criminal law system including the fact that evidence obtained illegally could be thrown out by the judge. "Viv did a great job finding the discussion on the BMOC fraternity chat site, but there wasn't a warrant for those files and none of the participants agreed to letting her log on. I'd been counting on the fact that Dalton would be trying the case himself. As long as he wanted that AG job more than following the letter of the law, I was sure he'd look the other way and get those files admitted. Now I'm not so sure."

"So you need an *actual* confession from one of the rapists."

"Yeah and with Victor Van Buren defending them, I can't imagine how that would ever happen."

"Hey, Cantori?"

Mackenzie could hear someone in the background calling Sam's name.

"Gotta go, Mac. I'm manning the precinct desk tonight."

Ten minutes after hanging up with Sam, Mackenzie was knocking on Viv's apartment.

"Perfect timing," Viv said, opening the door. "I need an opinion." Ushering Mackenzie into her kitchen, she pointed to an eight by ten sheet of matte paper laying on the kitchen table. "I'm going to scan it and enlarge it to eleven by seventeen tomorrow at school. What do you think?"

On the right half of her composition, in front of a collage of a group of black, white and brown women holding hands,

Viv had placed close ups of the faces of Maura, Josie Hunter and Sarah Nathan, each pulling duct tape off their mouths. SILENT NO MORE was written in red across the tape. On the left half of the piece were the letters R-A-P-E arranged in a large square. The effect was eerily striking.

"Wow, Viv. This is fantastic."

"Thanks. I hope my teacher agrees. Maybe we can use it for posters when the guilty verdict comes in."

Mackenzie shifted uneasily. "You didn't hear?"

"Hear what?"

"It looks like the Assistant DA may be pulling a double cross." Mackenzie repeated everything she'd just learned from Sam.

"Jeez, Mac." Viv's face registered disbelief. "Even I know Van Buren's reputation. If he's defending Tim and his buddies, there's a real chance they'll get off." Clearly upset, Viv began to pace. "You know what?" she lashed out. "Dalton's not going to honor his side of the deal? Then let's just release what we have on him. Ruin his career once and for all."

Mackenzie held up a hand. "Not yet. There's plenty of time before the November elections."

Viv stopped her pacing and regarded Mackenzie with narrowed eyes. "You didn't come here to check out my school project, did you?"

Mackenzie shook her head. "I came to see what you thought about my plan to get an admissible confession."

General Paulsen loosened his tie and unbuttoned his Army jacket as he settled into the first class seat in the third row by the window. The attendant had just announced that the doors were about to be shut, so he assumed no one would be occupying the adjoining seat. Glad to avoid conversation, he closed his eyes, hoping to catch a few hours sleep on the late night flight from Washington to Ft. Lauderdale.

"Pardon me."

The voice was too familiar. Couldn't be, thought Paulsen, opening his eyes. "Leyton?"

"My goodness, General. What a coincidence."

"What are you doing here?"

The politician held the general's stare for a few moments before flashing one of his famous inauthentic smiles. "Same as you. Making sure SEDO is secure."

"It's a real long shot." Viv announced as soon as Mackenzie finished explaining her plan. "And it won't be as easy to execute as that TV episode you remembered. CSI was it?"

Mackenzie shrugged. "Could have been Law and Order. Or maybe NCIS."

"Whatever." Viv frowned. "Everything depends on finding out if someone was taking pictures or video at the Alpha Beta Tau party Maura attended. Ideally a pledge not yet committed to the fraternity. Someone who's not even on the football team. Then of course, we have to hope this person caught what the prosecutor needs."

"And he has to agree to let him have it," Mackenzie added.

Viv made a face. "Like I said, a long shot."

"But you're not saying it's impossible?"

"No way. If the Assistant DA's gonna play dirty, I can too." Viv carefully put aside her graphic arts project before laying her computer on the kitchen table. "I think I'll start by reactivating Maura's webpage."

Mackenzie wasn't so sure that was a good idea. "You really want to get Dalton's attention?"

Viv produced her cat that ate the canary grin. "Actually I want to misdirect his attention." Without further explanation, she sat down, opened the lid of her laptop and started typing. "I need some alone time to figure out the rest of my strategy."

Mackenzie was almost out the door when Viv called out, "Oh by the way, Congresswoman Cooper emailed. She can meet Thursday at six p.m. in her Florida office. It's on Military. Even with heavy traffic you should be able to make it from the West Palm VA with time to spare."

"Guess I should I email her that it's okay."

"Already did." Viv replied without looking up from her computer.

Back in her own apartment, Mackenzie booted up her laptop and Googled the congresswoman to find the exact address of her Florida office. Looked like it wasn't far from the hotel where Craig would be staying. Maybe they could arrange to meet there after her talk with Cooper.

Mackenzie had already reviewed Elizabeth Cooper's impressive credentials and accomplishments both before and since she'd been elected as one of Florida's representatives in Washington. Now she was curious to find out more about the senior Republican representative from west Texas who was apparently backing Cooper's call for the subcommittee hearing.

Typing Leyton Fremont's name in the search engine, she located his website where his official photo and bio were prominently featured on the home page. Born in 1936 in Odessa, the white-haired grandfatherly looking seventy-two year old had served the eleventh district of Texas since 1982. For over twenty of those years, he had been a member of the Armed Services Committee. He was also a permanent member of the Select Committee on Intelligence. Among the issues he listed as important were Defense and National Security, the Second Amendment, Family Values, and Veterans.

Mackenzie clicked on one of the pull-down menus where she read his personal vow to ensure that veterans received the resources needed to obtain the care they'd earned. "We owe them nothing less," he'd written.

Amen.

The man had obviously spent his entire life supporting the military. Mackenzie couldn't help wondering why he'd volunteered to participate in a subcommittee hearing that would no doubt embarrass many of the generals he was glad-handing in the photos on his site. A cynical ploy for the female vote? An honest attempt to do the right thing? Or some reason in between? Whatever his motives, she guessed it was better to have such a high-powered player on board than not. It would be something to discuss with Congresswoman Cooper when they met.

About to log off, Mackenzie reluctantly decided to take a look at Art's flash drive. Tomorrow she would begin her mentorship with Dr. Mills. She'd probably be too busy once she started working with patients in the psych clinic. Retrieving the device from her bedroom, she returned to the kitchen and sat back down at the table.

She held her breath as she carefully inserted the flash drive into the USB port and waited for its icon to appear on the screen. Clicking to open it, she was startled by the message: **Enter Password to Unlock Drive.** Below the empty password box was another labeled **Show Hint.**

Jeez Art, what kind of secrets have you stored here that you need a password?

With no idea what it might be, Mackenzie asked for a clue. The letters T-F-E-P appeared.

What the heck?

Googling TFEP, Mackenzie discovered that the acronym represented at least five different entities: The Foundation for Entrepreneurial Partners, The Free Energy Project, Task Force on Electronic Publication, Task Force for Emergency Preparedness, and Tetrafluorethylene/propylene, a compound in synthetic rubber. After spending almost an hour checking out websites and learning about each, she was no closer to figuring out the password.

Picking up her cell, she speed-dialed Craig's new US cell number. Not surprisingly he didn't answer. It was ten p.m. in Florida, four a.m. in Germany. Depending on when his flight had left Berlin, Craig was probably somewhere in the air with his phone switched off.

Hoping to leave a voice mail, instead of the anticipated 'beep' prompt, the recorded message stated that his mailbox had not been set up. Just as well, she thought, there was time to deal with this when she saw him on Thursday.

Exhausted despite her nap, Mackenzie ejected the flash drive, shut down her computer and headed off to bed.

CHAPTER 22

Wednesday, September 3, 2008

At ten after seven a.m., the sun had been up less than five minutes when Mackenzie stepped out of her apartment.

Viv was just coming down the stairs carrying her graphic arts project in a plastic storage tube.

"I have to be at the VA by eight," Mackenzie said. "What's your excuse?"

"Your fault. I want to scan the poster and print it for my professor before the machine gets busy. But then I need time to work on the plan we discussed last night."

"You really think you can find someone who took photos at the party?"

"I spoke with Maura. She's talking with other freshman and they're putting together a list of possibles. We'll see."

While the two walked in tandem down the rest of the peeling steps to the parking lot, Mackenzie told Viv about the flash drive she'd found and the clue to the password. "My brother-in-law Craig is coming to Florida on Thursday. He and Art were friends. Maybe he can tell me if TFEP is some Army reference I'm just not familiar with."

"Just four letters?" Viv's eyes narrowed in contemplation. "Want me to see if I can figure it out?"

"I hate to put more on your plate."

Viv grinned. "You know me, kid. I love a challenge."

Mackenzie reached into her purse and fished out the flash drive. She handed it to Viv who placed it in her pocket before carefully fastening the plastic tube to the back of her motorcycle. "I'll do an offline password guessing attack using my PRTK toolkit."

Mackenzie stared at her blankly. "Okay, in English."

"Sorry. Password recovery software. Beats guessing," she said as she straddled the bike and slowly revved up the motor. "I'll call if I crack it."

"Thanks," Mackenzie said. "And good luck today."

"You too," Viv replied as she carefully snaked her way around parked cars and out onto the main street.

Family.

Even if Assistant District Attorney Dalton hadn't had a restless night, the six a.m. panic call from his nephew ensured that he woke feeling tired and cranky. The nature of Tim's message didn't help. "The bitch's website's back up! What am I going to do?"

Up to now Dalton thought he'd done a brilliant job threading the political needle - committed law and order candidate arresting his own nephew, then recusing himself to dodge any accusation of favoritism while appointing a weak prosecutor who could never stand up to the tactics of ball-buster defense attorney Elliot Van Buren, the man he'd recommended his brother hire. Van Buren's love of delaying tactics would give Dalton enough time to win the AG election before the trial. By then he'd figure out some way to keep Sam Cantori from disclosing his campaign finance shenanigans.

"What is it?" his wife asked when he hung up with Tim.

"Nothing important," he whispered. "Go back to sleep."

The moment her breathing evened, he slipped out of bed and tiptoed into this home office where he kept his laptop.

Powering up the computer, he typed in the address www Tim Dalton is a rapist dot com.

Goddammit.

Despite the promise to take the website down, there it was again. Only this time Maura Holmes asked PBU grads who'd been raped on campus to share their stories. The original request for current students to come forward was gone.

Dalton laughed to himself. College students. Think they're so clever. Kid probably figured she could always argue that she'd kept her part of the bargain by removing the earlier text. Good thing she wasn't a lawyer, though. This Varsity Virgin game targeted freshmen. Even if some grad came forward alleging rape, there was nothing the law could do to Tim. He was a fifth year senior. Florida's statute of limitations for rape was four years.

Feeling as though he'd dodged another bullet, Dalton called his nephew and advised him to calm down, but keep his pants zipped.

"Just what do you think you're doing sitting at my desk, Ms. Dodd?"

Reacting to the sharp tone, Mackenzie jumped up. "Sorry, Mr. Henrick." She held out a stack of papers. "Dr. Mills asked me to come in early to fill out these forms for my mentorship. I didn't realize you'd mind." Stepping away, she offered the administrative assistant an apologetic smile. Although she didn't know him well at all, Donald Henrick had never shown a flash of temper before.

Without responding, he appropriated his seat, noisily opening and closing drawers, then arranging his pens and papers in precise positions on the desktop. Apparently satisfied that she hadn't permanently disturbed anything, he stood, affecting a more affable expression. "Always like to start the day with everything ship shape."

Anxious to maintain a good relationship with her new co-worker, she nodded. "Of course."

The elevator doors opened and Dr. Mills stepped out, waving. "Ah, my two early birds." He pointed to the completed application in Mackenzie's hands. "Mr. Henrick, can you get these to HR so they can have Accounting issue Ms. Dodd's stipend check ASAP?"

"Yes sir."

Mackenzie handed him her papers. "Thank you."

As soon as the administrative assistant had disappeared down the hall, Mills whispered. "Donald is a little obsessive-compulsive."

"I noticed."

"But he means well." Mills took her arm and led her into his office where he took a seat behind his desk. "Okay, are you ready to officially start your mentorship?"

Sitting across from Mills, Mackenzie took copious notes while the psychiatrist spent the next hour reviewing all the PTSD therapeutic modalities available at the VA: two types of cognitive behavioral therapy - cognitive processing therapy and prolonged exposure therapy - as well as eye movement desensitization and reprocessing.

"Unfortunately we're so understaffed at this facility, we can't offer CPT, PET or EMSR right now. Instead, we focus primarily on group therapy and for some patients, brief psychodynamic therapy," he said, adding, "but you'll need to understand the basis of every modality in order to qualify for your counseling credential."

He handed her a thick manual titled 'Veterans/Military PTSD Fact Sheet' along with a folder of articles from various psychiatric and psychology journals. "Homework."

"Thank you, sir. I can't tell you how much I appreciate this opportunity."

Mills nodded. "I've asked Mr. Henrick to schedule daily meetings so we can discuss the material. I want you to continue to participate in the group therapy sessions. You're already a member, so it might be awkward to take on a leadership role here. That's why I've decided to let you start with one-on-one sessions of your own. With my oversight, of course." Clasping his hands, he touched his fingers to his lips. "The vets you cared for on the orthopedics ward?"

"Yes, Zack Bolton, Garth Stinson and Andrew Jones."

Mills wrote down the names. "Tomorrow you can sleep in. HR wants you to have your required physical at ten o'clock. Meantime, I'll have a talk with the head of ortho to make sure there's no problem on his end. If he gives the okay, you can start those sessions tomorrow afternoon. How does that sound?"

Mackenzie smiled. "Wonderful."

Mills leaned forward. "There's a lot to learn, Ms. Dodd. Psychotherapeutic training is an ongoing process. Even for me," he said with a sigh. "Ultimately, though, the cornerstone of being a good therapist is trust. Otherwise your patients will never reveal the secrets that are at the core of their PTSD." He regarded Mackenzie intently.

The words "trust" and "secrets" triggered a pang of guilt in Mackenzie. This would be the perfect time to tell Mills about the Silent Survivors blog and the public post about her rape. She wanted to be straight with this man who had gone out of his way to arrange her mentorship. She was just afraid the Army might blame the psychiatrist for what she'd done. Tomorrow she'd talk with Craig. As a Jag officer, he always seemed to know how to deal with the brass.

"Any questions, comments?"

Mackenzie shook her head. "No sir."

It was after eleven a.m. before Elizabeth Cooper finally had her opportunity to address the House. She wasn't surprised that even the few colleagues who'd sat through the morning debates were already taking off for lunch meetings with donors. After all, these days a good part of a congressperson's job was raising funds for the next election.

Although the main chamber was almost empty, the gallery was packed with young representatives from feminist activist groups her chief of staff felt would disseminate Cooper's message through social media.

With a nod from the Speaker of the House, the junior congresswoman from Florida stood at her desk and began.

"Madame Speaker, I rise to speak about an abomination and I vow to continue to speak about it until this Congress does something more than give lip service. The military must acknowledge that female soldiers are being raped while serving their country and those that commit such crimes must be brought to justice. The fact that up to now the military has turned a blind eye to the issue is disturbing enough. Even worse, it is not our enemies abroad who are committing these horrific crimes, but American soldiers abusing many of our own. Often the perpetrators get no more than a slap on the wrist and sometimes, though it is hard to believe, they actually are promoted.

We have a military culture that condones and, in some cases, rewards the abusive and violent behavior against female soldiers who are more likely to be raped by fellow soldiers than killed by enemy fire. The longer we fail to address what is clearly a national disgrace, Congress becomes an accomplice to these crimes.

That is why I am calling for an Army Services subcommittee hearing to be convened as soon as possible. I have invited a young woman to be a star witness in the proceeding. She is only one of the thousands of female soldiers who have let fear of retribution and a failure to prosecute keep her from reporting her sexual assault. However, I have no doubt that when you hear her story, you will agree that it is high time we right this terrible wrong."

The gallery burst into loud applause, swiftly gaveled down by the Speaker.

"This is a problem we can fix," Cooper concluded simply. "We only have to want to. Our troops protect us. We have to protect our troops."

General Paulsen exited Christine Linton's home in Deerfield Beach just after five p.m. His driver jumped out of the town car to open the back door. As Paulsen slid inside, Leyton Fremont, who'd been waiting in the backseat, opened his eyes and checked his watch. "Almost an hour. Did the widow give you a hard time?"

"Not at all. Just wanted her to feel the Army was sincerely interested in our vets and their families." His expression was tight. "Thought as a Southerner you'd understand my observing the common courtesies."

"Sometimes General, less is more. Especially when you're peddling bullshit," Fremont replied, letting the obvious dig roll off his back.

Paulsen pressed his lips together and stared out the window. From the day Anders had introduced him to Fremont and convinced the two to join the SEDO project, there had been contention between the passionate military man and the pragmatic politician. Most recently, as the unintended consequence of their operation had become more apparent, Fremont refused to consider shutting it down, declaring 'the unpleasantness' easily handled with cunning and, when necessary, a little muscle.

Knowing Fremont had a ruthless side, Paulsen wondered if that muscle might someday be directed at him. He wasn't stupid. Booking the same flight to Ft. Lauderdale was certainly no coincidence. He had no doubt that Anders had somehow discovered the details of his trip and sent Fremont to bird-dog him.

As if sensing that he might have gone too far, Fremont broke through the silence, affecting a solicitous tone. "Hey, lighten up, old man. You did good with the widow and your diversionary plan with the congresswoman is on target, right?"

Paulsen turned back to Fremont, his face reflecting wariness. "So?"

"So it's time to celebrate. We've got twenty-four hours before we meet with M. Let me treat you to a great meal and a little extra." He leaned in and tapped the driver on the shoulder. "Take us to Rachel's," he ordered, rattling off an address in West Palm Beach.

"What's Rachel's?" Paulsen asked.

"Famous gentleman's club. Best steak in South Florida." He pulled out two diamond-shaped blue pills from his pocket and winked. "And the naked girls ain't too bad either."

That night, stopping only to buy a grilled chicken sandwich and fries at a Wendy's drive-through, Mackenzie arrived home from the VA, dog-tired, but happy.

After her morning orientation, she'd attended the regular group therapy session. Still a member, she couldn't help imagining herself in the role of leader someday. Where once she'd judged Mills to be too laid back, she began to recognize how deftly his easy manner worked to gain the trust of vets inclined to internalize feelings.

Today Marine Lance Corporal Wally Johnson, mustered out after two tours in Afghanistan, sitting quietly for so many weeks, suddenly raised his hand when Mills asked if anyone wished to speak. "I'm tired of drinking too much and fighting and feeling like I'm ready to kill anyone who looks at me the wrong way," he'd said matter-of-factly. "I have a job with a car dealership in Delray, but there are days I just can't cope. You know?"

A few nods and one "fucking right man" from members of the group who obviously could relate.

"What do you do when that happens?" Mills had prompted in a gentle tone.

"I go and sit in one of the models on the lot until I calm down. Eight months ago my wife got too scared to live with me, so she took my two-year-old daughter, moved back to Atlanta with her folks, and filed for divorce." A deep sigh. "But now I have a new girlfriend and I don't want to subject her to my breakdowns. That's why I'm here."

Before the session ended, Mills had helped Wally identify some of the stressors that triggered his feelings of anger and rage, then walked him through a few ways he might deal with these intense emotions. Addressing the group, the psychiatrist had acknowledged that PTSD was a terrible, unfortunate consequence of war. "But as long as you all are willing to come here and share your experiences with each other the way Wally has today, it is treatable."

Mackenzie had been saddened by the thought that PJ might be alive if he'd opened up in group. "Impressive," she said to Mills when everyone had filed out. "I hope I can be as good someday."

Mackenzie had noted a world-weariness about the doctor in his reply, "Frankly, Ms. Dodd, I hope you'll be better."

She'd skipped lunch to stop by Jake's room. Only a few weeks since he'd been admitted, and already his condition had deteriorated significantly. It broke her heart to see him struggling to say her name. She'd been down this road with her mother and knew it was only a matter of time until he'd need to be on a ventilator. She'd sat by his bed until he finally fell asleep, vowing as she left him to continue her search for the possible cause of his condition.

The remainder of the afternoon had been spent studying the VA's PTSD manual and reading some of the articles Mills had provided including one by the psychiatrist himself: a short 1998 research study published in the Journal of Psychiatry entitled "Treatment of Gulf War Vets with PTSD Using Brief Psychodynamic Psychotherapy." In it, Mills described many of the coping techniques he'd shared with the group. "The therapist must learn to pay attention," he wrote. "To listen beyond consciousness or words."

Now, seated at her kitchen table, finishing her fast food, Mackenzie marveled at her good fortune - apprentice to a man who seemed so caring, so devoted to helping traumatized vets.

A loud ping from her cell announced an incoming text. Mackenzie fished the cell phone from her pocket and read Viv's message:

Good news, weird news. Call me.

Mackenzie speed-dialed Viv. "Give me the good news first," she said by way of greeting.

"And hi to you too," Viv quipped. "Rough day?"

"Sorry, actually a very good day. What's up?"

"I'm still on campus. Spent most of the day tracking down leads. Just when I thought we were getting nowhere, a freshman in Maura's English lit class came forward. She didn't attend the party, but her twin brother did. And guess what?"

Mackenzie knew the question didn't require an answer, so she waited.

"He's a pledge."

"On the football team?"

"Nope. Tennis. Singles. So he doesn't have the same team loyalty." Viv chuckled. "Especially not to a bunch of football jocks."

"Tell me he took photos."

"Better. He was testing the video on his new iPhone that night. According to his sister, there's enough recorded to send Tim and his buddies to jail for a very long time. She convinced her brother to do the right thing and turn it over to the cops."

"Fantastic." Mackenzie couldn't believe their luck. "You need to call Sam right away. Let him take it to his chief. Maybe that will get him out of the dog house."

"Already did. He's manning the night desk at the West Palm precinct. I told him I'd deliver it myself."

"Wow. Maura must be thrilled."

"She is about the video. Not so happy about the death threat she got after I reactivated the Tim Dalton is a Rapist website or the Dean of Students pressuring her to drop her complaint."

"Unbelievable. What's she going to do?"

"I suggested she share the death threat and the Dean's meeting with the press."

Mackenzie smiled. Viv was clearly enjoying her spinmeister role. "Is that the weird news?"

"Actually no." Viv's tone suddenly morphed from excited to solemn. "Are you sitting down?"

"I am."

"Christine Linton got a visit from General Paulsen today."

Mackenzie frowned. "The general who came to PJ's funeral?"

"The same."

"What did he want?"

"That's what's weird, Mac. He brought Christine a copy of PJ's personnel records from the field."

"And?" Mackenzie prompted, anxious for the punch line.

"And it says he never took Flometa…whatever."

"Flometoquine," Mackenzie corrected.

"Right."

"That's impossible, Viv. We both saw the record you downloaded from the eVetRecs site."

"I agree. It's a puzzle. Look I don't know what's going on, but I didn't share what we know with Christine. She called to tell me how nice this general was, how he'd made a special trip from Washington just to show how much the Army cares, that he understood the Iraq war had taken its toll on good men like PJ and he was sorry."

Mackenzie pondered this. A five-star general flying down from D.C. to talk to the widow of a lowly private was weird enough, but how could the two records be different? "Boy I'd love to get a copy of what General Paulsen brought," Mackenzie said.

"Want me to ask Christine to fax it to you at the VA tomorrow? She's a teller at Suntrust, so she has access to a machine."

"Great idea. Hold on a sec. Let me get you the number to the fax in the admin office."

Before hanging up, Viv apologized for not having had time to check out Art's flash drive.

Mackenzie laughed. "You *should* be sorry, kid. You didn't accomplish enough today," she said with obvious sarcasm. "Me, I went to work and now I'm exhausted."

Still, as tired as she was, when she finally laid her head down on her pillow, jumbled thoughts of General Paulsen and PJ and unsolved puzzles kept her tossing and turning for most of the night.

CHAPTER 23

At five to six a.m. Mackenzie woke to a phone call from Sam. "Missed you," he said. "Double shifts are a bitch."

"Missed you too." Yawning, Mackenzie sat up and shook off sleep. "I heard about the pledge with the iPhone."

"Ex-pledge since he snitched. Though I bet by the time this is over, Alpha Beta Tau will be banned from campus anyway."

"So is this the admissible evidence you needed?"

"Irrefutable. Even if the judge throws out the hacked chat room files, as long as the kid agreed to turn over his phone, the video's in. Great end run, Mac. Viv told me it was your idea. Pretty clever." His voice was filled with admiration. "Can't wait to see Assistant DA Dalton's face when the chief tells him what we've got."

"Those boys need to go away for a long time," Mackenzie declared. "Did Viv tell you that the university's been pushing Maura to drop her complaint?"

"She also told me about the death threat," Sam said. "I've asked the campus police to post a watch on her dorm."

"You think there's real danger?"

"Doubt it. Probably some frustrated alum pissed about losing a football star, but better safe than sorry," Sam said. "Actually, it's you I'm worried about."

"Me?"

"Don't be surprised if your public condemnation of the Army stirs up a few crazies."

"You're serious?"

"Universities aren't the only institutions that hate to be challenged, Mac. Once you put your name out there, you're going to get all kinds of media attention. You'll just need to be careful."

"I appreciate your concern, but in my case I've got two powerful congresspeople in my corner - not to mention someone pretty high up in the Judge Advocate General's office." She told him about her conversation with her brother-in-law Craig and his sudden support of her going public about rape in the military.

"Okay, I guess that makes me feel better," Sam said. "Listen, I'm off this weekend. How about that swim in the ocean we said we'd take before the summer ended? We're already a week late."

Mackenzie laughed. "It's a date."

Employee Health was backed up with acute complaints, so the one doctor on call didn't get to Mackenzie until eleven thirty. By the time he'd completed her physical, drew her blood, and applied a TB skin test, it was close to one p.m.

Anxious to get PJ's personnel record from Christine before Mr. Henrick finished his lunch hour, Mackenzie raced to the administrative assistant's office and checked the fax machine.

Nothing.

Damn.

"Looking for this?"

"What?" Breathless from her run up five flights of stairs, Mackenzie pivoted, nearly crashing into Henrick who'd silently snuck into the room behind her.

He stepped back and held up two pages. "This came for you at noon." His mouth was turned down at the corners in something approaching a scowl.

Jeez, Mackenzie thought. The second day on the job and she'd already done something new to offend this man. "I'm sorry if… I mean…"

As quickly as he'd registered displeasure, Henrick was smiling. "Not a problem, Ms. Dodd," he said handing her the fax. "Just let me know next time you're expecting something. Especially if it's marked confidential like this one. That way if I'm not here, I'll make sure the door's locked."

His light gray eyes swimming behind thick glasses locked with hers. Unreadable. She turned away. "I will."

"Hey." Dr. Mills stepped into the office."Glad I caught you two. Mr. Henrick, I've been called to a budget meeting and may not be back today. Can you reschedule my afternoon patients?"

"Yes sir."

"And Ms. Dodd. I'm afraid we'll have to skip our session. But I did get the okay for you to begin counseling those vets on ortho." He pulled a folded piece of paper from the pocket of his white coat. "Bolton and Stinson."

"What about Andrew Jones?"

Mills shrugged. "Seems he was transferred to another facility early this morning."

A little after two thirty, Mackenzie sat in a quiet corner of the hospital cafeteria, eating her first real meal of the day - a tuna salad on whole wheat and a cup of coffee. Having just finished Zack Boltan's therapy session and with a half hour before her next with Garth Stinson, she finally had a moment to consider what had happened in the administrative assistant's office. First, the unfortunate run-in with Henrick, then blindsided by Mills' announcement that Andy Jones was transferred. Both had left her feeling off-kilter.

Pulling out the two folded fax copies from her pocket, she pushed her food tray to the side, discarded the cover page, and smoothed out the second sheet. Just as Viv had said, the document purported to be the personnel record for Philip Joseph Linton. Mackenzie hadn't printed out the one Viv downloaded the other day, but she was sure that when she compared the two, they would be identical except for the fact that according to this, PJ had never taken Flometoquine - not before any of his three Iraq tours. Instead, this document claimed he'd been given Malarone each time, the same as Mackenzie, Boltan and Stinson. What the hell was going on? She'd love to ask Dr. Mills, but that would mean exposing Viv's hack into the VA system and she couldn't betray her friend. Closing her eyes, she was lost in thought when she felt a tap on her shoulder.

"Mind if I join you?"

At the sound of the familiar Jamaican lilt, Mackenzie blinked. It was Annie Dopkin, orthopedics nursing supervisor. "Of course, sit." She pulled out the chair beside her. "How are you?"

"Great. Thought I'd grab a little fuel before my three to eleven shift." The buxom nurse indicated the unhealthy food choices on her tray with an embarrassed laugh. "I know, I know, 'do as I say, not as I do'."

Mackenzie pocketed the fax and made room on the table for Dopkin's fried chicken, corn muffin, mashed potatoes, and key lime pie. "Actually it looks pretty good."

"So I hear you're training to become a mental health counselor," Dopkin said once she was settled. "Congratulations."

"Thanks. I just spent an hour with Zack Bolton. It seemed to go well. I'm seeing Garth Stinson at three." Mackenzie sighed. "I was hoping to work with Andy Jones too, but just found out he was transferred."

Dopkin nodded as she split off a piece of muffin and spread a dab of butter on it. "Tough case. Lots of anger issues. None of our staff could handle him."

"Where'd he go?"

"Tampa. It's one of seven regional amputation centers. They provide comprehensive holistic rehab care there with the full gamut of therapists including psych."

"I guess he is better off with qualified therapists."

Dopkin regarded her with a critical eye. "Now see here, young lady. You may not have your credential yet, but T. told me you made the most headway of anyone. And that was with no experience. I'd say you're a natural."

Hearing the same words Sam had used brought a smile to Mackenzie's lips. "Appreciate your confidence."

"You're welcome."

While they finished lunch they shared small talk and hospital gossip.

At five to three, Dopkin wiped a few crumbs of pie crust from her ample bosom. "Duty calls." She stood and grabbed her cafeteria tray to bus. Mackenzie did the same.

A moment later, the two were stepping into the hospital elevator. "Annie, do you know who ordered Andy's transfer?" Mackenzie asked.

"Why yes," Dopkin replied, pressing the button for the fifth floor. "My clerk said the call came late last night from Washington."

From his top floor airport hotel room, Anders looked out at the Ft. Lauderdale skyline, cursing the fact that his instincts had been validated. He'd flown in early that morning as a last minute contingency plan, hoping he was being needlessly cautious. But then that's how he'd made it to the top of PsyOps - taking only measured risks, keeping his friends close and his enemies closer.

Paulsen had insisted his plan would divert the girl's interest in the drug while he eliminated any clues that could expose SEDO. Yesterday Fremont had called with a reassuring report. The widow had accepted the altered medical record; he was taking the general out for a celebratory evening at some local strip joint.

But that was yesterday. The message Anders had just intercepted confirmed his worst fears. He had a problem he could no longer ignore. Now he had to decide whether it was time to close the book on Mackenzie Dodd.

Mackenzie's hour with Garth Stinson went even better than her session with Zack Bolton. Garth was delighted to hear that Mackenzie would be his therapist.

"Full disclosure, I'm a therapist in training."

"Hmm. T-I-T. I'm all for that, Ms. Dodd," he'd joked.

"At ease, young man."

The fact that they'd already established an open relationship from the few nights Mackenzie had worked with him, made it easy to apply the probing techniques described in Mills' journal article. Together they'd established goals the twenty-three year old hoped to achieve, rating learning to communicate better with his family the one that might take the longest.

Mackenzie could certainly relate to that, wondering if she'd ever repair the rift between herself and her sister.

On her way out the door, she turned back around. "Hey, did you happen to talk with Andy Jones when he was here?"

Garth made a face. "The Marine? Yeah. That kid has a real stick up his butt, you know. We were both waiting for X-rays the other day and I tried to strike up a conversation. I mean seeing as we've got missing limbs in common. But he just made some crack about my not being a *real* soldier cause I was a truck driver in Afghanistan. Not a grunt like him." Garth made a fist with his one remaining hand. "Three fucking tours and he's got the nerve to dis me."

"He's angry at the world right now," Mackenzie said. "Lashing out at you like that. It's really not personal. He needs help. They've transferred him to Tampa."

"Well fuck him." Garth produced a thin smile. "And good riddance."

On the way back to the psych clinic, Mackenzie replayed her interview with the Army Specialist. She couldn't shake the feeling she'd overlooked the significance of something said about Jones' comment.

Not a grunt like him.

Mackenzie understood that Jones had used 'grunt', the military slang for 'infantry' to insult Garth.

I'm a grunt; you're not.

Could that be it?

She made a quick detour to the nurses' dressing room where she'd stored her purse, opened her locker and retrieved the list she'd made at home on her legal pad. Sitting down on the wooden bench, she stared at the names:

- Zack Bolton - Air Force - two deployments to Iraq - Malarone - no signs of ALS

- Garth Stinson - Army-three deployments to Afghani-stan -Malarone - no signs of ALS

- Andrew Jones - Marine - one deployment to Iraq - Flometoquine - signs of ALS

- PJ Linton - Marine - three deployments to Iraq - Flometoquine - signs of ALS

- Jake Cantori - Army - two tours in Afghanistan - Flometoquine - ALS

- Thomas Welkers - Air Force - three tours to Iraq - Flometoquine - signs of ALS

- Diane Carter - Flometoquine - ALS

Neither Zack nor Garth had signs of ALS.

Both Zack and Garth were given Malarone before their deployments, not Flometoquine.

Sam and Viv had asked her the same question. *What was different about them?*

Her mind raced as she considered what suddenly seemed obvious: Zack was an Air Force mechanic, Garth drove trucks for the Army.

Not a grunt.

Both may have been silent survivors, but Jones was right. Technically they weren't combatants. Truck drivers, mechanics, nurses were all support personnel. And they all got Malarone, not Flometoquine.

Excited, Mackenzie wanted to share her revelation. She fished her cell from her pocket just as it pinged with a text from Viv.

Great minds, she thought, glancing down at her phone to read the message:

Cracked flash pw
2 UR VA mail
Open STAT
then call me

Wow. Viv had figured out the password for Art's flash drive. Why the urgency? Knowing she was at work, Viv wouldn't insist Mackenzie drop everything unless it was important. But why not send it to her gmail account? That way she could have checked it on her phone. Now she'd need to locate a VA computer.

Mackenzie considered returning to ortho where she might find a free terminal in the nurses' station, but it wouldn't be private. Armed with a plan, she stood, slammed her locker shut, and hurried to the outpatient psych clinic. As she reached the administrative assistant's office, she pressed herself against the wall and peeked into his half-open door. Thankfully Henrick was occupied on the phone, his back to her.

Hurrying past, Mackenzie tried the knob to Dr. Mill's office. Unlocked. Nervously scanning the hallway, she slipped inside, quietly closed the door, and settled behind the psychiatrist's desk. It took a few minutes to log onto the VA hospital system and locate her in-house email, but when she saw what Viv had sent, her whole body tightened. It wasn't the word 'VIDEO' in the subject line that made her heart race. It was the message under the Quicktime icon:

Mac - open if I am dead.

Mackenzie held her breath as she clicked open the four minute video and pushed 'play'. Instantly Art appeared on the screen. His handsome face looked haggard, his kind eyes, deep circles, beyond fatigue. Seated behind a desk that she guessed was located in his Baghdad quarters, he cleared his throat. "Hi, it's Saturday, February 3, 2007. If you're watching this, I guess I failed as a whistleblower."

Mackenzie gasped. Art had died the following day.

"I always wanted to be a good doc," he was saying. "And I do love you, Mac. Just not the way you wanted, not the way you deserved. I'm so sorry."

Mackenzie pushed 'pause' to grab a Kleenex from the box on Mills' desk. She wiped the tears blurring her vision, before restarting the video.

"Okay. Here's what I need to tell you. I don't have much time. Understand I had no idea what was happening. I'd never do anything to harm our troops. Now I'm worried I may have harmed your mom as well."

Beads of sweat dotted Art's brow as he took a deep breath, then continued. "I just learned that the Army's been giving our combat troops a drug to make them more aggressive. It's a secret PsyOps operation called SEDO. Turns out some of the men have experienced serious side effects including permanent nerve damage."

Art jumped up and disappeared from the screen. It was close to a minute of silence before he reappeared. "Sorry, thought I heard someone in the hall," he whispered. "I've been warned that my life's in danger if I reveal what I know. So, in case the threat is real, take this video to someone you trust, Mac."

He twisted his neck to check behind him, then quickly turned back toward the screen. "Not M. Gotta go." His forefinger reached toward his keyboard and the screen faded to black.

Stunned, Mackenzie swiveled the desk chair to stare out the window. Outside, the sky had turned an angry slate gray, a preamble to rain. *So much for the weatherman's prediction of sunny weather in paradise.* The incongruous thought popping in her mind as she tried to process the significance of what she'd just heard from Art.

Bad enough the Army would use a drug on its own troops to make them more warlike, but knowing it might cause fatal side effects, that was too horrible to believe. Art hadn't named the drug, but she could guess.

I'm worried I may have harmed your mom as well.

His words.

It had to be the Flometoquine that he'd prescribed.

She'd been right when she'd figured that only combat troops got the drug. She just hadn't understood why.

Take this video to someone you trust…Not M.

Turning her chair back around, Mackenzie glanced down at the name plate on the psychiatrist's desk: Michael M. Mills, MD.

Reminded her of Theodor T. Torres. *You can call me T. Not M.*

A terrible suspicion burrowed into Mackenzie's heart. Could Mills be M.? Was it even possible that Art knew him?

Mills' 1998 published study on PTSD had been conducted at the Washington VA when Art was there as a resident. They might have also crossed paths in Iraq. Didn't Mills say he'd picked up his smoking habit touring the Bagdad hospital?

Mackenzie closed her eyes, trying to imagine the psychiatrist's duplicity, her mind a riot of conflicting thoughts. Up until PJ's suicide a few weeks ago, Mills had shown little interest in her. Then suddenly he was questioning how well she knew the Marine outside of the clinic, advising her to stay clear of the press, suggesting one-on-one therapy sessions. Mills made her believe he cared deeply about young men like PJ, calling him a "troubled soul", commiserating over "so many people coming back damaged from this war". What if he already knew why they were so troubled?

Except for Sam, Viv and Dr. Birken, Mills was the only other person with whom Mackenzie had shared her concerns about Flometoquine. Each opportunity to pursue her theory had somehow been thwarted. The list was long: Dr. Birken transferred to Iraq, Andy Jones to Tampa, cancellation of PJ's personnel records, theft of his diary, an eVetRecs system strangely out of service, then a doctored version of the records turning up. Perhaps what had first appeared as a series of coincidences were anything but.

Maybe the speed with which Mills had arranged her mentorship was only camouflage, a scheme to keep her close, to prevent exposing this secret operation. No doubt heads would roll if it did become public. *I'll do anything to prevent Washington from shutting down the VA*, he'd said.

Anything?

Including killing Art?

Distraught by that horrible possibility, she reached for her cell to call Viv. Seeing that the battery was very low, she pressed 'off' to save it, then picked up the desk phone and dialed the number she knew by heart.

"What the...?" Donald Henrick frowned when he saw the red light on the office extension turn to green. With Dr. Mills' gone for the afternoon, no one should be using his phone. Curious, he quietly lifted the receiver, surprised to hear Mackenzie Dodd's voice on the other end.

"Unbelievable." Viv produced a loud whistle once Mackenzie had filled her in on Art's message. "You know the password turned out to be SEDO."

"The name of the Army's secret operation. How'd you crack it?"

"His clue. TFEP wasn't anything fancy after all. Just a simple skip code. Instead of forward, Art went backwards. 'S' became 'T', 'E' became 'F' and so on. Pretty clever. Sometimes you have to think like an amateur."

"Maybe so, but I needed a geek to figure it out," Mackenzie said. "Thanks."

"I didn't watch the video, but I knew it had to be serious."

"Viv, I think Dr. Mills is M."

"You're kidding."

Mackenzie enumerated her list of reasons for suspecting her mentor.

"I hate to say it," Viv acknowledged after a long silence, "but it does make sense. Especially if the doctor has a contact high-up in Washington. Someone with the authority to transfer people and shut down the VA's eVetRecs system."

"I still don't know exactly how Art died. The official report was enemy fire. Nothing specific. What if it wasn't related to the war? As hard as it might be to think of Mills this way, what if Art was killed trying to share what he knew?" she asked, repeating Art's exact words: *If you're watching this, I guess I failed as a whistleblower.*

"If that's true, then you better be extra careful about who you tell what you know," Viv replied, the concern in her voice unmistakable.

It was the second time Mackenzie had been told to be careful that day. Trying to sound calmer than she felt, she said, "My brother-in-law Craig's in town. Staying at the Boca Marriott. If I tell him, he'll know what to do." She checked her watch. It was four-thirty. "I'm going to leave right now and stop at his hotel. I don't have to meet Congresswoman Cooper until six."

"Will you call or text me when you get there?"

Mackenzie had to smile at Viv's overbearing, but obvious well-meaning solicitude. "*Yes*, mom."

"Okay, then. Before you go, delete the email. You don't want anyone hacking into it," Viv said, permitting herself a small laugh. "Sorry, I had to send the video through the VA's server, but your phone couldn't support such a big file. I have the flash drive. I'll hide it in your apartment."

A crack of thunder made Mackenzie turn to look out the window again. "Rain's coming."

"It's already pouring here," Viv said. "Be safe."

Five minutes later, Mackenzie had deleted the email and logged off the VA system. Slowly cracking open the office door, she checked the corridor. As soon as she thought no one was watching, she slipped out and hurried toward the elevator.

Viv used her key to enter Mackenzie's apartment, glad that her friend had remembered to lock the door. Now that she understood what was on the video, she worried about Mac's safety. If Mac was right about Art's death, who knew how far someone might go to silence her as well.

Stripping off her hoodie, soggy from the rain, Viv walked into the kitchen and draped it over a chair. As she wandered from room to room, she searched for the least obvious place to hide the flash drive. Finally, she settled on a box of tampons in the bathroom underneath the sink. Concealing the drive in the middle of the pack, she placed the box behind two rolls of toilet tissue and shut the cabinet.

Gathering up her jacket, Viv was moving past the kitchen when the land line rang. Although she didn't feel right about picking it up, she couldn't help hearing the caller's voice drifting from the answering machine in Mackenzie's bedroom.

By the time Mackenzie retrieved her purse from the nurses' locker room and exited the hospital, the sky had opened up. Without an umbrella, she had no choice but to duck her head down and run as fast as possible to the parking lot. It didn't help that the rain was making the walkway slick, so that when she tried to race past a group of nurses blocking the path, she slipped and fell face first. Still on the ground, she felt a hand squeeze her elbow. "Ms. Dodd? Are you okay?"

From her prone position she turned to see Donald Henrick. Despite the official sunny weather report, he apparently had had the foresight to bring an umbrella to work which he held over her as she slowly got to her feet.

"Guess I wasn't watching where I was going," she said, embarrassed by her clumsiness. She produced a grateful smile, hoping Henrick wouldn't chastise her for leaving the clinic early.

Perhaps because he was doing the same thing, he said nothing about the time. Instead he offered to walk her to her car.

"Thanks, I'm just over here." She pointed to her Civic parked near the entrance of the uncovered lot.

Once they'd reached her spot, he helped her into the driver's seat and turned to walk away before she had a chance to thank him again.

The red light on the answering machine in Mackenzie's bedroom was blinking. Viv had only discerned fragments of the message from the kitchen, but what she did hear had set off alarm bells. Now she pushed the 'play' button, hoping her fears were misplaced.

Still parked, Mackenzie took a moment to catch her breath. Surprisingly, her polyester pantsuit was only slightly damp and she hadn't torn the fabric or cut herself when she'd fallen. She patted the spray of rain from her face with a Kleenex, then glanced in the rearview mirror. Dismayed by the sight of wet hair plastered like a cap against her ears, she tried to fluff it with her fingers, but the effort seemed moot. She'd have to wait until it dried before she could hope to improve the look. In the meantime, she turned the key in the ignition and pressed her foot on the gas to start the engine. Instead of a smooth purr, the motor made a 'rur rur rur' sound, refusing to turn over.

Shit.

She didn't have time for this.

Hoping the diagnosis wasn't a dead battery, she tried the maneuver twice more until the sound stopped altogether. Mackenzie checked her watch. Four forty-five. If she didn't leave soon, she'd never make it to Craig's hotel before her meeting with Cooper. Considering options, she realized that even if she had paid for triple A, a hotshot might not do the trick. She knew she was long due a replacement battery. Better to call a cab and deal with it later she decided just as she heard someone knock on her window. Lowering it, she saw that it was Henrick.

He leaned in. "Need help?"

"Battery's dead," Mackenzie said. "I'm late for a meeting in Boca, so I think I'll just call a cab."

"I'm headed that way. Why don't I give you a ride?"

Before she had a chance to object, the administrative assistant had opened her door and held out his umbrella. She ducked under it as he guided her toward the Corolla idling in front of her Civic. "I was heading out when I saw you were in trouble," he said as he helped her into the passenger seat.

Mackenzie watched him walk around to the driver's side. Just before he stepped in, he pulled out his cell and made a quick call.

"Had to let my cousin know I'd be a little late," he explained when he was finally settled inside.

Although she didn't feel totally comfortable with Henrick, Mackenzie had to admit his being there was fortuitous, his offer generous. "I really appreciate your taking me," she said, fastening her seatbelt.

Once she'd played the message for a second time and checked the name on Caller ID, Viv was certain she needed to phone Mackenzie right away and warn her she might be heading into trouble.

Outside the rain was falling in unrelenting torrents. The rhythmic to and fro of the windshield wipers added counterpoint to Henrick's softly humming 'God Bless America'.

Mackenzie waited until he had carefully negotiated the curved entrance to I-95 before attempting small talk. "You said you're visiting your cousin?"

"What?" Henrick stole a quick glance at Mackenzie before turning back to concentrate on the road. "Oh, yes. Actually the General's a distant relative, but I can never remember the exact nomenclature so I just call him 'cousin'."

"A General. Wow."

Henrick smiled. "Great guy. I owe him my career."

"Were you in the military?"

Henrick shook his head. "I wish." He pointed to his thick glasses. "Bad vision's on the military rejection list. The General knew how much I wanted to serve, so he got me the job with the VA. Been there since I was twenty. Sixteen years next week." The pride in his voice was unmistakable.

Thirty-six. That jibed with Mackenzie's earlier estimate of his age. While Henrick resumed his humming she studied his profile - short and slim, a pale, acne pitted face under close cropped blonde hair. Nondescript. Odd duck. But a decent sort she guessed.

As if he'd read her mind, Henrick swiveled his head to give her a reassuring look.

Just as happy to forego idle chitchat, Mackenzie let her eyelids drift slowly downward, focusing instead on what she'd learned from Art's video.

Viv was frantic. She'd first tried calling Mackenzie, then texting her. No answer. Mackenzie probably didn't want to pick up while driving in the rain. Viv checked the time. Not quite five o'clock. Okay, she'd give her ten more minutes before trying again. Even with the bad weather, Mackenzie should be at her destination by ten after and she'd promised to call as soon as she arrived. If Viv didn't hear from her by then, she planned to call the police.

In a half-dream state, Mackenzie's mind swirled, emotions in turmoil. How could the Army hurt its own men? The thought of her ex being murdered was too much to accept. Was it really possible that the laid-back, caring affect of the psychiatrist she'd believed in was just a ruse? She prayed that once she told Craig what was going on, he'd contact the highest officials and demand an immediate investigation. She couldn't wait to get to his hotel and share her burden.

Startled by a sudden, erratic swerve, Mackenzie opened her eyes.

"Sorry," Henrick apologized. "That exit was slicker than I realized."

Mackenzie shook herself to full alertness. "Where are we?" She peered through her window. Between the heavy downpour and the darkening sky, she couldn't discern landmarks.

"I, uh, have to make a quick stop over here for gas. Final ETA should be no more than fifteen minutes," he said as he pulled into a darkened Hess lot.

He'd jumped out of the car before Mackenzie could ask if the station was even open. According to her watch, it was a little after five. If she got to the Marriott by five-twenty, she'd have time to talk to Craig and make her meeting with Congressman Cooper at six. Worse case, she'd contact Cooper and explain her delay.

Reminded that she'd turned off her cell, she reached into her purse and depressed the 'on' button. Then, checking around for a cord to charge the phone, she opened the glovebox and peered inside. At first, she was sure her eyes had deceived her. She swallowed hard. It couldn't be. The light *was* dim. Frowning, she reached in and pulled out a frayed notebook and switched on the overhead map light. The cover page with the words: 'property of Sergeant Philip Joseph Linton' took her breath away. Henrick had PJ's stolen diary.

Mackenzie felt as though she'd been punched in the gut. What had the Delray Beach policewoman said when she'd found the figurines? .... *one workman thought he saw a white Toyota hanging around a few days before the robbery.*

The implication hit Mackenzie as soon as she realized that this car was a white Toyota. Henrick must have been stalking her. Somehow he'd found out that Christine had given her the diary - a document that chronicled PJ's symptoms - symptoms that the men involved in the SEDO operation didn't want revealed.

Fury at herself for the second time she'd misplaced trust instantly morphed into an overwhelming sense of panic. If the administrative assistant was part of the SEDO conspiracy, she had to get away. *Now.*

Taking a deep breath and letting it out slowly, she struggled to clear her head. Viv wouldn't know she hadn't taken her car tonight. Even if someone at the hospital saw her get into Henrick's car, it would be days before anyone would worry about her. She was on her own.

With the station unlit, Mackenzie had no idea where Henrick was. Marshalling her nerve, she cautiously opened the passenger door, desperate to make her escape. The torrential rain had not abated, so she grabbed the diary and pressed it against her chest, using her purse as cover. With her head tucked down, she had just stepped out when she heard a voice behind her.

"I always try to follow orders, Ms. Dodd, but you keep making it very hard for me."

Heart pounding, Mackenzie turned. She knew it was Henrick standing there, but the only thing she could focus on was the gun in his hand.

"How about you get back in the car? I don't think you want to meet the General soaking wet. He should be here shortly."

Viv had been anxiously watching the minutes tick by on her phone until she could wait no longer. Pressing Mackenzie's name with her forefinger, she speed dialed her friend, hoping this time she would answer.

The cell's ring seemed to surprise Henrick who was now seated on the driver's side holding his gun on Mackenzie. In the moment he looked away, Mackenzie bent down and grabbed her phone from her purse. Before she could answer, Henrick's hand grasped hers, tightening on her arm. His strength was unexpected. A sharp pain shot through her wrist and elbow as he snapped back her hand and the cell phone dropped on the floor. Mackenzie kicked it under the seat, but by then the ringing had stopped.

"Sam, thank God I reached you. Mac's in serious trouble. I've been calling and texting and she doesn't answer. We've got to find her before...." Viv's voice took on an hysterical edge. "Her life's in danger."

Though he tried to maintain a professional calm, the notion that Mackenzie might be in danger sent an adrenaline rush through Sam. "Okay, slow down. Tell me exactly what's going on."

Through gulps of air and as quickly as she could, Viv filled him in on what Art's video had revealed.

"Jesus, Mac *was* right about the drug," Sam declared. "I can't believe the Army's using it on combatants like Jake knowing it could make them sick." He expelled a bitter sigh. "Someone's head's gonna roll."

"Mac's on her way to meet with her brother-in-law. We've got to stop her."

"I thought she said he was a good guy."

"I thought so too," Viv said. "Until I overheard a message from Mac's sister."

The second she'd finished speaking, Sam understood the urgency and agreed to Viv's plan to locate Mackenzie.

Anxiety coiled like a serpent in Mackenzie's gut. In a last-ditch effort to appeal to the administrative assistant's better instincts she asked, "Donald, why are you doing this? You seem like a decent guy. Let me go. I won't say anything about your involvement."

"Decent guy?" Henrick mocked. He tilted his head. "Maybe that works on TV, Ms. Dodd. I already told you. I'm just following orders." The crunch of tires made him glance in the rearview mirror. "Ah, here they are," he said as approaching headlights bathed the Toyota's interior in a shimmering amber glow.

A moment later, the lights were extinguished. Darkness all around, sounds of falling rain, car doors slamming, heavy footsteps. Henrick's door was pulled open and a man with sandy-colored hair leaned in. "You can put that gun down, son."

"Where's General Paulsen?" Henrick asked, twisting his neck to view the intruder.

"Early retirement." Smiling, the man whipped out a syringe from the pocket of his trenchcoat, jammed it into Henrick's carotid and depressed the plunger. "Same as you." Almost instantly Henrick lost consciousness. As he slumped sideways, the man reached around and grabbed the gun from Henrick's limp hand.

"You're gonna kill me too?" Mackenzie screamed.

"No worries." The man pocketed the gun."You, I'm taking to your brother-in-law. He's in the town car over there and he wants to talk to you." He carefully arranged Henrick on the driver's side and lifted the umbrella from the backseat. "I'm Dr. Anders, by the way. Craig's brother."

Sam wasn't surprised that Viv knew the Florida police had access to a controversial cellular phone tracker. By now he'd recognized the accomplished hacker was far more familiar with the latest surveillance techniques and devices than he. As she explained, the advantage of StingRay was its ability to identify a phone or other cellular data device even while it wasn't engaged in a call or accessing data services.

Sam's department had recently acquired a Stingray which was initially developed for the military and intelligence community. The only problem for Sam was convincing his captain that this was an emergency and he needed to use the device. Fortunately with several cards to play, it took just one phone call to Brompton to get his go-ahead.

Holding the umbrella over both of them, Anders escorted Mackenzie to the town car and ushered her into the back seat where, true to his word, Craig was waiting.

At the sight of her brother-in-law Mackenzie's rapid heartbeat began to slow. "Thank God. I was on my way to talk to you. How'd you know I was in danger?"

Craig pointed to Anders pacing outside in the rain. "Doug works for Army intelligence. He's been monitoring the General's phone calls."

"The General? You mean Henrick's cousin?"

"Paulsen's a very distant relative, but yes, that general."

Of course Paulsen was involved in the conspiracy. He'd come to PJ's funeral and then brought Christine the doctored personnel record. He'd obviously ordered Henrick to stalk Mackenzie and steal the diary. She felt like a fool for not realizing it sooner.

"We were meeting at the hotel when Doug learned you were with Henrick. He decided to intercept," Craig was saying.

"Doug's your brother?"

"Actually step-brother. His father married my mother."

"Right. You mentioned that when you visited last week."

"What were you coming to tell me?"

Mackenzie took a deep breath. "You won't believe what the Army's been doing. Remember when I asked you about the malaria drug?" Stumbling over her words, she quickly described her investigation, reporting everything she'd learned about the secret operation. "Even though I suspected something was up, without Art's video, I would never have figured out why only the combatants were getting Flometoquine."

"You have the flash drive with you?"

"In my apartment. Don't worry, it's safe." She wrapped her arms around herself like a protective blanket. "I think Art might have been killed for what he knew, Craig. He wanted me to tell someone I trusted. That's why I was coming to you. You've got to tell your superiors and demand an investigation."

Craig tsked. "You know, Judith says you're irresponsible. That's not your problem, Mackenzie. It's your goddam relentlessness." His expression seemed to reflect genuine regret. "I tried to protect you, I did."

Growing uneasy, Mackenzie frowned. "I don't understand."

"Why couldn't you be satisfied with your notoriety as a rape victim? Paulsen had Fremont set it all up with that Florida congresswoman. He was sure you'd be too busy to play junior detective." Craig sneered. "But the general was wrong, wasn't he? You're like a dog with a bone. You'll never let it be."

Opening the door to the backseat, Anders slipped in beside Mackenzie. "Hope you two had a chance to catch up." He leaned over to talk to Craig. "It's getting late. We've got to get going, M."

Mackenzie gasped. Her mind raced as the true significance of Craig's identity registered. She'd convinced herself that Mills was the bad guy. "*You're* M?"

Anders chuckled. "Ah, yes. My fault, actually. I wasn't so nice to my new big brother when he came to live with us. See he was a stutterer as a kid. McMaster sounded like one big 'mmmm' when he had to pronounce his last name. So that's what I called him growing up. M." Anders snorted with derision. "Of course only a few close friends and family even know about the nickname these days."

Mackenzie felt a mixture of disgust and fear. "Art said not to trust M."

Anders shrugged. "I'd say it was the other way around. Art refused to appreciate what our Strategic Enemy Defense Operation meant for our country."

"SEDO," Mackenzie said quietly, reminded of the flash drive's password code.

"Right," Anders acknowledged. "Almost twenty years ago, as a postdoc in Australia I discovered a drug that could enhance the fighting ability of our military men. Big brother here connected me with Paulsen who persuaded the Army to buy the rights from Mossie Pharmaceuticals. Then he introduced me to Fremont. It's the congressman's membership on the Armed Services Committee that's kept the project funded all these years. The country got a drug that would help win future wars with fewer soldiers and I got to head up PsyOps. All in all, a win-win."

"You call winning using a drug that can make soldiers sick or worse, kill them?"

"An unfortunate and unintended consequence, true, but sometimes the end justifies the means, don't you think?"

"I could never justify that end," Mackenzie spat.

Unfazed, Anders nodded. "Yes, it does seem that you and Art share the same moral sensibilities. That's why we couldn't trust him not to divulge what he'd learned."

"Did you kill him?"

"Not me. Big brother here arranged some friendly fire."

Anders' statement left Mackenzie numb. She struggled to breathe. Looking to her brother-in-law. "Are you gonna murder me too?"

While her head was turned, Anders had pulled out a second prepared syringe from his coat pocket and plunged it into her left arm. "Not murder," he said as she fell against him. "An accident. With this heavy rain and the roads so slick, no one will question how a Toyota ended up in the C-15 canal."

The last thing Mackenzie heard was "I'm sorry" from Craig.

Based on Viv's information, Sam was driving the cruiser south on I-95, the most direct route he figured Mackenzie would have taken to the Boca Marriott. Sitting beside him, the police tech used a portable StingRay device known as the KingFish to track her cell.

Speaking above the whoosing noise of the windshield wipers, Sam asked, "Exactly how does that thing in your lap work?"

"This box mimics cellphone towers and gets the phone to connect to it even if the owner isn't making a call. We just need to ride around until we get a signal from the target phone while pinging it. Once a signal is found, this setup measures its strength and provides a general location on the map."

They passed by several exits with nothing from the device and then, just as they reached the Congress Avenue offramp, a loud pinging registered.

"Take the exit," the tech ordered.

Yanking the steering wheel to the right, Sam headed up the curved ramp. A fresh sheen of sweat broke out on his face as he stopped at the traffic light. "Could have given me a little warning."

"Sorry." The tech was staring at the map.

"Which way?" Sam asked.

"Make a left on Congress. I think we're close."

Anders moved Henrick's body so he could drive the Toyota while Craig followed him in the town car north to the Delray Canal. Also known as C-15, the canal ranged in width from eighty to one hundred seventy-five feet and averaged eight feet deep - perfect for what he planned. On sunny days, more than one avid fisherman might choose the hours just before sunset to take advantage of the nearly seventeen miles of freshwater. Today, however, the heavy rains guaranteed that the area was vacant.

Anders forced a long skid before braking on a modest slope one car length south of the canal. Concerned about fingerprints, he slipped on a pair of surgical gloves and used a towel to wipe off the steering wheel. After moving Henrick back to the driver's seat, he and Craig both lifted Mackenzie from the back of the town car, placed her on the passenger side of the Toyota and buckled her seatbelt.

"The body count's getting awfully high," Craig commented.

"If you hadn't mishandled Art, it might not have come to this," Anders snapped. Without another word he put the car in neutral. "Help me give this a push so we can get the hell out of here. We still need to get that flash drive from her apartment."

The police tech stared at his tracking device, using a second set of pings to triangulate the location of Mackenzie's phone more precisely. A few blocks north on Congress the signal strength grew decidedly stronger. "There." He pointed to a low burm on the west side of the street.

"You sure?" Sam asked, driving closer to get a better look. "I don't see a…" Slamming on the brakes, he yelled, "Oh my God." He grabbed the emergency hammer from the side pouch and threw open his door, exiting the cruiser just as the Toyota's front end began its slide into the canal. "Call 911. I'm going in."

Sitting in Elizabeth Cooper's Delray Beach office, Congressman Fremont made no effort to hide his annoyance. "You know I made a special trip down to Florida to meet your star witness, Liz. Thought you said she'd be here tonight."

"I'm so sorry, Leyton. Ms. Dodd should have been here twenty minutes ago. I've had my aide call her cell, but she's not picking up. I'm hoping it's just the bad weather that's keeping her."

Leyton raised bushy eyebrows suggesting his skepticism. "I wonder if the young lady hasn't gotten cold feet." He shook his head. "If her no-show means she's reconsidered appearing before your congressional hearing, that would be a damn shame."

Reluctant to admit that what he was saying might be true, Cooper nodded. Of course, she assumed Fremont was being sincere and felt guilty for inviting him down.

Because of its many canals, Florida leads the nation by a wide margin in the number of people who drown inside their vehicles each year. Well acquainted with the stats, Sam knew that once the car was completely submerged, any passengers would have no more than about two minutes to get out alive.

Luckily he'd jumped into the canal before the Toyota completed its descent, luckier still that he'd realized Mackenzie was probably not the driver. This wasn't her Civic. That's why he swam directly around to the passenger side. With most of that window visible above the water line, he could make out Mackenzie leaning back against the headrest. Though he didn't observe any obvious injuries, she appeared to be unconscious.

Anxious to rescue her before it was too late, Sam tread water, at the same time hoisting the hardened steel point of the hammer overhead. It took two tries before the spring-loaded mechanism shattered the glass. By that time, the car had sunk lower. Water began rushing in, equalizing the pressure and allowing him to slowly open the door. Sam took a deep breath, dove down and reached in to unbuckle Mackenzie's seatbelt. Perhaps because she was unconscious there was no resistance as he pulled her out, managing to bring her to the surface on his first attempt.

He floated her on her back all the way to the shore. As the tech held out a hand to help him up, the piercing wail of sirens announced the arrival of a Palm Beach fire truck and local ambulance. Glancing behind him, Sam saw the Toyota completely sink to the bottom of the canal.

Afraid his town car could be too easily identified, Anders found a parking spot a block away from Shady Palms. Holding the umbrella to shield their faces, he and Craig headed toward Mackenzie's building, planning to break into her apartment.

"This one's a coroner's case," one of the fireman announced after he and his partner had removed the driver from the submerged vehicle. "Tow boys can probably wait to bring up the car tomorrow when the rain stops. Any idea who the dead guy is?" He directed his question to Sam who was focused on the EMT evaluating Mackenzie. He'd determined that she was stable, though still unconscious and were placing her on a gurney to transfer her to Delray Hospital.

Sam took a quick look at the body. "I do know him. Donald Henrick. He works at the VA."

"Not one of our better Florida drivers," the fireman commented. "Must have skidded and done a nose dive into the C-15."

After what Viv had told him earlier, Sam wasn't ready to call this an accident, but he didn't share his suspicions. He'd already contacted the chief who was sending one patrol car to start the investigation here and another to the Marriott to arrest Craig McMaster. Right now Sam was only interested in Mackenzie. As he watched her being transferred into the back of the ambulance he made a quick call to Viv.

The ambulance driver slammed the door and turned to Sam who was pulling out the dry clothes he kept stashed in his trunk. "Okay we're off. You coming?"

Sam shook his head. "Just promised her friend I'd give her a ride to the ER. I'll meet you there."

Wearing surgical gloves, Anders and Craig went through Mackenzie's apartment methodically. They'd been opening drawers and cabinets and closets for fifteen minutes without success. They'd found Art's jacket, but the pockets were empty.

Anders balled his fists in obvious frustration. "Where the hell could that flash drive be?"

"She said it was in the apartment and it was safe," Craig responded.

"We should have made her tell us exactly where she hid it."

Miffed by the earlier criticism, Craig pointed out that they might have learned its location if Anders hadn't been so anxious to give Mackenzie the ketamine.

Anders blew air through his cheeks. "You need to be right, fine. But we're not leaving until we've turned this place upside down."

Viv was impatiently waiting under an umbrella when Sam pulled the cruiser up to the curb. She jumped into the passenger seat and gave him a hug. "Thank God you found her."

"If not for you, she might be dead." Sam shook his head. "It definitely doesn't look like an accident."

"I can't believe her own brother-in-law would try to kill her."

"We don't know that for sure, Viv."

"You didn't see the video and you didn't hear her sister's phone message. Art said not to trust M. Judith made it clear that M. is her husband."

"Do you have the video?"

"I hid the flash drive in Mac's apartment."

"Is there another copy?"

"No. Why?"

"Maybe you better get it. This is going to be a major scandal when it breaks. That flash drive is crucial evidence." He locked eyes with Viv. "They're killing Jake, they almost killed Mac. I don't want any chance for the men responsible for this secret operation to go free."

Viv nodded. "Sure. I'll just run up. Won't take more than a sec."

While Viv headed upstairs, Sam used the opportunity to make two calls. His first was to the officer who'd been sent to the Marriott.

"I'm here now, but the suspect's flown the coop. Manager says Colonel Craig McMaster checked out around four-thirty."

"Damn," Sam said. "Any clue where he's gone?"

"Nada. The hotel valet saw him get into a black town car. Chief Brompton's put out a BOLO for the colonel and the vehicle."

"Thanks." Hanging up, Sam's second call was to Delray Hospital's emergency room. The nurse manning the desk reported that a Mackenzie Dodd had just arrived by ambulance. "The team is working on her now."

Anxious to get to the hospital to talk to the doctors himself, Sam checked his watch, surprised that nearly ten minutes had passed and Viv hadn't returned. Deciding to hurry her up, he shut off the ignition, left the patrol car, and ran up the steps to apartment 2G.

Sam wasn't surprised to find Mackenzie's apartment door slightly ajar. After all Viv had promised to be quick. She'd probably just left it that way. He started to call out to her, but stopped himself when he heard muted voices coming from the far bedroom.

What the…?

On full alert, he texted his captain for backup, then slowly pushed the door open, drew his Glock and quietly stepped in.

In the soft glow of twilight he could see that the living room had been tossed. Mackenzie's photo album was scattered on the floor along with a few books and the cushions from the loveseat. Moving cautiously past the kitchen, he noticed cabinet doors flung open, contents spilled on the counter. The same was true of the bathroom except that when he looked down, there was an upended box of Tampons in one corner and drops of blood at the entrance that seemed to be leading down the hallway.

Jesus, they'd hurt Viv.

His heart raced as he edged forward. Nearing Mackenzie's bedroom, the voices became louder. At least two males. He stopped just outside, flattening himself against the wall to listen.

"You've got the flash drive. Can't we just leave her?"

"Are you kidding, M? She knows as much as your crazy sister-in-law. We can't risk her talking. Bring the town car around front so we can move her. We'll have to finish the job elsewhere."

Hearing that, Sam quickly tiptoed back to the front entrance and hid outside the front door. The moment Craig emerged, he held up his badge with one hand, pointing his gun with the other. "Police. Colonel McMaster you're under arrest. One word and I'll shoot."

Surprisingly, Craig made no effort to resist, raising his hands. "I can't do this anymore."

Sam snapped handcuffs on his wrists, then patted him down for a weapon.

"Doug's got the gun," Craig said.

"What did he do to Viv?"

"The girl? She's alive. He hit her over the head when she wouldn't give up the uh…"

"The flash drive? Yeah I know all about the secret operation you Army bastards are running. Your drug is killing my brother."

Craig produced a contrite expression. "I am sorry. Doug asked me to negotiate the deal to buy the rights. I didn't know there were problems until it was too late."

Sam was filled with rage. It was all he could do not to punch this man. Instead he shoved him back toward the entrance of the apartment and snarled. "Call to your brother. Tell him you've brought the car, to bring the girl."

Craig nodded and did as he was told. Sam positioned himself to the side, out of sight.

Less than a minute later Anders appeared in the doorway carrying Viv. He stooped to lay her down and glanced up at Craig. "Goddammit, M. Keep your voice down," he said in an angry whisper. "And don't just stand there. Kid's heavy. How about some help?"

When Craig didn't respond, Anders blinked in confusion. Then, as understanding seemed to register, his eyes went wide. "You fucking Judas." From his crouching position, he reached into his pocket for his gun and pulled the trigger. The bullet hit Craig in the shoulder. Before Anders had an opportunity to try again, Sam pushed Craig down and aimed his Glock at Anders. "Police. drop it. Now."

Instead of complying, Anders turned his gun on Viv who was beginning to stir. "You want the girl? Let me go."

Tensing, Sam considered options. He wasn't certain he could get off a shot without risking Viv's life. Knowing backup would be there any minute, he decided to keep Anders talking. "Why'd you do it?"

"Do what?"

"Give our troops that drug."

"Flometoquine?" Anders produced a tight smile. "It makes them better fighters."

"It also kills some of them."

Anders let out an exasperated sigh. "You don't get it, do you? This country's waging war in Iraq and Afghanistan today and who knows what other Middle East country tomorrow. You think you can do that with the small volunteer army we've got? No way. Not unless we send the men back in again and again. My drug lets us do that."

Sam couldn't keep the bitterness out of his voice. "My brother Jake fought in Iraq. Two tours. Now he has ALS. He's dying because of your drug."

Anders pursed his lips. "Every good military strategy has some collateral damage." Although his gun was pointed at Viv, his eyes drifted to Sam as he continued to justify himself. "Your brother's a casualty of war."

The ruthless recitation was just too much. Unable to control himself any longer, Sam shouted. "Casualty of war? You fucking bastard!"

In what would later play out in his head as a slow motion ballet, Sam caught Viv inching far enough away from Anders to provide a clear shot. Although he'd tell Internal Affairs that he couldn't remember pulling the trigger, he would never forget the sound of approaching sirens drowning out the volley of bullets that entered Anders body.

Two EMTs carried Viv down the stairs in a gurney. Her head wound had been bandaged over her neon blue wisps. Conscious, but woozy, she motioned Sam over with a crook of her forefinger.

"Did you find it?" she whispered.

He held up the flash drive he'd pulled from Anders pocket.

"And you saved Mac." She managed a weak smile. "You did good."

He smiled back, thinking how deceiving looks could be. Who would ever guess this waif-like girl, barely out of her teens, had almost singlehandedly solved the PBU rape case, ensured the arrest of a corrupt DA, and foiled a diabolical secret military plot that had nearly killed the woman he loved. Gently squeezing her hand, he said, "Actually, I think we both did."

At eight p.m. a maid at the Boca Marriott entering room 213 for the evening turn-down found the elderly occupant in bed. Assuming he was asleep, she tiptoed out. It would take another twelve hours before anyone realized that General Paulsen was dead, a few days more before the medical examiner confirmed that he'd been poisoned. Leyton Fremont, who'd served the general his fatal cocktail, was killed by a hit and run driver as he crossed Military Trail on his way out of Congresswoman Cooper's office. The driver was never found.

CHAPTER 24

Seated around Mackenzie's kitchen table, Mackenzie, Sam and Viv watched the local news anchor shuffle her papers before beginning Monday's evening news.

"Today Assistant DA Dalton was arrested for campaign fraud. Mr. Dalton, who was leading in his bid for Florida's Attorney General, had no comment when questioned by reporters after his arraignment. Earlier today, the same judge revoked bail for Dalton's nephew Tim and the three other members of the PBU football team accused of a series of rapes of freshman women at the school. ADA Victor Novak who is now prosecuting the case said he's in receipt of a video that will provide unequivocal proof of guilt. All in all, a bad start to the week for the Dalton family," the anchor proclaimed.

Mackenzie lowered the volume on the TV and cheered. Sam and Viv joined in. Since Mackenzie's discharge from the hospital on Saturday afternoon, Sam had been staying in her apartment, helping with her convalescence. Pleased with the way he'd handled the Dalton cases, Sam's chief had not only given him a few days off, but promised a promotion.

Viv, whose head injury had required a half dozen stitches, had been invited for a pizza dinner. "Hey, turn it up again." The tow truck displayed on the screen was removing a white

Toyota from a canal. "In a follow-up to our story about the near drowning of a Delray Beach resident on Friday night, police investigators have determined that the slick roads caused the car to veer off and plunge into the C-15 canal. The driver, a VA employee, was killed instantly."

Mackenzie clicked off the TV and said with a cluck of her tongue. "So they've started the whitewashing."

"They're not letting Craig off," Sam said. "He pled guilty for his part in the secret operation."

"Life in prison instead of what he really deserves for arranging Art's death." Mackenzie couldn't keep the bitterness from her voice.

"Hey, I thought after talking with Congresswoman Cooper and Dr. Mills you agreed to let the Department of Defense handle things internally." Sam said.

Mackenzie nodded. "They convinced me that exposing SEDO would only hurt the country, that nothing would be gained by the public losing trust in our military. They promised to make sure that not one more soldier gets Flometoquine, that every soldier sick from the drug will have the best care by the VA." She glanced at Sam, wishing there was more to offer Jake.

"And you'll hold them to that, Mac," Viv declared.

Mackenzie shrugged. "DOD has the only copy of the flash drive."

Viv produced a smug smile.

"What? You told me to delete the VA gmail and I did."

"Not really. Yesterday I hacked back into the system and retrieved it. Tonight I may try to download Anders' encrypted files."

Mackenzie laughed. "You really are a piece of work."

"I'll take that as a compliment."

Sam shook his head. "I'm off duty, so I won't say anything, but just out of curiosity, is there any honest work in your future?"

"Actually, I got a call this morning from a DOD recruiter. I have a meeting in Washington next week. I made the date to coordinate with Mac's appearance in front of the House Armed Services subcommittee." She turned to Mackenzie. "I've also emailed the congresswoman to let her know I'd be happy to help with social networking for the bill she's sponsoring on military sexual assault."

Mackenzie gave her a hug, reminded how much she'd come to think of Viv as a sister, how estranged she still felt from her own.

"Don't you owe your sister a call?" Viv asked, as if she'd read her mind.

Excusing herself, Mackenzie went into the bedroom and dialed Judith's home phone. It was almost midnight in Berlin, but her sister answered on the first ring. "Mackenzie?" It was clear from the timbre of her voice that she'd been crying. "I thought you'd never want to talk to me again. A representative from Defense came to see me today. He arranged for me talk to Craig by Skype. He confessed what he and his brother did to you. I'm so very sorry."

Judith's words reduced Mackenzie to tears. She'd waited so long for Judith's approval and now it had come in an unexpected apology.

"I have a favor," Judith said softly.

"Yes?"

"I'll have to leave Germany now that Craig is officially out of the Army. I'm filing for divorce. Would you mind a visit while I figure out where..." her voice cracked.

"A visit? Yes. You'll bring Craig, Jr and the twins." She realized she didn't know their names.

"The boy is Paul," Judith said. "He has our brother's blue eyes."

Mackenzie held her breath, waiting for her sister's usual reprove. Instead, there was yet another apology. "I should never have blamed you for his death. It was an accident. Not your fault."

"And the girl?" Mackenzie asked.

"I've named her Kenzie. Is that all right?"

A few minutes later Mackenzie returned to Sam and Viv, obviously lost in thought.

"Everything okay?" Sam asked.

Feeling as though a burden had been lifted, Mackenzie kissed Viv on the cheek, then put her arms around Sam. All this time she'd sought Judith's forgiveness when it really was her own she'd denied. Kenzie forgiving Mackenzie. A smile bloomed on her face as she decided her next Silent Survivors blog would be about forgiveness. She'd finally come full circle. "It is now," she said.

EPILOGUE

True to the promise, at the end of September, ALS was officially declared a disability by the VA. Jake did get the best care available, but he finally succumbed to the degenerative disease. Sam, his mom, and Mackenzie were by his side at the end. He was buried with honors in Arlington.

Judith's visit lasted a few weeks during which she and Mackenzie became closer. Once a month they drove together to the VA cemetery in Lake Worth, laying yellow and white dandelions on their mother's grave.

With the approaching demolition of Shady Palms, a move was necessary. Judith found an apartment in Deerfield Beach not far from Christine Linton whose mother offered to help watch the children while Christine and Judith worked at SunTrust Bank.

Mackenzie moved into Sam's Delray Beach apartment. Sam received his promotion and transferred to the state's new Special Victims Unit. Mackenzie completed her mentorship with Dr. Mills and became a mental health counselor. In addition to her official job with the VA, she decided to volunteer with three other nurses at the Voices and Faces Project. As she explained it to one of the many media outlets who sought her out after her blog became a national sensation: "When a rape victim goes to the hospital, one of us collects evidence and takes photos. I have the unique perspective of knowing what it feels like to be on both sides. But I never tell patients I was raped. At the time of the exam, it's not about me. It's about them."

Although Mackenzie's testimony in front of the Armed Services subcommittee was well received, as Leyton Fremont had predicted, Congresswoman Cooper's bill to take military sexual trauma out of the chain of command ultimately failed. Nevertheless it didn't stop Mackenzie from pushing for change. She continued to blog and use the money raised to support veterans' causes.

It took until 2011 before Don't Ask, Don't Tell (DADT), the US military's eighteen year ban on openly gay and lesbian service personnel was officially repealed, ushering in a new era for the country's estimated sixty-five thousand serving gay and lesbian servicemen and women. According to the non-profit watchdog and lobby group, the Service Members Legal Defense Network, more than fourteen thousand five hundred US service personnel like Dr. Art Dodd had been thrown out of military service since the DADT policy took effect.

Maura graduated college and established Silent No More chapters across the country, a program aimed at helping young women avoid rape on campus.

Viv dropped out of PBU to take a job with the government as an ethical hacker. Though she's a white hat, she still keeps a copy of Art's flash drive and Anders' files. Just in case....

THE END

ACKNOWLEDGEMENTS

I would like to express my very grateful thanks to Paul Willand and his family who appreciate the psychological effects of multiple tours to Iraq and Afghanistan wars from first hand experience and were kind enough to read through the manuscript to help me understand the true nature of these wars and their aftermath.

Thanks to EJ Manton, licensed clinical social worker and psychologists, Rosalyn Malamud, PhD and Tera Beaber, PhD who worked with trauma victims and who made the scenes in the PTSD clinic ring true. Thanks to Steve Tiplitsky for sharing his expertise as a policeman.

Special thanks to Beth Lazerick who not only tirelessly read and reread the manuscript, but lent her name to one of the characters. And to my new Canadian friend, Susan Gibbon, who tells me that much of this story could also apply to the Canadian military.

Thanks to early readers Joan Cochran, Alice Suna, Seena Peck, Rhona Altomari, Dennis Ackerman, Cathy Rogers, Bonnie Cossrow, Sharon Hanley, Joan Hutton and Donna Emory. Their critical eyes were most appreciated.

Becky Fein not only provided clinical insights, but also introduced me to her Powerful Voices Project which helps to educate, empower and enhance the conversation around sexual assault and its survivors. Thank you.

Thanks, of course, to my wonderful husband Joel who encouraged me to fly alone with this novel, but was always there to make sure I made a safe landing.

Finally, *Silent Survivor* would never have been written without Dr. Maria Hoertz who watched her mother die of ALS and was convinced that a malaria drug used by the Army was responsible.

AUTHORS NOTE

Silent Survivor is a work of fiction, but the main plot as well as the various subplots are based on very real contemporary issues.

For example Post Traumatic Stress Disorder (PTSD), a condition introduced into the Diagnostic and Statistical Manual of Mental Disorders (DSM) in 1980, is characterized by hyper-vigilance, emotional numbness and recurring flashbacks. According to experts, it is said to afflict as many as 30 percent of veterans of the Iraq and Afghanistan wars. Those staggering figures don't include some 27 million Americans believed to be PTSD survivors from other traumas including rape[1].

Because PTSD has been shrouded in secrecy and shame within the military, there has been a virtual epidemic of suicides attributed to the disorder. Since 2001, more US service members have taken their own lives than have died on the battlefield. In 2012, a US Office of Veterans Affairs (VA) study found that on average, 22 US military vets commit suicide everyday[2]. The Veterans' Crisis Center in Canandaigua, New York is the only call center in the US serving vets in crisis. Employing 250 responders, 25 percent of whom are veterans themselves, the center receives over 22,000 calls each month[3]

The issue of military sexual trauma (MST) has taken decades to gain public attention.

---

[1] The Evil Hours, A Biography of Post-Traumatic Stress Disorder by David J. Morris,2015 Houghton Mifflin Harcourt Publishing

[2] https://www.va.gov/opa/docs/Suicide-Data-Report-2012-final.pdf

[3] Veterans Crisis Center in Canandaigua, New York can be reached at 1-800-273-8255 Veterans Press 1

Today, the VA defines MST as "psychological trauma, which in the judgment of a VA mental health professional, has resulted from a physical assault of a sexual nature, battery of a sexual nature, or sexual harassment which occurred while the Veteran was serving on active duty." The VA further defines sexual harassment as "repeated, unsolicited verbal or physical contact of a sexual nature which is threatening in nature"[4].

At least nine separate bills (like the one proposed by our fictitious Congresswoman Cooper) have been introduced in Congress by a bipartisan mix of senators and representatives, proposing a range of fixes. According to a report filed by the Department of Defense's Sexual Assault Prevention and Response Office in March, 2010, there were 3,158 sexual assault complaints in that year alone. The Pentagon acknowledged that given the underreporting of MSTs, that number probably accounts for about 13.5 percent of the estimated 19,000 incidents that occurred that year. Only 20 percent of reported cases went to trial which represent half the rate of the civilian justice system[5].

In February, 2011, 25 female and 3 male vets who were sexually assaulted while wearing the uniform filed an abuse lawsuit (Cioca v. Rumsfeld)[6] alleging that Robert Gates and his predecessor, Donald Rumsfeld, had failed to curtail widespread rape in the military. However, within a month, the judge, dismissed the case[7].

---

[4] http://www.mentalhealth.va.gov/msthome.asp

[5] http://www.csmonitor.com/USA/Military/2011/0429/Unseen-foe-for-troops-sexual-assault-in-US-military

[6] http://www.thedailybeast.com/articles/2011/11/14/military-faces-mounting-pressure-to-crack-down-on-rape.html

[7] http://www.thedailybeast.com/articles/2011/12/13/judge-dismisses-epidemic-of-rape-in-military-case.html

A 2012 study of a subset of 213,803 Iraq and Afghanistan veterans of veterans diagnosed with PTSD from April 1, 2002, to October 1, 2008, found that 31 percent of the women and 1percent of the men screened positively for MST[8].

Contributing to PTSD suffered by survivors of military sexual assaults is the harassment of victims who make an official complaint. Ninety percent of them are eventually involuntarily discharged. Today women in the military are still more likely to be raped by fellow soldiers than they are to be killed in combat.

The issue of gays in the military is another real issue. In 2011, President Obama signed legislation to repeal the Don't Ask Don't Tell policy (DADT), which had been passed by Congress and signed into law in 1993 under then-President Bill Clinton. "As of today, patriotic Americans in uniform will no longer have to lie about who they are in order to serve the country they love," Obama said in a statement. "As of today, our armed forces will no longer lose the extraordinary skills and combat experience of so many gay and lesbian service members. Today, every American can be proud that we have taken another great step toward keeping our military the finest in the world and toward fulfilling our nation's founding ideals." According to the Pentagon, recruiters now accept applications from openly gay people.

In 2014, Federal investigators investigated whether 55 colleges and universities in 27 states and in the District of Columbia illegally handled sexual violence and harassment complaints[9]. A 2015 academic study[10] reported that during their freshman year of college 15 percent of women are raped while incapacitated from alcohol or drugs.

---

[8] http://www.ncbi.nlm.nih.gov/pubmed/21907590
[9] http://www.cnn.com/2014/05/01/us/colleges-sex-complaint-investigations/index.html
[10] http://www.jsad.com/doi/full/10.15288/jsad.2015.76.829

Finally, PsyOps (Psychological Operations) is very real. Between 2010 and 2014, PsyOps was renamed Military Information Support Operations (MISO), then briefly renamed PsyOps in Aug 2014, only to return to MISO shortly thereafter in 2015[11]. It is a fact that the Army has been investigating psycho-pharmaceutical agents and behavior modification techniques that can diminish mental performance of our enemies, reducing their ability to fight. While there is no drug called Flometoquine, the premise that someone like Douglas Anders, MD, PhD could develop a pill that enhances performance - increasing alertness and above all aggressiveness - is frighteningly plausible, especially at a time when the US is fighting wars in multiple locations with a small, volunteer Army.

---

[11] http://soldiersystems.net/2014/08/10/two-big-organizational-renamings-in-socom-this-week/

ABOUT THE AUTHOR

Deborah Shlian is a physician, healthcare consultant and author of numerous nonfiction articles and books as well as six award winning medical mystery/thrillers, three co-authored with her husband, Joel. Check out her other books at www.shlian.com